D0327226

THE END OF ORDER

Also by Charles L. Mee, Jr.

BOOKS
White Robe, Black Robe
Erasmus
Daily Life in the Renaissance
Meeting at Potsdam
A Visit to Haldeman and Other States of Mind
Seizure

PLAYS
Players' Repertoire
Anyone! Anyone!
Constantinople Smith
Wedding Night

Charles L. Mee, Jr.

THE
END
OF
ORDER

❧

VERSAILLES
1919

E. P. DUTTON ❧ NEW YORK

Grateful acknowledgment is made to the following for permission to quote from copyrighted material:

"The Pretty Red-Head" from SELECTED WRITINGS, Guillaume Apollinaire (translated by Roger Shattuck), New Directions, © 1948 by New Directions

"The Voice of Robert Desnos" from CORPS ET BIENS, Robert Desnos (translated by Michael Benedikt), Editions Gallimard, © 1953 by Editions Gallimard

TWO MEMOIRS, J. M. Keynes, Granada Publishing Ltd., © 1949 by J. M. Keynes

PEACEMAKING 1919, Harold Nicolson, Harcourt Brace Jovanovich, Inc., © 1933 by Harold Nicolson

AT THE PARIS PEACE CONFERENCE, James T. Shotwell, The Macmillan Company, © 1937 by James T. Shotwell

LETTERS FROM THE PARIS PEACE CONFERENCE, Charles Seymour, Yale University Press, © 1965 by Yale University

Copyright © 1980 by Charles L. Mee, Jr.

All rights reserved. Printed in the U.S.A.

No part of this publication may be reproduced or transmitted in any form or by any means, electronic or mechanical, including photocopy, recording or any information storage and retrieval system now known or to be invented, without permission in writing from the publisher, except by a reviewer who wishes to quote brief passages in connection with a review written for inclusion in a magazine, newspaper or broadcast.

For information contact:
Elsevier-Dutton Publishing Co., Inc.,
2 Park Avenue, New York, N.Y. 10016

Library of Congress Cataloging in Publication Data
Mee, Charles L., Jr.
The end of order, Versailles 1919.
Bibliography: p. 269
Includes index.
1. Paris. Peace Conference, 1919. 2. Wilson, Woodrow, Pres. U.S., 1856–1924.
3. Clemenceau, Georges Eugène Benjamin, 1841–1929. 4. Lloyd George, David
Lloyd George, 1st Earl, 1863–1945. I. Title.
D644.M43   1980   940.3141   80-16249

ISBN: 0-525-09810-0
Published simultaneously in Canada by
Clarke, Irwin & Company Limited,
Toronto and Vancouver

Designed by Barbara Cohen

10   9   8   7   6   5   4   3   2   1

First Edition

IN MEMORIAM

William Mee,
my grandfather,
who lost all 10 of his brothers
in World War I

CONTENTS

ix

CONTENTS

CONTENTS

ACKNOWLEDGMENTS

I am deeply obliged to Terka Julay, who first encouraged me to undertake this book; to Lisa Miles, who helped me in the early stages to compile a bibliography and to lead me to the heart of the journals and memoirs; to my daughter Erin, who did a great deal of reading for me and pointed me to some of the best materials; to Sarah Waters in London, Kate Lewin in Paris, and Maria Niecko in Washington, all professional archival researchers, who pursued research for me in archives, libraries, and private papers with thoroughness and imagination; to Diane Wolkstein, who helped me to understand the character of the participants; to my father, whose reading and conversations about my manuscript pulled me through a dark time; to Suzi Mee, whose advice on structure pulled me through another difficult time; to Jack Macrae, my editor, whose help on revisions was invariably thoughtful and sound; to Jane Alpert, who did the close editing of the final manuscript; and to Audre Proctor, whose ability to transform my handwriting to a typescript always makes it a pleasure to write.

PROLOGUE

At the end of World War I, the representatives of the victorious nations gathered in Paris to sort through the ruins and carnage of the war, and to see whether they could find some new form amidst the appalling desolation. The United States was represented by Woodrow Wilson, Great Britain by David Lloyd George, France by Georges Clemenceau—but these three were only the most conspicuous among the frock-coated Foreign Office men, the generals, motorcycle messengers, aides and gossip columnists, society matrons and modern dancers, Walter Lippman and Sarah Bernhardt, Ho Chi Minh and Lawrence of Arabia, Marcel Proust and the Maharajah of Bikaner, and the crowd of others who converged on Paris to press their cases before the mighty, the influential, the press, and one another.

They labored for six months, from January through June of 1919, and signed at last—at the Palace of Versailles—what came to be called the Treaty of Versailles. Ordinarily the happenings and significance of such diplomatic gatherings can be understood by examining each of the positions taken by each of the participants, standing back to watch the give and take, and summing up the outcome.

At the end of the Great War, however, the diplomats confronted a world in fragments, a world that seemed to be in the midst of a massive psychic breakdown, of a breakdown of old combinations of states and of empires, of the disintegration of economic orders, of nineteenth-century capitalism, of the eruption of sudden disaster, of riots and assassinations, of tyranny and disorder, of frivolity and despair, exhilaration and dread on such an order of magnitude as to numb the mind.

When James T. Shotwell—short, with square shoulders, straight back, and a full, forceful moustache, the size of half a cigar—arrived in Paris as the official librarian to the American delegation, he went to have tea at the studio of the expatriate painter Edwin Scott. The two of them had to eat johnnycakes and syrup, because there was no bread in parts of Paris. Scott stood by the window overlooking his garden where a shell from the German long-range artillery had destroyed the plantings and thrown up earth against the houses. Across the way, a bomb had smashed a house on the Boulevard Raspail, and Scott said that he had not been able to concentrate or rest and had done little painting during the war.

Winter in Paris was unpredictable—some days wet and cold, icy enough to freeze the blood. Food and coal were in short supply. Some days were mild and beautiful, with clear skies at night, not at all cold, no heavy frost, grass green in the parks, even some flowers in bloom, a false spring that came and went disconcertingly. Near the Place de la Concorde, on one of the quays by the Seine, a trio—girl with violin, man with guitar, chanteuse—sang of the *nouvelle époque.*

When Shotwell dined with Sylvain Lévi, a distinguished French orientalist, Shotwell noticed "ice-cold and pitch-black corridors and a little heat in a grate stove, which [the Lévis] seemed to find very comfortable after the real hardships of the war. Professor Lévi has begun his courses at the Collège de France, but he says that it is impossible to take up the old subjects again with anything like the detachment of the scientific mind. His interest in the archaeology of India is only casual compared with his interest in the present."

World War I had been a tragedy on a dreadful scale. Sixty-five million men were mobilized—more by many millions than had ever been brought to war before—to fight a war, they had been told, of justice and honor, of national pride and of great ideals, to wage a war that would end all war, to establish an entirely new order of peace and equity in the world.

But far from resolving the conflicts that had begun the war, the war had let loose even more turmoil. By November 11, 1918, when the armistice that marked the end of the war was signed, eight million soldiers lay dead, twenty million more were wounded, diseased, mutilated, or spitting blood from the gas attacks. Twenty-two million civilians had been killed or wounded, and the survivors were living in villages blasted to splinters and rubble, on farms churned to mud, their cattle dead.

In Berlin and Belgrade and Petrograd, the survivors fought among themselves—fourteen wars, great or small, civil or revolutionary, flickered or raged about the world. Thirteen million tons of shipping had been sunk; 10,000 square miles of northern France had been ruined; 1,200 churches were destroyed along with 250,000 other buildings. Hundreds of square miles of central and Eastern Europe were in even worse condition. In Poland, people traded with German marks, Austrian krönen, Polish marks that had been issued by the Germans, Russian rubles—all plagued by uncertain exchange rates and runaway inflation. Prices rose in Austria by a factor of 14,000, in Hungary by 23,000, in Poland by 2,500,000, and in Russia by 400,000,000. And people starved all across Europe.

In central Europe, a member of a relief commission reported that "in countries where I found wagons I found . . . a shortage of locomotives; where there were locomotives, there was a shortage of wagons; where coal lay at the pithead . . . there were no wagons and where wagons waited, men were not available to work the coal. . . . In many parts of Poland, children were dying for want of milk and adults were unable to obtain bread or fats. In eastern districts . . . the population was living on roots, grass, acorns, and heather." Those who managed to survive the war and the revolutions and the violence and the privations were stunned by an epidemic of influenza that struck and spread and struck and spread again in the last spasm of the war and killed yet another six million people.

Four great empires had fallen—the German, Austro-Hungarian, Turkish or Ottoman, and the Russian—and the Allied armies still fought on in Russia against the Bolsheviks, trying vainly to restore the White Russians to rule. The collapse of these empires gave birth to the great political drama that commenced at the Paris Peace

Conference and continues to rage today: the conflict among the major powers to move into the old imperial domains—and the struggle of the other nations to win independence altogether from imperialism.

Perhaps all of this turmoil could have been contained had the political collapse not occurred in the midst of a collapse of many of the traditional ideals and usages that had underlain the political order of the nineteenth century. But the war had discredited much of the rhetoric of national pride, honor, and sacrifice, as well as faith in the notions of reason, progress, humanism. Nor did the notions of God, representational art, or Newtonian physics appear to be in such good repair. The "modern" western civilization that had grown up since the Renaissance was under siege from outside, and from within, and offered scant support to the disintegrating political order.

By January of 1919, as the delegates gathered in Paris for the Peace Conference, the shallow graves of Verdun were being washed out by the rains; feet stuck out of the ground, and helmets with skulls in them rose up through the mud. In this atmosphere, the diplomats gathered—and, far from restoring order to the world, they took the chaos of the Great War, and, through vengefulness and inadvertence, impotence and design, they sealed it as the permanent condition of our century.

PART ONE

ARRIVALS

THE SAVIOR

Woodrow Wilson sailed to Europe aboard the S.S. *George Washington* and landed at Brest on Friday, December 13, 1918—a date, Wilson thought, that was destined to bring him luck: thirteen was his lucky number because it was, among other things, the number of the letters in his name.

At Brest, one of the president's aides thought he counted thirty American destroyers, fifty French and British ships—"a wonderful sight!"—all in perfect alignment, each ship's band playing the "Star Spangled Banner," the crews giving three rousing cheers. A boatload of admirals arrived, then another boat bearing the French dignitaries, Foreign Minister Stéphen Pichon at their head, and General John Pershing, "the grandest man I ever saw," said Charles Seymour, a young aide in the American delegation, "very tall, enormous in breadth but still not a hint of excessive weight ... walks with a touch of a swagger." The crowd was "*en fête*, the women in thin white crinoline hats and the men in thin broad sailors with ribbons hanging down behind." The Americans disembarked amid bunting, singing schoolchildren, sailors, field marshals, generals, the mayor of Brest, deafening salvos of artillery, cheers, Mrs. Wilson descending the gangplank with General Pershing, the president beaming, silk hat in hand, flags, handkerchiefs; and they made their way through the town, past the crumbling walls of the castle built by Julius Caesar, to the railway station where the French had set up a speakers' platform.

The president—stepping forward to speak—looked, and dressed, like a Presbyterian minister, with a three-piece suit, firmly buttoned, silver-rimmed pince-nez; but he had a very broad, toothy smile. He was not easy or outgoing: he had arrived at the White House after his election to the presidency with coal tar headache tablets and a stomach pump.

"He was fond of reading aloud in modulated tones from his favorite authors," his personal physician, Dr. Cary Grayson, said. "On the library table close at hand for reference was a copy of Burton Stevenson's large anthology of verse, from which he would sometimes read John Burroughs' poem 'Waiting.' . . . Then from the same book he would read from Lear's nonsense verse and W. S. Gilbert's swinging lyrics—he was especially fond of the Duke of Plaza-Toro."

He loved all things familiar—old southern songs, the Princeton song, such hymns as "The Son of God Goes Forth to War" and "How Firm a Foundation"; he liked to read the same books over and over, to take the same automobile rides repeatedly, to revisit the same vacation spots in the English Lake Country, to wear the same old cape and, quite particularly, an old gray sweater that he had bought on a bicycle trip through Scotland some years before; he liked his favorite walking stick, and he liked to repeat often some of his father's favorite stories. Once he got hold of something that he liked and that was comfortable, he hated to let go.

The president had been born in Virginia in 1856, the only son of a severe Presbyterian minister and of a mother whom he recalled affectionately but infrequently. He had two older sisters; his relationships with women were generally accounted normal and commonplace, perhaps somewhat dull. He had been an indifferent or poor student, who did not decipher the alphabet until the age of nine, and did not read until the age of eleven. He was instructed in reading and writing, painstakingly, by his father, and had, by adulthood, so compensated for his early difficulties as to have made written and spoken eloquence one of his most noticeable assets—although it seemed at times that once he had arrived at a verbal formulation he became especially reluctant to abandon it, as though, if he allowed himself to let go of the construction so carefully built, he would be lost in disarray.

He was sick all his life, given to dyspepsia and nervous breakdowns, and evidently had suffered a succession of minor strokes—in 1896, at the age of thirty-nine, in 1900 and again in 1904, and particularly in 1906, when a more serious stroke left him blind in his left eye. As a youngster he had had to drop out of school a number of times. He dropped out of a small Presbyterian college in North Carolina where he had gone to study for the ministry. At Princeton, where he started over again at the age of nineteen, he had an undistinguished academic record. He studied law at Virginia and failed in trying to begin a legal practice, returning to Johns Hopkins to study history—which at last he taught at Bryn Mawr and Princeton.

He rose by the powers of his rhetoric. Everywhere he went as a student, he formed debating societies. At Princeton, he formed the "Liberal Debating Club," composed a constitution for it, and was elected its prime minister; at law school at the University of Virginia, he joined the Jefferson Society, became its president, and revised its constitution; at Johns Hopkins, he urged the members of the Hopkins Literary Society to turn themselves into the "Hopkins House of Commons," for which Wilson wrote a constitution; when he taught for a time at Wesleyan, he reorganized the students' debating society for them, turned it into a "House of Commons," and wrote a constitution for it.

He believed in words, in their beauty, in their ability to move people, in their power to give shape, and structure, and cohesion to the world—in their power, he appeared to believe, to transform reality.

His conviction in the force of language, and his unusual talent for using it, moved others along with him: the sentiments he expressed were fine and ennobling; he believed in their truth and he communicated to his audiences his conviction that what he said could be made to come to pass. Even as a young man at the University of Virginia, he drew such large audiences to hear his speeches that his appearances in debates often had to be scheduled in larger halls in order to accommodate the crowds.

He debated, he spoke, he read poetry, he wrote letters, and he practiced, every day, his techniques of elocution and composition. In time, he wrote several books, one on Congress, one on the Civil

War, a biography of George Washington, and *A History of the American People*. He attracted the attention of his colleagues; he worked assiduously as a professor at Princeton for twelve years—drawing large numbers of students for his lectures—and he seemed to slip naturally into the role of spokesman for the faculty of the political science department. As his reputation as a speaker spread outside the immediate bounds of Princeton, he made speeches to community groups, businessmen, political gatherings in New Jersey, New York, and elsewhere. He began, too, to receive invitations to assume the presidency of a number of universities, all of which he declined. At last, in 1902, he was asked to become president of Princeton University, an offer he accepted with alacrity.

As president of Princeton, he introduced a reorganization of the curriculum, requiring students to major in a single subject and integrate their courses into a consistent program—rather than to choose courses by a free elective system which had come to seem, to some, disorderly. He instituted, too, a system of tutorials that were designed to supplement large lecture courses with small group discussions, miniature debating societies.

In time some of Wilson's other ideas for reforms seemed to strike at the foundations of social privilege at Princeton, and he met the resistance of Andrew Fleming West, the dean of the graduate school. Wilson was uncompromising—some thought rigid—and because he would not bend, he was broken, fell ill, and was forced to resign in 1910.

He was elected governor of New Jersey in 1911. Because of some of his proposals for Princeton, he was seen as a man of democratic, almost populist, temperament, and, in 1913, he was swept—by this impression of his populism, and by his graceful, uplifting eloquence—into the presidency of the United States.

"He was a Southerner not merely in the superficial sense," the historian Gerald Johnson wrote, "—in the soft inflections in his speech, his normal courtesy toward friends and associates . . . but in more essential ways. For one thing, he was Southern in his deification of women and his strong urge to protect them, and in his belief that women should govern their own sphere and not soil themselves by participation in practical affairs . . . he demanded, not forthrightness and a masculine type of give-and-take in his friendships, but a loyalty that never questioned . . . and inevitably yielded to his own will . . . he had few intimates and broke sooner or later with most of them ... his most enduring friends were admiring, uncritical women."

His first wife, Ellen Axson, was the daughter of a Presbyterian minister. Her mother had died, and she had taken over as mistress of the parsonage, looking after her father, her two younger brothers, and her baby sister, and had vowed never to marry. Wilson called at the parsonage, and, as one of his biographers, Arthur Walworth, wrote, "when the caller asked pointedly about [the minister's] daughter's health, Ellen was summoned to the parlor and the young man was given an opportunity to exhibit his conversational charm on the question: 'Why have night congregations grown so small?' "

Ellen Axson's literary style was remarkably like Wilson's own—not merely arch and formal, as was so common in the late nineteenth century—but doubly indirect, agonizingly flirtatious: "Very unwillingly," she replied to one of Wilson's invitations, "and with the firm conviction that I am the most unfortunate of mortals, I write ... that I won't be able to go on this picnic either." And to his suggestion that they go on a walk: "There is no reason nor even—strange to say—*disinclination*, to prevent my saying most truthfully that I will be happy to walk with you this afternoon."

Wilson proposed; to be a bachelor, he told her, was to be "an amateur in life." She accepted. "Of course," he wrote to a friend, "it goes without saying that I am the most complacently happy man in all the 'Yewnighted States.' " Ellen had grown up, he said, "in the best of all schools—for manners, purity, and cultivation—a country parsonage."

Their marriage, which lasted until Ellen's death twenty-nine years later, in August of 1914, was entirely successful. All who knew them were impressed by the harmony of their home, the unfailing affection they displayed for one another, the complete contentment they found in one another and in their two daughters.

Wilson was a flirtatious man. "His powers of talk," Walworth has written, "ran riot in the presence of ladies whom he thought 'charming and conversable.' . . . He liked to air his literary fancies before what he regarded as the 'deeper sensibilities' and 'finer understanding' of intelligent women. He particularly enjoyed the 'lightly turned laughter' of ladies of the South. . . . Feeling that she was not by nature 'gamesome,' Ellen Wilson encouraged and shared her husband's friendships with brilliant ladies."

Wilson seemed genuinely to please the women he knew, in

conversation and in marriage, and he had at least one love affair: he met Mary Allen Hulbert Peck on a vacation that he took to rest, on doctor's orders, in Bermuda. Ellen Wilson had stayed at home to mind the children, and Mary Peck, whose first husband had died in an accident and whose second husband lived apart from her, was taken with Wilson's wit and after-dinner talk. He loved to walk along the shore with her and read to her from the *Oxford Book of Verse*, and she saw in him, according to Walworth, "a Christlike quality, a serene radiance that reminded her of Phillips Brooks." The affair lasted from 1906 into the early teens, when Wilson was president.

To Ellen Wilson, during their marriage, Wilson wrote a thousand love letters; to Mary Peck, he read poetry; he invariably enchanted women with his noble sentiments, clothed in fine language with a nimble wit. When Ellen Wilson died, and Mary Peck receded from his life, Wilson met and courted a forty-three-year-old widow named Edith Galt. Mrs. Galt met Wilson in the White House in 1915—she had come with a friend to have tea; and the two of them hit it off when Wilson took out a book and began to read to her. He read for a long time, and then took to interrupting himself with questions whether the author might have expressed himself more clearly.

"If I had written that when I was a boy," the president said of one passage, "my father would have made me rewrite it until I really said what I meant!"

He went on talking at length about his father, and Mrs. Galt replied with recollections of her father ("I had so exactly the same reverence for my father," she recalled), of her childhood in Virginia, and of "the faithfulness of the old negroes to their masters and mistresses." Within two months, Wilson proposed to Mrs. Galt.

As his marriage plans took shape, Wilson heard that some old letters that he had written to Mary Peck threatened to surface. Wilson was thrown into a panic. He determined that he must tell Mrs. Galt the complete truth about his relationship with Mary Peck and leave it to Mrs. Galt to decide whether or not she could proceed with their intended marriage.

But, when he sat down to write a letter to her he discovered that he could not bring himself to admit even to an innocent flirtation, let alone the love affair he had had with Mary Peck. He decided to point out instead that it might be difficult for Mrs. Galt to marry a man whose profession subjected him to backstairs gossip and malicious slander. That is to say, he decided to lie.

When he sat down to write, according to Dr. Grayson, "He went white to the lips, and his hand shook as I sat watching him try to write; his jaw set, determined no matter what it cost him, to spare [Mrs. Galt]; but after a long time he put the pen down and said: 'I cannot bring myself to write this; you go, Grayson, and tell her everything and say my only alternative is to release her from any promise.' "

When Grayson went to do Wilson's lying for him, Mrs. Galt heard out the doctor and then wrote a note to the president, saying that she would stand by him, giving him her complete trust and love. She sent off the note and waited for Wilson to reply. But, having seduced her with eloquence, he now became completely passive, and waited for her to act. "The day passed," she said, "with no word or reply . . . the next day and the next followed, and I felt humiliated and hurt. About noon of that third day Dr. Grayson came." Grayson asked her somberly to come to the White House. When she entered Wilson's bedroom in the White House, the curtains "were drawn and the room dark; on the pillow I saw a white, drawn face with burning eyes dark with hidden pain. Brooks, the coloured valet, was by the bed. No word was spoken, only an eager hand held out. . . . I never asked why he had not answered my letter, only had it reached him. He said, 'Yes.' "

They were married three months later.

During his presidency, American entry into World War I was a matter of violent dispute. He was opposed by those who saw no vital issue involved in the war for the United States, who saw, instead, the loss of many lives for no good purpose, or, even worse, for the purpose of turning the United States into an internationalist, interventionist power with all of the strain on the Constitution that comes of the foreign entanglements that the Founding Fathers had warned against—of the tendency, in an internationalist country, for political power to flow from the villages and cities and states to the federal government and, within the federal government, for political power to flow away from the legislative and judiciary branches into the executive, the tendency to lose the republic itself to the sway of an imperial presidency.

The war had started with the assassination in June of 1914 of the Archduke Franz Ferdinand of Austria-Hungary and his wife, as they rode in an open car through the streets of Sarajevo in Bosnia. Austria-Hungary blamed Serbia for the assassination, since the young assassin had come from Serbia. With the support of the Germans, Austria-Hungary made certain demands of the Serbians, who satisfied most but not all of them. On July 28, 1914, Austria-Hungary declared war against Serbia.

No one, or too few people, hated war in 1914. They remembered too little of war, and what they did remember was of such brief wars as the Crimean War of 1854–56, or the Franco-Prussian War of 1871, which had been decisive, glorious, advantageous for the victors—and fought by professional soldiers. To suggest, in 1914, that disputes might be settled peacefully, seemed to reveal a lack of courage and national pride.

Since 1871, too, the European nations, out of a general sense of anxiety, had bound themselves into an elaborate, interlocking set of alliances—so that, should war come, the old alliances and ententes would drag nations willy-nilly into the conflict.

At the same time, the world engaged in an arms race, led by Germany and Britain. Admiral Alfred von Tirpitz, who labored to build up the German fleet, declared that "without sea power Germany's position in the world is like a mollusk without a shell." The British, who had the strongest fleet in the world, responded to the German challenge by building a fleet of dreadnought battleships, thinking the Germans would be so impressed that they would give up their ambitions. The Germans produced their own dreadnoughts. And then the French, to challenge the supremacy of the German army on land, commenced to build up their army.

War is a great unifier of nations, a great organizer of disorder: if a politician is fortunate enough to find an external enemy, he need only direct the anger of his constituents toward the external enemy, and discipline his country against the outsider. For Germany, whose heavily industrialized economy was mortally threatened by rapidly rising prices of imported agricultural goods, an external enemy was a godsend. For Russia, whose czarist dictatorship was threatened by social upheavals, an external enemy was a godsend. For Austria-Hungary, whose fragile collection of Hungarians, Poles, Slavs, Rumanians, and others, was stirring against the central government, an external enemy was a godsend.

Meanwhile, in North Africa, Morocco and Algeria jostled with one another. Algeria was a French colony, Morocco a place where

French and German businessmen competed. When competition led
to crisis, and crisis almost to war, and Britain backed the French, the
Germans concluded that the French and British were joined in conspiracy to prevent Germany from gaining colonies.

In the Balkans, the Serbs tried to make a new nation—as the
Germans and the Italians had done not long before. The Serbs, with
the backing of the Russians, thought they would combine with
Montenegro and Albania; and, in the small Balkan wars of 1912 and
1913, Serbia emerged stronger than ever. "The first round is won,"
the Serbian prime minister said. "We must now prepare for the second, against Austria." And so, when the Serbian assassin shot Franz
Ferdinand and his wife, all the elements came together with a fury.

Wilson declared the United States "neutral"—although, in
practice, he was more neutral toward some countries than toward
others. When England violated the principle of the freedom of the
seas, Wilson ignored the violation. When the Germans violated the
principle, Wilson went to Congress for a declaration of war.

The United States entered the war late: the 1st Division did not
land in France until June of 1917; the 2nd Division did not follow
until September. And, once in the war, America suffered relatively
light casualties; about 114,000 American soldiers died in battle,
about the same number as the Bulgarians lost. Nonetheless, the arrival of the American expeditionary force marked the turn in the
fortunes of the war. The Americans seemed, and not only to themselves, to have won the war—and the speeches of Wilson seemed, in
the war's final year, to have distilled from the bloodshed its reason
and transcendent purpose.

The war was fought, said Wilson, not simply to defeat Germany, but to defeat the very causes of war, to substitute for the old
system of alliance and balance of power politics a new order based
upon justice and upon the rights of all people to determine for
themselves their own governments. Wilson's principles were laid
out in a speech in January of 1918 in the form of Fourteen Points
(given in detail later, in the chapter called "Basis of Negotiations").
The first five of the points were general: diplomacy was henceforth
to be open, not secret; the high seas were to be open to all nations;
world armaments were to be reduced; economic barriers to free
trade were to be removed; all colonial claims were to be adjusted according to impartial standards of justice. The succeeding eight
points were addressed to specific territorial questions (Alsace-Lor-

raine was to be returned to France; an independent Poland was to be established), all of which were specific applications of the principle of self-determination. The fourteenth point called for the organization of a League of Nations to ensure that all these principles were carried out in perpetuity.

In the following months, Wilson added to his Fourteen Points his four principles and five particulars—repeating, and putting into ringing phrases his notions that people must not be traded about as though they were mere pawns in the hands of politicians, that the genuine aspirations of people for self-government must be recognized, that the peace settlement must be based on justice and not on a passion for revenge or an acquisitive greed for new colonies or dominions.

Young people especially were thrilled by Wilson's speeches. Many of the young felt that the war had been started by old men, that the old men had sent the young to die, and the young men felt at the end of the war that it was time for them to take over and make the peace, to be certain that the peacemaking was not surrendered again into the hands of the old men. Wilson seemed to give voice to their greatest hopes and ideals, and they made him their champion, the victor of the war, the prophet of the peace. Young liberals spoke of national health care and the nationalization of railroads, of the internationalization of the brotherhood of labor, of politics based on morality, peace based on the true needs and wishes of the common people, and as the Allies commenced to push back the German forces at the second battle of the Marne in the summer of 1918, the hopes that overcame the young French and English and Americans had taken on the character of delirium.

The Germans, too, had listened attentively to Wilson's speeches, and, when their plight became unbearable, they turned not to the French or the English to sue for peace but to Wilson, whose speeches had promised again and again a peace of justice for all.

On October 7, the Germans sent a note to Wilson asking for an immediate armistice and requesting that the president call together all the belligerents to negotiate. "The German government accepts," the note said, "as the basis for its negotiations, the program laid down by the President of the United States."

During the next several weeks, Wilson exchanged notes with the Germans, making it clear that, among other things, the Allies would not be able to negotiate with the "monarchical autocrats of Germany." The Germans took the hint, and General Erich Ludendorff, who had risen through the ranks to become de facto military dictator of Germany, was forced from office. In time, Kaiser Wilhelm II—declining the suggestion that he go out into the trenches to seek a hero's death among the soldiers—fled secretly aboard his private train across the border into the Netherlands, where, under the protection of Queen Wilhelmina and her husband, the German Duke Henry of Mecklenburg-Schwerin, he formally abdicated as emperor of Germany.

The uncertain German government that remained—a military dictatorship undergoing a hasty refurbishing job to make it resemble a republic—agreed to pull back from France and Belgium as soon as the armistice was concluded, and to grant such preliminary military concessions as would make a resumption of the war impossible for Germany. Under these conditions, Wilson informed the French and the English of the German request for negotiations, and, on November 11, in the Forest of Compiègne, a German delegation signed the armistice agreement in the presence of Marshal Ferdinand Foch, general in chief of the Allied Armies in the West.

In all these concluding months of the war, President Wilson had achieved an astonishing personal triumph. All the world, it seemed, delivered itself to him to be remade according to his vision. In America, too, he enjoyed enormous credit. True enough, some could be heard to criticize his harsh repression of dissenters during the war; in general, Americans were inclined to let Europeans worry about European problems once the war was over, and to be preoccupied with questions about the cost of living, just when the "boys" would return home, and what jobs the returning soldiers would find. But, nonetheless, Wilson's notion for a League of Nations was popular, if only vaguely apprehended; the thought of having some sort of organization to make sure another great war would not soon break out seemed a worthy idea.

Wilson had made, perhaps, only one crucial mistake. In the congressional elections that had been held in the autumn of 1918, the president, riding high on his successes, made a special appeal to the American voters. He had always, in the past, insisted that the war must never be subject to party politics (must never, some complained, be subject to criticism), that the conduct of the war must have bipartisan support. But in the autumn of 1918 he broke his own rule. He called, illogically, for a sort of vote of confidence. He asked the American people to deliver a Democratic majority to him in the Congress.

"If you have approved of my leadership," Wilson said, "and wish me to continue to be your unembarrassed spokesman in affairs at home and abroad, I earnestly beg that you will express yourselves unmistakably to that effect by returning a Democratic majority to both the Senate and the House. . . . The leaders of the minority . . . have been antiadministration. . . . The return of a Republican majority . . . would, moreover, certainly be interpreted on the other side of the water as a repudiation of my leadership."

In truth, the Republicans had supported Wilson devotedly through the war, and his charge against them—his vainglorious call for a personal electoral prize—enraged them. They threw themselves into the campaign, and, when the final vote was tallied, of the forty contested seats in the Senate, the Republicans had taken twenty-five. The party ties in the Senate thus broke down as follows: forty-eight Republicans, forty-seven Democrats, one Progressive. And, once the Republicans had come to be the majority party in the Senate, they appointed as chairman of the Senate Foreign Relations Committee the Republican senator from Massachusetts, Henry Cabot Lodge, who hated Wilson and his internationalist policies and, in particular, his League of Nations.

"Our allies and our enemies," former President Theodore Roosevelt wrote from his deathbed just before Wilson set sail for Europe, "and Mr. Wilson himself should all understand that Mr. Wilson has no authority whatever to speak for the American people at this time. His leadership has just been emphatically repudiated by them. . . . Mr. Wilson and his Fourteen Points and his four supplementary points and his five complementary points and all his utterances every which way have ceased to have any shadow of right to be accepted as expressive of the will of the American people."

The European leaders did indeed take note of the American elections; only Wilson seemed to be oblivious to them. He basked in the pleasure of being a world figure; he was the first president to journey, while in office, to any foreign country; and he sailed abroad like a conquering hero aboard a former German ship that was renamed the S. S. *George Washington.*

In 1895, when Wilson had written his biography of George Washington, his first thought, his first sentence, was that Washington "was bred a gentleman and a man of honor in the free school of Virginian society.... Virginia gave us this imperial man and with him a companion race of statesmen and masters in affairs. It was her natural gift, the times and her character being what they were; and Washington's life showed the whole process of breeding by which she conceived so great a generosity in manliness and public spirit."

Wilson went on at length about Washington's childhood, sprinkling his paragraphs with such archaic—for Wilson's time— expressions as " 'twas," "but" for "only," "ere" for "before." Washington grew up, said Wilson with an adopted nostalgia, in a home that "stood upon a green and gentle slope that fell away, at but a little distance, to the waters of the Potomac.... The spot gave token of the quiet youth of the boy, of the years of grateful peace in which he was to learn the first lessons of life, ere war and the changing fortunes of his country hurried him to the field and to the council."

Washington's father, wrote the son of the Presbyterian minister, served in the House of Burgesses, "where his athletic figure, his ruddy skin, and frank gray eyes must have made him as conspicuous as his constituents could have wished. He was a man of the world, every inch, generous, hardy, independent. He lived long enough, too, to see how stalwart and capable and of how noble a spirit his young son was to be, with how manly a bearing he was to carry himself in the world; and had loved him and made him his companion accordingly."

Writing about the first battle of the Revolution at Concord, Wilson noted that three hundred soldiers had "gone to a last reckoning." Wilson did not otherwise notice much suffering, bloodshed, maiming, or death during the war, and, when he came to measure the effect of the Revolution on Washington, he observed only that strangers, who had previously "remarked the spirit and life that sat in Washington's eyes," after the war "found those eyes grown pensive ... touched a little with care, dimmed with watching."

Wilson saw Washington's presidency, in sum, as a succession of *tableaux vivants:* Washington's "unmistakable figure" out for a stroll, or the president on horseback "riding in his noble way" with "something in his air and bearing." Washington was seen as a child sees a remote father, as a figure at a distance, elevated, in a variety of postures, making certain gestures, possessing certain qualities—but never performing specific acts in the nasty business of bloody war or politics.

"There was that in his proud eyes and gentleman's bearing that marked him a man to be made friends with and respected. A good comrade he proved, without pretence or bravado, but an ill man to scorn, as he went his way among them, lithe and alert, full six feet in his boots, with that strong gait as of a backwoodsman, and that haughty carriage as of a man born to have his will."

In Paris, the cheers of the crowd, the tremendous throngs, the drums of the mounted band, the bunting, the shouts, *Vive* Wilson! airplanes overhead, the roar of the people, the muzzles of the captured cannon, the crowds by the Arc de Triomphe, the Champs Elysées, the Place de l'Opéra, the president with an amiable sweeping gesture of his hand, the bugles sounding "Aux Armes," the sun breaking through the clouds, blue skies and balmy weather, dominant colors among the crowd blue and khaki of the soldiers and the black of the women, cuirassiers galloping down the lane, Mrs. Wilson in a carriage heaped with flowers ("well dressed," Seymour said, "and at a short distance very good-looking"), many workingmen in the crowd, socialists who pinned their hopes on Wilson, regarding him as too moderate, yet, even so, knowing they needed a good peace to advance their cause and so trying to capture him for their own, the president's face glowing, his hat off, the "deep delight," the newspapers said, "the entire city a great stage vibrant with light and color," and "ecstasy of abandonment," lasting into the night, fresh outbursts, the hope of the common people, a citizen of humanity, the great hope, the new order, the new world come to save the old, his bold and measured words, head of the richest and most powerful nation, a new Europe, posters proclaiming *Wilson le juste,* war to end wars, make world safe for democracy, the people in tumult, eddies and waves, cheering crowds, some weeping.

"If," the president said on his arrival, responding to this universal fever for a just and lasting peace, "we do not heed the mandates of mankind, we shall make ourselves the most conspicuous and deserved failures in the history of the world." The peace, President Wilson said, must be based upon justice and upon the aspirations of all the common people of the world—or else, he declared, the diplomats would live to see "another breakup of the world, and when such a breakup came it would not be a war but a cataclysm."

The mass of people think, said Seymour, that "Wilson is the savior."

THE TIGER

Georges Clemenceau stepped forward—a short, powerful man with a solid, square body, short legs, a barrel chest, freckles, age seventy-eight. He resembled, one of the Americans said, "in face and figure a Chinese mandarin of the old empire. . . . He had the sallow complexion, the prominent high cheek-bones, the massive forehead with protuberant brows, the slant of the dark eyes, the long down-curving gray mustache, the short neck, the broad, rounded shoulders." He had been known for decades in French politics as a ferocious scrapper, sarcastic, cutting, a man who thrived on infighting, commonly called "The Tiger." He wore, as he always wore, indoors and out, morning and night, at work or at the dinner table, a pair of gray suede gloves when he reached out, as he approached the president, and firmly grasped both of Wilson's hands.

Clemenceau was born in 1841, and from earliest childhood he had no close friends; he almost never mentioned his mother; he found his brothers and sisters tedious; he preferred books that were scientific or, at least, rationalist.

"I think," he said to his secretary, Jean Martet, "the only influence which had any effect on me was—yes, my father's. . . . In the ordinary course of the day I didn't see my father much—he didn't do a great deal, and like all people who don't do anything, was always very busy. But at table—my father wasn't a man who attached great importance to the pleasures of the table—he spoke largely of his reading, enunciated his philosophy in fits and starts and, little by little, I absorbed it. He used to talk about Danton. I must say that I wasn't for Danton."

His father was a medical doctor whose father and grandfather had been doctors and small landowners. "Luckily he never had a single patient—he'd have killed them abruptly." The Clemenceaus lived in the country, in the Vendée, rugged farmland facing the Atlantic, country of hedgerows, stone cottages, conservative and Catholic. Clemenceau's own family had been a prickly, unconventional lot—rationalists, anticlericals, supporters of the Revolution, republicans against the monarchists, against Napoleon III. "At Nantes, my father used to go to a reading room . . . where people came to read and gossip—old folk, who had seen the Revolution and Napoleon. My father pointed one of them out to me and said, 'Do you see that man over there. He's an old friend of Marat.'

"I wasn't very clear as to who Marat was or what he had done, but Marat was a colossal name which struck me because of its association with all that blood, that bathtub, Charlotte Corday. Therefore I had a great respect for this old fellow."

In 1858, a would-be assassin fired at Emperor Napoleon III and missed. The police rounded up "malcontents" throughout France—including Dr. Clemenceau; they jailed the doctor and sentenced him to deportation.

"I remember going with my mother to see him in prison, and bringing him his little valise, for he was going to be sent to Algeria; in front of the spies I went up to him and said, 'I'll avenge you!' He answered, 'If you want to avenge me, work!' "

In the midst of this trauma, one of the doctor's daughters was struck with catalepsy, or, as Clemenceau said, went mad, and could not speak.

The doctor was taken to Marseilles, to be put aboard a ship for Algeria; but, by this time, his friends in Nantes had raised such a protest that, just as the doctor was about to embark, "the order came to let him return. Then there was a terrific scene between my father and the prefect of police. My father, shouting at the top of his lungs, said to the prefect, 'You'll see, I've no need to bind my son to Hannibal's vow. You'll have enough trouble with this lad yet!' "

Two years later, Clemenceau went to Paris to study medicine, and he took up immediately with radical republican circles—with a letter of introduction from his father to Etienne Arago to smooth the way—and he wrote articles for a small radical journal, *Travail*, to which Emile Zola was then contributing verse.

By 1862, Clemenceau had attracted the attention of the police and was jailed for two months for organizing a prorepublican parade. When he was released from jail—more cautious if not at all subdued—he decided to leave Paris for a while, and he went to England where he met John Stuart Mill and arranged to translate Mill's essays on Auguste Comte and positivism into French.

He proposed marriage to a well-to-do young woman, Hortense

Kestner, who was a year older than he was and who was not greatly attracted to him. Her father did not like Clemenceau either—considering the young man too domineering—and rejected his suit.

By 1865, with an allowance from his father in his pocket, and outfitted in a new frock coat and black satin breeches, Clemenceau set out to improve his English by living in the United States. He lived in Sheridan Square in Greenwich Village, and acquired an idiomatic command of American English, which he spoke in an accent that blended the guttural French *r*'s with a New England broadness. "I can cuss, too," he said, "but your slang is my baby."

He earned his money in America by writing dispatches for *Le Temps* about Reconstruction, the impeachment of Andrew Johnson, and other political affairs. It has often been said that the problems of Reconstruction after the American Civil War were the closest historical parallel to the problems of healing after World War I—but Clemenceau had little interest in them, except that he loved a good fight, and admired a man who stuck to what he believed. He did say, in expressing some reservation about Andrew Johnson's "moderation and generosity," that perhaps it was "too expansive," and that it would "allow the Southern states to resume the share of power which they held so long, and that the spirit of compromise, which plunged the United States step by step into the Civil War, will once again obscure the issues. . . . There is a feeling that the South is now at the mercy of the North, and that for the first time the opportunity is at hand to quell definitely, once for all, the temper of oligarchical pride which worked such disaster to the Republic."

To pick up some extra cash, Clemenceau taught horsemanship and French at a seminary for young ladies in Stamford, Connecticut, where he met, courted, and married Mary Plummer, the daughter of a dentist from Massachusetts. When the couple returned to France in 1870, Clemenceau plunged into politics and love affairs. He was a dashing young boulevardier who enjoyed the opera, theater, ballet, and such women as the opera singer Rose Caron (his "most dazzling conquest," it was said, "in the world of the theater"), the "ravissante" Comtesse d'Auray, and Léonide Leblanc, a middle-aged actress of whom it was said, "Put her on the summit of Mont Blanc, she will still be accessible."

Clemenceau and his wife had three children toward whom Clemenceau was always remote: when he saw them, which was infrequently, he spent his time showing what a good taskmaster he was. In time, Clemenceau and his wife separated, and in 1894, when he discovered that his wife had a lover, Clemenceau immediately moved to divorce her on the grounds of adultery and had her deported to the United States. He destroyed every photograph of her that he had, and every drawing, and then he took up a hammer and completely demolished a marble bust of her. Afterwards, Clemenceau had many "conquests" and especially enjoyed the admiration of much younger women and the innocent company of adolescent girls, but it is not clear that Clemenceau ever in his life, from earliest childhood, loved anyone.

His introduction to politics occurred in 1871, when the Germans invaded France. Clemenceau, still the young radical, was appointed mayor of one of the arrondissements of Paris, and served through the invasion, the fall of France, the abortive Commune—in which he played roles revolutionary, radical, conservative, and reactionary. When at last he could not prevent a Parisian mob from executing two French military officers, he retreated to his office, put his head down on his desk, and cried. It is the only recorded instance, this moment of complete impotence, of Clemenceau's ever having cried. He never forgot the experience—or the date on which the French capitulated to the Germans, agreed to suffer an army of occupation, pay an indemnity of a billion dollars, surrender Alsace and Lorraine, and sign a treaty guaranteeing all this at the palace of Versailles—on January 18, 1871.

In the years that followed, he labored for a restoration of the French republic. He combined careers in medicine, politics, and journalism for the rest of his life—keeping long hours, rising at four or five in the morning, going to bed at midnight, affecting a carelessness about his clothes—wearing battered hats, an umbrella hung from his side pocket, wrinkled topcoat—and a harshness about his manner. He was troubled by insomnia, a disordered liver (which gave a yellow cast to his complexion), a bad stomach, and what he thought was poor circulation.

He spoke for freedom of the press, for the substitution of a citizen army for the French professional army, for the abolition of capital punishment, the complete republicanization of the government, including the election of all public officials. He campaigned for the eight-hour workday, prison reform, and an end to religious influence in the schools. He regarded French imperialism as a means by which administrators and small groups of rich investors gouged money from the taxpayers. He championed the poor, the hungry, beggars, prostitutes, the unemployed, juvenile delinquents, bastards, and orphans.

Because he was always in the opposition, because he was a brilliant polemicist, because he used his own political journal to attack the government, he became known as a wrecker of ministries, a man who destroyed one premier after another. In sixteen years he brought down eighteen governments.

He was elected himself to the municipal council of Paris, to the chamber of deputies, to the Senate, and, from 1906 to 1909, he was premier of France. He was, withal, a man schooled in the fierce give-and-take of parliamentary politics, a man who thrived on, relished, and was superior in the arts of close combat.

When Alfred Dreyfus, a captain on the French general staff, was convicted of selling secrets to the Germans—and Clemenceau discovered that a cluster of conservatives and anti-Semites had faked the evidence—Clemenceau attacked the military establishment and the government mercilessly. It was Clemenceau who published Emile Zola's famous attack on the government, *J'accuse!* (and Clemenceau, incidentally, who thought of that inflammatory title for the article), and Clemenceau who stayed with the case long after others had grown tired of it, including Dreyfus himself, who was willing—to Clemenceau's disgust—to settle for a mere pardon. Clemenceau persisted until Dreyfus had not only been pardoned and set free but fully restored to his military rank. It took eight years, and Clemenceau's collected editorials, polemics, and essays on the case fill seven volumes.

He spent much time out of political office, much time despised, and he spent some of his years of disfavor writing dreadful novels and plays. He made many friends and acquaintances among artists and writers; he knew Oscar Wilde; he fought over an American woman, Selma Everdon, with Auguste Rodin. Perhaps his closest and most enduring friendship was with Claude Monet, whose impressionist paintings of water lilies Clemenceau especially loved.

Clemenceau enjoyed visiting Monet, sitting with Monet in the painter's garden, urging him on when the painter began to go blind toward the end of his life. "Monet was a supreme lyricist," Clemenceau said in a book he wrote about his friend's paintings of water lilies, "and this lyricist was a man of action. These two traits are not necessarily a ground of commendation in the eyes of our contemporaries." Monet was born, said Clemenceau, "palette in hand, and conceived living merely as standing before a canvas upon which to inscribe the flux of luminous energy through which the protean universe settles itself by means of its own reflection into a semblance of fixity. Feeling, thinking, willing as a painter. . . . He stood with bow well bent, with arrow on the string, ready for the will to let go."

Clemenceau loved to listen to himself write; everything he did had a vast element of hot air. "Silent each morning before his pond," he said of Monet, "he passed hours watching clouds and patches of blue sky slip by in fairylike processions, across his garden of water and fire. . . . He sought to fix the moments . . . of a light reflected from things radiating through the endless universe." Concerning the forehead of a self-portrait by Monet, Clemenceau wrote: "It is the seat of command, the imperious stronghold of the idea, of authority. The eyes are half closed, the better to savor the inner dream."

For all the nineteenth-century romanticism, however, Clemenceau's prose was not lax or passive; he remarked in Monet what he saw in himself: a sense of destiny, a sense of being alive amid great cosmic flux, an indistinct tendency toward positivism, a readiness to risk an impression of the ever-shifting truth and to seize upon the moment, to relish the sense of chance.

When World War I broke out, Clemenceau used his newspaper to whip up war fever in every way he knew how; he castigated "defeatists," called upon the secret police to root out "dissidents," and excoriated the uncertain government. He called for more arms, more energy, more will, more resolve. In 1917, some felt that there was a possibility for a negotiated peace; and it has been argued since that a negotiated peace might have staved off the collapse of some of the old regimes of Europe, sidetracked the rise of totalitarianism, and possibly saved millions of lives. But Clemenceau would have none of this defeatist talk. "The winner," he said, "is the one who can believe for a quarter of an hour longer than his enemy that he is not beaten."

All the French refer to their country in the feminine gender; but few have written with as much passion as Clemenceau about their love for France. "From the sea to the mountains," he said, the French countryside "transpierces" a Frenchman "with an intense spirit of dedication, a passion which embraces all the attributes of a soil now prodigal, now niggardly, all the lively dreams cradled by the hearthside, all the hopes of heaven which, even if deceptive, have none the less guided the soul on its march toward the stars, a march in which the journey, perhaps, is better than the goal. From the cloudy horizons of the ocean, from the translucent blue of the inland lakes which fashion the soul for high endeavor, from the jagged peaks of the Pyrenees and the Alps, from the radiant valleys with their flashing streams and bountiful harvest." This was the countryside that, in Clemenceau's view, in 1870 and again in 1914, had been raped by the Germans.

Clemenceau's attacks on the government were so persistent, so devastating, that they brought down every war ministry that President Raymond Poincaré could form—something for which Poincaré never forgave Clemenceau. At last, in desperation, since no one else could stand up under Clemenceau's attacks, Poincaré called Clemenceau himself to take over as premier.

Without hesitation, Clemenceau purged the lower ranks of the army, fired prefects and subprefects who had not been zealous enough in curbing defeatist propaganda, imposed censorship on the press and had one of his aides systematically plant stories, and prosecuted for treason any members of the government who seemed suspiciously lax. To take over command of the French Army, Clemenceau appointed Marshal Foch; but he kept a close watch on Foch, too. It was Clemenceau who had said, "War is too serious a matter to be left to the generals."

He went to the front lines, to the trenches, repeatedly, continuously, tramping along the duckboards in mud-covered shoes, mounting the parapets, surveying the battlefields, shouting insults at the German soldiers across the barbed wire in no-man's land, exposing himself to enemy fire repeatedly, courting death time and again. "At the first," one of his biographers wrote, "he exposed himself so ostentatiously to shell and machine gun fire that even Mordacq [an almost worshipful aide] . . . felt ashamed of what he rightly called his chief's *coquetterie.*"

Clemenceau managed to hold together a gaggle of socialist factions and right-wingers through the war. With the end of the war, however, the great cause that had kept the French together had vanished, and their unnatural harmony disintegrated once more. The militarist and industrialist right wing wished to use the war, and the peace, to ensure that the Germans would never again be either a military or commercial threat to France, to crush the Germans in order to punish them for the past and mutilate them for the future. The socialists wished to use the peace to build a new order, both internationally and domestically. Surely the time for socialist reforms had never seemed more propitious: social welfare legislation had been making great strides in Britain since the turn of the century; socialists had been working their way into positions of great influence in European parliaments; and the Russian Revolution announced that the day of complete transformation was at hand.

The crowds that welcomed Wilson to Paris were not an anonymous mass; Clemenceau and Wilson, and the other politicians who were practiced at seeing such things, saw an unusually large, disproportionate number of workingmen, of socialists lining the streets. The socialist crowd that welcomed Wilson to Paris understood that they were cheering an imperfect hero. On domestic matters, and on the more general questions of capitalist economy and society, they knew that Wilson was conservative. They believed, however, that he shared their wishes in international politics to do away with the old reactionary alliances and to help bring into the world new governments based on the principles of democracy. They believed that the president had not sailed to Europe for mere reasons of vanity. They expected Wilson to insist upon his new order by using the enormous economic strength of the United States—undamaged by the war—to pressure the Allies. And, while Wilson exerted this external pressure, the socialists believed, they would exert the internal political pressure.

On December 27, Clemenceau was forced to go before Parliament to request 10 billion francs for the civil and military budget for the first quarter of 1919. The socialists seized on the moment to ensnare Clemenceau in a debate on his foreign policy, to force him to speak about his intentions at the peace conference, to make him commit himself to a Wilsonian policy at the conference.

The socialists declared themselves opposed absolutely to the idea of a harsh peace; they were opposed, too, to the idea that France needed to honor all the secret treaties concluded in the course of the war—with Italy, for instance, to entice the Italians to enter the war. They were opposed, too, to the attempt that the Allies seemed to be making to roll back the Russian Revolution by supporting the White Russians in their efforts to overthrow the Bolshevik government. Indeed, the socialists declared, it seemed, even before the peace conference had begun, that the conference was to be dedicated to nothing but the repeal of history, the attempt to reestablish discredited nineteenth-century usages, that the world had gone through vast, irretrievable changes—because of great historical trends that had been building for years, because of the war, because of revolution in Russia and elsewhere—and now it appeared that all the French government thought to do was to make the conference a tremendous effort at counterrevolution.

Ernest Lafont rose to speak: apparently all the government could think to do in Russia, said Lafont, was to join with the remnants of the *ancien régime* to try to overthrow bolshevism.

Clemenceau, who had been silent until that moment, interrupted. The government had no thought of interfering in the internal affairs of Russia. The government's policy was merely to ensure a continued *cordon sanitaire,* to keep bolshevism from spreading into Europe.

Lafont was taken with the expression *cordon sanitaire,* an expression that had been used in the French newspapers but not in the chamber of deputies. "Let us call things by their real name," he shot back at Clemenceau. "It is a blockade. . . . The plan is to intervene militarily along the periphery, together with [the White Russians] in order more effectively to isolate Greater Russia from the rest of the world. . . . Will this mark the beginning of the League of Nations in this world? . . . Will it be assigned the task of restoring old forms of autocracy in those places of the world where these have been overthrown by natural popular movements?"

The socialists, Lafont declared, would never approve a budget that allocated even one sou "for this reactionary police action across Europe." Nor did Lafont wish to be misunderstood by the other members of the chamber of deputies. He did not object only to the Russian policy. "What is particularly disturbing to us . . . is that the same spirit which informs your Russian policy is being manifested in your policy in other parts of Europe."

At last, at about midnight, Clemenceau spoke. "But rather than go to the rostrum," as Arno Mayer has written, "and as if to show his scorn for these proceedings, he addressed the *chambre* from his seat for three quarters of an hour."

He did not wish, he said, to keep Parliament in the dark about his plans for the peace conference—nor did he think he could be accused of having kept Parliament uninformed in the past. On the contrary, he had often told the deputies just what the government intended to do, just what it was doing. At the moment, however, he had no intention of telling the deputies what he would do at the conference: "Even though I will press certain claims . . . I am not disposed to define these here . . . because I may have to sacrifice some of them to a higher interest."

Nonetheless, in general terms, he was prepared to declare himself: some deputies might affect to disdain the *vieux système* of diplomacy—of securing the borders of one's homeland, of maintaining a strong army, of arranging alliances so as to secure a balance of powers on the continent. Indeed, the *vieux système* might seem somewhat "prosaic" to some; but "in part," said Clemenceau, he "remained faithful to it."

International guarantees, he said, referring elliptically to Wilson, are "more difficult to establish in reality than in either speeches or books." And so, for the time being at least, France would see to her own defenses, would rely upon the time-tested devices of the old diplomacy to guarantee that more French lives would not soon need to be sacrificed, and would, at the same time, of course, "gladly" accept any other "supplementary" guarantees that might be made available.

As for the suggestion that he ought to abandon the old diplomacy in favor of some new, untested notion of peaceful order—and then just hope for the best—Clemenceau could not muster sufficient scorn. Balance-of-power politics was not simply a nineteenth-century fashion that had gone out of style; balance-of-power politics was necessary because "since remote times people have been going at each other for the satisfaction of their appetites and of their selfish interests, [and] neither I nor you have made this history."

The question of the budget was called to a vote. The socialists were able, on some questions, to count on as many as 100 or 140 votes. On the budget, they had hoped to pull a good many moderates over to their side. They had not reckoned, however, on Clemenceau's uncompromising facing down of the chamber. The socialists first proposed a couple of amendments—which were voted down 380 to 134, and 386 to 88. And then, when the main question was put to a vote, and the question had been transformed, in effect, into a vote of confidence in the government, Clemenceau's budget was approved by a stunning margin of 414 to 6.

During the war, Clemenceau had been asked to explain his policy in the chamber of deputies, and he had declared: "I wage war!"

(*Je fais la guerre*—the way some people might say *Je fais l'amour*).
"In domestic politics, I wage war. In foreign policies, I wage war.
Always, everywhere, I wage war.... And I shall continue to wage
war until the last quarter of an hour!" His policy had not changed.

HOTEL CRILLON

The delegation from the United States was put up in the Hotel
Crillon, whose windows opened onto the Seine toward the south,
the Champs Elysées to the west, the gardens of the Tuileries and the
Louvre palace across the Place de la Concorde. The old elevators
moved slowly from floor to floor, sometimes hanging halfway until
the water augmented itself sufficiently to overbalance the weight of
the passengers and lift them ponderously upward.

"I had an awful time with the French elevator, going up," Seymour wrote home, "... and kept figuring what I should do if it
didn't stop. Then if you please it *didn't* stop when it should; I saw
myself being crushed against the roof, and hastily pushed all the
buttons in sight; the result was a sudden stop between floors. I
pushed another button and dropped 20 feet; then on trying another
I soared way over my floor and within two feet of the roof. Finally I
got expert and with trembling knees emerged."

The rooms were agreeably proportioned, with high ceilings,
white paneling, fireplaces, enormous bathrooms, and a "very comfortable bed all done in rich old rose."

Breakfast, said Seymour, "turned out to be about the best in
our experience—bread very nearly white and with the finest crust,
the most perfectly fried sole I ever tasted, plenty of delicious butter
and all the sugar we wanted. The coffee has a good deal of chicory in
it." The hotel provided free matches for the guests, and shined their
shoes. "As to clothes I may have to get a top hat and morning coat
for state occasions."

Wilson was put up at the Palais Murat, a splendid eighteenth-
century pile, three stories high and eleven French windows wide,
surrounded by trees and set back from the street near the Parc

Monceau: the rooms, Shotwell observed, "have costly paintings and the ceiling is filled with original frescoes, but the most distinctive note of decoration is that afforded by the electroliers which give an indirect lighting through a mass of crystal and twisted bronze. These lights are multiplied by huge wall mirrors, so that one can hardly tell how many rooms are real and how many only reflections."

When Clemenceau came to call on the president, they adjourned to a small library on the second floor. This, their first meeting, lasted for an hour. Clemenceau spoke almost not at all. He listened, and by the end of the meeting, he was saying that he had originally been opposed to Wilson's attendance at the conference as a delegate (Clemenceau and Lloyd George were prime ministers, but Wilson was a head of state, comparable to Britain's king or France's president). Now, however, Clemenceau said he hoped Wilson would step right into the negotiations as America's chief delegate. When an American aide escorted Clemenceau downstairs after the meeting, the premier expressed his "keen delight" with Wilson.

Their next meeting, on the next day, lasted for an hour and a half. Again Clemenceau listened. Wilson spoke at length about his understanding of the principle of the freedom of the seas; and this led him to more general considerations of others of his Fourteen Points, and then, these questions led him in turn to a consideration of the importance of the establishment of the League of Nations.

Clemenceau returned a third time to the Palais Murat to visit Wilson; and once again the premier said little, trying instead to be agreeable and to draw Wilson out. But it seemed that Wilson was not to be drawn out—or else that he had already been drawn out, that he had no ulterior designs on territory or reparations, on colonies or gold, or any of the other ordinary spoils of war, that he had no thought of getting anything in payment for the American lives spent in the war, that he had indeed come to Paris to secure one thing and one thing only, the League of Nations, that the French, by giving Wilson his league, were about to get, for themselves, something for nothing.

During the debate in the chamber of deputies over the appropriation of the 10 billion francs—which occurred just after these meetings with Wilson—Clemenceau had remarked, in passing, on his impressions of President Wilson. Clemenceau believed, he said, that the president was a man of "noble candeur." The socialist deputies had leapt to their feet with cries of protest, shouts of "shame!" The word *candeur* is an ambiguous one, meaning both "frankness" and "simplemindedness."

THE GOAT-FOOTED BARD

Not all the delegations had yet gathered in Paris; the peace conference could not yet begin; and so Wilson set out once again, this time to London.

He was greeted there by King George, Queen Mary, Princess Mary, and the entire British cabinet, and taken down the Strand to Trafalgar Square, through the Mall and around Piccadilly in the royal coach, drawn by six black horses; the Grenadier guards played the "Star Spangled Banner"; two hundred thousand cheered in front of Buckingham Palace; and the socialists and liberals—some of them members of Parliament, some of them members of the British delegation to the peace conference—applauded Wilson at the Guildhall and the Mansion House and in Manchester when he denounced the old "balance of power" politics and spoke of a new order, a "common devotion to right," and a "mandate of humanity."

After his speech, the president was invited to go along to Number 10 Downing Street, where he might settle in for some hours in private with Lloyd George, as an insider in one of the more intimate moments in politics. Lloyd George, in order to make certain that his political house was in order before setting out for Paris, had called for a general election; he had invited Wilson to be with him to watch the returns coming in. "Around the table," said Billy Hughes, the prime minister of Australia, "were seated representatives of Britain and the Dominions of all shades of political opinion, together with . . . Wilson. We had been discussing some of the problems of the 'peace presently to be made,' but in a disjointed, perfunctory way; for we found it impossible to switch our minds from this great human drama then rushing swiftly to its climax.

"Lloyd George sat there outwardly unmoved—alert, smiling,

throwing in a word here and there about 'the peace . . . ,' opening telegrams, which continued to fall in a spate on the table at his elbow."

The prime minister was a short, stocky man, with a large head and a great shock of white hair that he wore in a flowing mane that fell below his collar. "He was inordinately proud of his large head," one unsympathetic observer said of him; "such are the foibles of great men that he always measured his contemporaries by the size of their heads. Neville Chamberlain, for example, was dismissed as a 'pinhead.' "

Quicksilver sprang to the minds of his contemporaries when they thought to characterize Lloyd George; he was a man constantly in motion, impossible to pin down, a quick and ruthless opponent in debate, shrewd and witty, always at the ready with a swoon of romantic oratory, a swift riposte, a man who would pounce and move on, whirl and impale his opponent, shift to new ground, and vanish.

Born on January 17, 1863, the son of a schoolmaster who died when the boy was one year old, David George was raised by his mother and his mother's brother—surnamed Lloyd—a shoemaker in Wales. The shoemaker learned Latin himself in order that he might teach the boy, and David became a lawyer at the age of twenty-one, married a farmer's daughter, Margaret Owen, at the age of twenty-five, and at the age of twenty-seven was elected to Parliament, where he sat as the member for Carnarvon Boroughs for fifty-four years.

A champion of the weak and the poor, the author of much of the legislation that established the modern welfare state, fearless opponent of the landlords, a resourceful, tenacious, devious, crafty conniver for the rights and interests of the lower classes, he realized, at some point during his career, that his passions—shared as they were by a large number of people—brought him growing power; and he commenced to tailor his passions to suit his ambitions rather than, as he had at first, to tailor his ambitions to suit his passions.

"He was an expert in every device of the intriguer's art," said Alfred Gollin.

"He had really no principles at all," Sir Colin Coote said of him, "only emotions."

He had, said L. S. Amery, "no central core of . . . conviction."

"I have to go to a far greater man than myself to find any description apt for him," a conservative opponent, Stanley Baldwin, later said of him. "I remember that Thomas Carlyle in describing another great man ... used these words which might have been written of the leader of the Liberal party: 'He spent his whole life in plastering together the true and the false, and therefrom manufacturing the plausible.' "

"You could hardly imagine," said Winston Churchill, one of Lloyd George's admiring cabinet members, "two men so diverse as [the former prime minister, Lord] Curzon and Lloyd George. Temperament, prejudices, environment, upbringing, mental processes were utterly different and markedly antagonistic. The offspring of the Welsh village whose whole youth had been rebellion against the aristocracy ... had a priceless gift. It was the very gift which the product of Eton and Balliol [Curzon] had always lacked—the one blessing denied him by his fairy godmother, the one without which all other gifts are so frightfully cheapened. [Lloyd George] had the 'seeing eye.' He had that deep original instinct which peers through the surface of words and things—the vision which sees dimly but surely the other side of the brick wall or which follows the hunt two fields before the throng. Against this, industry, learning, scholarship, eloquence, social influence, wealth, reputation, an ordered mind, plenty of pluck, counted for less than nothing. Put the two men together in any circumstances of equality and the one would eat the other."

"How can I convey," said John Maynard Keynes, then a young economics expert in the British delegation to the peace conference, " ... any just impression of this extraordinary figure of our time, this syren, this goat-footed bard, this half-human visitor to our age from the hag-ridden magic and enchanted woods of Celtic antiquity? One catches in his company that flavour of final purposelessness, inner irresponsibility, existence outside or away from our Saxon good and evil mixed with cunning, remorselessness, love of power, that lend fascination, enthralment, and terror to the fair-seeming magicians of Northern European folklore.... Lloyd George is rooted in nothing ... he lives and feeds on his immediate surroundings; he is an instrument and a player at the same time which plays on the company and is played on by them too; he is a prism ... which collects light and distorts it and is most brilliant if the light comes from many quarters at once; a vampire and a medium in one."

Lloyd George, like Wilson—and, for that matter, like Clemenceau, too—behaved toward the world as he behaved toward women.

He married Dame Margaret, née Margaret Owen, the daughter of a moderately well-to-do Welsh landowner, in 1888, and they had five children together. One child died in late adolescence; of the others, by the time of the peace conference, all but one had grown up and left home: only seventeen-year-old Megan, whom Lloyd George loved having with him wherever he went, was still living with her parents.

Lloyd George had his first extramarital affair three months after he was married—with a young widow he met in an amateur dramatic society that gathered for musical evenings in private homes. ("Nothing gave him greater pleasure," his son Richard wrote of Lloyd George, "than an evening of entertainment amongst professional performers, sopranos, young actresses of distinction, famous beauties, artists and their friends.") Lloyd George and Mrs. Jones took to rehearsing duets at her home, and presently she gave birth to an illegitimate son.

One time, while on a speaking tour of Wales, he spent the night with Dr. and Mrs. Edwards in Monmouthshire. Subsequently, Mrs. Edwards signed a paper admitting that her second child was the offspring of Lloyd George—an admission she later retracted, saying her husband had forced it from her at knife point.

In London, of a Sunday afternoon, Lloyd George enjoyed strolling out with a few of his children and dropping in at the home of Mrs. Davies. While the children were sent to play in the garden, Lloyd George would converse with Mrs. Davies. One afternoon, Richard came in from the garden unexpectedly and found his father "eating" Mrs. Davies's hand.

Recently, Colin Cross has written that "It was at times difficult to run [Lloyd George's] private office because the typists were able to give themselves such airs."

Wherever he traveled, innuendo followed. During a wartime visit to France, one newspaper reported, "Mr. Lloyd George, after a hard day's work in Paris, drove to the Latin quarter in the evening to see what life there during the wartime was like."

"I remember sitting in a restaurant with him," Richard recalled, "through which passed cohorts of fashionable, handsome creatures. A most statuesque enchantress passed our table, conscious of being the center of masculine attention, dipping and swaying like a yacht with all its sails engaged. I made some youthfully appreciative remark; but father hardly raised his eyes from his soup plate. 'Handsome. Like one of Rosebery's fillies. And about as exciting,' was his indifferent comment."

In time, Margaret became accustomed to her husband's promiscuity, and, by the time Lloyd George met Frances Stevenson, Margaret was ready to accept her presence completely.

Frances Stevenson was one of Megan's schoolteachers, aged twenty-three when Lloyd George, then forty-eight years old, met her and asked—in his customary fashion—whether she would like to be his secretary. By the time of the war, Lloyd George was spending nearly every weekend and many weeknights with Frances, although Margaret was often coming into London from the country, too. In time, Frances took a flat in Chester Square, Margaret spent a great deal of time in London—to her husband's apparent delight— and Lloyd George himself took a flat in Saint James's Court.

Margaret apparently never complained; Frances did, a lot; but Lloyd George continued to enjoy both of his "wives" and an unknown number of mistresses, as well as the companionship of Megan, and his grandchildren. Obliged, for decades, to choose between Margaret and Frances—as he was often forced in politics to choose between one loyalty and another—he chose them both.

Amidst the general elections whose returns Lloyd George awaited in the company of Woodrow Wilson, the party managers had complained to the prime minister that the campaign seemed to be falling a bit flat. The English, having suffered long and bitterly during the war, began to suspect now that the government was going "to let the Hun off." Widespread sentiment in Britain called for making the Germans pay sufficient reparations to get the British economy—which had been ravaged and placed deeply in hock to the United States by the war—back on its feet.

Lloyd George understood, as Keynes and others had explained, that Germany had been the very "spark plug" of the European economy; some war damages might in fact be paid—but not so much that the German economy would itself be destroyed. If the German economy were destroyed, so would the European economy be, so would the English economy be, so would the world economy be—and so, by the way, would President Wilson's view of a new order for the world, led by a League of Nations that would welcome Germany back into the world community.

And so, when Lloyd George came to insist that Germany pay

for the war, he insisted very carefully: "When Germany defeated France she made France pay," he said. "That is the principle which she herself has established. There is absolutely no doubt about the principle, and that is the principle we should proceed upon—that Germany must pay the costs of the war up to the limit of her capacity to do so."

The prime minister's statement was unexceptionable—and not very exciting. The *Times* complained decorously, but Lloyd George continued to speak discreetly and loftily. He left it to his associates to take the flatness out of the campaign, to seize the opportunity. "I," shouted one of the members of the war cabinet in the closing weeks of the campaign, "am for hanging the kaiser," and, with that, the Liberal party was off and running.

"We will get out of [Germany]," Sir Eric Geddes declared in a speech at the Guildhall in Cambridge, "all you can squeeze out of a lemon and a bit more. I will squeeze her until you can hear the pips squeak."

To squeeze Germany "until the pips squeak" became the rallying cry of the election. In the end, most people thought Lloyd George had said it. The popularity of the Liberal party revived speedily, and Lloyd George was ebullient: the trick was turned.

"From about nine o'clock," said Billy Hughes, "the returns came pouring in thick and fast, pointing to a victory for Lloyd George; and as time went on, this became more and more assured. . . . Congratulations poured in. . . . All . . . were caught up in the whirl of excitement; the reserve that normally cloaked their emotions was cast aside. They did not shout or stand on tiptoe, but they dropped all pretence of calm deliberation about the problems of the peace. The people of England had spoken; and the thunder of their voices shut out all lesser sounds. One after another congratulated Lloyd George, and leant across the table to shake his hand.

"But President Wilson held aloof and sat stiffly in grim silence. He was the honoured guest of the Government of Britain. . . . It would have been a gracious gesture to have said a few words of personal congratulations. But the President remained silent."

In the days following, the president was given testimonial dinners and driven about, presented to enthusiastic audiences, complimented and pampered and praised, until some of Lloyd George's associates commenced to notice that Wilson had not made any reference in his speeches, not even once, neither brief nor passing, to

Britain's suffering during the war, nor to Britain's great achievements during the war.

Lloyd George himself at last remarked of one of the president's speeches that it was notable for its "perfect enunciation, measured emphasis, and cold tones."

CROSSING THE CHANNEL

A placard had been posted by the crew in the wardroom of the channel ferryboat: "Politicians are requested not to be sick where we live."

HOTEL MAJESTIC

"When I eventually reached Paris," said Keynes, " ... it was as I had expected, and no one yet knew what the Conference was doing or whether it had started. But the peculiar atmosphere and routine of the Majestic were already compounded and established ... the feverish, persistent and boring gossip of that hellish place had already developed in full measure the peculiar flavour of smallness, cynicism, self-importance and bored excitement that it was never to lose."

The principal British delegates occupied two hotels, the Astoria and the Majestic. "The great hall of the Majestic," the young Harold Nicolson wrote in his diary, "was gay with the clatter of tea cups: the strains of dance music echoed from below the stairs. . . . The purlieus of the Majestic clattered to the sound of motor cyclists. A fleet of army cars facilitated our movements."

Many of the young English liberals such as Keynes and Nicolson, despite their dry, cynical style, were buoyant with hopes and expectations. It was clear to them that the real revolution that presented itself to the world at the end of the war was the Bolshevik revolution. The danger was that the counterrevolutionary old guard would line up against the Bolsheviks to provoke yet another dreadful confrontation. The historic opportunity that the young liberals saw was to champion Wilsonism—not because it was "the new order" but because it was a compromise between the truly new order and the old order. Some combination of Wilsonism, English liberalism, and French democratic socialism seemed to offer a genuine, desirable alternative to Communism. The young Englishmen saw their role as that of joining with the young Americans to keep Wilson from backsliding toward his conservative instincts and to keep Lloyd George from shilly-shallying.

The members of the British delegation to Paris possessed, among their briefing papers, a slim little volume about the Congress of Vienna which the younger diplomats perused with care, until they had acquired a faint sense of disdain for the mistakes that had been made in the time of the Emperor Joseph and Prince von Metternich, as Harold Nicolson said, by "the misguided, the reactionary, the after all pathetic aristocrats" who had met at the great conference a century before. "They had worked in secret. We, on the other hand, were committed to 'open covenants openly arrived at'; . . . they had believed in the doctrine of 'compensations': they had spoken quite cynically about the 'transference of souls.' We for our part were liable to no such human error. We believed in nationalism, we believed in the self-determination of peoples. 'Peoples and Provinces,' so ran the 'Four Principles' of [Wilson], 'shall not be bartered about from sovereignty to sovereignty as if they were but chattels or pawns in the game.' At the words 'pawns' and 'chattels' our lips curled in democratic scorn.

"Nor was this all. We were journeying to Paris, not merely to liquidate the war, but to found a new order in Europe. We were preparing not Peace only, but Eternal Peace. . . . We were bent on doing great, permanent and noble things."

That the position of these fine, intelligent, idealistic, young English liberals was inherently hypocritical had occurred to none of them, and would not occur to them for several decades.

Nicolson tried to convince his immediate superior, Sir Eyre Crowe, later permanent undersecretary for foreign affairs, that England had acquired Cyprus by a "disreputable" trick, that Cyprus was wholly Greek and would under the principle of self-determination, choose union with Greece, and that Britain would be in a false position if the British insisted on self-determination for other people's colonies but refused to surrender any British possession.

"Nonsense, my dear Nicolson," said Crowe, sacrificing the whole of British liberal idealism without a second thought, "you are not being clear-headed. You think that you are being logical and sincere. You are not. Would you apply self-determination to India, Egypt, Malta, and Gibraltar? If you are *not* prepared to go as far as this, then you have no right to claim that you are logical. If you *are* prepared to go as far as this, then you had better return at once to London."

&

LA SCALA

Still, not all of the delegations had yet arrived in Paris; and so the president reembarked upon his triumphal tour.

In Rome, as the guest of King Victor Emmanuel, Wilson was given a tumultuous demonstration, "rivalling those at Paris and London," said one reporter. The president was a personal guest of the king, received by the two chambers of Parliament, declared a citizen of Rome, and shown the Baths of Diocletian, the palace of the Caesars, and Queen Helena in person. He was given luncheon with the Queen Mother, and a state dinner, and an opportunity to speak himself, which he did "in English, as is his custom, so that comparatively few of those about him understood. But there was constant applause."

Italy's prime minister was Vittorio Emanuele Orlando, a man of "ruddy complexion," according to a British diplomat, "and his head is crowned, hedgehog-like, with iron-grey hair without parting." He wore close-fitting jackets, kept tightly buttoned; he was short, about the same height as Lloyd George, amiable, tenacious rather than quick in conversation, logical, a trained lawyer, "willing to shift," as Seymour said, "to whichever side seems to be getting the upper hand."

Orlando's foreign minister was Baron Sidney Sonnino, "white-haired and white-mustached," Robert Lansing said of him, "with a florid complexion and a genial smile . . . belonged to the diplomats of the old school, and was disposed to practice their methods. Practical and deliberate in urging his views, which were little affected by ide-alistic considerations." A former premier, self-confident, apparently less liberal than Orlando, Sonnino impressed the British, Nicolson later said, as a man of "independence, high-mindedness, a nimble wit and the humanities. These are immortal assets. They enabled Baron Sonnino to be protractedly unreliable before we found him out."

Wilson wished he could find some way to get around the Italian leaders and speak to the socialists, who regarded the president as their great hope; and Wilson wished even more that he could find an opportunity to speak directly to the Italian people; but Prime Min-ister Orlando and his aides were apparently intent upon keeping the president confined to formal receptions at the royal palace, the na-tional legislature, the Capitol. Once, when he had been promised a quick stop in the Piazza Venezia, the driver whisked him off to an-other place instead, and, when Wilson asked if this were the place where he was supposed to speak, he was told it was too late. On his last night in Rome, when he thought he would speak from a balcony of the Quirinal Palace, he was told there was no audience, which was quite true, since troops had cordoned off the plaza so that no one could get near the palace.

At last, in Milan, Wilson got his chance after a gala dinner—at-tended by some of Italy's most prominent socialist leaders as well as Benito Mussolini, then the popular editor of *Popolo d'Italia*, who was in the midst of founding his new Fascist party—and followed by scenes from the second act of *Aïda:* he presented himself finally to the crowds at La Scala, and the Italians responded enthusiasti-cally, screaming and blowing kisses to the president. Wilson, so re-nowned for his Presbyterian constraint, was overcome by the dis-play of Mediterranean passion, and he suddenly unbuttoned himself and threw kisses back to the crowd—and so he had closed his triumphal tour of Europe with the delirious Milanese, blowing kisses back and forth.

THE BRITISH DELEGATION

"The world," said Lord Riddell over dinner with Lloyd George and Andrew Bonar Law, former chancellor of the exchequer, "is demanding a revaluation of human effort. People are asking whether one millionaire is worth more to the world than, say, five thousand coal miners or engine drivers, or whether one lord chancellor is of equal value to a hundred sea captains, schoolmasters or professors." Bonar Law, Riddell confided to his diary, "was pleased with this point of view. L.G. commented on the difference between the situation of the wealthy and the poor.... Bonar Law said he spent a week-end at Curzon's some time ago, and the conversation turned on the changed conditions of the various classes. B.L. remarked to Curzon, 'Three hundred years ago I should have been a serf on one of your estates!' L.G. laughed and said, 'I should not have been a serf. I should have been a rebel!' "

The British worried that their telephones were being tapped, and the French authorities said they were unable to do anything about it. London experts were brought in but said nothing could be done. The prime minister was consulted on the matter. "It's no good setting the code makers to work at this stage," said Lloyd George, " . . . we'll use Welsh."

One other concern, said Nicolson, preyed upon Mr. Alwyn Parker who was responsible for the general comfort and well-being of the British delegation: the possibility of British delegation members contracting disease. To cope with that prospect, Mr. Parker "engaged an obstetric physician of the very greatest distinction."

The librarian of the British Foreign Office had prepared a colored chart of the relative positions and areas of concern of the Dominion prime ministers and delegates and other ambassadors, assistants, area experts, secretaries, aides, and motorcycle messengers, the whole chart color coded in red, green, and blue and designed with such neatness and order that when Lloyd George saw it, he laughed out loud.

When Lord Castlereagh went to Vienna in 1815, as representative of the British government, he took along a staff of fourteen men. In 1919, the British delegation filled five hotels. The Americans, at their high point, numbered 1,300 persons, maintained in Paris at a cost of $1,500,000. The Folies Bergère, it was said ("more moral if anything than formerly, some very pretty costumes, quite modest *nudités*"), presented such an array of tasseled hats, exotic designs of fir trees, suns, wildcats, Indian heads, gold braid, stiff red collars, plaids, derbies, and khaki that it was difficult to keep attention focused on the stage.

When Shotwell came to call, he noticed that the Majestic was attended by a group of "very solemn butlers and detectives at the door to look you over—or look over you, as they mostly do"—or did with the short Shotwell. The dining room was at least twice the size of that at the Crillon, and the scene was the most remarkable, Shotwell said, that he had ever witnessed: at different tables "sat the delegations of the different parts of the British Empire . . . Australia . . . the Indian Empire . . . the maharajah of Bikaner . . . Canadian table . . . discussing the fate of Arabia and the East."

Lord Robert Cecil, with whom Shotwell dined one evening, was "a very tall man—six feet three or more. When he sits down he slides into the chair and lets his body get under the table, so as he and I sat opposite and looked across at each other, we were both comfortably fixed with our eyes above the tablecloth."

"After luncheon," Nicolson recorded in his diary, "go with Allen to see Goga—a Transylvanian poet and politician. A young Transylvanian Virgil Tilea is there. They say they are 'too ashamed to speak of internal questions.' On external questions, however, they show no shame at all, demanding most of Hungary."

Mr. A. J. Balfour, foreign minister of Great Britain, loved to read thrillers, to play Ping-Pong, and to stroll on the Champs Elysées. He was known for his encyclopedic knowledge, apparent optimism, and complete detachment. Having been prime minister himself, from 1902 to 1905, he was an interested student of the office, and he watched Lloyd George, one of his colleagues said, "like one entranced by the beauty of a firefly; or like a schoolboy enraptured by the subtleties of cricket as it can be played by a Ranjitsinhji. He revelled in the game, as one of the flanneled fools, brilliantly eloquent, devastatingly critical, but"—because of the coolness of his own temperament and the combustiveness of Lloyd George's—"utterly ineffective."

Shotwell said that Balfour played tennis every morning and could not be got down to work until two-thirty in the afternoon, "so it is very difficult to get details to his attention. The story goes that a memorandum on Armenia was handed to him last night and he read a page of it, and then dropped it on the floor and kicked it into the farthest corner of the room, with the remark that as long as he was at this Conference he was not going to read any more memoranda, that he knew now all he wanted to know about the Armenians or anyone else; dismissed his secretary and went to bed."

❦

PRECONFERENCE ANALYSIS

Complaints began to appear in the editorial columns of newspapers about the dilatoriness of the diplomats in getting around to starting the peace conference. Food was not getting delivered to starving children; governments continued to crumble; civil war still raged in Russia; riots spread through Germany. The delay alone, some said, might sabotage the work of the conference before it had begun. Some political analysts thought that the delay was due to Lloyd George's wish to have a general election before the conference; others thought that President Wilson had wanted to have a grand tour of Europe before the conference began; others thought Wilson only toured Europe because the conference was delayed after Lloyd George called a general election; others pointed out that the agenda had not been drawn up, that some delegations had not yet arrived, that Clemenceau wanted Wilson to make a tour of the battlefields before the conference began.

The French quietly proceeded to set January 18 as the opening day for the conference—the date, as Clemenceau certainly recalled, on which France had signed its treaty of surrender to Germany in 1871.

PART TWO
THE AMERICAN OFFENSIVE

JANUARY 18

On January 18, Shotwell said, "A single company of soldiers on the Quai along the other side of the street, and another company in the courtyard with a trumpeters' band and kettledrums blare out a note of welcome for a big automobile from which emerges Woodrow Wilson. Cameramen turn their films busily while Wilson takes off his silk hat and smiles to the crowd. Almost no cheering and very few spectators."

The Ministry of Foreign Affairs, on the Quai d'Orsay, surrounded by a tall iron fence, was built in 1853 and filled with Gobelin tapestries, marble, white enamel, gold leaf, red silk hangings, cupids dancing along the frieze of the rococo ceiling, and, in the room where the delegates gathered for the first plenary session of the Paris Peace Conference of 1919, the *Salon de l'horloge;* a small clock in an ornamental mantelpiece. But the room had been renamed the "Salon of Peace," and, in front of the mantelpiece had been placed a large, vulgar, and unconvincing Statue of Liberty, or Peace, holding aloft a torch of Civilization.

The table, covered in green baize, shaped like a giant horseshoe, had nine red leather chairs at the head, fifteen down each side, inside and out, making, in all, sixty-nine, and the five large windows overlooking the Seine let in the uncertain sunlight.

Lord Esher, who had spent most of the war years in Paris doing political intelligence work under cover of working for the Red Cross, had provided Lloyd George with a quick rundown on the Frenchmen who would be in the room:

Clemenceau	Masterful—at a dangerous age. Life behind him instead of before him. "Capable de tout."
Pichon [French foreign minister]	Would never get half round the course at Aintree.
Jules Cambon	Old and foxy.
Marshal Foch	Cyrano de Bergerac.

Of the other members of the French delegation, Louis-Lucien Klotz, the minister of finance, was, said Clemenceau, "the only Jew who can't count."

The general secretary of the conference, charged with seeing to the efficiency of its operations, was M. Paul Dutasta, "a weak, flustered, surprised but not unamiable man," said Nicolson. "It was said that he owed his appointment to the intimate relation in which he stood to M. Clemenceau. . . . M. Dutasta would stand from M. Clemenceau a greater degree of abuse and insult than might have been expected from any person more detached."

It was Pichon, however, who followed Clemenceau, carrying the premier's briefcase. Pichon, said Lloyd George, "is frightened to death of the old boy." Clemenceau took the advice of none of the men, and, when they offered it, they risked being treated with rudeness of a high order.

Lloyd George, too, disdained the advice of his colleagues. Curzon said that Lloyd George was inclined to follow his own bent ("opportunistic and hand to mouth"). Lloyd George was accompanied by Balfour, his foreign secretary, whom Clemenceau commenced to call "cette vieille fille," and by Andrew Bonar Law, two of whose sons had been killed in the war. "Lonely and austere by nature," Beaverbrook said of Bonar Law, "almost every idle moment he passed in playing bridge and chess. His meals—which consisted generally of vegetables, rice pudding and a glass of milk—were swallowed swiftly. . . . Upright and straightforward in conduct . . . rejected all offers of honours and decorations." He seemed not to have much energy and was dispatched back to London by Lloyd George to keep an eye on the domestic political scene. Nor did Lloyd George pay much attention to the other principal member of the British delegation, Viscount Milner, the colonial secretary, a sixty-five-year-old bachelor who had the disconcerting habit of half closing his eyes "if he does not agree with you," said Clemenceau, "like a lizard." Educated in Germany and at Balliol College, Milner was "impressive," Beaverbrook thought, "but not attractive."

When Dutasta and his assistants lost things, Sir Maurice Hankey found them; he was, said one of the British delegates, "secretary of everything that mattered. A marine of slight stature and tireless industry, he grew into a repository of secrets, a Chief Inspector of Mines of information. He had an incredible memory, not like that of Barthou or Philippe Berthelot who learned verse every morning to keep theirs oiled, but an official brand which could reproduce on call the date, file, substance of every paper that ever flew into a pigeonhole."

Wilson was accompanied, too, by a delegation whose advice he ignored. General Bliss "sat perfectly still," one of the American aides said, "the very personification of the gruff, silent, honest soldier . . . a strongly built man . . . a little stooping at the shoulders . . . thick gray eyebrows, bristly gray moustaches, thick hair on his neck, and . . . bald." The general believed in pacifism, disarmament, and Wilsonism—even more strongly, some suspected, than Wilson himself.

Henry White was the only Republican in the American delegation—a sop to Wilson's political opponents in the Senate, who did not appreciate the gesture. An "old dear," Seymour called him: "Just as nice as he can be but he is certainly doddering." Though he was only sixty-nine years old, White dwelt largely in the past, a good companion for a drive through the Bois de Boulogne on a misty, gray-blue morning: tall, thick white hair, a full voice, walked with a cane. When Ray Stannard Baker published his memoirs of the conference, he went over the manuscript and deleted this sen-

47

tence: White "has had no doubts for thirty or forty years, since he came into the diplomatic service and stopped thinking."

Secretary of State Robert Lansing—cool, aloof, timid—sat silently through the speeches, doodling, and sketching unkind caricatures of the other delegates on the note pad that he balanced on his left knee. Seymour thought Lansing looked very tired. "He walks very slowly," Seymour said. Lansing told one of the young American aides that "he is bothered by his heart."

Wilson ignored all of the members of his delegation except for Colonel Edward M. House—who was unable to attend this opening session of the conference because of a slight illness. House, whom the delegates would meet later, was rumored to be the one man in whom Wilson confided.

The French, British, and Americans sat at the head of the horseshoe table; down along the sides were Hughes of Australia, Generals Louis Botha and Jan Smuts of South Africa, Ignacy Paderewski of Poland, the maharaja of Bikaner, Emir Feisal, Edvard Benes of Czechoslovakia, Prince Charoon of Siam.

Raymond Poincaré, a slight, round figure with a Vandyke beard, who occupied the ceremonial office of president of the French republic, opened the conference with an address to the delegates: "On this day, forty-eight years ago, on the eighteenth of January, 1871, the German Empire was proclaimed by an army of invasion in the Château at Versailles. It was consecrated by the theft of two French provinces [Alsace and Lorraine].... Born in injustice, it has ended in opprobrium. You are assembled in order to repair the evil that it has done and to prevent a recurrence of it. You hold in your hands the future of the world."

When Poincaré finished, the delegates stood to honor him, and he turned at once and left the hall. Clemenceau quickly slipped into the presiding officer's chair—his head bent forward, an expression on his face, an American journalist said, that "led one to think that he had a remarkable witticism in reserve and meant to tell it at the first opportunity."

Wilson rose to deliver the prearranged speech nominating Clemenceau chairman of the conference ("more nations are represented here than were ever ... fortunes of all peoples are involved ... a universal cataclysm ... danger is past ... victory has been won for mankind.")

Monsieur Paul Mantoux translated from French to English,

English to French; to the disgust of Clemenceau, English had been accepted as a second official language of diplomacy for this conference. Mantoux, who had a great shock of red hair and a beard, was dazzlingly bilingual, able to listen to a speech for fifteen or twenty minutes before the speaker paused and then, with the aid of only a few words he had jotted down, render the whole of the spoken passage, with remarkable accuracy, flourishes and eloquence intact or polished, and the appropriate shadings of sonority, tremulousness, anger, contempt, mockery, begging.

Lloyd George, who arrived late, as would be his custom, plunged extemporaneously into a seconding speech. Mantoux made an uncharacteristic mistake on this opening day; where Lloyd George referred to Clemenceau as "the grand young man of France," Mantoux slipped and translated Clemenceau into the "grand *old* man of France." Both Lloyd George and Clemenceau leapt to their feet at the same moment, amid general amusement, to demand a correction.

Clemenceau then moved briskly into the business of the conference—his head "thrown back," said Lansing, "between his broad, humped shoulders, with the knuckles of his gray-gloved hands resting on the green table in front of him, and with his thick, shaggy brows drawn partially over his dark eyes, which fairly sparkled as he addressed the delegates. He [spoke] in a deliberate and rather monotonous voice, but with no hesitation or break in the even flow of his words. As he proceeded, he became more and more emphatic, while the rapidity of his utterance increased until it suggested the drumming of a machine gun. He had none of the arts of oratory, but his distinct and incisive delivery compelled attention. . . . He seemed to hurl his words at his listeners. . . . Free debate and actual voting by the delegates had no place in the proceedings with M. Clemenceau in the chair."

Having listened to the fine expressions of sentiment about the historic importance of the conference, the urgent needs of justice and humanity, Clemenceau curtly said that the questions to be addressed now were: who was responsible for starting the war, how war criminals were to be punished, and how, and to what extent, the losses of the war were to be paid for.

"The greater the bloody catastrophe which devastated and ruined one of the richest regions of France, the more ample and splendid should be the reparation." Without pause, he proceeded to say that any nations that wished to express some opinion on a matter before the conference should submit a memorandum to M. Dutasta, and that the next plenary session of the conference would take up the question of the League of Nations. "No one has anything further to say? The sitting is closed."

PROTOCOL

At dinner, Balfour told Nicolson that after the official opening of the conference, Balfour walked down the steps with Clemenceau. "A.J.B. wore a top hat: Clemenceau wore a bowler. A.J.B. apologized for his top hat: 'I was told,' he said, 'that it was obligatory to wear one.' 'So,' Clemenceau answered, 'was I.'"

THE FEW AND THE MANY

Such plenary sessions as the meeting of January 18—requiring the appearance of "open covenants openly arrived at," and the presumed equality of all nations, great and small, in the deliberations concerning a treaty of peace—were, Nicolson noted in his diary, of a "purely fictitious character." Only five more such splendid meetings would be convened in the course of the conference.

Already there were too many nations in the world demanding a voice in their destinies, and the collapse of empires had let loose even more—the Poles, the Hungarians, and other Eastern Europeans. Some of them were represented in Paris by more than one delegation insisting upon recognition. Sheer numbers, betraying the dispersion of political power, made the world more complex.

The major powers constituted themselves at once into a Council of Ten, which consisted of five nations, each represented by a president or prime minister and his foreign secretary: Clemenceau and Pichon; Lloyd George and Balfour; Wilson and Lansing; Orlando and Sonnino; and, for Japan, Makino and Chinda, who were so polite that it was not clear that they understood what subjects were being discussed.

These ten were accompanied by their aides and advisers, and, when the fate of one country or another was under discussion, representatives of that country would be invited into the Council of Ten. The council room was about forty by sixty feet, with a high, domed ceiling, carved doric panels, three vaulting windows with green silk curtains, massive bronze chandelier, other fixtures here and there that were turned on one by one as the light of day began to fade, Gobelin tapestries representing the domestic life of Henry IV, an Aubusson carpet with a border of swans. Little high-backed gilt chairs were set out all around the room, with small individual tables in front of them.

Lloyd George persisted in arriving late for the meetings, but cheerfully, and, having little idea of the topic at hand, or of the position Britain meant to take, would begin to speak. In this way, one of the young English delegates said, he might start "most eloquently arguing the very case we were concerned to oppose. Hankey would scribble a note in his large, legible hand which Lloyd George would glance at without interrupting the flow of his argument. Presently he would blandly explain that he thought he had done full justice to a view which, however, the British Government did not share, and would now expound our own real attitude."

Clemenceau, said Shotwell, "had his desk in front of the fireplace with his back to the chimney. . . . Settled back, half-sunk in his armchair, with his eyes on the ceiling, he gave the impression of not listening more than half the time." His voice and his eyes, Shotwell thought, were his most arresting attributes—a rich, sad voice, "musical but not resonant," not the shrill, metallic voice Shotwell had expected—and eyes that were large and dark, "kindly and inscrutable; they seem to be trustworthy and yet to suggest that perhaps there is something concealed, not dishonestly, but simply going beyond the thought expressed, so that one hardly knows at what stage of agreement one has arrived—puzzling, deep-set eyes."

Usually, when he was tired of a subject, he was direct. He would frame a proposition or resolution and in rapid fire ask: "Y a-t-il d'objections? Non? . . . Adopté"—and bring down his gavel with a resounding crack. Nicolson noted in his diary that Clemenceau was "extremely rude to the small Powers: but then he is extremely rude to the Big Powers also." When the premier had grown tired of the whole session—especially if mealtime approached—he would pounce on any lull in a speech, declare *c'est tout*, drop his gavel on the table, "rise from his seat," one of the Englishmen said, "regardless of pleas or protests of would-be speakers" and walk out of the room.

Clemenceau presided, said Lord Robert Cecil, "with drastic firmness."

BASIS OF NEGOTIATIONS

"The armistice terms were humiliating," Botha, premier of South Africa, said over lunch. "I felt sorry, when I read them, that any nation should stoop so low as to accept such terms. Even barbarians will not surrender their cattle without a struggle. It would have been more dignified had the Germans said, 'We will not agree to your terms. You must do what you think best.' "

The Germans had in truth thrown themselves on the mercy of the Allies: they depended, in part, upon the Allied promise to base the final peace settlement on Wilson's Fourteen Points and four principles, applied impartially to all, including Germany.

Wilson's first point ("open covenants openly arrived at") had already been compromised several months before when Colonel House had met privately with Clemenceau and Lloyd George and assuaged their misgivings about the Fourteen Points by agreeing to a common "interpretation" which was committed to paper. The interpretation became a gloss on the Fourteen Points that Wilson, Lloyd George, and Clemenceau agreed tacitly to follow. Among other things the first point was interpreted to mean that open covenants would not, of course, preclude confidential negotiations concerning those open covenants.

Wilson's second point ("absolute freedom of navigation upon the seas") was interpreted not to mean that the weapon of blockade was to be abolished—since Britain, lord of the seas, considered naval blockade one of its principal defenses.

The third point ("removal . . . of all economic barriers") was interpreted to mean that a country could still protect its home industries by use of tariffs.

The fourth point ("national armaments will be reduced to the lowest point consistent with domestic safety") was interpreted to apply especially to Germany.

The fifth point ("a free, open-minded and absolutely impartial adjustment of colonial claims" with due regard for "the interests of the populations concerned") was not taken to mean that Germany might retain any of its colonies, even if the people of the colonies desired it.

The remaining points were not greatly altered by the interpretation: the sixth point addressed the need to welcome Russia into the international community "under institutions of her own choosing," and, to assist in that end, to withdrawing of all foreign troops from Russian soil.

The seventh and eighth points called for the restoration of Belgium and France, and the return to France of Alsace and Lorraine, which had been taken by Germany in 1870–71.

The ninth point called for an adjustment of Italy's frontiers in accord with "recognizable lines of nationality."

The tenth through thirteenth points called for the establishment of independent nations out of the shattered Austria Hungary; the restoration of Rumania, Serbia, Montenegro; sovereignty for Turkish portions of the Ottoman Empire; and the establishment of an independent Poland.

The fourteenth point called for the establishment of a League of Nations, to afford "mutual guarantees of political independence and territorial integrity to great and small States alike."

Wilson's four principles were left uninterpreted: the first stated that each part of the final settlement "must be based upon the essential justice of that particular case"; the second stated that "peoples and provinces must not be bartered about from sovereignty to sovereignty as if they were chattels or pawns in a game"; the third stated that all territorial questions had to be settled "in the interests of the populations concerned"; and the fourth that all "well-defined national elements"—such as the Hungarians and Serbs—were to be given "the utmost satisfaction that can be accorded them without introducing new, or perpetuating old, elements of discord and antagonism."

On the basis of these points and principles, Germany had laid down its arms, and the Europeans had welcomed Wilson almost deliriously, not having heard that the Fourteen Points had already been "interpreted."

THE AIMS OF CLEMENCEAU

Clemenceau wanted, first and last, to ensure security for France. Yet, although his aims were simple, his methods were wonderfully complex. He seemed to the English and Americans to be an uncommonly harsh man, a man filled with a sense of rage and vengeance, determined to crush Germany, to smash Germany's army, bankrupt Germany's economy, destroy Germany's empire, and keep Germany from ever making war again.

Part of Clemenceau's harshness was his nature, part of it was a performance meant for home consumption—to outflank the right wing in France that was calling for even more draconian measures than Clemenceau dreamed of considering—and part of it was apparently meant to hide his aims from his allies: at the same time that Clemenceau was calling for the complete disarmament, crushing, and bankrupting of Germany, the French were secretly sounding out the Germans about the possibilities of postwar economic and political cooperation.

The complete ruin of Germany was one option that Clemenceau toyed with, but not one that he wished to embrace. His instincts were more fluid. He demanded, as a matter of course, the return of Alsace and Lorraine—and this demand was met at once. He demanded in addition the complete disarmament of Germany west of the Rhine, full reparations payment for all war damages done to France (and, in order to guarantee that reparations were paid, the right of French troops to occupy the Rhineland until such time as reparations had been paid in full), a share of the surrendered German colonies, a specific guarantee that German Austria and Germany could never be reunited, assurances that Austria-Hungary would remain shattered, the secure establishment of the new states of Poland, Czechoslovakia, Yugoslavia (to assist in making certain that France had no large rival on the continent, but did have some small counterbalances to use in diplomacy), and some other minor bits, including recognition of French interests in Syria, Lebanon, Silesia, Palestine, and Armenia.

The English and Americans were impressed by Clemenceau's unwillingness to compromise on any of these matters, but in fact the premier was ready to entertain any number of combinations and permutations. All of his demands were suspended in a shifting, variable relationship to one another. To rebuild France after the war, he might prefer to take loans from America instead of reparations from Germany. Instead of insisting on reparations, he might enter trade agreements with Germany—perhaps using the club of reparations to induce the Germans to make a favorable deal. He might be less severe on the matter of German disarmament if the Americans and English would agree to a military alliance to protect France against possible German aggression. Rather than insist that Germany pay reparations, perhaps he would be content if the Germans paid nothing: if they would—or could—pay nothing then France was entitled to continue to occupy the Rhineland for ten, twenty, a hundred years.

On the other hand, if Allied cooperation did not continue after the war, if the Americans would not help France rebuild, if the Americans and English would not join in an economic combination with France, or would not join in a military alliance with France, then France would resort to a harsh peace with Germany to attempt, with whatever prospect of failure, to hold Germany down.

For Clemenceau's aim was to lead Europe, not ruin her, to dominate the continent, not devastate it, to hold Germany down and let her up again under French terms, to keep Germany divided for a time and let her up into a Europe knit together in a customs union dominated by France—in short, to pursue a policy not unlike the one the Allies would adopt after the end of the Second World War.

Whether France could in fact dominate the continent was another, and doubtful matter; but that, more than mere vengefulness, was Clemenceau's grand idea. To ensure French dominance, there were many possibilities, and Clemenceau could afford to hold out for a settlement, to delay and delay, waiting for the others to come around. For, after all, unlike the English and the Americans, whose armies clamored to go back home, Clemenceau lived there.

THE AIMS OF LLOYD GEORGE

Lloyd George, for his part, wanted to get some spoils for Britain and to see that the German high seas fleet (already held captive by the Allies) was neutralized so as to ensure continued British supremacy of the seas. He wanted a share of reparations money—if he could get it without ruining Germany—not only because he had promised it to the English voters, but because Britain, like France, needed the money, and disliked being so deeply in debt to their principal creditor, the United States.

He wanted, too, to eliminate competition from the German colonial empire by dividing up and scattering the German possessions and, less importantly, to distribute some of these colonies among British Commonwealth countries. On this last point, Lloyd George was not greedy: the essential thing was to break up the German Empire, not to swallow it, to ensure the continued pre-eminence of the British Empire, not to extend it.

In addition, Lloyd George had some lesser items on his shopping list: in order to entice Italy over to the Allied side during the war, England had agreed, in the secret Treaty of London in 1915, to give Italy a chunk of territory to its north. This secret treaty, and one with Japan, and some other minor agreements, needed to be honored—or, at least, Britain needed to seem to want to honor them—in order to keep Britain's word burnished in diplomatic circles.

Lloyd George wanted, too, to frustrate Clemenceau's plans to make France dominant on the continent—perhaps by seeing to it that Germany was not completely undone—and to ensure that Britain kept the upper hand in the ancient Anglo-French rivalry. He could not say this; and so he said instead that Clemenceau was a harsh, vengeful old man, who was trying to impose a Carthaginian peace on Germany.

THE AIMS OF WILSON

No one quite knew what Wilson wanted. "We sacrificed little," one of the Americans said, "in announcing that we would take no territory (which we did not want) nor reparations (which we could not collect) . . . our geographical position was such that we could advocate disarmament and arbitration with complete safety."

The young American idealists saw Wilson as the selfless champion of a new world order based on justice and a right regard for the aspirations of all people—a lofty, perhaps impractical idealism—an idealism that was being frustrated by the cynicism and vengefulness of Clemenceau and the shilly-shallying of Lloyd George.

The English diplomat James Strachey Barnes suspected, on the other hand, that Wilson had kept America out of the war to conserve her strength, then intervened when American power could seem the decisive factor in victory, and thus entered the world scene with a set of principles that provided a gloss for a pax Americana. So, in time, America "with her immense wealth and growing population, with the aloof detachment which her geographical situation afforded her, might thereby easily become the virtual arbiter of the world's destinies. . . . It was *realpolitik* with a vengeance."

No one in Paris could quite sort out what Wilson wanted. As time went on, he seemed neither as idealistic nor as cunning as he was thought to be. Evidently it was enough for Wilson to be the one who took America into the world—modestly, without arousing jealousy or resistance—simply to begin what was to become the American Century.

THE AIMS OF ORLANDO

Orlando's aims were a travesty of the aims of all the others. Italy had remained neutral at the beginning of the war, and then, in a remarkably forthright manner, inquired of both the Germans and the Allies what might be in the war for Italy. After sniffing around both sides, the Italians were offered more generous promises from the Allies: the Treaty of London, secretly concluded in 1915, promised Italy a slice of the Dalmatian coast with its offshore islands, the southern Tyrol up to the Brenner Pass, Trieste, the islands of the Dodecanese, and some other lesser items. In exchange for these concessions, Italy promised to give the port city of Fiume to what was to become Yugoslavia, and to join the war.

Sir Edward Grey, who negotiated much of the treaty on behalf of England, had to retire—he was ill, he said—temporarily to the country. The Foreign Office permanent undersecretary who was left in charge could not resist making a cynical remark to the Marchese Imperiali. "You speak," said the marchese self-righteously, "as though you were purchasing our support." "Well," the Englishman replied contemptuously, "and so we were."

The Italians did not keep their part of the bargain. They declared war on Austria-Hungary, but did not declare war against Germany for more than a year. Even then, the French and British felt the Italians had not fought with much enthusiasm. By the time of the Paris conference, it had dawned on Clemenceau and Lloyd George that the concessions along the Dalmation coast were no longer the properties of the enemy Austria but of the new and friendly nation of Yugoslavia, the "Kingdom of the Serbs, Croats and Slovenes," as it was then called. No one had fought more valiantly during the war than the Serbs. Then, too, these concessions to Italy flagrantly violated the principle of self-determination; if the Treaty of London were to be honored, Italy would be handed dominion, as Nicolson noticed, over "some 1,300,000 Yugoslavs, some 230,000 Germans, the whole Greek population of the Dodecanese, the Turks and Greeks of Adalia, all that was left of the Albanians, and vague areas of Africa." Wilson ought, as Nicolson pointed out, to refuse to honor the treaty at all, if he were to remain true to his Fourteen Points.

Perhaps because he realized he needed a new bargaining lever to hold the Allies to these concessions, perhaps because he became greedy, or perhaps simply to see what more he could get, Orlando demanded, in addition to everything else, the port city of Fiume.

The diplomats in Paris were disgusted. Aside from all other considerations, the Italians had no real use for Fiume, whereas it was the only port that Yugoslavia could possibly use. The Italians had no reason to demand Fiume except to ruin Yugoslavia as a competitor in overseas trade. Yes, Orlando agreed—as though with a shrug—that was true; but, then, Italy had been offered excellent concessions by Germany, and if Orlando did not get a good deal at Paris, the Italians would ask "why Italy had troubled to join the Allied side."

The Italians, said Balfour, were "swine."

THE AIMS OF OTHERS

The ambitions of the Big Four were not the only ambitions to be sorted out at Paris. One day when Shotwell looked in, Chekri Ghanem, "an Arab-looking gentleman with a long, forked, grey beard" spoke on behalf of some Syrian interests, in a speech that took him two and a half hours to deliver. In the middle of the speech, one of the young American aides slipped a note to Wilson, saying that Ghanem had not been in Syria for thirty-five years, having lived in France all that time. Presently, Wilson got up, strolled across the room, and, with his hands under his coattails, gazed out the window.

Clemenceau hissed at Pichon in a stage whisper: "What did you get the fellow here for, anyway?"

Pichon shrugged. "Well, I didn't know he was going to carry on this way."

Ghanem stopped reading his speech, looked around the room, apologetically asked if he was taking too long. In his nervousness he let a few pages that he had just read slip back onto the pile of manuscript on his desk. Clemenceau told him to finish; Ghanem started in again, not noticing that he was repeating the few pages he had just read.

When Ghanem left, and Clemenceau was about to adjourn, Wilson took the floor and said that he had promised a women's group that he would ask whether the conference might consider taking up some questions of special interest to women.

"Ah," said Clemenceau. "It's suffrage?"

That was, said Wilson, one of the questions.

Clemenceau said that he was deeply interested in suffrage, but that the conference was not the right place to consider it.

Balfour rose to say that he had long fought for women's suffrage.

Sonnino took the floor to say that he had stood up for women's suffrage in Italy "under the most difficult political conditions."

Makino rose to deliver a brief speech expressing his "appreciation of the part played by women in civilization; but he, too, agreed that this was not the place to recognize their political rights."

Clemenceau again turned to Pichon and asked in his stage whisper, and in the tone of voice in which one might inquire about a gnat, "What's the little fellow saying?"

❧

THE TRANSCRIPT

A. J. Sylvester, the official shorthand writer for the British delegation, had, as his colleagues, "Miss Painting and Miss Mitchell, two of the best note-takers I have ever worked with." The three of them worked in shifts, ten minutes per shift; at the end of each shift, the notetaker would take the notes into an adjoining room, transcribe them immediately, usually by dictating to a speed typist, and have them sent on for duplicating. A meeting might consume 250 foolscap pages, of which 100 copies were required.

The British had hand-crank duplicating machines; the Americans had electrically operated duplicators which could make thousands of copies while the British were making dozens. The British and Americans teamed up.

"The duplicating machines were working at full speed," Sylvester recalled, "and soon there were great stacks of paper piled up in the office.

" 'This is where we show you American methods,' I was told, as I stared at the stacks of paper and watched the duplicators turning out hundreds of pages, to add to the big piles reaching almost to the ceiling.

"It looked magnificent, but unfortunately, in their haste the American experts had forgotten to number the folios, with the result that the first page was about the only page that anyone could say for certain was in the proper order."

THE LEAGUE OF NATIONS, I

Whatever imperfect arrangements might be made, whatever improvisations might be adopted in negotiations, however many lives had been lost—all this and more, Wilson said, would be redeemed by the covenant for the League of Nations.

Wilson's first objective was to persuade Clemenceau and Lloyd George to agree to include the covenant for the league within the body of the treaty of peace. In this way, no matter what the treaty might say, the league would exist, and America, as part of the league, would belong to the international community. A number of United States Senators, and a number of Americans, were opposed to American membership in the league. But, Wilson calculated, if he could make the league absolutely part of the treaty, then he could get it past the Senate: the Senate, he thought, would not have the temerity to reject the treaty of peace.

It turned out to be astonishingly easy to persuade Clemenceau and Lloyd George to put the league into the treaty. Clemenceau said of Wilson, one American journalist wrote in his diary, "What Lord

Castlereagh said of the Czar at the Vienna Congress: 'It is necessary to group him.' " Or, as Clemenceau confided to Mordacq, "When the moment comes to claim French rights, I will have leverage that I might not have at this moment." Wilson should have been alarmed, but he was not.

The first meeting of the commission to draft the covenant of the league was held late in the afternoon in a dining room of one of the private apartments at the Hotel Crillon. The linen had been removed from the dining table, and a green baize cloth had been spread. Fifteen men sat around the table—one representative each from five "small" powers (Belgium, Brazil, China, Portugal, and Serbia), and two representatives each from Japan, Italy, France, Britain, and the United States.

Wilson ran the meetings, and loved them. His idea was to have a league that would provide a permanent organization for the peaceful settlement of disputes, a place to which imperfections in the treaty itself could be taken in the future for adjudication and adjustment—not a military alliance, but a forum where arguments could be settled before nations resorted to military alliances.

"In the main tenets of his political philosophy," Nicolson wrote of Wilson, "I believed with fervent credulity. In spite of bitter disillusionment I believe in them today."

The president was superb in his work on the league, said one of his aides. "He seems to like it and his short talks in explanation of his views are admirable." And he was tireless. "The President is a quaint bird," Lord Riddell noted in his diary. "This afternoon he came from the Conference Room and gave instructions for someone to telephone for his typewriter. We conjured up visions of a beautiful American stenographer, but in a short time a messenger appeared, bringing with him a battered typewriter on a tray. By this time the Conference had finished. The typewriter was placed in a corner of the Conference Room and the President proceeded to tap out a long memorandum, the purport of which had been decided upon by him and his colleagues. It was a strange sight to see one of the greatest rulers in the world working away in this fashion."

"The rest of us," said Lloyd George, "found time for golf and we took Sundays off, but Wilson, in his zeal, worked incessantly."

The president wanted, he explained to his colleagues, to call the document that they produced a covenant, because "I am an old Presbyterian." On occasion, Wilson seemed to have forgotten entirely where he was. At one point he amazed Lloyd George and Clemenceau by explaining how the league would establish a brotherhood of man where Christianity had not been able to do so. "Why," Lloyd George recalled Wilson as saying, "has Jesus Christ so far not succeeded in inducing the world to follow His teachings in these matters? It is because He taught the ideal without devising any practical means of attaining it. That is the reason why I am proposing a practical scheme to carry out His aims."

Clemenceau, said Lloyd George, "slowly opened his dark eyes to their widest dimensions and swept them round the assembly to see how the Christians gathered around the table enjoyed this exposure of the futility of their Master."

(Already the delegates were smiling at remarks attributed to Clemenceau: "Wilson talks like Jesus Christ," the Tiger was rumored to have said, "but acts like Lloyd George." Or, "How can I talk to a fellow who thinks himself the first man for two thousand years who has known anything about peace on earth?" Or, "Wilson has Fourteen Points, but God had only Ten.")

Although Wilson had made the league his own, he was, in truth, something of a latecomer to the notion of an international government. The negotiators for Great Britain were Jan Smuts of South Africa ("Dine with Smuts. . . . We talk religion," Nicolson noted in his diary, "anthropology [pigmies, bushmen, hottentots, golden bough], on which the General knows a good deal in a picturesque way. He is simple and intricate")—and Lord Robert Cecil (". . . the play of a smile on a rather stern face," said Shotwell). Both Smuts and Cecil had plans for a league. Wilson had, in fact, looked especially closely at the Smuts plan and incorporated much of it into his own.

Lord Robert's plan, said Lansing, called for "a Quintuple Alliance which would constitute itself primate over all nations and the arbiter in world affairs, a scheme of organization very similar to the one proposed by General Smuts.

"Lord Robert made no attempt to disguise the purpose of his plan . . . to place in the hands of the Five Powers the control of international relations . . . based . . . on the right of the powerful to rule. Its chief merit was its honest declaration of purpose"—to place "the destiny of the world . . . in the hands of a powerful international oligarchy possessed of dictatorial powers."

Lansing was not that much more enamored of Wilson's plan,

which called for an executive council dominated by the five major powers, which only seemed more democratic without being so. Lansing thought that Wilson opposed Cecil's plan only because it "too frankly declared the coalition an oligarchy of the Five Powers, and that there should be at least the appearance of cooperation on the part of the lesser nations."

But Smuts and Cecil were not the only veterans of world government. Even the French had a promoter of the European peace movement on the league commission.

"Is there really a permanent court of justice at The Hague?" one of the commission members asked.

"I," said Léon Bourgeois, "have the honor to be one of its members."

He was an "elderly gentleman," Cecil said of Bourgeois, "with unsatisfactory health. His eyesight was bad and he was extraordinarily sensitive to cold. I have a vision of him attending a committee at my room in the Majestic Hotel which was reasonably warm. He, however, found it so cold that he borrowed a fur rug of mine which he wrapped round himself, with the red cloth lining outward, so completely that he looked like a gigantic red caterpillar! Apart from this peculiarity, he was a courteous and able colleague with a great power of pouring out a stream of French reasoning, admirably phrased, in an even delivery without special emphasis. He told me that he had once been making a speech and that, in the course of it, he went to sleep. When he awoke a few minutes later he found that he had continued his speech without any interruption."

Bourgeois had only one proposal to put forward; and he proposed it again and again, monotonously: that the league have a permanent, standing international army, led by French generals. French policy—Clemenceau's policy—had the virtue of consistency: Wilson could have his league, but the league must resemble nothing so much as an old-fashioned military alliance—directed against Germany. Bourgeois was the perfect embodiment of Clemenceau's ideas for the league: it must be either militaristic—and led by the French—or irrelevant.

THE LEAGUE OF NATIONS, II

All of the major powers at the conference were agreed that Germany was to be stripped of all its colonies and possessions. A difference of opinion arose, however, as to what to do with these colonies. Nearly everyone at Paris naturally assumed that they would be divided up among the victors as the spoils of war. Wilson—committed to the principle that "peoples and provinces" were not to be traded about like "chattels and pawns in a game"—had another plan.

Wilson's plan was this: all colonies would be set free, then, all colonies would be taken under the protective wing of the League of Nations. The league would see to it that the colonies were governed freely and democratically and not bullied by larger nations. To oversee the former colonies, the league would appoint one country or another as guardian. Thus, for example, Australia might become New Guinea's guardian, and New Guinea would become a "mandatory" under the League of Nations.

Billy Hughes, the prime minister of Australia, did not understand this scheme. If Wilson's plan were a genuine proposal to abolish colonies, then it would be a great threat to the whole British Empire, and to Hughes's plan in particular to annex New Guinea. On the other hand, if Wilson's plan were merely a polite device to disguise the real nature of colonial control, Hughes thought it contemptible.

Hughes was not the only one to find the notion of mandatories confusing. When one of the Chinese delegates to the conference inquired about a certain troubling point, he was informed that it would be settled by mandatory.

"Who," the Chinese delegate asked, "is Mandatory?"

The dispute spilled over from the league commission into a Council of Ten meeting. Hughes—a small, deaf, pugnacious old man with an electric earphone, and a tendency to pretend (in order to irritate Wilson) to be more deaf than he was—told the president bluntly that he wanted New Guinea, and he did not care what others might decide to do about mandatories or anything else.

The president was moderate, conciliatory, and condescending. Surely Hughes did not mean to have New Guinea if he were opposed by the wishes of the whole world?

Hughes, his hand to his ear, shouted: "Yes, that's about it!"

Wilson was taken aback by the man's manner. The president did finally concede, however, that a vote could be taken of the natives to determine their wishes.

"Do you know, Mr. President," said Hughes, "that these natives eat one another?"

Wilson looked at Hughes sourly and declined to reply.

Hughes thought Wilson was both inflexible and weak, an idealist with feet of clay, and, perhaps even worse, a man without a sense of humor.

Lloyd George tried to come to Hughes's assistance, to let Hughes show Wilson and others that he was a reasonable, well-intentioned man, not an implacable foe—in short, a man ideally suited to have the mandate for New Guinea.

"And would you," Lloyd George asked gently, "allow the natives to have access to the missionaries, Mr. Hughes?"

"Indeed I would, sir," replied Hughes, "for there are many days when these poor devils do not get half enough missionaries to eat."

PRIMITIVE PEOPLE

When Shotwell had lunch with Viscount Milner, Britain's colonial secretary ("quiet, but forceful, not reticent in comment but carefully choosing his words when giving an opinion, much like a philosophical lawyer"), the conversation naturally turned to the question of colonies and possessions. Milner mentioned that he rather thought Britain had done well—where she had really tried—"in handling primitive peoples," but that it was extremely difficult to succeed in colonial administration when "the people governed were of about the same grade of intelligence as their governors."

Shotwell was impressed by Milner's cool, olympian view, and intrigued by his explanation.

The great question in statecraft, Milner said, was to determine "at what stage, and how far, a people of capacity but immaturity should have their rights of self-government admitted." Milner thought that the moment to grant self-government had arrived when the people in question "began to express themselves in abstract terms, that is, in the demand for constitutions and institutional bodies, instead of in terms of personalities."

Britain, said Milner, had always done superbly at training colonial administrators—men of "dependable character and good common sense"—trained not so much in technical matters as in "the humanities, especially the classics," which suited them well to govern "savage tribes." In this way, the products of the British public school system would tend "both by position and by racial prejudice . . . to take a position of aloofness and have an innate sense of their own superiority which primitive peoples readily recognize as a sign of leadership."

Shotwell wondered whether Milner could define more precisely the moment at which the subjects of colonial administration had begun to think in abstract terms.

Milner thought that this stage could not be defined exactly (perhaps, though Milner did not mention it, the stage had not even yet been reached in England or America), but it seemed to him that, "as nearly as one could state it, it was about when a people began to demand written or formal safeguards for their rights . . . as soon as they ceased to look to the personal qualifications of those governing them as the essential basis of relationship."

❧

GRAND TURK

"Dined with the P.M.," Riddell wrote in his diary, "who gave an amusing account of some of Clemenceau's observations at the Peace Conference. The question of the disposition of Heligoland arose, whereupon Clemenceau remarked, pointing to Wilson, 'He will hand it over to the League of Nations.' When Constantinople was under discussion, Clemenceau said, turning to Wilson, 'When you cease to be President, we will make you Grand Turk.' "

Riddell: "Did Wilson appreciate the joke?"
Lloyd George: "No, I don't think he did. . . ."

❧

WILSON'S TOUR OF THE BATTLEFIELDS

When the president first arrived in France, Clemenceau urged him to ride out for a tour of the battlefields. Wilson declined, saying that he would take a day off at intervals after the work of the conference got under way. During the month of January, Wilson's aides were nudged by the French diplomats to speak to the president about a tour of the battlefields, but the president still put it off. Presently the French newspapers—ever ready to do the government's bidding—began to attack Wilson for his apparent indifference to the blood shed during the war.

Why Wilson avoided the battlefields became a subject for gossip among the delegates. Some thought that Wilson suspected the French were trying to get him to take the tour so that the sight of the devastation would make him "see red" and he would come to share Clemenceau's wish (this school of gossips assumed it was Clemenceau's wish) to gouge heavy reparations out of the Germans. Perhaps the president found it difficult to look, for instance, at the Meuse-Argonne battlefield, where the men he had summoned to fight had suffered 150,000 dead and wounded.

Wilson had never liked raw facts. As a student at Johns Hopkins University, when he wrote his dissertation about congressional government—later developed into a book—he never actually went to Washington to have a look at the subject of his study, although Johns Hopkins was only an hour's train ride from Washington.

His habits did not change: after some years of apprenticeship as an academic historian, when he wrote his biography of George Washington, he avoided primary sources and wrote the book entirely out of secondary sources. When he was president he rarely read the daily newspapers and only cursorily glanced at the weekly press summaries that were prepared for him.

When at last, toward the end of January, the president did

drive through the part of the countryside where the Americans had done their heaviest fighting—Château-Thierry and Belleau Wood—returning by way of the battered cathedral at Rheims, where the archbishop gave the president a conducted tour, he did not linger.

The president, said Billy Hughes, "went right through the great areas affected in a closed limousine, stopping nowhere and seeing nothing. Along the route the sorely stricken inhabitants—whose homes had been battered to ruins, whose once smiling pastures and fertile farm lands were now barren, hideous heaps and cavernous depths—had gathered in little knots to welcome the great man about whom they had heard so much, and perchance to speak to him and to hear from him some words of sympathy. . . . But he passed them by without so much as a wave of the hand or a nod of the head.

"I came to Beauvais a few minutes after he had passed through and presented myself to the Colonel in command. He was almost in tears. . . . He told me that his men had been standing there all day, under the broiling sun, to receive President Wilson—but the President had swept past without even acknowledging their salute!"

Some of the other members of the American delegation drove out into the battlefields, too. Shotwell drove along a route similar to the president's, and at Belleau Wood Shotwell was transfixed by the shell holes, the splintered trees, shrapnel embedded in the roads, shallow graves blown open by shells, the grave of Joyce Kilmer, the chill in the countryside, the low-lying white mist, shards of farmhouses in the haze, the chalky rock at Craonne along the Chemin des Dames smashed to a fine powder, no grass, no ruins, only a fine powder covering all, nothing above ground, the remains, here and there, of cellars, the Chemin des Dames itself, the Ladies' Road running along the crest of the hill, disappeared in a wilderness of shell craters. "Even if one could trace it for a distance, there would be danger of getting lost, because there is no sign of direction."

Rheims, said Shotwell, was as dead as Pompeii, "and the ruins remind one somewhat of those of antiquity. In fact, from Rheims on, as far as Soissons, we all had the impression . . . of having passed out of the modern world back into a vanished civilization." Rheims gave way to a tract of utter desolation, an uninhabited desert, trenches, "white chalky parapets," barbed wire, and silence—no living thing, no bird, no animal broke the silence. They were in no-man's-land, a landscape unspeakably bizarre, death white, cratered, cold.

"When I came back to Paris," Shotwell said, after touring the Marne, Château-Thierry, Belleau Wood, Verdun, "I gave my clothes to the chambermaid to be cleaned, and remarked that the white mud was hard to get out, that it was the dust of Verdun. She took the clothes reverently and said with a tone that I shall never forget, 'That is very precious dust, sir.' "

SACRIFICES

Klotz began to read a pamphlet that described the terrible destruction visited on certain of the occupied regions of France. Wilson interrupted, saying, "This evidence might no doubt affect [the delegates'] frame of mind, but what effect would it have on their plans?"

Lloyd George had insisted that representatives of the Dominions be given room at the council table; Wilson opposed the plan. Lloyd George reminded Wilson that Australia and Canada, with far smaller populations than the United States, had both lost more lives than the Americans.

The small powers objected to the way that Clemenceau excluded them from meetings of the Council of Ten. "The five great powers, I am obliged to say," Clemenceau replied, "are in a position to do so. At the time of the armistice they had together twelve million men under arms on the battlefields. Their dead can be counted by millions."

The power of a politician—the degree of his strength or ability to lead in his own country—is measured by the amount of blood he can persuade his followers to spill. That fact, though difficult for Wilson to face, was referred to repeatedly in Paris. The corollary of this principle was often mentioned as well: nations expected to get their way in proportion to the number of lives they had lost, and they expected to be compensated for their losses not in hopes for the future but in something as tangible as dead soldiers—in land, factories, coal, gold, or money.

"A scheme has been propounded," Riddell said to Lloyd George, "whereby the Americans would forgo the debts due to them from the Allies. The Americans are being allowed a voice in the Peace Conference far beyond what their sacrifices justify. They might well pay their footing, and bear a larger portion of the cost of the war."

LLOYD GEORGE TO THE FRONT

Every Sunday during January of 1919, Lloyd George gathered a few friends and colleagues and drove out to see the battlefields, "through towns and villages," recalled one of these colleagues, "which were unrecognizable but for the sign-boards which indicated their names: through country intersected with trenches and rusty barbed-wire entanglements and swathes of poppies . . . for L.G. it seemed almost an obsession and he gloried in it."

Lloyd George relived the war for his companions town by town—north of Paris in an arc toward Holland, through Compiègne, Amiens, the battlefield of the Somme, Arras, Lille, Loos, Neuve Chapelle, Ypres, Passchendaele. The prime minister had visited some of these battlegrounds during the war. "When we reached General Cavan's quarters [during the battle of the Somme]," he recalled, "there was a heavy bombardment going on from our eight-inch howitzers assembled in the valley below, known to the soldiers as the Happy Valley. The roar of the guns beneath and the shrill 'keen' of the shells overhead were deafening. We could hardly carry on a conversation."

The battle of the Somme ranks with Verdun as one of the bloodiest battles ever fought. After four and a half months of battle, casualties on both sides exceeded a million. It was, said Lloyd George, a "bullheaded fight," with only a small ground gain to show for all the relentless slaughter of "the choicest and best of our young manhood." The battlefields of the Somme, Churchill said, "were the graveyard of [war minister Lord] Kitchener's army."

The generals, Lloyd George said, "lavished the lives placed at their disposal in foolish frontal attacks on impregnable lines, in spite of the lessons of every war since modern weapons were perfected. They then sent home requisitions for more units to bring their depleted battalions up to strength. . . . Whilst hundreds of thousands were being destroyed in the insane egotism of Passchendaele, every message or memorandum from [British commander in chief Sir Douglas] Haig was full of these insistences on the importance of sending him more men to replace those he had sent to die in the mud."

The general headquarters, said Lloyd George, never witnessed, "not even through a telescope, the attacks it ordained, except on carefully prepared charts where the advancing battalions were represented by the pencil which marched with ease across swamps and marked lines of triumphant progress without the loss of a single point. As for the mud, it never incommoded the movements of this irresistible pencil."

In one area, General Gough reported that "men of the strongest physique could hardly move forward at all and became easy victims to the enemy's snipers. Stumbling forward as best they could, their rifles also soon became so caked and clogged with mud as to be useless." It was into this terrain that Haig, from a distance, ordered tanks and cavalry to charge.

Elsewhere, an officer from general headquarters, making his first visit to the battlefront, grew "increasingly uneasy as the car approached the swamp-like edges of the battle area; he eventually burst into tears, crying 'Good God, did we really send men to fight in that?' "

Men and pack animals were caught in the mud, drowned in the overflowing streams, sank beyond recovery into impassable bogs that stank of blood, gas, and latrine. Robert Graves, who fought at the Somme and at other battlefields nearby, recalled that "every night we went out to fetch in the dead of the other battalions. . . . After the first day or two the corpses swelled and stank. I vomited more than once while superintending the carrying. Those we could not get in from the German wire continued to swell until the wall of the stomach collapsed, either naturally or when punctured by a bullet; a disgusting smell would float across. The colour of the dead faces changed from white to yellow-grey, to red, to purple, to green, to black, to slimy."

For months, hundreds of thousands of British troops fought

through this mud, sleeping in shell holes with the rats, drowning in the filth, guns choked with ooze, the survivors storming the trenches opposite and being thrown back again. And the British press, Lloyd George said, "rang with praises of the ruthless courage, untiring calm and undaunted tenacity—of the Commander-in-Chief!"

Walking along one day, "whistling 'The Farmer's Boy,' to keep up my spirits," Graves recalled, "suddenly I saw a group bending over a man lying at the bottom of the trench. He was making a snoring noise mixed with animal groans. At my feet lay the cap he had worn, splashed with his brains. I had never seen human brains before. . . . Beaumont . . . also got killed. . . . He had his legs blown against his back."

According to the guidebooks to the battlefields that were published by Michelin, the battle of Verdun was "a battle of . . . mutual annihilation. The method was to concentrate the fire of all the guns, not over a line but on a zone. . . . The simile that best expresses it is no longer that of a battering ram striking against a wall, but that of a rammer falling perpendicularly and hammering an encircled zone. . . . Here the wounded in deep-dug aid-posts went mad from lack of air. Here often a mug of water meant life or death to a man. This encircled zone was bounded by a narrow stretch of ground which the opposing artilleries tried to spare because the infantry were fighting there hand to hand, with bombs, machine guns, and flame-throwers."

To visit the site of the battle of Grurie Wood, which took place "without quarter day and night" for more than a year in the early phase of the war, the Michelin guide suggested that a motorist turn right at Le-Four-de-Paris east of Verdun along G.C. 67 toward La Harazée and then follow a path to Fontaine-aux-Charmes. Here begin the streams and ravines where rival French and German trenches were no more than thirty yards apart, sometimes only ten yards apart, with masses of barbed wire between them. Here and there, the trenches crossed over enemy lines. The countryside was a desolate landscape of burned tree trunks and rubble, and the front trenches had crumbled under the onslaught of aerial bombardment and mine explosions, "which completely demolished the frail barricades often made up of human corpses."

Across these lines, the French and Germans attacked and counterattacked, driving one another back a yard and a half at a time, regaining the loss, retreating again. During one such battle, a

Captain Juge stood upright on the parapet, his revolver in his hand, cheering on his men. "He fell wounded but got to his feet again shouting: 'Stand your ground, stand your ground, my men, and be brave.' He was wounded again but refused to be taken back to the rear." His men, like Captain Juge, stood on the exposed ground and fired "point blank at the enemy who were making incessant attacks. Captain Juge was wounded a third time. By this time the company was reduced to one officer and 23 men, with no bombs and almost no cartridges." Two other companies came up to assist Juge's men. The two new companies counterattacked against the Germans, and then found themselves attacked by the Germans from the rear. They retreated—by now out of ammunition—covering themselves by building barricades across the trenches through which the Germans came. They retreated a hundred yards, building nineteen barricades as they went, fighting hand to hand at each barricade, until, at last, they held the Germans with bayonets and the butt ends of their rifles.

Robert Graves describes the conclusion of another such fight:

"The din was tremendous. [The company commander] saw the platoon on his left flopping down, too, so he whistled the advance again. Nobody seemed to hear. He jumped up from his shell-hole, waved and signalled 'Forward!'

"Nobody stirred.

"He shouted: 'You bloody cowards, you are leaving me to go on alone?'

"His platoon-sergeant, groaning with a broken shoulder, gasped: 'Not cowards, Sir. Willing enough. But they're all f——ing dead.' "

THE AGE OF THE SMILE

"This," Sir George Riddell told Churchill as they drove out toward Amiens for a tour of the battlefields, "is the smiling age. In former days, statesmen were depicted as solemn, stately individuals with the cares of the world on their shoulders. Today, the smile is in fashion. The Lloyd George smile. The Wilson smile, and so on. Even great sailors and soldiers are depicted smiling."

Churchill, aged forty-five, secretary for war and air, answered "that he had had a happy life on the whole. Now he was happier than he had ever been before. . . . He spoke much of L.G., whom he described as a delightful companion; a man with unerring judgment, etc. (It was not always thus, but one could hardly expect it.) Winston said that he never bore malice, and never believed unfriendly things reported to have been said of him by his friends. He thinks that [former prime minister] Asquith is done. He missed his tide, and should have become Lord Chancellor when L.G. formed his first Government."

Churchill was in Paris to lobby for "an army of one million on a compulsory basis" to send into Russia to fight the Bolsheviks. "I want to build up the nation," Churchill said, "with the gallant men who have fought together. I want them to form the basis of a great national effort. I want them to combine to make an even greater England."

Riddell thought people would want "more than high sounding phrases. . . . They are sick of promises."

Churchill agreed, "and spoke strongly in favor of better conditions—cheap houses, higher wages, etc."

They had started out at nine o'clock in the morning. By midday they had reached a ruined château that had been Foch's old headquarters at one time during the war: they lunched at the château and then got back in the car to continue on a course that meandered two hundred miles through the countryside, past, among other things, some small cemeteries, to which Churchill pointed through the window, saying: "Poor fellows! I wish they had lived to see the end of the war!"

Eventually, Churchill fleshed out his plan to raise an army against the Bolsheviks by suggesting that the Allies reach an agreement with Germany to have German troops join forces with Britain, France, and America to conduct operations against Russia.

When Churchill's name was mentioned one evening over dinner at Lady Astor's, Lloyd George was irritated. Churchill, said Lloyd George, "has bolshevism on the brain."

THE LEAGUE OF NATIONS, III

One of Wilson's phrases called magnanimously for the equal treatment of all religious minorities. Wilson had in mind, specifically, the equal treatment of the Jews under immigration laws around the world. The Japanese—whether because they wished to secure the rights for themselves, or else because they wished to establish a diplomatic bargaining position to use to trade for other things they more urgently wanted—proposed to include two innocuous words in the expression "religious equality." The Japanese wished to have the phrase read: "religious and racial equality."

Billy Hughes bridled. Open Australia to a flood of yellow immigrants? He told the Japanese forthrightly that he would not tolerate it. More than that, he trotted out to the press club where he cornered some American newspaper reporters: "The story lost nothing in the telling," Hughes recalled happily. "I directed my remarks particularly to . . . those who did the cables for the Pacific states—California, Washington and Oregon. I pointed out what this thrice accursed clause would mean to the people generally . . . a policy which would bring disaster to the people on the Pacific slopes and gravely imperil those in the adjoining states. . . . Send out the cables [Hughes importuned the reporters] breathing fire and slaughter—aye and worse still, defeat at the next elections."

Wilson was covered with confusion and dropped the topic from his conversation.

INITIATIVE

Wilson seemed uninterested in any issue save the league and his Fourteen Points. He had, aside from these two general sets of goals, no complete outline of terms for the peace. He gave no instructions to the junior members of the delegation about any aim to pursue; and, when the legal staff of the American delegation tried to repair this situation by drawing up a skeleton treaty, Wilson remarked acidly that he did not intend to have the treaty drawn up by lawyers.

"The consequence," Lansing said, "was that the general scheme of the treaty and many of the important articles were prepared and worked out by the British and French delegations." The British and French proposals set the terms of the discussion, and Wilson lost the initiative from the beginning. The glow of the triumphal tour, the support of the cheering crowds, the enormous influence that all the other delegates expected the president to exert because of his great popularity—all this was dissipated in the grand, quiet salons of the Quai d'Orsay.

Occasionally, if the president expressed some very definite view on a matter, Clemenceau, as presiding officer, would ask Wilson if he would like to draft a resolution embodying his point. Then, like a schoolboy with an assignment from his father, "Mr. Wilson would at once take a pencil," as Lansing recalled, "and without hesitation and without erasures work out in his small, plain hand a resolution couched with exceptional brevity in unambiguous terms . . . the exactness of his thought and his command of language were clearly exhibited." Wilson was better at this sort of thing, Lansing thought, than any other member of the Council of Ten—and, had he done it more often, "it would have been he rather than the French or British who initiated action by the council." But Lansing could not recall that Wilson ever prepared a resolution except at the suggestion of Clemenceau or one of the British delegates. "If he prepared one voluntarily, I do not remember the occasion."

Often, after a subject had been thrashed out by the council, "often to the point of weariness," Clemenceau would turn to the president "and ask his opinion as to the action which ought to be taken." Wilson, said Lansing, would reply in precise English, without hesitation, "though he usually evaded a decision by a general review of the points made by both sides during the argument."

When the president finished, Clemenceau would ask for opinions—from Lansing, Lloyd George, Balfour, and so on—and then turn to the president again and ask, "Well, what shall we do?"

"The President frequently answered, 'Perhaps it would be well

to refer the matter to a committee of experts'; or, 'May I ask if anyone has prepared a resolution?'

"If the last question was asked, it was apt to bring a response
from Mr. Lloyd George, whose secretaries had drafted a resolution
while the discussion was in progress."

❧

THE GERMANS

Some of the younger aides wondered where the Germans were and
when they were expected to arrive. But the Germans, as it turned
out, had not been invited.

The younger aides, some of them, understood at once then that
the French, English, and Americans and all the other victorious
powers were assembled for a preliminary conference—and that,
once the victors had agreed on things among themselves, the Germans would be invited and the real conference would begin. But
this was not the case.

The younger aides thought that the treaty provisions that they
were writing up for their superiors were position papers and drafts
of notions that would be debated first by the Allies and then compromised in negotiation with the Germans. But this was not the
case, either. Position papers were often taken wholesale and incorporated into a final draft of a treaty that, somehow, was no longer a
negotiable document. With growing horror, the younger men realized that they were writing the final treaty for the final peace conference and that, once they had finished their work, it would be thrust
upon the Germans, and they would be forced to take it. The peace
conference, as it turned out, was not to be a conference at all in the
traditional sense of the term. An awesome sense of unreality spread
over Paris—a sense that sprang from the feeling that Germany did
not exist.

As the conference went on, although the negotiations were
conducted primarily in terms of arriving at a treaty with Germany,
in fact "Germany" was often simply a manner of speaking and the
Germans, who were not represented in Paris, were quite naturally

ignored. What the negotiations really dealt with were the relations among the victor powers—couched in terms of Germany, settled almost invariably at Germany's expense, but almost never with any sense of what Germany was, or what Germany had become, or whatever might be going on in Germany at the moment.

Paris, for all its gossip, for all the rumors of turmoil and war that reached it from elsewhere in Europe, was closed in on itself, hermetically, impervious to the world.

AUSTRIA-HUNGARY

"Friday evening," Seymour wrote home, "I had one of the most interesting dinners yet. We invited H. Wickham Steed and Seton-Watson. Steed is the foreign editor of the London *Times*. . . . Seton-Watson is a publicist of means who has given up his life practically to studying Austria-Hungary, living there for many years; Steed is also a specialist on Austria. These two . . . work and live together and you could not imagine a more complete contrast: Steed is tall, elegant, distinguished in appearance, with a grey imperial beard and long silky grey hair brushed back; and with a very assured manner. Seton-Watson is a little Scotchman, hesitating in speech and insignificant in appearance, modest in his statements; in talking of Hungary which he knows better than any other Anglo-Saxon he always ends a statement 'Isn't it?' or 'Don't you think so?' They make a fine pair."

Seton-Watson was the editor, too, of *The New Europe*, a magazine dedicated to conjuring a new world order composed of new nations, "whom we regarded," Nicolson said, "with maternal instinct, as the justification of our sufferings and of our victory."

The Austro-Hungarian Empire, which had been—with Russia and the German Empire—one of the three main constituents of the European balance of power, lay in shambles. What had been a heteromorphic agglomeration of nations and peoples, languages and histories under the Hapsburgs, had fallen apart into fragments that none of the victors wished to put back together again.

"My attitude towards Austria," said Nicolson, "was a rather saddened reflection as to what would remain of her when the New Europe had once been created. I did not regard her as a living entity; I thought of her only as a pathetic relic. My feelings towards Hungary were less detached. I confess that I regarded, and still regard, that Turanian tribe with acute distaste. Like their cousins the Turks, they had destroyed much and created nothing. Buda Pest was a false city devoid of any autochthonous reality. For centuries Magyars had oppressed their subject nationalities. The hour of liberation and retribution was at hand. For the Bulgarians I cherished feelings of contempt."

With these feelings came notions on the part of Nicolson or others that eventually found their way into the final settlement of the treaty—that Bosnia, Herzegovina, Croatia, and Slovenia should be united with Serbia and Montenegro to create Yugoslavia; that a chunk of Hungary should be given to Rumania, and Hungary made independent; that the Czechs and Slovaks should be put together into the new state of Czechoslovakia; that Istria, the South Tyrol, and Trentino should be given to Italy; and that Austria should be left as a small German-speaking area, of six million population, lying principally to the east of Vienna.

Many of these shufflings and tradings and rearrangements would sort out old confusions—the part of Hungary transferred to Rumania was inhabited mostly by Rumanians; Istria and Trentino, Italian-speaking areas, seemed logically to belong with Italy rather than Austria. However, not all questions were considered strictly along the lines of self-determination, or according to apparent requirements of justice or history. Many were considered along the lines of what would benefit France, what would enfeeble Germany, what would make useful counterweights in the balance of power. Sometimes old confusion would be replaced by new confusion: millions of Magyars would be transferred with the Rumanians to Rumania. And sometimes the new rearrangements would create new resentment and bitterness as well: only two-thirds of Poland's population would be Polish, as millions of defeated Germans came under its rule; and fewer than 10 million of the 14 million inhabitants of Czechoslovakia would be Czechs or Slovaks, as millions of defeated Germans would be placed under the rule of Czechs. Then, too, although the principle of self-determination might work relatively well in western Europe, it tended toward absurdity in parts of east-

ern Europe where political groups were often less important than—
or intermingled with—ethnic or linguistic groups, or religious or
social groups. When the diplomats finished their work, Europe
would be littered with new causes of war.

"Bratianu presented the case of Rumania," Seymour said; "he
is . . . Prime Minister and head of the delegation. He is large with a
black beard, a rather somber-looking man with a strong nose. . . . He
did not stress the Treaty of 1916 [another secret treaty used to entice Rumania into the war by promising part of Hungarian Tran-
sylvania and another chunk of territory to the southeast of Rumania,
the Banat of Temesvar] . . . but argued on grounds of justice and
future peace.

"Vesnic answered for the Yugoslavs, speaking with more oratory, then Bratianu again, then Trumbic again for the Yugoslavs.
Pasic was there but spoke very little."

Bratianu, said Nicolson, "is a bearded woman, a forceful humbug, a Bucharest intellectual, a most unpleasing man. Handsome
and exuberant, he flings his fine head sideways, catching his own
profile in the glass. He makes elaborate verbal jokes, imagining them
to be Parisian."

"The Commissioners seemed rather puzzled by the discussion," Seymour wrote home. "Lloyd George asked where the
boundaries of the Banat were. . . . Sonnino kept his eyes closed during most of the talk; I think he went frankly asleep at least once;
when he opened them he scowled at the Yugoslavs; he probably
doesn't love them very much.

"Only once did all the Commissioners wake up. That was
when Vesnic said that certain parts of the Banat would be shown to
be Serb by the candidacy of Serbs in the elections. Here at last was
familiar ground. 'You mean to say that a majority of candidates returned in those districts was composed of Serbs?' said Lloyd
George. . . . It was screamingly funny. Inasmuch as elections in
Hungary mean less than nothing, since the majority of anti-Magyar
candidates are thrown into prison by the authorities."

The conference had a terrible tendency to go adrift. The
American league offensive had lost momentum, bogged down in a
swamp of annoying questions and complexities. The conference had
taken on the aura of the war just passed: this was, like the trench war
of the preceding years, the diplomacy of attrition, and the principal
object was often not to win but merely to keep going without any

clear aim in view. Nor would it do to doze off or allow oneself to be lulled by the atmosphere of inconsequence; for one never knew, if one were inattentive for even a moment, but that an advantage might be taken.

Nicolson noted in his diary on January 31, "Bratianu . . . is evidently convinced that he is a greater statesman than any present. A smile of irony and self-consciousness recurs from time to time. He flings his fine head in profile. He makes a dreadful impression.

"A.J.B. rises, yawns slightly, and steps past his own armchair to ask me for our line of partition in the Banat. . . . Vesnic replies to the Rumanian case. . . . He attacks the Secret Treaty. . . . President Wilson gets pins and needles and paces up and down upon the soft carpet kicking black and tidy boots."

Benes, foreign minister of the provisional government of Czechoslovakia, presented the case for the Czechs—"a delightful little chap," Seymour called Benes, "just as friendly and as moderate as one could wish . . . the translator, Mantoux, is always a joy. He puts more spirit into his translations than the principal puts into his original speech. Mantoux never says, 'Mr. Benes claims this territory on the ground of historic rights.' He says, 'We feel by virtue of our noble history, etc.,' with his voice shaking with emotion and fervor."

Benes spoke eloquently, covering his case in detail and clearly—but it took him three hours. Then Karel Kramarz, the president of the provisional government of Czechoslovakia, wished to speak, and when he asked for the floor for a half-hour, Clemenceau said, "Oh, we'll appoint a special commission and you can talk to them for a couple of hours. Now we had better have a cup of tea."

Meanwhile, none of the pieces stayed put. All was fluid; all was in turmoil; riots and fighting broke out, governments toppled; Bolsheviks took over; nothing was stable, or certain; and the Italians—fearful of the implications of the collapse of the Austro-Hungarian Empire, fearful that a new German Austria would eventually press down upon Italy's northern border, fearful of a powerful new nation in Yugoslavia, argued desperately, and without making a favorable impression on anyone. "The Italians were very dramatic," said Seymour, "waved their arms around, tears came into their eyes."

IMPROVISATION

Jules Cambon, French elder statesman, age seventy-four, former ambassador to the United States, former general secretary of the Ministry of Foreign Affairs, was heard to say, upon leaving a meeting of the conference, to one of the young British diplomats: "Mon cher, savez-vous ce qui va résulter de cette conférence? Une *improvisation.*"

THE MPRET OF ALBANIA

Prince William of Wied, who had reigned as mpret, or monarch, of Albania until 1914, fled to Germany then because of domestic political problems. The throne of Albania was still vacant in 1919, and no one knew what to do about it. Because the Anglo-Persian Oil Company had a stake in Albania, Lloyd George took an interest in the throne, and he loved a suggestion that a young Englishman made after looking up Albania in the British Museum: the two rival factions in Albania, the young Englishman said, were similar to warring clans of Scotland.

"This is a balkanized version of Scotland," Lloyd George declared confidently to Lord Curzon. "We must make the country work on a clan basis. What they want is a king and what could be better than a king who has a personal knowledge of the Scottish clan system. I know the very man—Atholl."

"Personally," said Curzon, "I should rather be the Duke of Atholl than King of Albania."

"The comparison between the two countries is too marked not to take advantage of the fact," said Lloyd George. "The tribes are just like clans, and those distinguishing patterns of their white wool jackets are on the same principle as tartans."

The duke of Atholl declined. Lloyd George then thought he might advertise for a king, but in the end he adopted a more discreet means; he enlisted an aide, Maundy Gregory, to look for suitable kings. Gregory wrote one peer: "I am requested to submit to you a proposal of a highly confidential nature. As you are doubtless aware, the future of Albania has for some time been a problem which has occupied a great deal of the Prime Minister's time. He is both anxious that this country should have a monarch and that the links which have been established between Albania and the United Kingdom should be maintained. I am therefore authorized to ask you whether you would kindly consider accepting the dignity of kingship for Albania."

The peer was apparently interested, and he arranged to meet with Gregory in London for a quiet chat about the proposition. His interest vanished when Gregory mentioned how much the peer would have to come up with to close the deal: £250,000.

The first Lord Inchcape did not condescend to meet Gregory, but wrote instead: "I duly received your letter of the 29th ult. and am sorry I have been so long replying. It is a great compliment to be offered the Crown of Albania, but it is not in my line. Yours sincerely, Inchcape."

In the end, Gregory failed to find a king for Albania, but not before he had received some seventy applications for the job, including this letter from a man in Streatham: "I am not a country gentleman myself, but I come from country gentleman's stock on my mother's side. I stand six feet two inches in my socks and measure forty-four inches round the chest. I take the greatest interest in the welfare of the working classes. I accordingly believe I would do very well by you."

FEISAL, AND LAWRENCE OF ARABIA

"The Emir Feisal was the most striking and picturesque figure in the Conference," said Billy Hughes. "He was a magnificent man, with dark flashing eyes and regular features set off with a black beard trimmed to a fine point. Clad in a long white robe stretching down to his heels, his shapely head crowned with a white turban, he looked what he was: the great fighting chieftain of the warlike tribes of the Arabian desert."

Feisal, descendant of the prophet Mohammed, had come to the conference, Lansing thought, for the purpose of establishing an Arab kingdom out of the wreckage of the Ottoman Empire—an Islamic kingdom "extending northward from the desert wastes of the Arabian Peninsula to the Taurus Mountains and the borders of old Armenia, and from the Euphrates to the Mediterranean." Feisal's desires seemed to "include Palestine within the boundaries of the proposed state"—and he impressed all the delegates with the forcefulness and grace of his arguments.

Britain and France had agreed during the course of the war to divide the Turkish Empire between them—recognizing Syria as falling within the French sphere of influence, and Iraq, Palestine, and Trans-Jordan as part of the British sphere—but recognizing, too, the right of all these areas to independence. It was Feisal's delicate task to play the French and British ever so slightly against one another, easing the grip of each on the Middle East so that the area might achieve enough independence to fall within Feisal's own grasp.

He was followed everywhere by Colonel T. E. Lawrence. "Cannot understand him," Nicolson confided to his diary. "His foreground is so different from his background, and he hops from one to the other." Nicolson's postconference description of Lawrence can only be described as bitchy: "And Colonel T. E. Lawrence the while would glide along the corridors of the Majestic, the lines of resentment hardening around his boyish lips: an undergraduate with a chin."

Shotwell was more impressed than Nicolson by the legend of Lawrence as a student of medieval history who used to sleep by day and work by night at Magdalen College, and "take his recreation in the deer park at four in the morning." He was said to have ingratiated himself with the Arabs and fought against the Turks in the desert. Lawrence arrived at one meeting with Shotwell dressed in the uniform of a British colonel, but wearing his "Arab headdress to keep his friend [Feisal] company.... His veil over his explorer's helmet was of green silk and hung down over his shoulder with a tassel or two of deep red. Around his head was a similar double strand of big, corded braid . . . about three-quarters of an inch in diameter and looking much like a crown . . . a Shelley-like person, and yet too virile to be a poet. He is a rather short, strongly built man of not over twenty-eight years, with sandy complexion, a typical English face, bronzed by the desert, remarkable blue eyes and a smile around the mouth that responded swiftly to that on the face of his friend."

Shotwell especially loved hearing Lawrence say that there were two ways of automobiling across the desert—one was to have a Rolls-Royce and fly along at fifty miles an hour, just catching the tops of the bumps. "The other way is to have a series of Ford cars stretching across the desert, so that as soon as one breaks down another can be taken. Either one beats camel riding."

Feisal and Lawrence, said Shotwell, were "obviously very fond of each other. I have seldom seen such mutual affection between grown men as in this instance. Lawrence would catch the drift of Feisal's humor and [translate] the joke . . . while Feisal was still exploding with his idea; but all the same it was funny to see how Feisal spoke with the oratorical feeling of the South and Lawrence translated in the lowest and quietest of English voices."

When at last Feisal's opportunity came to address the conference, "he stood in his place," Hughes said, "speaking in a strong resonant voice. He had no notes but he never hesitated for a word. There was a cadence about his voice that held his audience."

Hughes had on his staff an air force man, Sergeant James, who had served in the Middle East and knew some Arabic. Before Lawrence translated the speech for the delegates, Hughes asked James in a whisper whether he could understand what Feisal was saying. James thought Feisal was quoting from the Koran but he was not certain; yes, just as Feisal finished the first part of his speech, James leaned over to Hughes and whispered, "That last bit was from the Koran all right—I've heard it hundreds of times."

When Colonel Lawrence translated Feisal's speech into English, he spoke with force and eloquence, setting out the Arab case persuasively; however, there was no reference to the Koran. Feisal rose to continue his speech. "Try to follow him," Hughes said to James. Sergeant James listened carefully, and every few seconds he would lean over to Hughes triumphantly and say, "*That* was from the Koran all right."

When Lawrence translated this next section of Feisal's speech, he was once again commanding and eloquent, but he neglected once again to quote from the Koran.

"I looked at the Emir sitting there with unruffled front," said Hughes, "and, as I caught his eye, he bowed, and with a smile returned my greeting. On the spur of the moment I moved to his side, and congratulated him on his speech. To my surprise he smiled and said, 'Thank you.' Although thinking this to be 'curiouser and curiouser,' I followed it up by asking him if he would join me in a cup of coffee. He said, 'I would be very pleased.' Just that! The Emir Feisal, who but five minutes ago I believed could neither speak nor understand English was now talking good colloquial English. We walked together into the coffee room, chatting in a most friendly way. It was evident that he had understood Colonel Lawrence's bowdlerized interpretation of his speech perfectly, and that his quotations from the Koran were designed to give the Colonel the widest possible latitude in setting out the case for Iraq on lines best calculated to commend it to the Conference."

❦

THE NEWS

The reporters in Paris were in a swivet. No one told them anything. They could not attend any meetings of importance; they were told a lot of lies. The newspapers, said Nicolson, had sent "their best people here, and they are given no information."

As a result, little news of the conference got out of Paris. Rumors circulated: it was reported that Clemenceau was holding things up until Wilson would have to return for a visit to the United States, and then the French would rush matters forward. Impressions were reported: a feeling of vague dislike toward President Wilson had spread through Paris because he had delayed so long in visiting the battlefields. But anything like a fact was hard to come by.

In London, frivolity broke out in the newspapers. Articles about the war were considered a "dud." The *Daily Mail* announced, in "This Jazz Age," that people were "dancing as they have never danced before." Yachting, professional cricket, polo, and the Derby all revived terrifically. Veterans were looking disconsolately for the "homes for heroes" that Lloyd George had promised them—and for jobs that many of them were unable to hold because of lingering symptoms of shell shock. Pedigreed puppies were almost impossible to buy, since dog breeding had suffered during the war. It was hard, once again, to get seats on buses; restaurants were full; and poetry seemed to have suffered a decline. American chewing gum was being sold in the streets of London, and young Englishwomen were adopting the fashions of short hair and short skirts as part of the new freedom that the breakdown of old standards had allowed; tobacco restrictions were ended; food coupons would soon be done away with. The Guards Division marched through London. The Australians had a parade. The Canadians had another parade.

From time to time, newspaper readers learned something of the peace conference ("enough to sober the thoughts of any serious person")—but attention was hard to capture for sober thoughts in the first months after the war. In the United States, news of the conference did not spread far beyond the readers of a few newspapers, and such serious journals as the *New Republic* were still running high-minded editorials about the hopes for a new age of democratic socialism.

ૐ

A RIOT IN A PARROT HOUSE

The conference seemed to Nicolson to resemble a "riot in a parrot house" that occurred amid "the slouching queues of prisoners still behind their barbed wire, the flames of communism flaring, now from Munich, and now from Buda Pesth . . . the machine-gun rattle of a million typewriters, the incessant shrilling of telephones, the clatter of motor bikes . . . the cold voices of interpreters, 'le délégué des Etats-Unis constate qu'il ne peut se ranger . . .' the blare of trumpets . . . the rustling of files . . . the crackle of Rolls-Royces upon the gravel of sumptuous courtyards, and throughout the sound of footsteps hurrying now upon the parquet of some gallery, now upon the stone stairway of some Ministry.

"... the infinite languor of Mr. Balfour slowly uncrossing his knees, a succession of secretaries and experts bending forward with maps.... Si cette frontière était prise en considération, il serait nécessaire de faire la correction indiquée en bleu ... Telegram from Vienna. Count Karolyi has resigned and according to telephone message received by ... Fate of Allied Missions uncertain ... Wir wissen das die Gewalt der deutschen Waffen begrochen ist. Wir kennen die Macht des Hasses, die uns hier."

"Apart from the actual strain of continuous labour," Nicolson wrote to his father, "there is the moral exhaustion of realizing one's own fallibility and the impossibility of extracting from the lies with which we are surrounded any real impression of what the various countries and nationalities honestly desire." The conference came to be shrouded, Nicolson said, "in mists of exhaustion, disability, suspicion, and despair."

And yet, he said, "there is a definite inarticulate human element behind it all somewhere, and somewhere there must be a definite human desire behind all these lies and lies."

THE LEAGUE OF NATIONS, IV

Wilson was to have his way with the League of Nations—for the most part at least. He was to have his executive council (the "oligarchy" as Lansing called it) that would dominate the more democratic assembly; the league would have its secretariat and secretary general to carry out the administrative chores. It would undertake, as one of its first items of business, to plan for a worldwide reduction in armaments; it would insist that members bring their disputes to the council for arbitration, and "in no case ... resort to war until three months after" the council had reported its findings; it would provide, especially, a means of resolving any disputes that arose out of the treaty settlement. It would oversee the creation of mandates for former colonies in accord with the principles of self-determination and the other Fourteen Points and complementary principles.

The only problem was the French insistence that the league

have a standing army. The provision of a standing army was not merely an addition to Wilson's notions for the league: it was a direct contradiction of the entire philosophy of the league. It would substitute for the league's idea of arbitration the threat of military sanction, the threat of military punishment at the hands of an army controlled by the league's executive council. It would be—the French idea did not change—a reborn military alliance directed against Germany.

Wilson would have none of it. But Léon Bourgeois was adamant. Wilson would not compromise. Bourgeois would not withdraw his demand.

The pressure of time began to prey upon Wilson's mind. He had said that he would return to the United States for several weeks' visit in midconference to attend to business, in particular to the closing of the current session of the Congress. He wanted—as everyone knew—to be able to take back with him a completed covenant of the League of Nations, to return from the conference, as he had arrived, in triumph, to lay the covenant before the Congress at this moment, while his standing in the world was at its highest, so that he might carry the domestic Republican opposition before him.

His ship was scheduled to leave Brest on February 15.

Then, on February 10, Wilson was attacked in the French press. "President Wilson," said the editor of *Figaro*, "has lightly assumed a responsibility such as few men have ever borne. Success in his idealistic efforts will surely place him among the greatest characters of history. But failure will plunge the world into chaos and will make the author responsible for this chaos one of the most pitiful figures that history has ever presented."

The jibe was not surprising—nor was its inspiration a mystery. All the diplomats understood that Clemenceau, that old journalist, could plant any story he wanted in the French papers. To make certain the editorial was not dismissed as a coincidence, Clemenceau granted an interview for the same issue of the paper. The premier said nothing about the president but only warned in passing against sacrificing France to the "attainment of high but vague general ideals."

Wilson was incensed. One of the president's aides was instructed to inform a member of the committee on public information that the president had "given intimations of a very definite character that the removal of the Peace Conference away from Paris to another capital, or to Geneva, was under consideration."

That afternoon, Premier Clemenceau was seen arriving at the Hotel Crillon, where he went to have a private conference in the quarters of Colonel Edward M. House.

❧

COLONEL HOUSE

The rooms at the Hotel Crillon in which the delegates met to talk about the league were those of the only man that President Wilson trusted, Colonel Edward M. House.

House had been born in Houston in 1858, the seventh son of one of the richest men in Texas. He grew up in a rough-and-tumble household in which the favorite game was War and learned at an early age to ride, shoot, hunt, and play pranks. Some of the obstreperous behavior of the House youngsters was not timid: Edward on two occasions almost killed a playmate; one brother fell from a trapeze and died of a brain injury; and House's eldest brother had one side of his face shot off.

When he was twelve years old, Edward was playing on a swing when a rope snapped. He injured his head, and then, in the course of recovery, he was stricken with malaria. He never regained his strength after this double assault: for the rest of his life he was frail, unable to tolerate the heat of summer in the South, limited in his physical energies. Rather than leaping into activities himself, or taking a leading part in fights or pranks, he learned to live by his wits, and, to some extent, to live vicariously. "I used to like to set boys at each other," he told one of his biographers, "to see what they would do, and then try to bring them around again."

He was an indifferent student (who avoided hazing rituals at prep school by keeping a large knife and a six-shooter at hand), less interested in academics than in excitement, techniques of cutting corners, and in politics. He was a little fellow, short and shaped like a slender pear, with sloping shoulders, large ears, a receding chin, and a poor speaking voice: a man without the physical presence to make a public leader, a man destined for a place in the background.

After quitting Cornell, he returned to Texas to pursue business and to educate himself in professional politics. He politicked for four Texas governors—one of whom bestowed the title of "Colonel" on him. And at last, after a dozen years of rooting around for a congenial politician on the national level, he discovered Woodrow Wilson, then governor of New Jersey. One of Wilson's most pressing problems in 1912 was to cajole William Jennings Bryan, the former Democratic presidential nominee, into supporting him for president. House had been Bryan's next-door neighbor for a year in Austin, and the Colonel commenced assiduously to try to deliver Bryan to Wilson.

House wrote letters to Wilson ("I have been with Mr. Bryan a good part of the morning . . ."), whetting Wilson's appetite for more news, for fuller information, gradually leading Wilson to believe that House exerted useful influence over Bryan, over Texas politicians, and over others—influence that House wanted to use in Wilson's behalf, out of sheer admiration for Wilson, with no hope or wish for any reward, simply to be of use. House was not issued the customary invitation to come to meet the candidate: rather, Wilson came to call on House at the colonel's New York apartment.

William Allen White said that House possessed an "almost Oriental modesty, a Chinese self-effacement." He seemed, said White, to be "in constant and delightful agreement with his auditor. . . . He is never servile, but always serving; gentle without being soft; exceedingly courteous. . . . He is forever punctuating one's sentences with 'That's true, that's true.' "

Wilson was captivated. They agreed about everything. "What I like about House," Wilson later said, "is that [all] he wants to do is to serve the common cause and to help me and others."

The hour of their first meeting, House said, "flew away. . . . Each of us started to ask the other when he would be free for another meeting, and laughing over our mutual enthusiasm, we arranged an evening several days later when Governor Wilson should come and have dinner with me."

During the next several months, Wilson called on House from time to time, courting the colonel, until, at last, Wilson was able to write House: "My dear friend, we have known one another always." House, for his part, understood Wilson's need for praise and encouragement, and during the several years that followed, addressed Wilson as "my great and good friend," often saying such things of the president's actions as, "I think you never did anything better"—or, "My faith in you is as great as my love for you—more than that I cannot say." Or, again: "I think of you every day."

House invariably shrank from publicity, declined credit for any good advice he gave, forgot any instance when his good advice was ignored, and subordinated all his wishes and ambitions to those of the president. He thought he was uncommonly talented at helping other men come to agreement, at finding compromises, at cajoling or seducing others into harmony. In fact, he was superb at doing all the dirty work that Wilson considered unseemly. He stayed always in the background; he never asked a favor. When offered a cabinet position, he declined. He never wished to take an active role in any endeavor—except one: he wished that the president would not attend the Paris peace conference but would instead appoint House the chief of the American delegation, so that the colonel would finally be able to exercise his powers on a suitably grand stage.

"It is amusing," Ray Stannard Baker wrote in his diary, "going about as I do, to discover [everyone at the conference], more or less surreptitiously, keeping diaries. . . . House dictates, sitting on his long couch, with his legs coddled in a blanket, to his stenographer and secretary, Miss Denton. He speaks in a soft, even voice of the celebrities he has had in conference and what he would do with them if only he had the power. As he talks he brings his small hands together softly from time to time, sometimes just touching the finger tips, sometimes the whole palms."

Baker detested House. "I had a long talk this evening with Colonel House," Baker recorded on another occasion, "who was sitting on his lounge with a figured blanket over his chilly legs—quite serenely dictating his diary to Miss Denton. More and more he impresses me as the dilettante—the lover of the game. . . . He stands in the midst of great events to lose nothing . . . and plays at getting important men together for the sheer joy of using his presumptive power. He is an excellent conciliator, but with the faults of his virtue, for he conciliates over the border of minor disagreements into the solid flesh of principle. I found him tonight quite cheerful—quite optimistic. He told me that if *he* had it to do he could make peace in an hour!"

THE ANCIENT GREEKS

"There's nothing beyond Aeschylus," Clemenceau once said to his secretary Martet, "nothing beyond Plato, nothing beyond Socrates. It all ended in bloodshed and domesticity. Well, perhaps it's the history of all peoples, in all times. Baber, my friend Baber, the conqueror of Persia, used to have a pile of heads brought to him every morning, and when the pile was a little smaller than usual, he would say, 'It's pretty small, this pile. My men are getting slack.' Nevertheless, it was the same Baber who said, 'There are sighs which arouse the world to action.' Men are like that. And one may even wonder if all that blood and all that brutality were not necessary for the making of an Aeschylus and the building of an Erechtheum. Gentle and kindly men are pleasant to have about, but in general they don't create masterpieces."

THE LEAGUE OF NATIONS, V

On February 11, there was no change in negotiations in the league commission. If anything, the atmosphere had become worse. Bourgeois went on and on about the need for an international army. When Wilson told him that such an army—ready to march at any time that its international command gave the word—would violate the American Constitution, Bourgeois was unmoved. When Bourgeois became tired of talking, he turned to one of the other members of the French delegation, who took up the same theme. The French were evidently conducting a filibuster. At the end of the day, President Wilson declared that negotiations were at a deadlock and that there was no point in meeting the next day.

On February 12, Colonel House and Lord Robert Cecil conferred. Wilson was not a party to their discussions.

On the morning of February 13, at the meeting of the league commission, Lord Robert spoke. He would speak, he said, "very frankly." The French must understand, said Lord Robert, that the League of Nations was not anything from which America or Britain had much to gain; the league was practically a gift of American support for Europe. The Americans could well afford to go their own way in the world—so could Britain—and leave France alone on the continent, with Germany. The alternative to Wilson's League of Nations was not a military alliance led by France; the alternative was—here came Cecil's emphatic threat—"an alliance between Great Britain and the United States," leaving France out entirely.

On the afternoon of February 13, Bourgeois permitted the issue of the standing army to be brought to a vote by Lord Robert. The idea of the army was voted down. The stumbling block to the league had been removed. The league covenant was completed. The most significant piece of diplomacy to have taken shape in the conference thus far had been concluded.

Colonel House telephoned the news to Wilson. The covenant had been finished on the thirteenth of the month; it contained twenty-six articles, twice thirteen. "When I telephoned the President at seven o'clock that we had finished, he was astonished and delighted."

Perhaps Cecil's speech had done the trick. Or perhaps Clemenceau was not much moved by Cecil's threat. Perhaps the Tiger had merely shifted his strategy to the final stages of "grouping" or entrapping Wilson—by letting the president claim his victory, letting him return to the United States in triumph, letting him rest his reputation on the achievement of the league, letting him make speeches about what a great boon had been conferred upon the world, and then, when Wilson returned to Paris after his Washington trip, to hand him the bill.

On February 14, the President read the covenant to a plenary session of the whole conference. "This covenant," said Wilson, "is definite in the one thing that we are called upon to make definite. It is a definite guarantee of peace.

"Many terrible things have come out of this war, gentlemen," the president said, "but some very beautiful things have come out of it. Wrong has been defeated, but the rest of the world has been more conscious than it ever was before of the majesty of right. People that were suspicious of one another can now live as friends and comrades in a single family. . . . The miasma of distrust, of intrigue, is cleared away. Men are looking eye to eye and saying, We are brothers and have a common purpose . . . and this is our covenant of fraternity and friendship."

When Wilson had finished his speech and sat down again, Colonel House passed him a note: "Dear Governor, Your speech was as great as the occasion—I am very happy—EMH." And Wilson replied: "Bless your heart. Thank you from the bottom of my heart. WW."

Several hours later, accompanied by aides and other diplomats, by Clemenceau and others of his French hosts, Wilson, smiling, boarded a train at Gare du Nord. Just before the president boarded, House wrote in his diary, Wilson "bade me a fervent good-bye, clasping my hand and placing his arm around me."

The president, having arrived in Europe in triumph, left in triumph. His League of Nations had been outlined and approved and made the very centerpiece of the treaty that would shape the twentieth century. Although the president had had to work his way through a mire of old rivalries and obstacles to achieve his end— and, in the end, did not know how he had achieved—few politicians can ever have felt the keenness of pleasure that Wilson must have felt, to have given shape to the entire world by the sheer force of his character. Nor would Wilson himself ever again have such a feeling of triumph.

PART THREE
ENTR'ACTE

THE ASSASSINATION

On the morning of February 19, Clemenceau was being driven from his home in the Rue Franklin to a meeting with Balfour and Colonel House, to try to speed up the conference affairs. Emile-Jules-Henri Cottin, a twenty-three-year-old man, dressed in rough corduroy garb, a woodworker known to his friends as "Mildou," stepped out of the shadow of a kiosk at the intersection with the Boulevard Delessert, raised his hand, and fired a pistol twice into Clemenceau's limousine, crying out, "I am a Frenchman and an anarchist!"

Cottin ran after the car and fired, according to some reports, another nine shots, according to others six shots, according to others ten. One of them hit Clemenceau who slumped forward, saying, "The animal shoots well."

Clemenceau's driver turned the car around quickly and sped back to the Rue Franklin, where the premier told those who helped him into his house: "It's nothing."

Three physicians were summoned and discovered that he had been hit in "the posterior portion of the right shoulder blade, with no vital injury." This, Clemenceau told the nun who was sent to care for him, "simply proves that I am well in with the good Lord."

The bullet had passed, however, quite close to his lung; and Clemenceau was put to bed coughing.

When the pope sent his blessing by telegram, Clemenceau at once replied by sending his own blessing to the pope.

"It is the one sensation that I hadn't yet had," he told Martet, when the young man arrived at the Rue Franklin. "I had never yet been assassinated."

"Dear me," said Balfour (always on the lookout for diplomatic signals) when he heard of the attempt on Clemenceau's life. "I wonder what that means."

Sarah Bernhardt wrote to Clemenceau on one of her small monogrammed cards: "I beg you, let me have some news of you. It is for me! For me alone! Thanks with all my heart!"

Toward one o'clock, Clemenceau started to cough more violently, and to spit up blood, and it was discovered that the bullet had come to rest in the mediastinum, the space between the two lungs where the heart and viscera are. Sarah Bernhardt sent another message: "Will you please forgive me; but I so much want to have news; I feel myself utterly unnerved by the rumors. Just now Clemenceau is France. I have always loved him, and since this war I devoutly worship him."

Clemenceau was not unaccustomed to bullet wounds. He fought his first duel, when he was a student in Paris, with a young man whom he had never met and never saw again. The young man, named Prompt, had made some insulting remarks about Clemenceau in the presence of one of Clemenceau's friends. They met in the forest at Clamart and exchanged two shots without wounding one another.

In the course of his life, Clemenceau fought perhaps another dozen duels, seven with pistol and five with épée. He was superb with either weapon, although he preferred the sword, perhaps because he knew that he could, with the sword, inflict a wound without killing his opponent. With the pistol, he usually fired first, and into the air, and in return his opponent usually fired into the air—although Clemenceau bore several scars from occasions on which his opponent had not been so generous. With épée, he liked to disarm his opponent at once with a sudden and stunning *coup en seconde*, which almost paralyzes the arm. He would then wait until his opponent's sword was retrieved before inflicting a wound at will.

"I was never one to believe that a wrong could be righted by a bullet or a sword-thrust. But, following my upbringing, I made up my mind to give a proper account of myself if provoked to a point where a duel was unavoidable. . . . A few times my rage of the moment blinded me into going after blood. More often . . . I had the good sense to cool off, and to fire in the air. . . . Seems kind of silly now, doesn't it? But then, I am too old now. I gave up dueling after seventy."

Cottin was put on trial at once. It was discovered that he was not only an anarchist but that he also attended evening meetings of a Communist group. Nothing else seemed as much worth reporting in the newspapers as this. Cottin was convicted and condemned to death. Clemenceau interceded. "We have just won the most terrible war in history, yet here is a Frenchman who misses his target six times out of seven at point-blank range. Of course the fellow must be punished for the careless use of a dangerous weapon and for poor marksmanship. I suggest that he be locked up for about eight years, with intensive training in a shooting gallery." He commuted Cottin's sentence to life imprisonment, of which Cottin served five years before he was granted—without Clemenceau's help—amnesty.

Within eight days, Clemenceau was back up on his feet and had returned to the meetings of the conference. The delegates were reminded from time to time of the attempt on his life when Clemenceau would be seized by a fit of coughing—prolonged, deep, rumbling, calling up visions of blood in the lungs, and of the bullet, which still lodged at the center of Clemenceau's chest.

The premier never mentioned his wound, except in jest; cartoons appeared in the newspapers of the indestructible Tiger—gray suede gloves covering his claws. The world seemed more than ever subject to chance—as, assuredly, it was. In an instant, Clemenceau had replaced Wilson as the hero of the conference. Having shot Clemenceau, the assassin had wounded Wilson.

SABOTAGE

With Clemenceau in bed, Wilson in America, and Lloyd George popping back to London to keep tabs on domestic politics, the second-rank diplomats stepped forward to continue negotiations, and to show how much better they could do than their superiors. Pichon's moment of glory was the briefest of all: Clemenceau was still able to give directions from his sickbed.

House, who had been waiting for decades to arrive at such an opportunity, had prepared his ground carefully. Before Wilson left Paris, House noted in his diary, "I outlined my plan of procedure during his absence: we would button up everything during the next four weeks. He seemed startled and even alarmed at this statement." House quickly reassured the president that the point would not be to come to any final conclusions but only to have things ready for Wilson when he returned. Wilson seemed, vaguely, to think this a fine plan.

Balfour, as foreign minister, naturally assumed full powers in Lloyd George's absence. "Tall, slim and good-looking," Lord Beaverbrook said of Balfour, "like Asquith he was much admired. His intimate friends were few in number, and it is just possible that he didn't believe in anything or anybody." Clemenceau decided in the end that Balfour was "the Richelieu of the congress."

"A general feeling of impatience," Balfour declared in a secret session of the Council of Ten, "is now becoming manifest in all countries on account of the apparent slow progress the conference is making in the direction of final peace." Indeed, a general feeling of impatience had been manifest for weeks, but it had not been to Balfour's advantage to notice it before. Now that Wilson was gone, and it had become possible for Balfour and Clemenceau to direct their attention to the issues that they cared about, "it would be folly," Balfour said, "to ignore altogether the danger that feeling [of impatience] might produce."

And so Balfour introduced a resolution, as Baker said, "to bring about a preliminary treaty with Germany, containing not only the military terms but practically everything else except the League of Nations." Balfour's resolution called for all the groups of experts to submit their final reports by March 8, the week before Wilson's scheduled return. Finally the conferees agreed to issue an invitation to the Germans to send a delegation to receive the treaty terms about ten days after Wilson's return. And, during this intermission in the meetings of the heads of state, Wilson's League of Nations was referred to a committee.

ENTROPY

Fifty-eight committees were formed in the course of the conference, "some mainly as sops to starved vanities," as one of the young Englishmen said, and others mainly as places for the senior negotiators to bury unwanted issues. During Wilson's absence, as more and more questions of morality and justice were referred to the committees, the conference was infused with a new sense of organization and disorder, purpose and uncertainty, knowledge and ignorance, reason and irrationality, books and maps, statistics and frontiers, salients, corridors, watersheds, dossiers, partitions, counterproposals, drafts, droning testimony, articles, amendments, colored inks: "Things," Seymour wrote home, "are getting more rather than less complicated."

The conference was overwhelmed by detail, and Seymour was even losing his ability to talk. "If the French make a proposition which is perfectly rotten and the chairman asks your opinion, you can't say 'I don't like it,' but rather: 'At the present moment I feel that my government would have some hesitation in accepting the proposition of the French without reserve; may I suggest that a modification in the following sense would perhaps provide for a settlement which might, in the eyes of the inhabitants concerned, appear more equitable.' I find that I am losing all capacity to say just plain 'no' or 'yes'; it has to be, 'I should be rather slow to agree,' or, 'at the present moment I should feel inclined to concur.' "

On the Czech committee, Seymour had to oppose the French,

who "wanted to give more to the Czechoslovaks than we have believed to be fair or even wise for their welfare." Jules Cambon represented France on that committee. "He is old, short and fat, with
white mustache, rather bent and near-sighted. His charm lies in his
very genial smile and quaint expressions of humor." The argument
the old charmer made about Czechoslovakia, however, was vexingly
to the point: if the principle of self-determination were applied according to strict ethnological criteria, they would end up with "a
country as discontinuous as the spots on a panther's skin." Such an
end, Cambon ventured, was not what the conference wished to
achieve.

The Italians were represented by Salvago Raggi, a "typical diplomat of the old school, very suave, outdoing himself in politeness,
playing his hand very carefully." When Cambon would ask Raggi to
set forth Italy's position, Raggi would say, "I ask myself whether it
is not wiser, at this stage, to put at least two possibilities before ourselves." And then, as Seymour said, he would say nothing. Or, if he
wanted to delay matters, "he would say, 'I don't quite understand,'
and use up 15 minutes in having explained to him what was perfectly evident from the start. And all this with the most magnetic
and friendly manner."

Sir Joseph Cook represented Britain. "He is blissfully ignorant
of everything European . . . but sometimes Sir Joseph thinks that he
has a good idea of his own and will fight like a steer for it. . . . Sir
Joseph insists that our duty is to reward the Czechs for what they
have done in the war by giving them all the population possible, regardless of whether or not it wants to be Czech citizens."

"You and I," Andre Tardieu said to Seymour one day, "will
not be able to travel in either Rumania, or Serbia, or Hungary, after
this commission has finished."

The more the committees learned of the countries they studied,
the more they realized that no amount of information, either accu-
rate or inaccurate, could disguise the essential horror confronted by
the conference: that the committees could not redeem all the confusion and anguish and bloodshed of the war.

Because the enormity of that realization was too dreadful for
the junior delegates to face, the committees continued to labor under
a massive burden of confusion and ambiguity, verbal generality and
exhaustion, to harbor hopes they no longer had, to pretend to a faith
they no longer shared.

Having started out to do something fine, the young diplomats began imperceptibly to shift their intentions to an aim more urgent, and even desperate: to try not to take a catastrophe and turn it into something worse.

❧

THE SMART SET

"One of the interesting developments in the life here is tea at the Quai d'Orsay," Seymour wrote home. "All the distinguished people in the building generally gather at 4:30 and we have an opportunity to see them and even sometimes to speak to them. I was talking to Le Rond the other day when Foch came up to him, and Le Rond introduced me to him. The marshal is certainly not distinguished looking at any distance, but he has a remarkable face, lined and with fine expression. I think that he looks with distrust on all civilians connected with the Conference, believing that they are not going to make the most of the victory that he has given them."

Admiral Lord John Fisher, first sea lord, "was a wonderful dancer," Lloyd George's mistress Frances Stevenson said, "and I enjoyed my gay waltzes with him around the ballroom at the Majestic. . . . Lord Fisher never seemed to get tired, and after one dance he said to me: 'Don't you think that is pretty good for an old man of nearly eighty?' "

Of the artists, said Frances Stevenson, Augustus John was the most picturesque. "His parties became celebrated, but sometimes riotous." At the opera one evening with a party that included Augustus John, Miss Stevenson felt "shy and awkward" when she was introduced to Puccini, who was in a box with two Russian ex-archduchesses.

Paris was "putting on her act," Vansittart, a young Englishman said, "which deceives most Americans, but beneath the make-up she remained her hard self. . . . There were a few modernizations, such as cocktail parties from which women barely tore themselves away in time to undress for dinner. Best-sellers were full of fornication. Sex, superseding slaughter, regained its place as topic of the hour, with new laxity towards *ces messieurs* of perversion. After four years a sag in probity went without saying."

Sarah Bernhardt appeared for luncheon parties, "still full of vitality and grace," Frances Stevenson said, although happily she was now "old and almost grotesque in her great gold wig." Paderewski, in Paris as prime minister of Poland, resolutely refused to play the piano, and Miss Stevenson was delighted when, after a dance at the Majestic at which the Royal Army Band played, "a heavy-looking Frenchman came up to Paderewski and shook him by the hand. 'I wanted to tell you,' he said, 'that I think you have got a very good band.' "

At a gala performance for a French charity, Miss Bernhardt was borne in on a float with white draperies, so that "she seemed to be emerging from clouds." The queen of Rumania, Madame Poincaré, and the wives of the American commissioners to the conference were there. One scene in the revue represented the great literary figures of French history—Balzac, Dumas, and so forth. When Dumas entered, one of the French women said brightly, "Voilà, Dumas." One of the American women "was instantly transformed from a languid, disinterested listener to a lion hunter keen on the scent. 'Oh,' she exclaimed, 'I didn't know he was in Paris; we must have him to dinner!' "

Ho Chi Minh was in Paris, too, although no one invited him to dinner. Ho, who had come to Paris during the war and worked as a pastry chef under Escoffier, as a retoucher of photographs, and as a designer of "Asian antiquities" manufactured in France, had been trying to get the attention of Clemenceau, Lloyd George, and Wilson. With two of his compatriots, he had drawn up an eight-point plan that called for an end to the colonial exploitation of Vietnam and a beginning of independence for his country. Unable to get the attention of any of the Big Three, he turned then to writing articles about Indochina for *Populaire* and so, attracting the attention of some of the leaders of the French Socialist party, entered politics.

Herbert Clark Hoover, "who has done such wonderful work in Belgium," as head of the American relief mission, was being mentioned as a possible candidate for president. Gertrude Bell was in Paris. Nancy Astor brought Ruth Draper to Paris, and Miss Draper performed her "impersonations" for the ambassadorial community. It was said that the cook at Lloyd George's house in the Rue Nitot made *langues de chats* especially for Clemenceau when the premier came to tea, and Clemenceau "enjoyed them like a child." There were plenty of good boxing matches in Paris even though Criqui, a great stylist, unfortunately had been wounded in the war. Arnold

Toynbee was in Paris, writing papers on Turkey and the Near East for the British delegation.

Gossip was that the queen of Rumania had gone on a shopping spree some weeks before and, at lunch with Balfour, had reeled out a list of all her purchases, which had included a pink silk chemise. She had mentioned to Balfour, then, that she expected to meet President Wilson. "What shall I talk to him about," she asked, "the League of Nations or my pink chemise?" "Begin with the League of Nations," Balfour had said, "and finish up with the pink chemise. If you were talking to Mr. Lloyd George you could begin with the pink chemise."

At the Opéra, when Paderewski entered the presidential box, the orchestra played the Polish national anthem, and handkerchiefs and cheers rose from the audience. Paderewski bowed: "Not a presidential bow," said Nicolson, "a concert platform bow. His wife looks like hell in orchids." It was said that Clemenceau, who enjoyed attending the opera, had been overheard murmuring, "Figaro here . . . Figaro there . . . he's a kind of Lloyd George."

Nicolson dined with Balfour, Berthelot, Jacques Blanche, Paul Claudel, and Anna de Noailles. "She looks like a hawk from some hieroglyph in a Temple at Luxor. Eve Francis declaims Claudel's poetry afterwards. He sits there in front of her, a sturdy man, managing to convey that his applause is directed at her masterly recitation and implies no praise of the poetry which she recites."

Throat germs were everywhere: from time to time a delegate would disappear for a few days; the American doctor would ask matter-of-factly whether the delegate was "spitting up blood"—and, if not, the doctor, unimpressed, prescribed aspirin and rest.

At dinner with George Creel, chairman of the committee on public information, some of the young American delegates learned that Vienna was "gayer than Paris, with lots to eat and amusements in full swing," Budapest and Hungary were "dead," famine in Slovakia.

Nonetheless, "the rain clears off nightly at Paris," Shotwell said gratefully, "and no matter what kind of a day, you can walk under the stars after any evening session." In a quiet little restaurant near the Sorbonne, one got sugarless coffee with lunch—cheese, war bread, in an unheated room. In general, the cost of living was atrocious. Sole cost sixteen francs a pound.

Admiral Sir Ernest Charles Thomas Troubridge told of the discomfiture of Miss Durham, a nurse. She had been a great admirer of the Montenegrins until one day, while caring for one Montenegrin hero in the hospital, she made the mistake of looking into a bag that he always kept with him, and there discovered sixty human noses.

Seymour was impressed with the quality of the junior members of the American delegation. Christian Herter, he said, was "just as nice as they make them," and Allen Dulles, Lansing's nephew, was "absolutely first class—just as nice as he can be," and Allen's older brother, John Foster Dulles, was "very charming," but Seymour was somewhat irritated by Vance McCormick.

On the issues facing the conference, McCormick was in favor of seizing all the art treasures of Berlin, Dresden, and Vienna and holding them as collateral. "He believes that Germany must not be pushed too hard now because of the danger of anarchy; he also thinks that she is certain to get economic control of Russia in the future, unless we Americans make a very bold, decided, and intelligent bid."

None of these opinions bothered Seymour, but he was upset when the conversation drifted to matters back home. "I talked with [McCormick] on reorganization at Yale for some time; he is on the corporation. He is a very fine man and very intelligent, but I think it unfortunate that men who know so little about a university or college should have the power to organize Yale so completely at the present time."

PROUST

"Proust is white, unshaven, grubby, slip-faced," said Nicolson, when he met Proust at dinner at the Ritz. "He puts his fur coat on afterwards and sits hunched there in white kid gloves. Two cups of black coffee he has, with chunks of sugar. Yet in his talk there is no affectation."

Proust asked Nicolson to tell him how the committees worked, and Nicolson began, "Well, we generally meet at ten, there are secretaries behind—."

"Mais non, mais non, vous allez trop vite. Recommencez. Vous prenez la voiture de la Délégation. Vous descendez au Quai d'Orsay. Vous montez l'escalier. Vous entrez dans la Salle. Et alors? Précisez, mon cher, précisez."

And so Nicolson told Proust everything: "The dominant note is black and white, heavy black suits, white cuffs and paper: it is relieved by blue and khaki: the only other colours would be the scarlet damask of the Quai d'Orsay curtains, green baize, pink blotting pads, and the innumerable gilt of little chairs. For smells you would have petrol, typewriting ribbons, French polish, central heating, and a touch of violet hair-wash. The tactile motifs would be tracing paper, silk, the leather handle of a weighted pouch of papers, the foot-feel of very thick carpets alternating with parquet flooring, the stretch of muscle caught by leaning constantly over very large maps, the brittle feel of a cane chair seat which has been occupied for hours."

"Mais précisez, mon cher monsieur, n'allez pas trop vite."

"A group of little men at the end of a vast table: maps, interpreters, secretaries, and row upon row of empty gilt chairs. The great red curtains are drawn, scarlet and enclosing against the twilight sinking gently upon the Seine. The chandeliers blaze. . . . To the adjoining banqueting hall we adjourn for a few minutes, for tea, brioches and macaroons. It is a large, slim room, and the tea-urn gutters in the draught. Then back again to our long table. 'Messieurs, nous avons donc examiné la frontière entre Csepany et Saros Patag. Il résulte que la jonction du chemin de fer Miskovec-Kaschau avec la ligne St. Peter-Losoncz doit être attribuée. . . .' On returning to the Majestic the sounds of dance music would reach us from the ballroom. . . ."

SHELL SHOCK

"I see that my next book," Proust wrote to Philippe Soupault, "though copy-read by M. Breton, contained so many mistakes that if I did not list an erratum I would be dishonored." It took Proust eight days to discover two hundred mistakes in twenty-three galley proofs. "But by no means," Proust concluded acidly, "let M. Breton take this for a reproach."

André Breton was clearly not interested in Proust's work, which memorialized a world that had, to Breton's mind, been completely destroyed in the war, in what Breton called a "cloaca of blood, stupidity, and mud."

Breton, who was a medical student when the war began, was assigned first to a hospital in Nantes and later to the psychiatric center of Saint-Dizier. At Nantes and Saint-Dizier, he was deeply—and permanently—moved by the deliriums, hallucinations, the waking dreads and the nightmares of the patients traumatized by shell shock.

What Breton saw let loose by the war—the anarchy of mind, the terror, the madness, as well as curious flights of fancy, startling new connections, beautiful juxtapositions, suddenly liberated images, chance associations—could no longer be contained by traditional forms.

He responded not to Proust, but to Rimbaud, Lautréamont, and to another soldier-poet, Apollinaire. In 1915, he began a correspondence with Apollinaire, whose *Alcools* had been published two years before. Apollinaire was in another hospital in 1916. He had been wounded in the head while he was preoccupied with reading a new issue of *Mercure de France*. Whether or not he fully appreciated the absurdity of having his head blown open while reading a literary journal, he did enjoy the opportunity afterwards—following two surgical operations—to sport the large white turban bandage on his head.

Unfit for further active service, Apollinaire returned to Paris and finished a second volume of poetry, *Calligrammes*. "Having seen the war in the Artillery and Infantry," Apollinaire wrote (in Roger Shattuck's translation),

> *Wounded in the head trepanned under chloroform*
> *Having lost his best friends in that frightful*
> > *struggle*
> *I know of the old and of the new as much as one man*
> > *alone can know of them*
> *And without being uneasy today about this war*
> *Between us and for us my friends*
> *I pronounce Judgment on this long quarrel of*

> *tradition and innovation Of Order and Adventure*
> *You whose mouths are made in the image of God's*
>   *Mouths which are order itself*
>
> *Be indulgent when you compare us*
> *To those who have been the perfection of order*
> *We who seek everywhere for adventure*
>
> *We are not your enemies*
> *We wish to offer you vast and strange domains*
> *Where flowering mystery offers itself to whoever*
>   *wishes to pick it*
> *There are new fires there and colors never yet seen*
> *A thousand imponderable phantasms*
> *To which reality must be given . . .*

The phantasms that Apollinaire and Breton saw were not created by the war alone. Freud had long since revealed dark areas of the psyche; Einstein had demolished classical physics. But the war had finished the job—and what had finally been released by the war—the huge upsurge of all the forces of the unconscious—could no longer be encompassed by reason, balance, morality, or ethics.

Pierre Janet, a professor of psychiatric medicine and one of Jung's teachers, had commended the practice of "automatic" writing. "Let the pen wander," he said, "automatically, on the page even as the medium interrogates his mind." In this way, as Anna Balakian has written, "the strictures of mental inhibition" will be loosened, and "the spontaneous workings of the mind [will] emerge into view." Janet believed that automatic writing would lead to a new understanding of the relationship between conscious and unconscious, a way to a complete knowledge of self.

Breton saw in Janet's work a way to enlarge his grasp on reality by recognizing, as equally real, both waking and dreaming, both the outer world and the inner, both reason and madness, and, in this way, to reveal "the marvelous." Breton believed, as he said, "in the future resolution of these two states, dream and reality, which are seemingly so contradictory, into a new kind of absolute reality, a *surreality.*"

Breton seized, too, on the work of the English scientist Robert Brown, who had demonstrated almost a century before that certain movements of molecules cannot be predicted according to simple laws of cause and effect. In the phenomenon of "Brownian movement," so many diverse causes and effects are interacting in such complex fashion that the behavior of any one molecule can only be guessed at within a range of possibilities and statistical probabilities. Once the influenza epidemic began in Europe, one might have been able to predict hundreds of thousands, even millions, of deaths; but no one could have foretold that two days before the armistice, the flu would kill Apollinaire.

It seemed that people were to be the victims of chance—and so, certainly, Breton's friend Apollinaire was. But Breton dealt with the upsetting prospects of chance and chaos by insisting upon their obverse: the way to avoid being the victim of chance was to turn the tables completely, and to seek chance actively, to make chance an ally of freedom, to search always for new possibilities to take advantage of.

And so Breton became a wanderer in the streets of Paris, seeking chance encounters in the Café de Flore, juxtapositions of characters, vistas, objects found on the sidewalks. In the apparent agents of catastrophe, in chance, and in the surrender of reason he hoped to find some sense of harmony with life. He sought the marvelous in—as Lautréamont's incessantly quoted phrase had it—"the casual meeting of sewing machine and umbrella on a dissection table."

In March of 1919, Breton, Philippe Soupault, and Louis Aragon put together the first issue of a new magazine, *Littérature*, dedicated to shaping this new vision. Soupault reviewed Charlie Chaplin's recent film, *A Dog's Life* (which President Wilson had seen one night on shipboard on his way to Paris). Cocteau, who was dining from time to time with Harold Nicolson, was noticed for his recently published *Le Coq et l'Arlequin*. Pieces by Lautréamont and Apollinaire were printed. Tristan Tzara contributed something.

Breton and Soupault soon embarked on another joint project—dictating to one another a stream of automatic writing. "By the end of the first day," Breton said, "we were able to read to ourselves some fifty or so pages obtained in this manner, and begin to compare our results. All in all, Soupault's pages and mine proved to be remarkably similar: the same overconstruction, shortcomings of a similar nature, but also, on both our parts, the illusion of an extraordinary verve . . . a considerable choice of images . . . and here and there, a strong comical effect." Some of the images were striking— rivers of milk, androgynous plants, a marvelous chain of keys, and, as Anna Balakian has pointed out, "the intimate network that connects the human with the earth in an image such as this: 'Do not disturb the genius planter of white roots my nerve endings underground.' " The text as a whole, though incoherent, was not marvelous; nevertheless, published under the title *Les Champs Magnetiques*, it was the first surrealist text, and it certainly represented, in Balakian's phrase, the "triumph of inscape over landscape."

Breton himself thought that, of all his acquaintances, the one most talented at inducing a trancelike state was Robert Desnos, whose first poems were published in *Littérature* in 1919. "The Voice of Robert Desnos" sounded (in Michael Benedikt's translation) like this:

tornadoes whirl around in my mouth
hurricanes bring if such a thing is possible color
      to my lips
tempests purr at my feet
typhoons if such a thing is possible start to paint
      my portrait
I accept the drunken kisses of cyclones
raging tides crash forward before my feet
the tremors of the earth make me tremble not at all
      but cause carnage at my call
volcanic smoke clothes me in wisps
and that from cigarettes becomes my cologne
while the smoke-rings from cigars create my crown
love affairs and even long-sought love itself take
      refuge here with me
lovers hearken to my voice
the living and the dead yield to me and greet me the
      first quite coddle the second with familiarity
gravediggers abandon their half-finished holes to announce
      that I alone can command their nocturnal labors
assassins salute me
executioners cry for revolution
cry my voice
cry my name
ship-pilots take their fix from my eyes
construction-workers suffer vertigo as they hear me
architects depart for the desert
assassins give me their benediction
human flesh pulsates at my call . . .

MISSION TO MOSCOW

Had the Russians not been inconvenienced by a revolution, they would have been represented at the peace conference, and Lloyd George had suggested that the Russians should be invited to patch up a truce among themselves so that they could send a delegation to Paris. Wilson approved of Lloyd George's idea, but Clemenceau and Orlando both objected. Baron Sonnino suggested that there were Russian émigrés in Paris at that moment who represented every shade of political opinion in Russia, and they could easily be invited to speak for Russia at the conference. Lloyd George declared that he had nothing to say against "these people, Prince Lvov, etc. We were told they represented every shade of opinion. As a matter of fact, they represented every opinion, except the prevalent opinion in Russia."

Wilson objected, mildly, that bolshevism was only prevalent "in some respects"; but Lloyd George was not to be put off. He "feared," he said, "the fact that it was prevalent must be accepted. The peasants accepted Bolshevism for the same reason as the peasants had accepted the French Revolution, namely, that it gave them land. The Bolsheviks were the *de facto* government. . . . To say that we ourselves should pick the representatives of a great people was contrary to every principle for which we had fought."

But Clemenceau was against the notion of having any Bolsheviks in Paris. "I never wanted to hold the conference in this bloody capital," Lloyd George complained. "Both House and I thought it would be better to hold it in a neutral place, but the old man wept and protested so much that we gave way, and this is what we get for the concession."

Wilson suggested that a meeting be arranged at Prinkipo, one of the Princes Islands in the Sea of Marmora, and that invitations be sent to all the Russian governments—there were, at this time, three, or perhaps four governments in Russia—but the White Russians refused to attend such a meeting, and the Bolsheviks said they would come only if the invitation were sent to them in such a way as to constitute a formal recognition of their government by the Allies.

Then, several days after Wilson had left Paris, Colonel House summoned William C. Bullitt to his rooms. With Wilson's permission, House and Lloyd George had decided to send a secret mission to Moscow to see what sort of deal might be struck with Lenin. The mission was to be kept secret not only from the world, but especially from Clemenceau, who was opposed even to speaking with the Bolsheviks.

Bullitt, a twenty-eight-year-old Philadelphian, a well-connected Yale graduate from a wealthy family, was a brilliant, impulsive, brash young man who, like House, was confident that he could solve great political questions if given the chance. For his mission, he chose to take along an ex-social worker named Captain Petit, a secretary named Lynch, and the left-wing, muckraking journalist Lincoln Steffens. In Sweden, the mission was taken under the wing of a Communist guide named Kil Baum, who, "added to Bullitt and Lynch," said Steffens, "made a murderous peace commission.

"Our conspiracy was to get through Finland. A new country with new officials is always difficult, and the Finns (and the Poles) felt that they were guardians, not only of their borders, but of European civilization. Bullitt managed the Finns ... when at the Russ-Finn border an arrogant Finnish officer drew up to stop and search us, Bullitt outdid him in arrogance—'Hands off, you. Telephone for orders. We pass.' "

Aboard the train, Steffens, ever the working journalist, considered how he would write the story he had not yet got—and, long before they reached the Russian border, he came up with a ringing phrase that became the famous conclusion of his first-hand, in-depth report: "I have been over into the future, and it works."

The Russians had been among the forces allied against Germany during the war; but, in March 1918, the Bolsheviks had signed the Treaty of Brest-Litovsk, concluding a separate peace with Germany. The Allies, feeling betrayed, deployed troops around the Russian border. The Allied countries thought first that they were protecting ammunition dumps—to keep the Russians from turning munitions over to Germany. Then the Allies thought they might encourage the overthrow of the Red government so that a new government might re-enter the war against Germany. In time, the Allies forgot both these motivations: they discovered that they had become the associates of the counterrevolutionary White Russian armies and that they were embroiled in a tremendous civil war.

Wilson did not care for the Bolsheviks, but he did not care for the monarchist White Russians either. Nor did he think that he could persuade many Americans to send soldiers or money to support the White Russians. Lloyd George could not send men or money either; indeed, he was fairly certain that the British Army would revolt if he tried to send it to Russia. Clemenceau was convinced that the Bolsheviks ought to be stamped out, but France had neither an army nor money. The French did propose that an army of Poles, Czechs, Finns, and Rumanians might be raised—paid for by the British and Americans, led by a French officer corps—but neither Wilson nor Lloyd George even deigned to take that proposal seriously.

Lloyd George was certain that world peace was not possible so long as Russia was left out of any settlement. It seemed clear to everyone that the Bolsheviks needed to be either smashed or accepted—but no one, save Clemenceau and the French, could conclude which course to take. Amidst the turmoil of the spring of 1919, it seemed that the world was being divided between the Left and the Right. The moderates, the liberals, seemed caught between contradictory wishes and sympathies, compromised even before they had begun. They seemed, even as they spoke of a new order, to be attempting to shore up an old order, stunned, paralyzed, unable to choose. Even the best of them, the bright, articulate young British liberals, were immobilized by their commitment to the Empire, and so, in the end, to the old order. While they hesitated, the Red Army chased the Germans out of Estonia and Latvia, prepared to move into Lithuania, and calculated that Germany itself would soon establish a Communist government. Moderates and bourgeois liberals drifted toward alliance with reactionaries and the new Right. As real change, real revolution appeared in Europe, liberalism's basic loyalty to the old order became more and more apparent. Confidence in moderation waned as people were drawn increasingly to one side or another during February and March—to the Communists or to the emerging Fascists.

"Petrograd," said Lincoln Steffens, "was a deserted city when we got there at night. Nobody was at the station, nobody in the dark, cold, broken streets, and there was no fire in the vacant palace assigned to us. I . . . was called out by our Swedish and Russian guides to go looking through dead hotels for officials at midnight teas. . . . I was led from one tea to another till at last the guide found and presented me to Zinoviev, one of the three commissioners appointed to deal with us."

Zinoviev asked Steffens whether the Paris mission was composed of plenipotentiaries. Steffens said no. "When he heard that . . . he turned away abruptly, and we never saw him again." What Zinoviev understood—what Steffens and Bullitt could not bring themselves to realize, bright and decent men that they were—was that even at this moment, even when Wilson and Lloyd George had gone so far as to send a mission to Russia, even so the western leaders had sent nobodies.

The Russians evidently debated among themselves what to do about the old journalist and his young sidekick; it was not even clear to the Russians who was the head of the delegation. Eventually, Lenin sent Tchicherin, the secretary of foreign affairs, from Moscow to Petrograd to see who these Americans were. Bullitt and Steffens persuaded Tchicherin that Wilson and Lloyd George would like to arrive at some understanding with the Russians that could then be presented to the French as an attractive deal. The Americans were taken onto a train by Tchicherin and Litvinov who had represented the Bolsheviks in London after 1917. The Russians escorted the Americans to Moscow, installed them in a warm palace with servants and gave them "piles and piles of caviar . . . caviar and black bread and tea. It was all they had, we guessed." The Russian leaders themselves apparently had little to eat and frequently turned up at the American palace at mealtime. "We had opera and theaters and music; we had the czar's box one night; but we never had a meal outside our own house, and the Russians were frequently at our table."

Lenin, said Steffens, was a "quiet figure in old clothes," who greeted the journalist with "a nod and a handshake. An open inquiring face, with a slight droop in one eye that suggested irony or humor." Steffens asked Lenin, among other things, "What assurance can you give that the red terror will not go on killing—"

" 'Who wants to ask us about our killings?' he demanded, coming erect on his feet in anger.

" 'Paris,' I said.

" 'Do you mean to tell me that those men who have just generaled the slaughter of seventeen millions of men in a purposeless war are concerned over the few thousands who have been killed in a revolution with a conscious aim—to get out of the necessity of war and . . . and armed peace?' He stood a second, facing me with hot eyes; then quieting, he said: 'But never mind, don't deny the terror. Don't minimize any of the evils of a revolution. They occur. They must be counted upon. If we have to have a revolution, we have to pay the price of revolution.' "

They spoke of the upper classes, who would not permit change; of the "fixed liberals," who were just as bad; of the conservatism of the peasants. Steffens asked whether the peasants were being given the land. "Not by law," Lenin replied. "But they think they own the land; so they do."

Lenin took up a piece of paper and a pencil. " 'We are all wrong on the land,' he said, and the thought of Wilson flashed to my mind. Could the American say he was all wrong like that? 'Look,' said Lenin, and he drew a straight line. 'That's our course, but'—he struck off a crooked line to a point—'that's where we are. That's where we have had to go, but we'll get back here on our course some day.' He paralleled the straight line.

" 'That is the advantage of a plan. You can go wrong, you can tack, as you must, but if you know you are wrong, you can steer back on your course.' "

Bullitt's dealings with Lenin were more businesslike. In fact, the brash young man came up with a superb deal. Lenin wanted the western powers to withdraw their own troops, to cease their support of the White armies, and to end the blockade they had imposed on Russia. In return for these concessions, the Bolsheviks would stop the civil war, allow the White Russians to remain in possession of whatever territory they controlled at the time, to declare a general amnesty, and to pay off some of the old czarist debts to foreign nations. Lenin insisted on only two other points. The offer of this deal must come from the Allies—that is, the western powers must commit themselves to the deal first so that Lenin would not appear to be begging; and the offer must come before April 10.

Bullitt was delighted with himself. He had rescued the world from a war between the forces of revolution and counterrevolution, and he could not wait to get back to Paris to announce the deal he had made.

POLISH JOKES

Shotwell was invited with several other junior members of the American delegation to a formal luncheon with some of the members of the Polish delegation at their headquarters in the Rue La Pérouse near the Etoile. Paderewski was not there—which was just as well. Although Paderewski lent a certain immediate distinction to the Polish delegation, with his "long flaxen hair," as Lansing said, "sprinkled with gray and brushed back like a mane from his broad white forehead . . . peculiarly narrow eyes and his small moustache and goatee that looked so foreign," nonetheless Lansing expressed the common opinion when he said that Paderewski was "absorbed in the aesthetic things of life rather than in practical world politics."

The Americans were treated to a full luncheon with champagne, a dignified speech by one of the Poles, who referred to the historic occasion that brought them all together, and then, after the guests adjourned to the drawing room, formal introductions and stiff handshakes with some twenty Polish leaders, each of whom treated the Americans to little set speeches about their wishes for Danzig, Posen, Lemberg, and so forth. Historians spoke of the history of Polish toleration; geographers and economists outlined the ways in which new borders would function for the common good. Maps and statistics were produced. The afternoon entertainments went on until five-thirty.

Halfway through the luncheon, it occurred to Shotwell that something was wrong; and then he figured it out. "We were being treated as plenipotentiaries. There was some mistake." The Poles were presenting their case to the wrong people. The greater joke was that it made no difference. Poland was to be created out of German, Russian, and Austrian territory not because of the claims of justice, history, aesthetics, or morality, but because Clemenceau wanted Poland to help stabilize Eastern Europe against both the Bolsheviks and the Germans.

But, the greatest joke of all was that in the event of another war, the borders of this Poland would be indefensible.

MISSION TO GERMANY

The rumor was, in Paris, that the Germans were starving. If the Germans were starving, the English said, then Germany would fall to the Bolsheviks. If they were starving, it was because of the Allied blockade—which ought to be lifted. The Germans, said Clemenceau, were not starving. (Or perhaps Clemenceau wanted them to starve.) The Americans, knowing nothing of Germany, could not be sure. However, it was true, Keynes said, that Herbert Hoover had promised American farmers "a minimum price for their hogs; the promise had overstimulated the sows of that continent; the price was falling." If the Germans were indeed starving, then the Americans, said Keynes, would like to "unload on Germany the large stocks of low-grade bacon which we now hold, and replace these by fresher stocks from America which would be more readily saleable."

Keynes was dispatched with a party to Treves to sort out just what was happening to the Germans and what might be done about it. "It seemed," said Keynes, ". . . an extraordinary adventure . . . to step on German soil. We wondered what the streets would look like, whether the children's ribs would be sticking through their clothes and what there would be in the shops. . . . One domestic scene remains in my memory. The town was at that time within the American sphere of occupation and in the hands of the American Army. . . . Accordingly we were taken round by an American lieutenant . . . to inspect one or two domiciles available for us. The first we entered was a typical upper middle-class German household, bare but spotlessly clean. With dejected but respectful faces the Frau of the house and her husband showed the alien conquerors round. I felt very much ashamed of the whole business. We talked loudly amongst ourselves, enquired after the bathroom, inspected the mattresses, declared that it would do on the whole and were given the latchkey." Keynes and his fellow Englishmen never returned to their German house; it was much more convenient for them to stay aboard their own train. Keynes realized, to his astonishment, that the entire episode of looking for suitable German quarters had only been an instinctive ritual of trying out the prerogatives of the victors.

Keynes's train had arrived in Treves at about breakfast time. The German delegation arrived a little later. The head of the delegation, Matthias Erzberger, age forty-four, a leader of the Catholic Center party, had earned the hatred of many of his fellow Germans by his avidity for the war at the beginning and then, in the summer of 1917, after he toured the front, his announcement that Germany could not possibly win the war. A man of raw ambition, ruthless and unprincipled, given to a nasty manner in debate, he might have been forgiven all had he not also been reckoned one of the most brilliant men in Germany, a man who was most often, if not always, right.

Keynes said that as Erzberger led his delegation down the station platform, he was "fat and disgusting in a fur coat. . . . With him were a General and a Sea-Captain with an iron cross round his neck and an extraordinary resemblance of face and figure to the pig in *Alice in Wonderland.* They satisfied wonderfully, as a group, the popular conception of Huns. . . . We watched them as sightseers. They walked stiffly and uneasily, seeming to lift their feet like men in a photograph or a movie. . . . How were we to behave? Ought we to shake hands? . . . They pressed into the carriage, bowing stiffly. We bowed stiffly also, for some of us had never bowed before."

Of the other members of the German delegation, Keynes especially noticed a representative of the Reichsbank, "elderly, broken, with hungry, nervous eyes, deeply middle class, looking somehow like an old broken umbrella, who lost the thread of the conference at the outset and never recovered it" and "a representative of the Foreign Office, his face cut to pieces with duelling, a sort of Corps student type, sly and rather merry, overanxious to catch the eyes of one or other of us with a cheerful grin."

So this, at last, was the enemy. They seemed a shattered lot—and, as the Allies moved into negotiation with them—strangely out of touch with reality. The Germans, Keynes gradually realized with astonishment and alarm, seemed much less anxious than the English about the prospects of starvation. Keynes would never be certain whether their casualness was the result of some secret knowledge on their part, perhaps of some concealed food supplies unknown to the Allies—or the result of the fact that the Germans did not understand their own plight.

Erzberger and the others of his delegation represented a government that was, at that very moment, in the midst of a violent revolution.

Kaiser Wilhelm had fled into exile in November. "A scapegoat had to be found," said one of the German politicians, "and there was the Emperor." But his fleeing in disgrace did not resolve Germany's problems. His flight had been followed by a mutiny among the German sailors stationed at Kiel, and their mutiny had spread until it became a revolution that swept through the northwestern part of Germany. Then, in southern Germany, an Independent Socialist leader, Kurt Eisner, had proclaimed Bavaria an independent republic.

In the meantime, however, the kaiser had formally abdicated. The chancellor, Prince Max, had entrusted the government to Friedrich Ebert, the leader of the Majority Socialist party, and the German republic was proclaimed.

In Berlin a struggle broke out between the Majority Socialists, who hoped for a gradual, nonviolent move away from capitalism, and the extreme left wing, the Spartacists, led by Karl Liebknecht and Rosa Luxemburg. By the end of December, the Spartacists had transformed themselves into the German Communist party and taken to leading marches and demonstrations that ended up in riots, police scuffles, and deaths. The left wing of the Independent Socialist party joined with Liebknecht and Luxemburg, and finally, on January 5, a demonstration began that would not end. Liebknecht called for revolution, and, within hours, the streets of Berlin had been taken over by two hundred thousand workers; the revolutionaries controlled the city with snipers; and the rumor swept Berlin that the remnants of the German Army would march to Berlin to support the revolution.

The revolution lasted for ten days. The government turned to some of the old army leaders who were assembling militias—*Freikorps*—in Berlin and asked them to put down the rebels. The Potsdam regiment went into action at once, opening up with trench mortars, howitzers, machine guns, grenades, and flamethrowers, and they turned against the largely unarmed rebels without mercy. Parades and demonstrations were banned; revolutionary leaders were jailed; the streets were patrolled by tanks and armored cars; and Liebknecht and Luxemburg were placed under arrest and, while they were under arrest, murdered.

In this atmosphere, an election was held for deputies for the new National Assembly which was to go to the ancient city of Weimar, draft a constitution, and make peace with the Allies. The new Communist party declined to take part in these elections. The Majority Socialists did well, winning thirty-nine percent of the vote. The Independent Socialists won seven percent. And the parties of the center, and, even more, of the conservative factions, did disconcertingly well. The new German National People's party, the party of diehard monarchists, industrialists, and large landowners, who might have been expected to have been discredited by the war, were able to poll a solid ten percent.

The new republican National Assembly convened in February to govern a nation that suffered from staggering dislocations, from a shortage of labor on farms and a mob of unemployed soldiers in the cities, from a drop of thirty-nine percent in industrial output compared with prewar levels, a drop of thirty-eight percent in agricultural productivity, a lack of farm machinery and of commercial fertilizers, from starvation, and a continuing blockade by the Allies so that no food or fertilizers or farm machinery could get into the country. Prices and currencies were in disarray, taxes had been vastly increased, the public debt had increased by a factor of twenty during the war—and that represented debt not to foreign countries but to German citizens, who stood to be wiped out by default or inflation, the supply of paper money had increased by a factor of five. Transportation and other facilities of commerce had been wrecked, while the largest and most successful industries at the end of the war were the ones dedicated to weapons production and so were now at once obsolete. Disease was rampant; so was continuing riot, fighting, revolutionary upheavals, and boiling resentment and rage.

Friedrich Ebert and Gustav Noske were the most important figures in the new German government. Ebert, a decent, commonsensical, hardworking, competent man, more than slightly dull, with a passion for methodical organization, was elected president. Gustav Noske, a weak and hesitant man who liked to dress in baggy, rumpled clothes, was deeply impressed by the glamour and power of the military. Appointed minister of defense, he came to love the idea that he was considered strong and somewhat cruel, that he was known as "the Bloodhound."

Between them, in order to defend the new government from assorted rebels and revolutionaries, Ebert and Noske raised, and permitted to flourish, a number of *Freikorps*. The *Freikorps*, some composed of a couple of hundred recruits, some composed of a thousand or more, appealed especially to young men who were upset by the anarchy of their times and wished to belong to a group that had clear sets of beliefs and strong discipline. Because the *Freikorps* organized themselves somewhat spontaneously, and because the government was too preoccupied with too many issues to provide much central organization, the members of the *Freikorps* tended to develop intense loyalty to the individual *Führers* of their groups.

Through January and February, as the *Freikorps* put down one revolt or another, they gained in strength, ferocity, efficiency, and independence. They gained a reputation for putting down rioters with utter ruthlessness, and they liked to compare themselves to the storm troopers, the *Sturmtruppen*, who had so seized the popular imagination during the war.

Of all the rebellious groups in Germany, certainly none was larger than the former kingdom of Bavaria. Traditionally independent-minded, the Bavarians—even when they had been united with Prussia in 1871—had forced Bismarck to leave them with their own postal service, their own army, and their own diplomatic corps. At the end of the war, the new Bavarian government, led by Kurt Eisner, published some documents from their diplomatic archives that tended to show Bavaria had been innocent of any evil intent at the beginning of the war. If anyone in Germany was responsible for the outbreak of the war, these documents were meant to suggest, it was the Prussians. Friedrich Ebert castigated Eisner and informed him that the new constitution would certainly call for more centralized authority in Germany. Two days later, Eisner announced that the Bavarian government had severed diplomatic relations with the Ebert government. Bavaria would make a separate peace with the Allies.

Eisner's cabinet would not support him, and a *Putsch* was attempted. Students demonstrated. Eisner, a Jew, was attacked as an "Israelite devil." On February 21 Eisner was assassinated by Count Anton Arco-Valley, a member of the Thule Society that took as its symbol, to show its anti-Semitism, a swastika, and whose members greeted each other with the salutation *"Heil!"*

A coalition cabinet declared itself—and had to flee Munich. A group called the Coffee House Anarchists ruled for six days. A Communist group took over. Gun battles occurred in the streets. A Red

Army was formed and, within two weeks, grew to a force of perhaps twenty, or even thirty, thousand. The cost of supporting the army finished bankrupting the Bavarian government.

Soon, thirty thousand of the toughest of Gustav Noske's *Freikorps*—by this time a force almost wholly independent of any government control—would advance in a pincers movement through Dachau and Freising toward the Bavarian capital of Munich. They would move with lightning swiftness to encircle the city. The Germans, having lost the war, would direct their rage against one another with breathtaking savagery.

"They could not exactly describe why they marched," Richard Watt has written, "but it was all bound up somehow with the joy of crushing underfoot the 'rotten' elements of German life—proletarianism, Judaism, and the 'November criminals' [the politicians who had signed the armistice agreement the preceding November] who had stabbed Germany in the back and caused her to lose the war."

The Bavarian government could not defend itself, and so the *Freikorps* goose-stepped, unopposed, into Munich. They shot the socialist military commander of the Bavarian government. They beat, with their rifle butts, the anarchist commissar of public education, and then kicked him to death. They happened upon a meeting of Catholic workingmen, herded them into a cellar and shot or bayoneted them to death. In all, the advance guard of the new reich killed about a thousand.

The *Freikorps* left behind a city seething with anger and a lust for vengeance in every street and alley—the hatred of socialists for the *Freikorps*, of Communists for monarchists, of royalists for Jews, of anarchists for industrialists, of nationalists for anarchists.

This was the country that was—or perhaps was not—starving. At Treves—in the railroad car with the Allied representatives—Matthias Erzberger proposed, logically but to the astonishment of the Allies, that food be shipped to Germany at once, and that it be paid for, since the Germans had no money, by a loan from the Allies themselves.

"I bent my efforts," Keynes said tactfully, "speaking coldly and very clearly, to an endeavor to impress it on them that they must banish this idea from their heads . . . and that they would waste precious time if they pursued it."

What Keynes did not mention was that the Allies were not unanimous in their humanitarian concern for the Germans. Clemenceau was not only unconvinced about the Germans' need for food; he was skeptical about their plight altogether. In addition, Clemenceau wanted neither to loan Germany money to buy food nor to allow the Germans to use their own assets to buy food. Clemenceau wanted Germany's gold and other liquid assets outright, as reparations payments. If German gold or liquid assets were given to America or Britain as payment for food, France would have nothing left to collect as reparations.

Nor could Keynes quite tell Erzberger about another subtle twist in the deal. The Allies had agreed among themselves that Germany's merchant marine would somehow be taken from Germany. So far, however, they had not quite come upon the proper pretext for laying hold of Germany's merchant marine. The English especially, with their historic interest in dominating the sea, wanted to make certain that Germany's commercial seaworthiness was ruined. Now, with Germany's need for food, the Allies saw a fine opportunity. The Germans were informed that the Allies had no ships available to deliver food to Germany: therefore, if Germany wanted food, the German merchant marine would have to be surrendered to the Allies.

Somehow, through all this, Keynes managed to keep his good cheer and a certain buoyant cynicism. Erzberger agreed finally to hand over 5 million pounds in gold and other currencies, and to *loan* their merchant marine to the Allies for the purpose of shipping the food supplies.

Back in Paris, when Keynes and his colleagues returned to submit a report on their negotiations, their superiors were not pleased. The Germans had agreed that the merchant marine be used for the food shipments but stipulated that this agreement did not "prejudice in any way the final disposition of these vessels"—which was not quite what the English, in particular, had in mind. And Clemenceau was utterly opposed to the deal to transfer 5 million pounds of liquid assets to his English and American friends.

Keynes was sent back to Treves. There the Paris mission met with Erzberger again. But Erzberger, too, had had time to confer with his superiors; and the Germans had another proposition to make. Their proposal was masterful: it attempted to turn the negotiations upside down. Instead of bargaining from the German need for food, the Germans bargained from the Allied desire for ships. Thus: the Allies claimed that they needed the German ships only because they had no others to transport food to Germany. But the

Germans could not afford to buy food from the Allies unless the Allies loaned them the money for the food. Did the Allies want the German ships? Then the Allies would have to loan money to Germany. Keynes appreciated the cleverness of his adversaries.

"The atmosphere was tense and sombre," said Keynes. Another of the German negotiators, "Excellenz von Braun, with the lips of his nose slightly eaten away, like a chipped Chinese mask," took up the argument: he appealed, he said, not so much to the "humanitarian sentiments" of the Allies as to their political "conscience." He raised the specter of the collapse of Germany and therefore of the "flooding of bolshevism over the whole of Europe" if the Allies did not discover some means of keeping Germany from starvation and chaos.

Von Braun had "raised questions," said Keynes, "far beyond our competence at that moment, and we turned our train towards Paris."

In Paris again, the question was considered by the experts, with consultations and memoranda among Clemenceau, Lloyd George, and—across the ocean—Wilson. The British and Americans were naturally eager to release some German gold and start food shipments; Clemenceau still resisted settlement.

Keynes and his colleagues left for another session with the Germans—Keynes's instructions still not clear—this time at Spa. Once a fashionable resort near the border of Belgium, Spa was later the headquarters of the German Army, and then the seat of the armistice commission that was charged with keeping the uneasy peace while a treaty was settled. The British occupied a villa that had been Ludendorff's quarters. "A few steps away was the Kaiser's villa and a little farther up the hill Hindenburg's. . . . The spot was melancholy with the theatrical Teutonic melancholy of black pinewoods . . . the horizon was bounded by the black line of woods, the sun sank behind them, and the trees behind the house sighed like a lovesick Prussian. . . . One can believe sometimes that no greater responsibility for the war lies on any one man than on Wagner . . . what was Hindenburg but the bass and Ludendorff but the fat tenor of third-rate Wagnerian opera? How else did they see themselves in their dreams and in their bath?"

Keynes and von Braun reached a deadlock at once, and the instructions of both sides kept them from reaching a compromise. The Allied negotiators ordered their train to return to Paris once more.

In Paris Clemenceau was up and about, recovered from his gunshot wound; Lloyd George had been back and forth to London and was then in Paris; Wilson was still in the United States; for a discussion of the food problem, fifty-nine persons attended a meeting of the Council of Four.

Lord Robert Cecil presented the report of the Allied negotiators to the council. Cecil suggested that Germany be informed at once that the Allies categorically would furnish food, that shipments would begin as soon as Germany delivered ships for the purpose, and that Germany's liquid assets, including gold, be used to pay for the food. In short, after all the travel, all the conferences and negotiations, consultations and exchanges of memoranda and passage of time, the situation had not changed at all—only now Clemenceau and Lloyd George were in the same room, and the impasse was unavoidable.

The Americans and the British stood to get something out of all this, still. The Americans would sell some foodstuffs; the British would boost their position as a sea power. But Clemenceau got nothing—and was asked to give up gold.

No way out of the impasse could be found. The Germans must be made to pay: the Allies were agreed on this. Whatever they worked out among themselves, it would be at Germany's expense. The Germans had nothing left to pay but their gold. Clemenceau would have to yield, and, as he continued to obstruct and delay, he seemed more and more to be denying a small boon to his allies, and risking general anarchy in Europe, all because of greed, and all for what was, when all the spoils of war were considered together, a trivial sum.

Lloyd George, said Keynes, was "rousing himself. He can be amazing when one agrees with him. Never have I more admired his extraordinary powers than in the next half-hour . . . he spoke; the creeping lethargy of the proceedings was thrown off, and he launched his words with rage. . . .

"The Allies were now on top, but the memories of starvation might one day turn against them. . . . The Allies were sowing hatred for the future; they were piling up agony, not for the Germans, but for themselves. [Lloyd George's man on the scene in Germany] General [Herbert] Plumer had said that he could not be responsible for his troops if children were allowed to wander about the streets half-starved. The British soldiers (with a characteristic shake of the head) would not stand that."

Clemenceau continued to resist. His information, he said, suggested that the Germans were just using the specter of Communism to frighten the Allies: there was no real threat of Communist revolution in Germany. The debate dragged on. Lloyd George spoke again. Then, suddenly, a secretary rushed into the council chamber with a sealed envelope for Lloyd George. The delegates were hushed. It was a telegram from General Plumer. In fact, the telegram had arrived—at Lloyd George's request—before the meeting began, but he knew that it would have a more sensational effect if it were delivered in this way. Lloyd George read it out in his most dramatic manner: "Please inform the Prime Minister that in my opinion food must be sent into this area by the Allies without delay. The mortality amongst women, children, and sick is most grave, and sickness due to hunger is spreading. The attitude of the population is becoming one of despair, and the people feel that an end by bullets is preferable to death by starvation."

The French were in retreat. Clemenceau agreed to deliver food. He insisted, however, that the Germans must agree first, before they were told about food, to turn over the ships. They must understand as a matter of principle—at the moment and for the future—that they must do what they are told and not haggle and try to turn negotiations upside down. Lloyd George agreed to Clemenceau's demand. Then, said Clemenceau, Marshal Foch would be sent to inform the Germans of this.

"It was said innocently; but Lloyd George was quick enough to see the trap. Evidently the Marshal might contrive to deliver this ultimatum in such a way that the Germans would inevitably reject it. No, said Lloyd George, discarding the rhetorical for his bantering and humorous method, this has to do with ships . . . and whilst he would defer to no man in his admiration of the Marshal on land, no, not to any man (stretching his hands towards Foch), was the Marshal equally at home on the sea? He, Lloyd George, had never crossed the Channel with him and so could not say for certain (smiling)."

Lloyd George thought he would be in terrible trouble back home if he did not send an English admiral for this errand. "The Marshal," said Keynes, "did not quite follow what was being said, but saw that he was being flattered and bantered; so he grinned and tugged his moustache."

Lloyd George had routed Clemenceau and Foch; but the field was not cleared. Now, from another quarter, Clemenceau's last sally was delegated to Klotz, the minister for finance, who still withheld the gold. The Germans might pay in some other way, he said—but not in gold.

"Never have I seen the equal of the onslaught with which that poor man was overwhelmed. . . . Lloyd George had always hated and despised him; and now saw in a twinkling that he could kill him. Women and children were starving, he cried, and here was M. Klotz prating and prating of his 'goold.' He leant forward and with a gesture of his hands indicated to everyone the image of a hideous Jew clutching a money bag. His eyes flashed and the words came out with a contempt so violent that he almost seemed to be spitting at him. The anti-Semitism, not far below the surface in such an assemblage as that one, was up in the heart of everyone. Everyone looked at Klotz with a momentary contempt and hatred; the poor man was bent over his seat, visibly cowering. We hardly knew what Lloyd George was saying, but the words 'goold' and Klotz were repeated, and each time with exaggerated contempt. Then, turning, he called on Clemenceau to put a stop to these obstructive tactics, otherwise, he cried, M. Klotz would rank with Lenin and Trotsky among those who had spread Bolshevism in Europe. The Prime Minister ceased."

The ships were surrendered, the food was delivered, and it was paid for in gold. As a concession to the French, the German gold was to be sent to Rotterdam where it would be exchanged for French francs; thus the French got actual possession of the gold—and, on the exchange of gold for francs, a profit.

TRACTATUS LOGICO-PHILOSOPHICUS

Perhaps the most meaningful diplomatic mission that Keynes performed in 1919 was to take a manuscript of some twenty thousand words from a prison camp at Monte Cassino and transport it, in his diplomatic pouch, to Bertrand Russell in Cambridge. The manuscript, the *Tractatus Logico-Philosophicus*, which helped to transform western philosophy, had been written by Ludwig Wittgenstein, a former student of Russell's and a friend of Keynes's, in notebooks that Wittgenstein had carried through the war in his rucksack.

Wittgenstein had enlisted in the Austrian army at the beginning of the war, served on the eastern front and in the Tyrol before he was taken prisoner by the Italians in November of 1918. One of nine children of a wealthy and sophisticated family—his father was a prominent man in the Austrian iron and steel industry who was especially interested in music, whose family was personally acquainted with Mendelssohn and Brahms among others—he was tutored at home until the age of fourteen. He was precocious, extremely demanding of himself, and not accustomed to taking clarity for granted. Having grown up in the collapsing Austro-Hungarian Empire, fought through the war, and lived to see three of his brothers commit suicide, he understood that lucidity was a struggle.

His notes, the drafts of his ideas for the *Tractatus*, his second thoughts and false starts all show a tortuous labor in the completion of his book—and his finished book had no ordinary beginning, middle, and end. It was composed of fragments—thoughts more or less complete, sometimes clear, sometimes incomprehensible, sometimes unfinished, sometimes contradictory, torn from his mind in the course of the war—and set down, finally, as numbered paragraphs or propositions abandoned to the page, left because Wittgenstein could not improve on them—and altogether not long enough or clear enough to be a finished book.

His confidence in what he had done was so tenuous that just two days after he had entrusted the manuscript to Keynes, he wrote to Russell: "I'm now afraid that it might be very difficult for me to reach any understanding with you. And the small remaining hope that my manuscript might mean something to you has completely vanished." He suggested that Russell might just as well send the manuscript back.

As it turned out, Russell wrote an introduction to the *Tractatus*. When Wittgenstein read it, he thought he ought to withdraw his manuscript from the publisher: Russell had not understood the book. After the *Tractatus* was published, and Wittgenstein was considered by many to be the greatest living philosopher, he was found to have taken a job as a gardener in a small Austrian village.

The essence, at least, of Wittgenstein's work is understandable.

Wittgenstein was struck by the fact that, in lawcourts in Paris, automobile accidents were reconstructed by means of toys and dolls. A collision between a car and a truck would be shown by putting together a toy car and a toy truck: presenting a three-dimensional picture, or model, of the accident.

A sentence, said Wittgenstein, is a picture. "A proposition is a picture of reality. A proposition is a model of reality as we think it to be." If we say, "My fork is to the left of my knife," we understand that the "fork" of the proposition corresponds to a real fork; the "knife" of the sentence corresponds to a real knife; and the structure of the sentence is a model of the spatial relationship of the fork and the knife in reality.

"At first sight a sentence—one set out on the printed page, for example—does not seem to be a picture of the reality with which it is concerned. But no more does musical notation at first sight seem to be a picture of music, nor our phonetic notations (letters) to be a picture of our speech. And yet these sign-languages prove to be pictures, even in the ordinary sense, of what they represent." Given proper explication any sentence could be broken down into its constituent pictures—if it was a model of the real world.

Objects are put together into relationships: the relationship, expressed by a sentence, is a fact. Every sentence—every picture, every model—represents, as Anthony Kenney has written of the *Tractatus,* "a possible state of affairs, which may be called its sense; it is a true picture if its sense agrees with reality, and otherwise a false picture. . . . A logical picture of a fact . . . is a thought. . . . The totality of true thoughts is a picture of the world. . . . " Not all models, Wittgenstein thought, needed to be sentences: pictures, paintings, photographs, sculptures, musical scores, maps, charts— all of these are models.

But not all things can be said in "picture" propositions. The statement "God is good" cannot be pictured: one cannot find an object in the world that corresponds to God, or to good. And so the statement "God is good" cannot be encompassed in logic.

Indeed, in Wittgenstein's view, most of what is truly important cannot be encompassed in logic: ethics, values, ideas of beauty, justice, religion, and morality—all these are in a realm beyond models, and philosophers ought to keep their hands off such things, cease to believe that such matters could be reduced to logic—leave them to poetry, satire, irony, music. "Whereof one cannot speak," the *Tractatus* concludes, "thereof one must be silent."

Language could provide models of reality. But what if one attempted to make logical constructs about God, or goodness, or justice? Such constructs could only be nonsense. Considerations of justice might be important—far more important than matters of logic—but to attempt to deal with them as though one were dealing logically was to create confusion. A logical picture of a fact is a thought: a construct made without models of relationships of facts is—thoughtless.

Wittgenstein had nothing to say about the diplomacy of Versailles, but when his methods of analysis are applied to the peace conference, the vision is appalling. The diplomats dealt in a world of wishes, not of what was but of what they wished would be, of questions of justice and of intention, of bitterness and uncertainty, of formulations of hope and resentment that had no correspondence with any facts about the world; and, then too, what facts there were kept changing.

Wittgenstein might have said that no language could have been drafted to correspond rigorously to the facts. "The world," his first sentence of the *Tractatus* states, "is everything that is the case." But Wilson spoke as though the League of Nations was the case; and Clemenceau as though French hegemony was the case, and Lloyd George as though the survival of the empire was the case. Strictly speaking, the models of the Dadaists and the Surrealists were more firmly grounded in the real world than the formulations of the diplomats. Wittgenstein would have known at once that the diplomatic formulations were hopelessly meaningless.

❧

NOIR CACADOU

Historically, dadaism had preceded, and given way to, surrealism. But history was a wreck, and dadaism continued after the war, to reappear, even though it was dead.

In Zurich, Tristan Tzara spent the month of March bringing together the painters and writers and musicians and dancers for Noir Cacadou, an evening of dada entertainment at the Club Voltaire. As Tzara recalled the evening, "1500 persons filled the hall already boiling in the bubbles of bamboulas. Here is Eggeling connecting the wall with the ocean and telling us the line proper to a painting of the future; and Suzanne Perrotet plays Erik Satie (+ recitations), musical irony non-music of the jemen-foutiste gaga child on the miracle ladder of the Dada Movement. But now Mlle Wulff appears/superhuman mask 1/2 o/o & ?/ to accentuate the presence of Huelsenbeck and Laughter (beginning) the candy makes an impression a single thread passes through the brains of the 1500 spectators. . . . "

Viking Eggeling believed in a system of contrapuntal opposites, of the mutual attraction and repulsion of pairs; thus he believed in the simultaneity of form and chaos, reason and madness, chance and determination, idiocy and sense, the rationalism of Keynes and the absurdity of Schwitters, the realism of dreams and the irrealism of the waking world, in somberness and laughter—beliefs so deeply held and thoroughgoing that he would not eat both milk and eggs at the same meal because they were too "analogous." His lecture—the opening event of an evening supposed to be entertaining—was at once so boring and so novel, so ponderous and so *outré*, that the audience was restless and disturbed because it was not disturbed.

Hans Richter and Jean Arp painted the sets for the dances of Suzanne Perrotet and Kathe Wulff, performed to the music of Satie and Schönberg. The sets were covered with shapes that Richter decided resembled nothing so much as gigantic cucumbers.

"This is what things have come to in this world," one of Richard Huelsenbeck's poems (in Hans Richter's translation) begins,

> *The cows sit on the telegraph poles and play chess*
> *The cockatoo under the skirts of the Spanish dancer*
> *Sings as sadly as a headquarters bugler and the*
> *   cannon lament all day*
> *That is the lavender landscape Herr Mayer was talking*
> *   about when he lost his eye*
> *Only the fire department can drive the nightmare*
> *   from the drawing-room but all the hoses are broken*
> *Ah yes Sonya they all take the celluloid doll for*
> *   a changeling and shout: God save the king*

On this evening, Huelsenbeck's poems drew the first laughter and catcalls from the audience. And then, as Richter recalled, "all hell broke loose."

Tzara recited a *poème simultané.* Tzara's poems were not merely spoken, declaimed, and sung, not merely accompanied by whistles, shouts, sobs, cowbells, banging on the table and on empty boxes, screams, and drums. A simultaneous poem would have two, three, or four different parts—all recited simultaneously by two, three, four—or, on this evening, twenty—poets, one of them reciting (fortissimo):

rrrrrrrr   rrrrrrrr   rrrrrrrr   rrrrrrrr   rrrrrrrr
while another poet recited (in variations of fortissimo, piano, and forte):

$$OOO \quad OOOOO \quad OOOOOO \quad OO \quad OOOO$$
Huelsenbeck might join in with:
   hihi Yabomm hihi Yabomm hihi hihi hihiiiii
while Tzara recited:
   can hear the weopour   will   arround   arround the hill
with accompaniments of:
   *shal shal shal shal shal Every body is doing it doing it
   doing it prrrza chrrrza prrrza rouge bleu rouge bleu i
   love the ladies i love to be among the girls Peltschen
   um die Landen tata taratata tatatata oh yes oh yes oh
   yes oh yes*

with variations and flourishes of crowing, stuttering, sighing, cursing, yodeling.

And the audience shouted, laughed, whistled, chanted in unison—joining, as it were, in the recitation of the poem, assuming, as Tzara said, "menacing proportions islands spontaneously in the hall, accompanying, multiplying underlining the mighty roaring gesture and the simultaneous orchestration. Signal of the blood. Revolt of the past, of education. Feverish fiction and 4 acrid macabre cracks in the barrack."

"Dada not only had *no* programme," Richter said, "it was against all programmes. Dada's only programme was to have no programme...." The "official belief in the infallibility of reason, logic and causality seemed to us senseless—as senseless as the destruction of the world and the systematic elimination of every particle of human feeling. This was the reason why we were forced to look for something which would re-establish our humanity.... We had adopted chance, the voice of the unconscious...."

And yet, even so, dada gave rise to new programs willy-nilly, hand over fist. In 1919, Paul Kammerer published his *Das Gesetz der Serie* (*The Law of Seriality*) and Hugo Ball published *Kritik der deutschen Intelligenz* (*A Critique of the German Intelligentsia*). Kammerer's book tried to develop a theory that explained "dreamlike" associations and, as Richter said, "to discover the laws which govern acausal relationships." He tried to explain how events occurred not in relationships of cause and effect but rather in relationships of synchronicity, producing a book that would have greatly relieved, or profoundly disturbed, the minds of the diplomats in Paris.

Ball's book attempted an analysis of the psychic climate in Germany and foretold—not because of politics, economics, sociological forces, but because of a cataclysmic psychic breakdown—the rise of nazism. Ball himself dropped out of the dada movement ("I have examined myself carefully, and I could never bid chaos welcome") and moved to Ticino to live a life of religious poverty.

When Kurt Schwitters walked the streets in Hanover in 1919, he picked up bits of thread, envelopes, tram tickets, pieces of glass, cigar bands, small sticks, old shoes, tufts of hair, feathers, rags, nail files, anything to stuff in his pockets, wire, women's corsets, chunks of plaster, wood, cheese wrappers, cardboard, stamps, and pieces of paper money.

One evening, in the Café des Westens, he presented himself to Hans Richter, as Richter recalled:

" 'My name is Schwitters, Kurt Schwitters.' I had never heard the name before.

"We sat down and I asked, 'What do you do?'

" 'I am a painter and I nail my pictures together.' "

He liked chance. He liked spontaneity. He liked dirt and things that showed the signs of deterioration. He liked to make sculptures that moved and emitted sounds.

"When he was not writing poetry," said Hans Richter, "he was pasting up collages. When he was not pasting, he was . . . washing his feet in the same water as his guinea pigs, warming his paste-pot in the bed, feeding the tortoise in the rarely used bathtub . . . cutting up magazines . . . "

Over a period of years, he spent part of his time working and reworking a column—something of a full-scale monument to humanity—which was always changing, never finished. Made of plaster, it was riddled with niches, into which Schwitters placed things from his friends—a lock of hair, a piece of shoelace, a nail paring, a dental bridge, a urine specimen.

The column grew—occupying half of a moderate-sized room, reaching to the ceiling. Layer after layer of bits of his friends' lives, and of his own life, covered one another, until there was no more room to add to the breadth of the column. And so, because Schwitters had inherited the house from his father and was the landlord, he evicted the upstairs tenants, broke a hole in the ceiling, and continued the column on up through the house.

"One day in 1919, finding myself in rainy weather in a town on the banks of the Rhine," Max Ernst wrote, "I was struck by the obsession exercised upon my excited gaze by an illustrated catalogue containing objects for anthropological, microscopic, psychological, mineralogical and paleontological demonstrations. There I found such distant elements of figuration that the very absurdity of this assemblage . . . gave birth to a hallucinating succession of contradictory images, of double, triple, and multiple images which were superimposed on each other with the persistence and rapidity characteristic of amorous memories and of hypnagogical visions."

To clippings from these catalogue pages, Ernst added, by drawing or painting, *"what was visible within me*—a color, a pencil line, a landscape . . . the desert, a sky . . . to obtain a set and faithful image of my hallucination": and so, from fragments of the outer world and visions from an inner world, Ernst made the first collages, and proceeded to define what he had done. "What is the noblest conquest of collage? The irrational. It is the magisterial eruption of the irrational in all fields of art, poetry, science, fashion, the private life of individuals, the public life of nations."

Or, as Ernst wrote elsewhere:

" . . . Half-grown, women are carefully poisoned / they are bedded in bottles / the little American girl we are launching this year amuses herself by suckling sea-dogs / the human eye is embroidered with batavic tears of curdled air and salted snow. . . .

" . . . The dog that shits / the well-coifed dog despite difficulties of terrain caused by an abundant snow / the woman with the beautiful throat / song of the flesh. . . . "

"We were beside ourselves," said Marcel Janco, "with rage and grief at the suffering and humiliation of mankind."

After Tristan Tzara's *poème simultané* at the Club Voltaire, some of Arp's poems were recited. Arp, too, was enamored of chance: he liked to make a drawing, tear it to pieces, throw the pieces on the floor—and then glue the pieces of this random pattern onto another sheet of paper. He loved all chance associations, and tried to let accidental juxtapositions lead him through his poems, as in:

> *Their rubber hammer strikes the sea*
> *Down the black general so brave.*
> *With silken braid they deck him out*
> *As fifth wheel on the common grave.*

At the Club Voltaire that evening, Arp's recitations were greeted with cries of "Rubbish!"

By the time Walter Serner took the floor to give a rendition of his *"Letzte Lockerung"* (or "Final Dissolution"), the audience was ready to come apart. Serner, dressed in striped trousers, gray cravat, black cutaway, carrying a headless dummy and a bouquet of flowers, sat in a chair with his back to the audience and commenced his reading of his anarchist manifesto to an audience ominously silent. Dissolution was not, to Serner, an unavoidable misfortune: it was a positive good, an end to be sought—the complete wreckage of the world as it was, everything torn to shambles, everything pulled out of place, everything given over to the positive glorification of riot, bewilderment, turmoil, destruction.

First came the catcalls, then the shouts, derisive, enraged; chairs and pieces of balustrade broken up for clubs; young men leapt onto the stage, irrelevant rantings about Napoleon, the tailor's dummy smashed, the bouquet stomped. A reporter from the *Basler Nackrichten* grabbed Hans Richter by his necktie "and shouted ten times over, without pausing for breath, 'You're a sensible man normally.'"

The "unchained hurricane frenzy siren whistles," said Tzara, "bombardment song the battle starts out sharply, half the audience applaud the protesters hold the hall in the lungs of those present nerves are liquefied muscles jump Serner makes mocking gestures sticks the scandal in his buttonhole / ferocity that wrings the neck. . . . Chairs pulled out projectiles crash bang expected effect atrocious and instinctive.

"*Noir Cacadou,* Dance (5 persons) with Mlle Wulff, the pipes dance the renovation of the headless pithecanthropes stifles the public rage . . . delirium in the hall, voice in tatters drags across the candelabras, progressive savage madness twists laughter. . . . "

PART FOUR
THE FRENCH OFFENSIVE

WILSON'S RETURN

"Again we landed at Brest," Edith Wilson said of the president's return to the peace conference—again on the thirteenth of the month, this time the afternoon of the thirteenth of March. Again an official welcoming party came out to bring the president ashore, "and among them we were surprised to see Colonel House." The president asked Mrs. Wilson to speak with the French, and he adjourned to his compartment to talk with Colonel House.

"I look back on that moment as a crisis in his life," Edith Wilson recalled, "and feel that from it dated the long years of illness . . . the wreckage of his plans and his life."

While Mrs. Wilson waited in her adjoining stateroom, the president and Colonel House talked until after midnight. It had grown very quiet aboard the ship when, at last, Mrs. Wilson heard her husband's door open and Colonel House take his leave. "I opened the door connecting our rooms. Woodrow was standing. The change in his appearance shocked me. He seemed to have aged ten years. . . . Silently he held out his hand, which I grasped, crying: 'What is the matter? What has happened?'

"He smiled bitterly. 'House has given away everything I had won before we left Paris.' "

House had agreed, in the interest of speeding up the work of the conference, to arrive at a "preliminary" treaty of peace with Germany. The preliminary treaty dealt with military terms for Germany, boundaries, reparations, and a number of other matters.

In the terms that had been negotiated for this preliminary peace the French had been gradually winning their diplomatic war of attrition on minor points—on the possible occupation of the Rhineland, on matters of disarmament of Germany, on the possibility that America and Britain would agree to defend France against military attack from Germany—until the treaty had come increasingly to resemble an arrangement for the permanent military and economic control of Germany by a military alliance of Britain, France, and America.

No wonder that Clemenceau had come to love House and had taken to hugging and complimenting the colonel (who was immensely pleased by the old man's attentions).

"He has compromised on every side," Wilson told his wife about the colonel's work; " . . . his own explanation of his compromises is that, with a hostile press in the United States expressing disapproval of the League of Nations as a part of the treaty, he thought it best to yield some other points lest the conference withdraw its approval altogether."

It may be that House's acquiescence to French wishes for military guarantees of security was the price he had had to pay—even before Wilson had left Paris in February—for French agreement to the draft of the league covenant. It may be that House felt he had to yield still more in Wilson's absence. It may be that House was simply seduced by Clemenceau.

But, whatever House had meant to do by making compromises to win the league, what was worst of all, from Wilson's point of view, was that House had also given away the league itself: the covenant of the league had been completely eliminated from the preliminary treaty. Some gossips were even saying that the present conference would establish a treaty—and then the league would be put off for a future congress to discuss.

In fact, House had kept the president tolerably well informed of the Paris negotiations while Wilson had been back in the States. But Wilson had not quite paid attention to the vague, persistent, wearing away of the American position.

"So," Wilson told his wife, "he has yielded until there is nothing left."

"Bursting with indignation, I stood holding my husband's hand. Before I got myself together, he threw back his head. The light of battle was in his eyes. 'Well,' he said, 'thank God I can still fight, and I'll win them back or never look these boys I sent over here in the face again.' "

WILSON'S COUNTERATTACK

"A new home awaited us in Paris," Edith Wilson said, "a house on the Place des Etats Unis, where Bartholdi's statue of Lafayette and Washington gives a friendly welcome. It was less ornate than the palace of the Prince Murat, and more homey. My first feeling was that here people had been happy."

She ran to show the president her bathtub—a sunken tub the size of a small pool, its walls tiled in a rich cream color and, in the four corners, tiled apple trees in bloom. On the bottom of the tub, in the porcelain, were some pink petals, as though they had dropped from the trees. Directly above, where the tree branches met on the ceiling, a chandelier was hung, and on the chandelier were perched birds of many colors. Butterflies hovered over the apple blossoms. The faucets were gold.

"I think," said the spoilsport, with a tight smile, "I could not live in this place."

For twenty-four hours, Wilson did nothing. He met informally with a group of delegates at the Hotel Crillon and talked, as one of the British delegates jotted in his diary, "of the League of Nations and other nonsense"—evidently with the thought that he would give Lloyd George and Clemenceau and the others a chance to redeem themselves. But no one picked up Wilson's broad hints about the league. Indeed, as Frances Stevenson wrote in her diary, "He has started to annoy D. [Lloyd George] ... by talking of matters that have already been settled as though they were still open for discussion & as though he intended to reopen them. I am very glad he has started to annoy D., as I think the latter was too prone to encourage & agree with him while he was here before. I do not think they will ever get a move on until President Wilson has been put in his place, & D. is the only person who can do it. Clemenceau cannot tolerate him at any price."

When no one picked up Wilson's hints, the president brooded for another twenty-four hours and then struck. On Saturday morning, the fifteenth, at eleven o'clock, he phoned Ray Stannard Baker on a secret phone line that ran from the house on the Place des Etats Unis to the Hotel Crillon. He told Baker to put out a press release announcing simply that there was no truth to the rumors that the League of Nations would not be a part of the treaty of peace.

"The President said today that the decision made at the peace conference at its plenary session, January 25, 1919, to the effect that the establishment of a League of Nations should be made an integral part of the treaty of peace, is of final force and that there is no basis whatever for the reports that a change in this decision was contemplated."

The statement struck Paris, said Baker, like a "bombshell"; it overturned "the only important action that the delegates had ventured to take during his absence."

❦

WILSON WOUNDED

Wilson's bombshell, as it turned out, was a dud. The president was no longer being taken quite as seriously as he had been back in February. Although Wilson did not seem to realize it, the essential weakness of his position had been exposed; some of the more decent, or squeamish, of the diplomats were even embarrassed.

When Wilson had first sailed to Paris, back in December, he had said to his advisers aboard the *George Washington* that he and the members of his delegation "would be the only disinterested people at the peace conference, and that the men whom we were about to deal with did not represent their own people." In truth, the exact opposite was the case: Lloyd George was then in the midst of a landslide election victory; Clemenceau was about to receive a clear vote of confidence from the chamber of deputies; Wilson's Democratic party had just lost badly to the Republicans in the November congressional elections.

The suspicion that Wilson was a four-flusher was confirmed when he returned to the United States in February and March. When he invited the members of the Senate Foreign Relations Committee to a dinner in the White House in February, Senators Borah and Fall declined the invitation. Senator Brandegee baited and harassed the president while Wilson tried to deliver an after-dinner disquisition on the league. Senator Lodge left early. The next day, Brandegee issued a remarkably derisive comment: "I feel as if I had been wandering with Alice in Wonderland and had had tea with the Mad Hatter."

Some of these men opposed American meddling in international affairs; but an even larger number of others had a different sticking point with Wilson's policies: what was to become of the Monroe Doctrine?

According to the Monroe Doctrine, the American continents were closed to European colonization. No European power could extend its system to any part of the Western hemisphere, and, at the same time, the United States would not interfere with any of Europe's existing colonies or with Europe's internal affairs. The Monroe Doctrine established an American sphere of interest in the Western hemisphere. The League of Nations, on the other hand, was to do away with spheres of interest and with colonies. Wilson's domestic political opponents insisted that the president have the other powers explicitly recognize that, whatever might happen to other spheres of interest, America's remained sacred. America might move into Europe; but Europe might not move into the Americas. Former President William Howard Taft drew up a list of six essential changes to be incorporated into the covenant for the league. The single most important change was the exemption of the Monroe Doctrine from any provision of covenant or treaty.

"The conservation of the Monroe Doctrine," the editor of the *Atlantic Monthly* wrote to Ray Stannard Baker, "is, to my thinking, certainly implicit in the [treaty], but, unquestionably there is a public demand that the subject should be specifically mentioned."

And so, in order to have some hope that his entire enterprise—league and treaty both—would not be repudiated in America, the president had to return to Paris with the embarrassingly hypocritical demand: that the conference recognize the sanctity of a doctrine that contradicted a number of the principles Wilson had asked the others to recognize.

Wilson's needs—to have his league, and to have the Monroe Doctrine affirmed—were at last clear, and so was the weakness of his political position. As the impossibility of Wilson's position became palpable the Europeans closed in on the president for the kill—and certain of Wilson's idiosyncrasies appeared, or became, more pronounced. "Well, my friends," he would say in beginning a sentence—then, smiling, "and we are all friends here . . . "

One of the British delegates watched this mannerism closely. Wilson spoke, the delegate said, "rather like a man preaching to the others, or like a professor addressing a class of students. . . . If the President had something nasty to say, one could always tell long beforehand by the very sweet and ingratiating tones he used. Always he would begin by saying, 'Well, my friend,' and everyone knew that another sermon was about to be delivered.

"Clemenceau got very tired of this. On one occasion just as the President had said, 'Well, my friend,' Clemenceau shouted, 'Mon Dieu! Don't say that again! Every time you do, you send a cold shudder down my spine!' "

The sniping had begun, the casualness, a certain lack of respect. Nothing could be done about it; nothing could protect him. On March 17 Riddell noted in his diary, "It is no joke to be a President. Wilson is guarded by detectives morning, noon and night. Today I saw one of them standing outside the lavatory watching over his chief."

❦

THE COUNCIL CHAMBER

Like Odysseus, said Keynes, "the President looked wiser when he was seated; and his hands, though capable and fairly strong, were wanting in sensitiveness and finesse. . . . But more serious than this . . . he was not sensitive to his environment at all."

In dealing with the "swift arrows of Clemenceau's Latin intellect," Nicolson said, "with the kingfisher darts of Mr. Lloyd George's intuition," Wilson seemed "a trifle slow-minded."

"The President's slowness amongst the Europeans was noteworthy," said Keynes. "He could not all in a minute, take in what the rest were saying, size up the situation with a glance, frame a reply, and meet the case by a slight change of ground; and he was liable, therefore, to defeat by the mere swiftness, apprehension, and agility of a Lloyd George. There can seldom have been a statesman of the first rank more incompetent than the President in the agilities of the council chamber."

The president lacked, Keynes thought, that "dominating intellectual equipment" that was necessary "to cope with the subtle and dangerous spellbinders whom a tremendous clash of forces and personalities had brought to the top as triumphant masters in the swift game of give and take."

Although Wilson had long admired the English parliamentary system, had written about it as a young man and a history professor, had perhaps even envied those who had made their careers in Parliament, he had not himself come up through such a system that gave the advantage to those who were quick and clever at infighting. Both Lloyd George and Clemenceau thrived on combat at close quarters; both sought confrontations; both had served long apprenticeships in the arena of such political grappling; both, indeed, had risen to the top of their governments because they were superior in just these arts—or this sport. Wilson was not suited to such stuff, either by temperament or training, nor was he accustomed to it. At Paris, just when he had dug his toes in for a prolonged argument, he would discover that his adversary had moved to an attack from another direction. "This blind and deaf Don Quixote," said Keynes, "was entering a cavern where the swift and glittering blade was in the hands of the adversary."

It seemed to Keynes, too, that the president's thought and temperament were not so much intellectual as theological. He was wedded not to conclusions that he had reasoned his way to, and so might consider anew, might revise according to the new information or possibilities that were presented to him, but rather to truths, to principles he held a priori, that he must apply to the new information brought to him, that could not be compromised.

"He could take the high line; he could practice obstinacy; he could write Notes from Sinai or Olympus. . . . But if he once stepped down to the intimate equality of the Four, the game was evidently up."

Lloyd George, said Keynes, would often, after he had finished a speech, while it was being translated into French, get up and cross over to the president "to reinforce his case by some ad hominem argument in private conversation," not giving the president the leisure to consider the points of the matter but proceeding to "sound out the ground for a compromise." The president's advisers would gather around them; the British experts would press in to learn what was being discussed; then the French aides would crowd in, "until all the room were on their feet and conversation was general in both languages."

Gradually, with vast and elaborate patience, Clemenceau was purchasing Lloyd George's support: in every instance that the old German Empire competed with the British Empire—the German Navy, merchant marine, colonies—Clemenceau let Lloyd George know that the French understood how to make deals on such matters.

It was more difficult for Clemenceau to cut Lloyd George in on reparations: the war had not been fought on British soil and there was no damage to be repaired. So Lloyd George argued that compensation should be paid not only for damage to property but also for "damage to persons"—including disability pay and the cost of pensions for widows. Clemenceau let it be understood that he might be persuaded to accept this notion and that, if he did, he would not be unalterably opposed to apportioning reparations so that fifty percent went to France, twenty percent would be divided up among a number of claimants—and thirty percent would go to Lloyd George. Still, the Tiger held off on closing any deals.

Clemenceau, said Keynes, "carried no papers and no portfolio, and was unattended by any personal secretary." He impressed Keynes as an old man who, although vigorous, was conserving his strength for important matters. "He spoke seldom, leaving the initial statement of the French case to his ministers or officials; he closed his eyes often and sat back in his chair with an impassive face of parchment, his gray gloved hands clasped in front of him. A short sentence, derisive or cynical, was generally sufficient, a question, an unqualified abandonment of his ministers, whose face would not be saved, or a display of obstinacy reinforced by a few words in a piquantly delivered English."

One day, Clemenceau asked an American newspaper reporter what the expression "for crying out loud" meant. When it was explained to him, Clemenceau "smacked his lips in smug satisfaction, and said he intended to 'try it out on Lloyd George.'"

"But speech and passion were not lacking when they were wanted," Keynes said, "and the sudden outburst of words, often followed by a fit of deep coughing from the chest, produced their impression rather by force and surprise than by persuasion.

"My last and most vivid impression is of . . . the President and the Prime Minister at the center of a surging mob and a babel of sound, a welter of eager, impromptu compromise and counter-compromise . . . on what was an unreal question anyhow, the great issues of the morning's meeting forgotten and neglected; and Clemenceau silent and aloof on the outskirts . . . dry in soul and empty of hope, very old and tired, but surveying the scene with a cynical and almost impish air; and when at last silence was restored and the company had returned to their places, it was to discover that he had disappeared."

WEEKEND AT FONTAINEBLEAU

On the weekend after the president returned to Paris, Lloyd George decided that it was time for him to make his move in the negotiations. He packed some of his chums into cars and drove out into the forests at Fontainebleau, to the Hotel France and England, where they took a sitting room. As Lloyd George wrote to his daughter Gwilym, they "spread maps all over it & worked hard & I think well."

Sir Maurice Hankey (Hanky-Panky, Riddell called him) was among the Fontainebleau group, the "slightly built, quick-motioned, clerical-looking soldier," as Shotwell thought of him. "He has been at every Imperial and Inter-Allied Conference since [1907], and I learn from others that no one else knows so much of what has taken place. He has kept a diary."

Sir Henry Wilson, Chief of the Imperial General Staff, was there—a fifty-three-year-old man who had never been able to gain admission either to Woolwich or Sandhurst (where he was turned down three times) but whose "intellectual gifts," Beaverbrook said, "outshone those of every other soldier."

The third member of the group was E. S. Montagu, financier,

secretary for India, who had served Lloyd George at the conference by talking "firmly" to the French about their demands for large reparations. ("Nothing like the right man in the right place," Riddell had said when Lloyd George delegated Montagu to be mean to the French.)

The group that Lloyd George gathered was notable for its lack of a foreign secretary, the lack of any experts, the lack of anyone who advocated a particular policy—no champion of the League of Nations was present, no young English socialist. The fourth member of the group was young Philip Kerr, a nephew of the Duke of Norfolk. Kerr was distinguished for charm and loyalty and an ability to swat up a smooth piece of prose.

Only the presence of Montagu tipped Lloyd George's hand: the prime minister had brought along one man who tended to be anti-French. The senior Foreign Office men were said to be in a state of "impotent dismay." Lloyd George, said Bonar Law, was not well suited to the delicate business of peacetime diplomacy; the prime minister had been "all right as a drummer in a cavalry charge in war but we did not want a drummer in a hospital." None of the Foreign Office men, wedded as they were to diplomatic niceties, appreciated Lloyd George's formidable talents as a deal-maker.

After some tramping about the countryside, the group got down to the serious business of playacting. Sir Henry Wilson was assigned two parts: he was to speak about the treaty as though he were, first, a German, and secondly, a Frenchwoman. Hanky-Panky spoke as an average Englishman. Montagu spoke, said Lloyd George, "from the point of view of a man from Mars." Philip Kerr took notes. And Lloyd George listened.

"I explained my present situation," said Sir Henry the German, "and my wish to come to an agreement with England and France, but saw no hope, for I read into the crushing terms they were imposing on me a determination on their part to kill me outright. As I could not stand alone I would turn to Russia, and in the course of time would help that distracted country to recover law and order, and then make an alliance with her. I would under no circumstances join so crazy and so rotten a thing as the League of Nations," which Sir Henry had described earlier as "a machinery set up to interfere with everyone's business."

Sir Henry had somewhat more difficulty entering into the part of the Frenchwoman, talking vaguely of "how sore she was both morally and physically, and how loath to look into the mirror of the future from a dread of what she might see."

Hankey, presenting the British point of view, argued first and naturally enough, for the limitation of German naval strength; secondly for stiff reparations payments for England—a total figure of 500 million pounds annually, fifty percent for France, thirty percent for England, and twenty percent for all others; thirdly for British mandates for Palestine, Mesopotamia, East Africa, South-West Africa, and the South Pacific Islands. In spite of his reparations demands, however, Hankey insisted that "penal terms on Germany" would be a mistake, driving the Germans toward bolshevism. Large chunks of German population should not be split off and given, for example, to Poland. The Rhineland should not be taken from Germany, but might be demilitarized. The coal basin of the Saar might be placed under French control for ten years, to compensate France for her losses of coal production, but the Saar should not be given to France for more than ten years. The kaiser should be tried. The League of Nations should be set up to deal with international quarrels— "and generally to keep *small states* [emphasis added] in order."

On Sunday, having ruminated on all this, and having relished lounging around the hotel playing his "peace games," Lloyd George had Philip Kerr draw up a "Fontainebleau memorandum."

"You may strip Germany of her colonies, reduce her armaments to a mere police force and her navy to that of a fifth rate power; all the same in the end if she feels that she has been unjustly treated in the peace of 1919 she will find means of exacting retribution from her conquerors." The prime minister argued that a "hard" peace would never work—trying to keep Germany in a permanent state of weakness was destined to fail—and so he proposed a "soft" peace. No large blocs of population should be shifted, no Germans placed under Polish control, no Eastern Europeans moved from one state to another. No humiliating peace should be drawn up that would push the Germans toward bolshevism. No reparations payments should be demanded that could not be paid by the generation that had made the war; future generations must not be punished for the sins of their fathers. No disarmament agreements ought to be applied to Germany alone; the Allies, too, ought to limit their armaments.

The Rhineland, said the Fontainebleau memorandum, should

remain a part of Germany. France would be compensated for this by a firm guarantee of military help from Britain and America until the League of Nations could guarantee French security. Furthermore, France was to be given either the Saar Valley or compensation for the loss of French coal mines.

Lloyd George returned to Paris on Monday, "with his plans all made," Frances Stevenson wrote in her diary. "He means business this week, & will sweep all before him. He will stand no more nonsense either from French or Americans. He is taking the long view about the Peace & insists that it should be one that will not leave bitterness for years to come, & probably lead to another war."

In short, Lloyd George served notice on Clemenceau that the Tiger had better come through on some of the deals they had been flirting about, or else Lloyd George knew how to make trouble. The prime minister felt enormously pleased with himself and with the impressive-sounding memorandum he had swatted up after a weekend of amateur theatricals.

On Monday night, Frances Stevenson and Lloyd George "had a jolly little dinner—some young people came up from the Majestic & D. was in very good form—absolutely mad. When he gets to the point of trying on other people's hats he is always most amusing. He tried on a Staff officer's hat & someone said he looked like Lord French. 'Oh no, that can't be,' said D. 'Lord French is *naughty!*' "

❧

THE BIG FOUR

They sat in a semicircle in front of the fireplace in Wilson's little study on the first floor of the house in the Place des Etats Unis— amid a Rembrandt, a Delacroix, a Hobbema, and several Goyas—"a dark, richly furnished room," said Ray Stannard Baker, "looking out upon a little patch of walled garden with an American sentinel pacing up and down the passageway."

It was Lloyd George who had suggested that the Council of Ten be dropped, and that he and Clemenceau and Wilson—and Orlando—get together by themselves, just the four of them, without foreign ministers or aides or experts or even translators, and finally get down to business. They sat in large, comfortable, brocaded arm-chairs: Lloyd George closest to the fireplace, then Clemenceau, then Wilson—then a table, and, on the other side of the fireplace, Orlando, and, next to the fireplace, an empty chair in case the Big Four wanted to call in a visitor from time to time.

For a while Orlando could not follow the conversation. Wilson, Lloyd George, and Clemenceau all spoke English. Orlando had mastered only "eleven o'clock," "good-bye," and "I do not agree." As a grudging concession to Orlando, Clemenceau called in Mantoux to translate the conversations into French for the Italian prime minister; after a while, the Big Three relented and allowed Orlando's Italian translator to take up a permanent place in another chair, between Orlando and the table.

At first—and for several weeks—they had no recording secretary, no one took notes, no one could be sure what had been decided, what had been tentatively concluded or finally settled, what had been discussed or only proposed, what had been delegated to a committee for research, what reports had been finished and brought back to the Big Four. The willfulness of the arrangement seemed intentionally designed to befuddle the president, who was least able to tolerate such lack of structure, to keep track of the decisions as they were made and remade, intentionally forgotten or slyly resurrected.

Clemenceau and Lloyd George thrived in this atmosphere—the atmosphere of the give-and-take of the journalist's office or the cabinet room, where no holds are barred, the talk is direct and dirty—and they both seemed able to keep dozens of points in mind at once, and to forget none of them. Orlando, even with his translator, could not keep up with the fast talk. Wilson, pretending he was up to it, was confused and soon began to exhibit symptoms of bewilderment and a loss of control: he commenced to misplace important pieces of correspondence. Clemenceau and Lloyd George, having at last got Wilson onto the sort of ground they relished, began to take the president apart.

Lloyd George directed the negotiations at once to the central, and nasty, issue of reparations. Too many issues remained variable in terms of one another; if the matter of reparations could be definitely resolved, perhaps the secondary and peripheral issues would fall into place.

Yet, once he had directly raised the issue, Lloyd George sidestepped into an exquisitely devious manner of confronting it. Clemenceau insisted on maximum reparations, to be paid in full, even if it took Germany a thousand years. Wilson argued for minimum reparations, for a specific figure to be placed in the treaty, and for a limitation of thirty years on payments: if the Germans could not pay the full bill by the end of thirty years—and a commission of the League of Nations would verify whether they could or not—they would be excused from further payments. (Wilson's position was doubly nice: it kept France from crushing Germany; it also ensured that France and Britain would remain deeply in debt to the United States.)

Lloyd George wanted the maximum amount to be paid—so that his thirty percent share would be worth something—but he still wanted the German economy to be allowed to revive. However, since it seemed impossible to arrive at a figure that was economically feasible, large enough to please Clemenceau and Lloyd George, small enough to please Wilson and not to ruin Germany—Lloyd George worked his way to a superb idea: no specific figure would be named. A commission would be appointed. The commission would work for two or three years first to see just how much Germany could pay; the commission would then set an assessment on Germany. If the assessment could be paid, fine; if it could not, it could be adjusted.

In this way, all options were left open. Something would seem to have been decided, but nothing specific could be pinned on Lloyd George or Clemenceau or Wilson. The voters of no country could blame anyone for having gotten too much or too little. Responsibility for the whole issue could be laid off on a commission; maybe the Allies would get some money, and that would be fine. The whole proposition resembled nothing so much as legerdemain, and it had a certain appeal for Clemenceau as well.

❦

WILSON FALTERS

"He is so busy," said Ike Hoover, the White House usher, "he never dresses for dinner anymore. He goes right to that meal in the clothes he has worn all day. This is so different from his usual custom that I mention it to illustrate what is happening to him."

Wilson's greatest weakness, thought Lloyd George, who was busily plotting and conniving to do Wilson in, was the president's "pervasive suspiciousness." Wilson had never been notable for openness and camaraderie. He had systematically cut himself off from Secretary of State Lansing, and the Republican delegate to the conference, Henry White; he met only five times during the entire peace conference with General Bliss; the experts complained that they could never get to him. And now he was cut off even from his old friend Colonel House; there were no more encouraging notes signed "affectionately." He seemed to have reached the point almost where he no longer trusted anyone. He had closed himself off not only to advice but also, to a large extent, to information.

Some of the delegates noticed that a muscle near Wilson's left eye had begun to twitch.

Lansing noticed that one of the President's old mannerisms— one that the secretary of state had only seen on one or two previous occasions, and then in such a subdued form as to be unnoticeable— was becoming quite florid: "a sort of little chuckle or half laugh which frequently interrupted his flow of language. . . . It seemed to be an involuntary act, caused by nervousness or embarrassment. It sounded almost apologetic."

THE TIGER'S TIGER

Clemenceau delayed, and postponed, raised old questions anew, reconsidered the League of Nations, continued to insist on matters even when all the others had refused to agree with him, allowed his colleagues to filibuster and ramble, called in useless witnesses to present their cases to the conference, adjourned the meetings, took long lunch hours, dawdled and procrastinated. Lloyd George thought he was not the same since he had been shot. "The old boy has lost his power of coming to decisions," said Lloyd George on the golf course at St.-Cloud.

In truth, Clemenceau had lost none of his powers. He simply waited. He held Wilson suspended, immobilized and talking, and while Wilson talked, Clemenceau quietly threatened to turn loose Marshal Foch.

"Foch strikes you at first," said Shotwell, "as a meditative type of man, with eyes that seem half dreamy at times, gray eyes something like those of Sir Douglas Haig—in fact both look like Scotchmen. Later when he spoke there was fire in his voice; but it was not the ringing voice of a young vigorous man but rather the tired voice of an old man."

Tired or vigorous, Foch was one of the great heroes of the war. He was always ready to fight: the Germans again if need be, the revolutionaries in Eastern Europe, the Communists here and there, the Russians, or, if he could not get his way, Clemenceau. Clemenceau's idea was to use Foch as a specter to frighten Wilson and Lloyd George into the kind of settlement the premier wanted: better to settle with the Tiger, Clemenceau told the others, than to demand too much, force Clemenceau from office, and then have to deal with extremists like Foch.

Foch's idea was to try, as he had tried throughout the war, to use Clemenceau as a malleable politician to be led to greater and more complete victories. On October 8, 1918, in the closing stages of the war, Foch wrote to Clemenceau: it was essential, the marshal said, for France to seize the left bank of the Rhine, "which would serve as a pledge for security as well as for reparations." If France could get certain hold of the Rhine, said Foch, "she may be at rest, for she can be sure of reparations and security; without the Rhine she has neither. . . . We must have the Rhineland; we want nothing more and will take nothing less."

The Rhineland and reparations—these were the absolute aims of the marshal—and he asked Clemenceau to give him the name of the fellow in the Ministry of Foreign Affairs with whom he, Foch, could coordinate these military and diplomatic affairs. Clemenceau wrote back at once to tell Foch to keep his place: diplomacy was for diplomats (and for Clemenceau), not for military men.

Although Clemenceau pursued the same two aims as the marshal, he pursued them with less than military straightforwardness—with an instinct for the main chance that left Foch baffled, suspicious, and angry.

During November of 1918, six possible plans were drawn up by the War Office, all of them permutations on the objective of securing the Rhineland. But the annexation or occupation of the Rhineland was not the only notion that Clemenceau entertained. Evidently he did not consider the possibility of splitting Germany exactly in half, but he spent a great deal of time searching for a similar formula. The closest he came to the idea of dividing Germany was to fragment it—to shatter Germany into many small states, such as those that existed before Bismarck unified the nation.

Gabriel Hanotaux, a former French foreign minister, tried to clothe this notion in Wilsonian rhetoric. Hanotaux's plan called for the "federalization" of Germany; the new Germany would have the Rhineland sliced away and then be composed of six or eight little states—all this under the rubric of self-determination for the inhabitants of these little states.

Although Clemenceau could never arrive at a perfect formula for his idea, the notion of dividing Germany into at least three autonomous republics remained his foreign policy always. Just before Wilson returned to the conference in March, Clemenceau grumbled that "the more separate and independent republics were established in Germany, the better he would be pleased," especially—though he did not say it—if they could be somehow tied to France through some sort of customs union or commonly regulated market.

Clemenceau's variable notions were never appealing to Lloyd George or Wilson, both of whom considered them measures that would create many new Alsace-Lorraines, many new causes of war. And Clemenceau did not insist on fragmenting Germany. But whenever the prime minister or the president would attack Clemenceau's more moderate ideas as too extreme or draconian, the Tiger would shrug and threaten to resign and leave French policy in the hands of men like Poincaré and his friend Foch, who spoke of nothing but armies, invasions, and the outright annexation of the Rhineland.

THE SQUEEZE

It seemed to Wilson that the French were intentionally delaying the negotiations by their endless talk, but the French newspapers were blaming Wilson for the delay. They said that he was reopening old issues, distracting the conference from the hard questions by talking always about the League of Nations—and the English newspapers, when they were not blaming Lloyd George, were carping at Wilson, too.

Clemenceau's remarks were being collected and recounted among the delegates.

"Mr. Wilson," the Tiger said on one occasion, "if I accepted what you propose as ample for the security of France, after the millions who have died and the millions who have suffered, I believe—and indeed, I hope—that my successor in office would take me by the nape of the neck and have me shot before the donjon of Vincennes!"

"You wish to do justice to the Germans," he said to Wilson on another occasion. "Do not believe that they will ever forgive us. They will seek only the chance of revenge. Nothing will suppress the fury of those who hoped to dominate the world and believed success so near."

"Pray, Monsieur Clemenceau," Wilson asked the premier at one point, "have you ever been to Germany?"

"No, sir!" said the Tiger. "But twice in my lifetime the Germans have been to France."

The principal issues were assuming a certain clarity by this time—a balance, a relationship that suggested some natural trades. The French stood to get two for one in the trade that appeared to be taking shape: Wilson would get the Monroe Doctrine, and Clemenceau would get his way on reparations and the Rhine. Wilson refused to deal.

In the president's study, before the fireplace, the Big Four discussed reparations in the morning and the league in the afternoon. On the next day they talked about reparations all day. On the following day, they talked of reparations in the morning and the Rhine in the afternoon. On the next day, they talked about the Monroe Doctrine. On the next day they talked about the Rhine and the Saar in the morning, and, in the afternoon, they spoke again of reparations.

"In getting at the amount of war damages," Charles Thompson wrote of the reparations question, "the French first made their estimate of 200 billion dollars and the English of 120 billion dollars; and these were gradually scaled down to 40 billion dollars. But here the progress halted, the American members of the commission were not satisfied that enough had been done.... The proposal as it stood was that the 40 billion dollars should be spread over a period of 40 years—a billion a year for Germany to pay. But with interest on this outstanding sum it would amount in 40 years to something like 80 billion dollars."

The Americans proposed a far more modest sum. American financial experts estimated that the absolute maximum that the Germans could pay—taking all available resources at home and abroad—was only $12 billion, including $8 billion in assets outside of Germany, including such items as the German merchant marine, mines and railroads in Alsace and Lorraine, foreign securities and properties in East Africa, Shantung, and elsewhere, including also government and private wealth in South America and the United States. "Should all this be confiscated," Thompson wrote, it would "leave four billions to be paid" from other assets, and it was calculated that Germany "could meet this balance in about twelve years."

Keynes observed that a journey "through the devastated areas of France is impressive to the eye and the imagination beyond description. During the winter of 1918–1919, before Nature had cast over the scene her ameliorating mantle, the horror and desolation of war was made visible to sight on an extraordinary scale of blasted grandeur. The completeness of the destruction was evident. For mile after mile nothing was left. No building was habitable and no field fit for the plow. The sameness was also striking. One devastated area was exactly like another—a heap of rubble, a morass of shell-holes, and a tangle of wire ... to the returned traveler any number of billions of dollars was inadequate to express in matter the destruction thus impressed upon his spirit."

But when the destruction was expressed in dollars—when the cost of restoring the destroyed areas was assessed in material terms—Keynes estimated the amount of reparations necessary to fix the damage to property was not as horrendous as it might appear, but was rather something on the order of $2.5 billion. René Pupin, a French analyst, placed the figure similarly at between $2 and $3 billion. Keynes estimated that what the Germans could possibly pay—never minding for the moment what they should pay—was about $10 billion.

When the Big Four gathered in Wilson's study—to talk of $100 billion or $50 billion, or $25 billion—the estimates that Keynes and other financial experts had made were largely irrelevant. The way that the Big Four were to settle a sum for reparations had much less to do with facts, with figures of wealth, industrial production, the real possibilities of postwar transfer payments, foreign credits, exports, price deflation, and tax policies than it had to do with whether Britain and France were to be in debt to the United States.

Was the Monroe Doctrine crucial to Wilson? Was the president determined to have his League of Nations? Then Germany could easily pay $100 billion in reparations. Was the Monroe Doctrine less vital to the president? Was the United States prepared to give economic assistance to France? Then Germany had only $25 billion worth of assets. Facts would not be allowed to determine politics; politics would determine facts.

Nothing of importance had yet been settled; everything remained fluid; all elements in a grand, elusive algebraical formula remained variable; and, until one element could be fixed to everyone's satisfaction, no elements would be fixed. One of the president's old admirers cabled to Wilson, knowing that the president faced the prospect of unseemly deal-making if he were to continue negotiations at all, and urged the president to withdraw from the conference and return to the United States. Wilson paced up and down the floor after receiving the cable, pondering whether to trade or quit, whether to play the game or go home, knowing, apparently, that the only possible course for him if he were not to give up all his magniloquent words, was to haggle and deal. "My God," he said at last, "I can never go through with it."

❧

WILSON YIELDS

On March 27, Wilson commenced to go through with it, by making an essential concession to the French. Were the French concerned about their security? Were the provisions about occupation of the Rhine, and the high reparations bill, measures to ensure protection against Germany? Then Wilson and Lloyd George would reassure the French: "We hereby solemnly pledge to one another our immediate military, financial, economic and moral support of and to one another in the event Germany should at any time make [an] unprovoked and unwarranted attack against either one or more of the subscribing Powers."

In short, Wilson agreed to the military alliance that he had been resisting for so long. Constitutionally, of course, as he had pointed out to Clemenceau before, he was unable to give such a military guarantee. Theoretically, his League of Nations made such a military alliance irrelevant, and wrong. Nonetheless, Wilson gave in— and then looked for what he would get in return.

What he got were more demands from Clemenceau.

On March 28, after days of hopeless wrangling, after yet another morning of profitless nattering, Wilson told Clemenceau that the United States could not conceivably consent to French demands for the Rhineland. Then, Clemenceau said, he must insist on ownership of the Saar Basin. The Saar Basin: no one, Wilson said impatiently, had ever even heard of this French demand for the Saar until quite recently. The Saar was indisputably German territory, and its inhabitants wished to remain German. It had been German for its entire history, except for two brief interludes when it was seized by Louis XIV and again by Napoleon. But in all history it had only belonged to France for a total of twenty-three years. For Clemenceau now to raise the question of the Saar was an outrage.

Clemenceau called Wilson pro-German.

No French prime minister, said Clemenceau, could possibly sign a treaty that did not satisfy French demands for the Saar. Perhaps, Clemenceau hinted, he would resign if the other leaders did not wish to deal with him, and then Wilson would see: Foch and Poincaré would make certain that a much more hard-line prime minister took Clemenceau's place.

"Then," said Wilson darkly, "if France does not get what she wishes, she will refuse to act with us. In that event"—he resorted to his ultimate threat—"do you wish me to return home?"

"I do not wish you to go home," Clemenceau replied, "but I intend to do so myself." And, with that, Clemenceau got up and walked out.

The meeting was over; the delegates dispersed; Wilson was in a panic. To several younger members of the American delegation who called at his house, Wilson said, "I do not know whether I shall see Monsieur Clemenceau again. I do not know whether he will return to the meeting this afternoon. In fact, I do not know whether the peace conference will continue. Monsieur Clemenceau called me a pro-German."

The president was isolated. Clemenceau had been doing his work well. Lloyd George might still be standing by Wilson on some of the matters before the conference, but the British prime minister was certainly not a staunch ally: he had been, as it turned out, as easy for Clemenceau to seduce as Colonel House had been.

"The truth is," Lloyd George said to Riddell as they drove out of Paris for a picnic lunch and a tour of Versailles, "that we have got our way. We have got most of the things we set out to get. If you had told the British people twelve months ago that they would have secured what they have, they would have laughed you to scorn. The Germany Navy has been handed over; the German mercantile shipping has been handed over, and the German colonies have been given up. One of our chief trade competitors has been most seriously crippled and our allies are about to become her biggest creditors. That is no small achievement."

Lloyd George was, said Riddell, in a jolly mood. In fact, Lloyd George was so delighted by what he was getting for the good of the empire that he seemed to have lost sight, at least for the time being, of what he was giving to Clemenceau on the continent.

House tried to save Wilson. The colonel persuaded the president to call in some financial experts to work over the French proposals on the Saar and reparations and try to arrive at some compromise. The British and Americans were so close to agreement, said House, that it would not look good for the United States to "take a stand in which she was not supported by Great Britain. I advised yielding a little in order to secure harmony, so that the accusation could not be made that we were unreasonable. He promised to do this."

"The whole world wants peace," Lansing noted. "The President wants his League. I think that the world will have to wait."

Clemenceau sent André Tardieu to Colonel House. The French suggested that passions be allowed to cool while each of the Big Three appointed a "consultant" to try to work out a compromise. Tardieu, the former French high commissioner to Washington, and the man who had greeted Wilson back in December when the President arrived at Brest, would represent France. Lloyd George named J. W. Headlam-Morley, the Foreign Office historian and an expert on Germany, "a quiet, scholarly man of good common sense," as Shotwell said, "and a kindly sense of humor." Wilson appointed Charles H. Haskins, a Harvard professor whose specialty was the Middle Ages in Europe, but whose range of knowledge was extensive. Wilson had known Haskins since the days they had both been students at Johns Hopkins and remarked of the professor that he was one of "the rare New England historians who did not regard the westward march of the American frontier as an aspect of the expansion of greater Boston."

The consultants haggled dispassionately and arrived at a proposal for the Saar: a special administrative regime would be established to ensure French operation of the coal mines; after fifteen years a plebiscite would be held to determine whether the inhabitants of the Saar wished to be a part of Germany or of France.

"The President tried to get me to admit," House noted in his diary, "that the solution which our experts have proposed and which Clemenceau might be willing to take as to the Saar Valley was inconsistent with the Fourteen Points." House gave Wilson no sympathy. "I replied that there were many who thought otherwise."

Wilson yielded—and still, Clemenceau was not satisfied.

The question of reparations was raised once again in front of the fireplace in Wilson's study. The French and the British had agreed to drop their demand for reparations for indirect costs of the war—such as demobilization allowances and interest charges on war loans—and Wilson agreed to include soldiers' pensions in costs to be reimbursed by Germany. Thus, the manner in which the British would get their cut was established. Still, no one could agree on a definite dollar sum. And the French had come to love Lloyd George's proposal that no specific sum be named, but that the final fixing of an amount be left to a reparations commission. At last, Wilson yielded on this point, too.

And yet Clemenceau was not satisfied. The Americans were negotiating for an indefinite sum to be paid in a maximum period of thirty years; but the French, backed by Lloyd George, meant to set a maximum period of forty years. Each time Wilson yielded to Clemenceau, he discovered a new demand: on the matter of reparations, Clemenceau demanded unconditional surrender.

On April 2, Baker called on the president. Wilson was, said Baker, "at the end of his tether." The president said, Baker recorded, "that it could not go on many days longer; that if some de-cision could not be reached by the middle of next week, he might have to make a positive break."

WILSON BREAKS

On April 3, at six o'clock in the evening, following an afternoon in which he had seemed fit and fine, the president was suddenly "seized," as Dr. Grayson reported, "with violent paroxysms of coughing which were so severe and frequent that it interfered with his breathing." He was ordered to bed at once.

Grayson was alarmed; Mrs. Wilson was shaken. Grayson sus-pected at first that the president had been poisoned. Wilson's tem-perature rose to 103, and he sank quickly into exhausted coughing, vomiting, and diarrhea that went on through the night and the next day, through the night of April 4 and on into April 5. Grayson re-vised his diagnosis to influenza.

Dr. Grayson had become a member of the presidential "fam-ily," and an agreeable man to have around, a confidant, a bearer of personal messages; but his medical knowledge was perhaps not as penetrating as that of some of his contemporaries. "If the present universal use of automobiles and elevators is continued," Grayson once said, "we may expect our great, great, great grandchildren to be born without legs." Horseback riding, Grayson thought, would cure nearly anything. "The outside of a horse," the doctor enjoyed saying, "is good for the inside of a man." Riding, he said, "gives a perfect and thorough massage to the entire system . . . this exercise is a most direct and active tonic to the digestive functions . . . the exercise is delightfully comfortable and gratifying and the associa-tions pleasant, for a horse is one of the most friendly and agreeable of companions . . . when a man doesn't like a good horse," Grayson said, "or a good-looking girl, why he isn't right, that's for certain."

Had Grayson inquired more particularly into Wilson's back-ground, he would have learned that at Princeton, Wilson had com-plained of occasional headaches, dizziness, and stomach upset—a phenomenon that Wilson came to call "turmoil in Central America." At the University of Virginia Law School, his headaches and dyspepsia continued, and, after graduation, when he made his short-lived attempt at a law practice in Atlanta, he was troubled by what he said was "biliousness"—but which his father diagnosed as difficulty with his *"mental* liver."

At Johns Hopkins, his complaints of headaches became more frequent—which Wilson attributed to the pressures of overwork, and to a longing for Ellen Axson. At Bryn Mawr, bowel disturbances were added to his headaches, and, by the time he had returned to Johns Hopkins to teach graduate courses, he had acquired his own stomach pump, with which he treated himself.

In May of 1896, while he was spending a weekend at Princeton, he noticed a numbness in the fingers of his right hand, and a sensation of weakness and slight pain in his right arm, and he was not able to write well with his right hand again until March of 1897. To strangers or acquaintances, Wilson was casual about these inconveniences. He learned to write—and to play golf—left-handed. To his family, he expressed great worry, and received great sympathy—frequently mentioning his problems with left-handed penmanship, and his suffering from hemorrhoids.

On May 28, 1906, he woke up in the morning completely blind in his left eye. An ophthalmologist diagnosed the trouble as a broken blood vessel in the eye and told Wilson that it was a symptom of high blood pressure.

"The sequence of episodes of paresthesia in one hand and blindness in the opposite eye," Edwin Weinstein has recently written, "is characteristic of occlusive disease of the internal carotid artery, the major supplier of blood to the brain. This vessel gives off a branch, the ophthalmic artery, whose continuation, the central retinal artery, goes to the homolateral retina, and continues on to supply the cerebral hemisphere. . . . Thus, the combination of symptoms indicates that there was blocking of the left internal carotid artery."

The sense of weakness in hand and arm abated, as is common; the slight impairment of sight persisted for the rest of Wilson's life, as is also to be expected. He had another minor attack against his right hand in 1908, but no other episodes. An associate of the ophthalmologist who examined Wilson in 1906 made some observations that Weinstein records as follows: "Woodrow Wilson suffered from a very high blood pressure and his fundi (retinas) showed hypertensive vascular changes with advanced atherosclerosis (thickening of vessel walls), angiospasticity (spasm of retinal vessels), retinal hemorrhages and exudates."

After his problems of 1906, Wilson seemed markedly more irritable and impulsive, "more openly aggressive," as Weinstein noted, "and less tolerant of criticism and opposition." Such personal characteristics are often associated with cerebral vascular difficulties, although they are not necessarily caused by brain damage. Another person, with a different psychological makeup, might respond differently. In any case, Wilson's tenseness and intolerance did not help to alleviate his high blood pressure.

In the spring of 1915, Wilson was stricken repeatedly, for several days, with blinding headaches—at a time that coincided with some crucial decisions on foreign policy. "I am interested in neutrality," he said in a speech to the Associated Press on April 20, "because there is something so much greater to do than fight; there is a distinction waiting for this Nation that no nation has ever yet got. That is the distinction of absolute self-control and self-mastery."

Over the next several months, Colonel House encouraged Wilson to take an increasingly active role in world affairs. In August, the president consulted his ophthalmologist about persistent headaches. On October 8, Wilson approved a plan prepared by House that called for an initial attempt to exert diplomatic pressure against Germany; and, failing that, American entry into the war.

In early 1916, Wilson showed increased irritability and intolerance of the criticism or opposition of others. On April 6, 1917, the president led the country into war against Germany. Thereafter, Wilson's neurological symptoms, psychological idiosyncrasies, and political activities became so inextricably intertwined that it becomes increasingly difficult to separate the different strands from one another.

In April of 1919, the fusion of inner and outer worlds, of inscape and landscape, became so complete once again in the person of Wilson that it was possible at last to describe the president and the world in the same terms: both had had a dreadful breakdown; both suffered from a disorder so complexly fabricated of wishes and fears, politics and psychic disarray, hard facts and utter hallucinations, reality and imagination, power and impotence as to defy any single analysis or prescription, or any hope of a full recovery of a former, Victorian self.

WILSON'S DEFEAT

The negotiations continued in front of the fireplace in Wilson's study: Clemenceau and Lloyd George and Orlando were there, and sitting in for Wilson was Colonel House. From time to time the colonel would rise, move to the back of the room, open what appeared to be a solid, well-filled bookcase, and step through a secret passageway into Wilson's bedroom, where the president lay ill. As well as he was able, Wilson would guide House in closing the deals Wilson could not bring himself to make.

Clemenceau, Frances Stevenson confided to her diary, "was very pleased at Wilson's absence, could not conceal his joy. 'He is *worse* today,' he said to D., and doubled up with laughter. 'Do you know his doctor? Couldn't you get round him & bribe him? ! . . .' The old man did not attempt to conceal his feelings on the subject."

Grayson told Baker that Wilson might have caught influenza from Clemenceau, whose deep, racking cough was so much a topic of conversation. "I hope," said House genially, when Baker relayed this speculation, "that Clemenceau will pass on the germ to Lloyd George."

Now, with Wilson out of the way, and with Clemenceau's friend Colonel House sitting in on the negotiations, a secretary was suddenly allowed into the room to make notes on the agreements. Colonel Hankey was called into the study, and he did not leave until Clemenceau and Lloyd George had written the heart of the treaty, paragraph by paragraph, clause by clause, all of it recorded, painstakingly, in precise detail.

The remaining item to be settled was reparations. "The problem of Reparations came up on the morning of April 5," according to the papers of Colonel House, "as Sir Maurice Hankey prophesied . . . [it was] 'a turning point in the thorny question.' " The session began badly; although the experts thought they had reached an agreement on the issue, it turned out that the French and British expected still more concessions. The Americans had understood that, although no specific sum was to be mentioned in the treaty, reparations would be limited by the amount Germany could pay in thirty years. The French insisted that the reparations commission should not take into account Germany's ability to pay in thirty years, but that damages should be assessed, and then paid for, no matter how long it took. "To the disappointment of the Americans," according to House's papers, "Mr. Lloyd George also opposed the principle of a thirty-year limitation."

"I do not accept," said Clemenceau, "that the commission should have power to declare the capacity of payment of Germany . . . we are not prepared to accept any limitation now. We shall see what is possible and what is not, we shall take into account the question of accumulated interest. . . . We are willing to let the door [remain] open to every liberal solution.

"But . . . what the enemy owes to us should be declared (if not by means of [a fixed] sum, at least by determining categories of damages to be compensated for). We shall retain our faculty of allowing time to pay. Let us fix a limit of thirty years, as thought desirable by most of us. If everything has not been paid for during thirty years, then the commission will have the right to extend the period."

Everything came out just slightly different after Clemenceau had rephrased it. He accepted the thirty-year limit—with the proviso that the time limit could be extended. When all the verbiage and vagueness was cut through, the effect of Clemenceau's position was strikingly clear: he accepted no limitation of any kind on reparations, neither the naming of a fixed sum, nor the limitation of time.

In the end, House drafted an agreement that constituted a compromise of a compromise of a compromise on wording, such that it gave everything away to Clemenceau while seeming to do the opposite. "The schedule of payments," said House's draft, "to be made by the Enemy States shall be set forth [by the commission], taking into account, in the fixation of the time for payment, their capacity for payment." Such language—language that seemed to say one thing while permitting the contrary—was quintessentially Wilsonian. The president accepted it: his defeat was complete.

Some of the young Americans were astonished that Wilson had agreed—when it came to drawing up the list of things for which Germany would have to pay reparations—not only to assess Germany for damage to property and a long list of other actual costs of wartime civilian damage but also the cost of pensions for veterans, thus enormously inflating the possible reparations bill. When some of the experts told him it was simply illogical, Wilson exploded, "Logic! Logic! I don't give a damn for logic!"

WILSON RALLIES

On Sunday morning, April 6, Wilson rose in his sickbed, suddenly struck by what he had done, and called for Colonel House. The colonel was on an outing to Versailles for lunch when the president's summons to a four o'clock meeting caught up with him.

At four o'clock, sitting up in bed with his old sweater around his shoulders, Wilson spoke to House, Lansing, White, and Bliss. "It was determined," said House, "that if nothing happened within the next few days, the President would say to the Prime Ministers that unless peace was made according to their promises, which were to conform to the principles of the Fourteen Points, he would either have to go home or he would insist upon having the conferences in the open."

Later in the evening, Wilson summoned Bernard Baruch to his bedside. Baruch, chairman of the War Industrial Board during the war, and head of the economic section of advisers at the peace conference, was brought into the president's bedroom by Dr. Grayson. Wilson was sitting up, still in the old sweater, and Mrs. Wilson sat next to him, knitting.

Wilson told Baruch that he had come to the end of his patience, and he had decided to squeeze the British and French somehow. What did Baruch advise? Baruch thought the president might consider stopping the financial credits on which the British and French were virtually living at the time. Wilson accepted the recommendation and cabled at once to the secretary of the treasury to cut off any new credits.

Then, as a final flourish, Wilson told Grayson to call up the S.S. *George Washington*, to be ready to take the president home to the United States, and to make certain that the word got out that he had called for his ship. When Clemenceau heard the news that Wilson had sent for the *George Washington*, he said, "It's a bluff, isn't it?" Grayson replied, "He hasn't a bluffing corpuscle in his body."

"I have told you," White loyally declared to the press, "we would not stand around here doing nothing forever."

Secretary of State Lansing, ever the diplomat, when asked about the president's call for the S.S. *George Washington*, stated that the action "justified speculation as to its meaning."

APRIL 7

The French response to Wilson's histrionics was phlegmatic. Louis Loucheur, who handled the economic negotiations for France, told House calmly that the French had no difficulty in settling matters just as Wilson wanted them. Loucheur assured House that Clemenceau had read the reparations agreement that Wilson had proposed and "approved it in toto."

Of course, there were one or two minor points of phrasing that Loucheur wanted to go over. And then, "Loucheur told me time and again after we had accepted and voted over a few verbal and unimportant changes, that it was the last, and yet, when the very next sentence was read, suggestions for changes would be made. . . . At six o'clock I left. . . . We wasted the entire afternoon, accomplishing nothing, for the text when finished was practically what it was when we went into the meeting."

That evening, when Ray Stannard Baker came to see the president, Baker found Wilson "fully dressed, in his study, looking thin and pale. A slight hollowness of the eyes emphasized a characteristic I had often noted before—the size and luminosity of his eyes . . . and he looked at one with a piercing intentness."

Wilson told Baker why he had asked the *George Washington* to be readied, and Baker urged him to put out a press release, setting out once and for all a clear, specific program that applied his Fourteen Points to all the issues before the conference—a final, protean attempt to write the whole treaty. Wilson said he was doubtful about doing that, but that he thought it would be good to issue a statement saying simply that he intended to stand on his principles.

"Then Italy will not get Fiume?"

"Absolutely not—so long as I am here."

"Nor France the Saar?"

"No."

THE SAAR

Clemenceau could not help but notice that Wilson did not get aboard the *George Washington* to return to America. On the morning of April 8, the subject of the Saar was raised. Lloyd George—by this time working in wonderful harmony with Clemenceau—suggested that the Saar not be annexed to France, but that it be split off from Germany and made into a separate state, like Luxembourg, and enlarged somewhat to bring in the industrial area on which the Saar Valley depended, "an independent state in the customs union of France."

House did not like this idea, but he suggested as an alternative that the Saar be split off from Germany and then not put into a customs union with France but rather taken under the protection of the League of Nations.

The French coal mines in the Nord and Pas de Calais areas had been destroyed in the war. France would need 50 million tons of coal a year—coal it could now get only from Germany. Thus, Clemenceau feared, unless he got the Saar, Germany could virtually fix French industrial prices by the price of coal and so dominate French economic policy.

In the afternoon, Wilson returned to the meetings of the Big Four. By no means would he agree to take the Saar from Germany, the president declared. To be sure, he recognized that France needed coal, and he was prepared to see France get its coal from the Saar Valley. And so, he was prepared to envision a case in which Germany was to own the *soil* of the Saar Valley, and France to own the *sub*soil.

This marvelous solution to the Saar problem would doubtless

create difficulties, which could be solved, Wilson thought, by a commission of arbitration.

Wilson's amazing suggestion was taken up and worked over by Tardieu and Charles Haskins. In the process of neatening Wilson's proposal, the negotiators settled on this solution: German sovereignty was to be suspended for fifteen years; during that time an administrative commission of the League of Nations would have full rights in the Saar, which would be exercised to ensure a supply of coal for France; at the end of fifteen years, a plebiscite would be held to determine the ultimate sovereignty of the Saar.

THE MONROE DOCTRINE

"Today," Baker noted in his diary for April 10, "when I went into his study, he looked old and worn. Things are not going well. . . . I saw him standing with Grayson close to the window. The sash had been thrown up and Grayson was exercising the President by standing with him foot to foot, and with clasped hands pulling him vigorously back and forth. The President turned to me with the remark, 'Indoor golf.' "

That night, the president attended a meeting of the negotiators who were finishing the covenant of the League of Nations. They were meeting once again in Colonel House's rooms at the Hotel Crillon, and one of the French delegates was once again endlessly talking, still frustrating Wilson's need for specific recognition of the Monroe Doctrine.

Some time after midnight, the president rose to reply. He gave, one of the young Americans said, "an extempore speech of witching eloquence . . . which left the secretaries gasping with admiration, their pencils in their hands, their duties forgotten, and hardly a word taken down."

"At a time when the world was in the grip of absolutism," said Wilson, the Europeans turned to America to "take some political step to guard against the spread of absolutism to the American Continent." America replied by proclaiming the principles of the

Monroe Doctrine. "Now that a document was being drafted [the covenant for the league] which was the logical extension of the Monroe Doctrine to the whole world, was the United States to be penalized for her early adoption of this policy? . . . Was the commission going to scruple on words at a time when the United States was ready to sign a covenant which made her forever part of the movement for liberty? Was this the way in which America's early service to liberty was to be rewarded?"

More than eloquent or witching, the President's speech appears to have been so heated as to have been alarming to some. Léon Bourgeois had a hurried, whispered conversation with another member of the French delegation, and then the French declared that they would not wish by any means to raise a serious objection to anything so close to the President's heart.

THE DEAL

On the next day, however, it turned out that the French wanted to discuss the whole issue again. Coincidentally, they wanted to discuss the subject of the Rhineland, too. During the next three days, with House running back and forth between them, Clemenceau finally accepted Wilson's acceptance of Clemenceau's proposed counteroffer to Wilson's compromise position. The German side of the Rhineland would be demilitarized along a strip fifty kilometers wide. On the French side, French troops would occupy the western Rhineland in three strata; the first stratum would include Coblenz, the second Mainz, and the third would be contiguous to the French frontier. The French troops would withdraw from these three strata piecemeal, at three five-year intervals. However, if the Germans did not pay their reparations bill in full, the French would occupy the Rhineland until reparations were paid.

"The President made a wry face over some of it," House said, "particularly the three five-year periods of occupation, but he agreed to it all."

On the fifteenth of April, House went to the Ministry of War to see Clemenceau. "I said to him, 'I am the bearer of good news. The President has consented to all that you asked of me yesterday.' He grasped both my hands and then embraced me."

In that case, the Monroe Doctrine was accepted.

"At last," Clemenceau said to Mordacq, "I've got almost everything I wanted."

WILSON'S NIGHTMARES

"Even while lying in bed," Ike Hoover had noticed, "he manifested peculiarities, one of which was to limit the use of all the automobiles to strictly official purposes, when previously he had been so liberal in his suggestions that his immediate party should have the benefit of this possible diversion, in view of the long hours we were working."

Once out of bed, said Hoover, "his peculiar ideas were even more pronounced." He became obsessed with the idea that "every French employee about the place was a spy for the French government." No one could disabuse Wilson of this idea. "He insisted they all understood English, when, as a matter of fact, there was just one of them among the two dozen or more who understood a single word of English."

At the same time, Wilson was seized with a sense of personal responsibility for all of the furniture in the house that he occupied. On two occasions, Wilson thought that pieces of furniture were missing, and the president, said Hoover, "raised quite a fuss. . . . Upon investigation—for no one else noticed the change—it was learned that the custodian of the property for the French owner had seen fit to do a little rearranging."

Edwin Weinstein, who wrote of Wilson's neurological difficulties with such interest, has observed of these reports that automobiles "were a favorite figure of speech. . . . In 1906 [Wilson] had predicted ominously that the automobile would spread socialism in the United States because it gave people the picture of the arrogance of great wealth. . . . Along with golf, motoring was his favorite relaxation and recreation. In the White House, motoring was a daily activity with each trip numbered and no deviation permitted from a set route."

"The delusion that all the French servants were spies who spoke perfect English," Weinstein says, "is a highly condensed symbolic representation of his problem with the French. . . . In a delusion, one represents his problems in symbols that explain and impart a particularly vivid feeling to the experience by reason of the way the language is an expression of personal identity."

The temptation to lapse into Freudian language is irresistible—Freud and Wilson having done so much to make one another's worlds. Weinstein's more customary style sounds like this: "The episode of April 2 to 5 suggests that he sustained a lesion in the right cerebral hemisphere extending to include deeper structures in the limbic-reticular system . . . he now had evidence of bilateral damage, a condition affecting emotional and social behavior more severely than a unilateral lesion. With such involvement, there occur changes in the patient's perception and classification of his environment, so that his designation and recall of issues, events, and people tend to become *metaphorical* representations of his own problems and feelings."

❦

BENEFACTORS OF HUMANITY

"Baker and others of our entourage have been after me for several days," House wrote in his diary for the fifteenth, "concerning attacks in the French press, not only against the President but against the United States." After his embrace from Clemenceau, House mentioned, "I cared nothing about it individually, but I did care about the good relations between the United States and France and I hoped he would stop [the newspaper criticism of the President]." They were agreed now on the Rhine, reparations, and about the Monroe Doctrine.

Clemenceau summoned Martet "and told him in French, with much emphasis, that all attacks of every description on President

Wilson and the United States must cease; that our relations were of the very best and that there was no disagreement between our two countries upon the questions before the peace conference."

The effect was "magical." On the next day, April 16, all the Paris papers published lavish, enthusiastic praise of President Wilson: "We have seen him; we have admired him; our descendants in their turn will wonder at it all, and the work of President Wilson will remain one of the legends of history. President Wilson will appear in the poetry of the coming ages, like unto that Dante whom he resembles in profile. . . . This man of law, this jurist of Sinai, this Solomon of Right and Duty . . . before he is made memorable in bronze and marble, let us salute in our hearts, in the temple of our gratitude, the image of this forever memorable man. Honor to President Wilson, High Priest of the Ideal, Leaguer of the Nations, Benefactor of Humanity, Shepherd of Victory and Legislator of Peace."

From that day on, said Colonel House, "it was clear that the crisis had passed."

PART FIVE
LOOSE ENDS

FIN DE LA SAISON

A telegram was dispatched to the Germans, inviting them to send a delegation to Paris to receive the peace terms, but the feeling that pervaded the conference was not of a world restored to harmony but of a world in utter wreckage. "Nothing much counts any more," Ray Stannard Baker wrote in his diary. "A treaty will be made, but it may never be signed, or if signed it will have little meaning. We are plunging inevitably into an unknown world full of danger."

"Really," Seymour wrote home, "the last week has had almost the air of a *fin de la saison* [*sic*]. No more commission meetings, very few conferences, a great deal of dope as to what was being decided by the Big Four and a general clearing up of offices." Seymour had even had a warning to get his maps ready to be packed at short notice. "This doesn't mean . . . that the conference is over. But it does mean that the most important questions are settled in their broad lines, and that if Europe doesn't break up on our hands the rest is largely a matter of details."

Among the "details"—now that the treaty with Germany was nearly settled—were the treaties with the smaller states, with Austria, Hungary, Turkey, and Bulgaria. Some of these treaties were on their way to being settled. But, once the treaty with Germany was presented to the Germans, and signed, the conference would adjourn and leave the "minor" treaties to a council of the League of Nations to complete.

"Everyone feels," Seymour said, "that the main necessity is to sign with Germany and send the conference home, after which we shall have, at least nominally, a condition of peace."

❧

THE HOUSE OF COMMONS

In London, in the House of Commons, Kennedy Jones began to circulate among conservative members to say that Lloyd George, having come under the influence of President Wilson, was betraying the interests of France and Britain. He was giving in on reparations and settling for a soft peace with Germany.

Colonel Claude Lowther, another member of Parliament, circulated a memorandum to the other members showing how Germany could pay the vast sum of £25 billion. Meanwhile, Lord Northcliffe, proprietor of the *Daily Mail*, instructed his editors to print the same banner over every report from Paris: "They will cheat you yet, those Junkers! Having won half the world by bloody murder, they are going to win the other half with tears in their eyes, crying for mercy." Having "lost the war by fighting," one of the *Daily Mail* reports said, "the Germans hope to win a favourable peace by whining."

At the end of the first week in April, Lloyd George received a telegram from London: signed by 370 conservative members of Parliament, the telegram urged the prime minister to stand firm and to "present the bill in full" to Germany for the war.

On April 16, Lloyd George returned to London to annihilate his opposition before it grew any larger. His dilemma was neat: just how he might answer his critics—without telling the truth—was not clear. Yet, as he had said to Riddell on the day that Wilson collapsed and took to his bed: "The chief difference between ordinary and extraordinary men is that when the extraordinary man is faced by a novel and difficult situation, he extricates himself by adopting a plan which is at once daring and unexpected. That is the mark of genius in a man of action."

In this situation, Lloyd George did not want to declare that he had given his efforts either to a hard or to a soft peace: he did not want to lose the support either of the conservatives or of the liberals. Nor did he wish to get into the rat's nest of the substance of the Paris negotiations, which would force him to reveal all sorts of embarrassing compromises and deals—to show how much he had become the tool not of Wilson but of Clemenceau. Nor, certainly, was he ready at all to reveal how he had arranged to pass the question of reparations to a commission. Instead, believing that the best defense is an attack, he returned to the House of Commons, made a few bland and circumspect criticisms of the more conservative views of some members, and then lambasted Lord Northcliffe.

It was said that the conservatives took their information about the way negotiations were going from a "reliable source," a certain newspaper that Lloyd George did not mention by name. "Reliable! That is the last adjective I would use. It is here today, jumping there tomorrow, and there the next day. I would as soon rely on a grasshopper."

It was hard for a man, Lloyd George said (carefully avoiding any mention of Lord Northcliffe's name), when he had deluded himself into thinking that only he knew how to run the world, to find that he had received no direct call to help sort it out; when a man thought only he knew how to win a war, but was not asked to lead the nation or to serve in the cabinet.

"And then the war is won without him! There must be something wrong! And, of course, it must be the Government!"

At any rate, such a man—such an outsider, such a *journalist*— will surely decide that he is the only man then to sort out the peace. "The only people who get near him tell him so constantly, and so he prepares the peace terms in advance and he waits for the call.

[Here, loud laughter filled the House of Commons.]

"It does not come.

"He retreats to sunny climes—waiting!

"Not a sound reaches the far-distant shore—

[laughter]

—to call him back to his great task of saving the world.

"What can you expect?

"He comes back and says,

" 'Well, now, I cannot see the disease, but I am sure it is there!
[laughter]

" 'It is bound to come!'

"Under these conditions I am prepared to make allowances, but let me say that when that kind of diseased vanity—

[here Lloyd George tapped his forehead]

"—is carried to the point of sowing dissension between great allies whose unity is essential to the peace and happiness of the world . . . then, I say, not even that kind of disease is a justification for so black a crime against humanity."

[Loud cheers.]

By the time Lloyd George finished his speech, he was positively buoyant. "D. returned," Frances Stevenson wrote in her diary the next day in Paris, "in the highest of spirits, & very pleased with himself. He had a wonderful reception, & gained complete mastery of the House, while telling them absolutely nothing about the peace conference."

THE ITALIANS

The disposition of the Italian claim to Fiume had not yet been settled. Orlando continued to insist on having Fiume in trade for his approval of the League of Nations. The president had let the opportunity slip by for a fast, principled stand, and the young American experts feared that Wilson was about to give in to Orlando. Seymour and some of his colleagues sent a letter to the president, urging him not to compromise with the Italians. This letter was followed by a memorandum from the ignored American delegates—Lansing, Bliss, and White, who had come to be known, among the Big Four, and the representatives of other great powers, as the Lesser Three.

Thus, the Lesser Three and all six of the territorial specialists on the American delegation took a Wilsonian position against giving Fiume to Italy. Lloyd George, saying that he wished to honor the Treaty of 1915, was prepared to have the question decided either way. Clemenceau, although he despised the Italian claim, saw the issue in entirely unprincipled terms: if Orlando did not sign the treaty, the French told Colonel House, then the united front of the Allies would be broken, and Germany might take advantage of that disarray to refuse also to accept the treaty. "The goodwill of Italy," said Tardieu, "is more important to the peace of the world than the ultimate disposition of a miserable Dalmatian fishing village." Then, too, Tardieu said, "I fear that the Italians, unless they are 'sweetened,' will turn pro-German."

Such complexities did not seem to be amenable to compromise; on the contrary, the very messiness of the situation seemed to propel each of the Big Four back into his essential attitude: Lloyd George to his lack of commitment, Clemenceau to his unscrupulousness, Wilson and Orlando to their rigidities.

At last, on Easter Sunday, April 20, a day that Seymour remarked as a "warm perfect day" on his way to high mass at the Madeleine ("beautiful service, a Mozart 'Kyrie' and 'Sanctus,' with two organs"), the Big Four gathered in Wilson's study to settle the Fiume question. Lloyd George had especially asked to have the meeting start at ten in the morning so that he and Frances Stevenson could set out afterwards for a picnic lunch in the country.

Orlando had worked himself into a most delicate position over Fiume. He had spoken so often to the Italian people about Italy's demands at the peace conference that the Italians—and Orlando's political opponents—were now uncompromising about their wishes. Whatever Fiume's worth might have been to Italy, it was by this time crucial to Orlando's own survival as a politician.

Orlando brought Sonnino to the meeting of the Big Four, and Sonnino spoke of Italy's need to establish good strategic positions in the north. He was scornful of the League of Nations: no one, said Sonnino, could foresee what problems might come up in the Balkans. "Placing the control of all or any part of this region in the hands of a League of Nations that is not made powerful with an adequate military force is an absurdity; more, it is a criminal action."

"We are pledged," Wilson insisted testily, "to establish a new basic principle, a new international morality, one that has been so often ignored in the last century. . . . You are placing a great burden upon me; but I shall not shirk the responsibility you impose. If you insist, I shall have to state openly to the world the basic reasons of my objections. I cannot accept for myself or for the United States responsibility for principles which are in direct contradiction to those for the maintenance of which we entered the war."

It seemed that Wilson and Sonnino could not engage in a constructive exchange that morning, and so the Big Three asked Orlando to have his foreign minister withdraw from the room. The presence of the Italian foreign minister, they said, was *incomodo*.

Orlando could be just as inconvenient as Sonnino, however. At one point in their dispute over Fiume, Orlando invoked point nine of Wilson's Fourteen Points: "A readjustment of the frontiers of Italy should be effected along clearly recognizable lines of nationality." Sometimes Orlando liked point nine; at other times he insisted that he had entered a reservation on the point. When no one remembered his having done so, he said he had done it the previous November. No one had heard it: he must have mumbled it. In any case, when Italy was given a piece of territory that included 230,000 Tyrolese, he forgot it entirely. As for Fiume, Orlando once again embraced point nine, shouting with deep passion at the president: "Mr. Wilson, there are at least thirty thousand Italians in that most Italian of cities. We cannot abandon them to the by no means tender mercies of the Yugoslavs—treaty or no treaty."

But Wilson, who had learned by this time to treat his Fourteen Points as cavalierly as the next man, when it suited his convenience, replied: "Signor Orlando, there are at least a million Italians in New York, but I trust that you will not on this score claim our Empire City as Italian territory."

Lloyd George tried to rescue the situation (and move things along in time for his picnic) by chiming in with one of his eloquent, heartrending improvisations. He began by recalling all that he and Orlando had gone through together—the hardships of the war, when both had led their countries through dark times, the moments of discouragement and despair, the hope. Scarcely had Orlando taken office, Lloyd George recalled, when the Italians had suffered a terrible rout at Caporetto. A conference was called at Rapallo to discuss the catastrophe, and there, at Rapallo, Orlando had declared that Italy would never give up. The Italian Army would, if necessary, retire to the toe of Italy—no, into Sicily itself; but still Italy would never give up, Italy would fight back. No sacrifice would be too great for the sacred cause of the Allies.

Could not, Lloyd George asked, could not Italy now make one more sacrifice for the cause of peace?

Orlando sniffled. And then he wiped his eyes. Whether he thought of the old days, or of future elections, he could not contain his emotions. He rose, and turned, and went over to the window, and took out his handkerchief, put his head in his hands, and sobbed.

Lloyd George stopped, somewhat surprised at the effect his speech had had.

Clemenceau stared at Orlando's back with a cool and cynical regard.

Wilson rose from his chair and went over to Orlando, and shook his hand sympathetically.

The interpreters, Mantoux and Aldovrandi, glanced at each other in embarrassment.

Balfour, when he was told of the incident later, said unsympathetically, "I have heard of nations winning their way to empire by bribery, cajolery, by threats and by war, but this is the first attempt I have heard of by any statesman to sob his way to empire!"

"In his Fourteen Points," Clemenceau remarked to Colonel House, "Wilson promised to Italy 'a rectification of her frontiers according to the recognized lines of nationality'; but unfortunately these lines are far from clear. . . . Have you ever thought, my dear House, how absurdly patient the poor hoodwinked people are? Rarely, very rarely, do they hang a diplomat."

"The situation is perfectly clear," Colonel House told the president later. "Orlando will not give up Fiume because he is convinced that if he does his ministry will fall, and Page [the American ambassador to Italy] wires from Rome that the Sicilian's conclusion is perfectly correct. He asserts that no ministry that signed the treaty without Fiume as part of the booty would survive." Indeed, some of the politicians speculated that if Orlando's ministry fell, the Italians would elect a government that would be pro-German. The *Giornale d'Italia*, the *Idea Nazionale, Gazetta del Popolo,* and *Perseveranza* all demanded that Italy simply annex all territories that were occupied by Italian troops. The Fascists held a rally in Milan and planned demonstrations in Turin, Rome, and half a dozen smaller cities.

Under the circumstances, Clemenceau and Lloyd George favored giving Fiume to Italy at once and putting a stop to the burgeoning demands. Orlando, House wrote in his diary for April 22, "has ceased to attend the meetings of the Council of Four and relations are very strained. The whole world is speculating as to whether the Italians are 'bluffing' or whether they really intend . . . not signing the peace unless they have Fiume. It is not unlike a game of poker."

Wilson decided to call Orlando's bluff. Counting on the vast affection the Italian people had shown for him during his triumphal tour before the conference had begun, the President decided to speak directly to the Italian people, to take his case over the head of Orlando and win the Italians to his cause by himself.

Wilson informed Clemenceau and Lloyd George that he intended to issue a manifesto addressed to the Italian people, and Clemenceau and Lloyd George carefully did not oppose him but sat back silently, and let the president go. More than that, and ominously: Orlando, who heard that the president planned to resort to this ploy, also sat back and let Wilson proceed.

"It seems strange," Riddell said to Lloyd George before dinner, "that after all the secrecy that has been observed, one of the plenipotentiaries should appeal to the peoples of the world over the head of one of his colleagues with whom he has a difference of opinion, and in particular to the nation represented by that colleague. Which of the Fourteen Points does that come under?"

Lloyd George, Riddell noted in his diary, "only laughed."

Before Wilson delivered his statement to the press, he read it to Clemenceau and Lloyd George. Wilson, Lloyd George told Riddell, "is very pleased with it. Old Clemenceau said it was very good. He is an old dog."

"America," Wilson declared to the Italian people, "is Italy's friend . . . she is linked in blood as well as in affection with the Italian people. . . . Interest is not now in question, but the rights of peoples, of states new and old, of liberated peoples and peoples whose rulers have never accounted them worthy of right; above all, the right of the world to peace and to such settlements of interest as shall make peace secure. These, and these only, are the principles for which America has fought . . . only upon these principles, she hopes and believes, will the people of Italy ask her to make peace."

The president's manifesto was wonderfully eloquent. The reaction to it amazed him. Orlando, who had known Wilson's appeal was coming, announced at once that he was abandoning the conference and returning to Italy. Let the Italian people, Orlando said proudly, "choose between Wilson and me."

Orlando had been thinking for some time, House said in his

memoirs, of walking out of the conference, in order to show he was serious about not signing the treaty unless Italy's demands were met. Wilson's appeal, House thought, furnished Orlando "with an opportunity for a spectacular departure . . . and provoked a tremendous popular sympathy for him in France and at home."

When Orlando arrived back at the train station in Rome, he was greeted by a huge crowd, crying "Down with Wilson! Down with Wilson!" The portraits of Wilson that had been put up for his visit to Italy were now torn down. The president had played his strongest card—a direct appeal to the people—but he was three months late. His prestige, such as it had been, was utterly gone.

As for Orlando, who waited victoriously in Rome for the Big Three to beg him to return to the conference and accept Fiume at last: no call came.

"Well," one of the Italian delegates who stayed behind said to Clemenceau, "I see that your press is behind us."

"Yes," said Clemenceau, "but you know as well as I do what that means. I have a list here of the French papers which have been purchased by the Italian propagandist bureau, and the price paid for each paper."

Nicolson jotted a note in his diary about the Italian departure: "Good riddance."

Yet, although Orlando could go away, the Italian question would not. Why, asked the Italian editorial writers, did Wilson want to impose "absolute justice" on Italy alone? Why not address a proclamation to the British about the former German colonies they were taking? Why not address a proclamation to the French about the Saar Valley? And why not speak to the Yugoslavs about some of their acquisitions? And why not speak to the American people, too, about the Monroe Doctrine?

Why had Wilson not asked Britain to abandon Malta, Suez, and Gibraltar? If Britain were to be allowed the right to protect herself by occupying these pieces of territory, "why not recognize Italy's right to protect herself in the Adriatic by occupying those islands off the Dalmatian archipelago which would make her coast secure?"

In his newspaper *Popolo d'Italia* Benito Mussolini assured his countrymen that the ever-vigilant Fascist party "would not neglect Paris." The president may be contemptuous of "little Italy," but he need not think Italy was so puny as to submit to Wilson's swindle.

Gabriele d'Annunzio, flamboyant poet, addressed a national revival meeting:

"Our epic May begins. I am ready. We are ready.

". . . today only Italy is great . . . today she alone is pure. . . . Against us I see only big and small merchants, big and small usurers, big and small forgers. . . .

"In the face of criminal intrigues Italy must be bold. Powerless against defeated and distintegrating Russia, Germany, and Hungary, will the peace conference prevail over the most victorious of all nations, over the nation which saved all other nations?

"Fiume, Zara, Sebenico . . . Spalato . . . creatures of life, more alive today, in this Italian hour, than in all the past centuries of Rome and Venice, today more beautiful than yesterday and less so than tomorrow, impregnable flowers of Latin beauty, covered with the dew of blood and tears. . . ."

The Yugoslavs, Mussolini declared, would only "grit their teeth," if Italy chose to take Fiume—and whatever else Italy chose to take—for, after all, Yugoslavia did not have the wherewithal to oppose Italy; Yugoslavia lacked the "field artillery, machine guns, airplanes, ammunition, provisions and . . . internal cohesion."

THE JAPANESE

The Japanese suffered—silently, but intensely. Their proposal for a recognition of the principle of racial equality had been quashed. Then, when Lloyd George had returned from Fontainebleau, the Japanese—members of the Council of Ten—had been squeezed out of the Council of Four. It was explained that the members of the Council of Four were all chiefs of state or prime ministers—and, although Makino had once been premier, he was not the Japanese premier at the time of the conference. Colonel House took pains to inform Makino and Chinda that, for the time being, the Big Four were discussing only matters of European concern; when broader questions were raised, they would be called back in on an equal basis with the others. When told this, Makino "beamed with satisfaction."

Nonetheless, the Japanese still wanted Shantung, and, while they continued to smile, they were not amused, and they continued to insist on Shantung with stony determination.

Shantung, a Chinese province, had been taken over by Germany in 1898. Then, during the war, the Japanese had taken it from the Germans. In 1919, the question was whether the province was to be restored to China, or given to Japan. Clearly, the Chinese had the stronger claim to the territory. Unfortunately, in order to enlist Japanese aid against Germany during the war, the governments of Britain, France, and Italy had secretly promised to give Shantung to Japan.

Once again, Wilson could have saved the Allies by declaring that he would simply not honor that secret agreement. Once again, Wilson hesitated. And once again, the league was used as leverage against Wilson: the Japanese would vote for the league, if Wilson would give them Shantung. It was, Lansing remarked dryly, "a species of 'blackmail' not unknown to international relations in the past."

Wilson's dilemma was not nice: if he gave Shantung to Japan, China would not vote for the league; if he gave Shantung to China, Japan would not vote for the league; and, whatever he did, it had begun to come clear to all the delegates, if not quite yet to Wilson, that, whatever refined and dignified language the president might like to indulge himself in, he, too, was dealing in bribery.

"This afternoon," Colonel Stephen Bonsal wrote in his diary for April 24, "Makino and Chinda appeared by appointment, as solemn a pair of Dromios as I have ever seen. And only a few hours before we had learned that Orlando had run out on the conference. . . . Makino said he had come in all frankness to announce that Japan would not sign the treaty"—unless Japan was given control of Shantung. Makino must insist, he said, on "a definite settlement of this question . . . with the least possible delay."

The Japanese sense of timing was exquisite. With Italy gone from the conference, and, as Bonsal said, "with Russia absent and the Central Empires at least temporarily excluded, should the Rising Sun Empire withdraw, our World Congress, or whatever it is, could dwindle to the proportions of a rump parliament."

The Japanese also happened to possess a good deal of political credit with President Wilson. Makino and Chinda had made it their business to come to Wilson's aid repeatedly in debates; they had backed the president immediately and firmly when he asked to have the Monroe Doctrine recognized. Some cynics might say that the Japanese tried to ingratiate themselves with Wilson because America had historically been a friend of China. Nonetheless, Wilson and House understood that they had become indebted to the Japanese.

On April 26, Wilson called on House in the colonel's rooms at the Crillon. Lansing, White, and Bliss were present, and House noted in his diary that both Wilson and Lansing "lean toward China, while in this instance my sympathies are about evenly divided, with a feeling that it would be a mistake to take such action against Japan as might lead to her withdrawal from the conference."

A couple of days later, after a desultory formal meeting, Lloyd George took House aside and asked if the colonel could not get Wilson "in a more amenable frame of mind. He thought the President was unfair to Japan and so does Balfour.... The concession ... which the Japanese have taken over as a part of their spoils of war is bad enough; but it is no worse than the doubtful transactions that have gone on among the Allies."

"President Wilson," Sir Maurice Hankey wrote to Lady Hankey, "with his wretched, hypocritical Fourteen Points, has already alienated the Italians, and is now about to alienate the Japs."

In Lansing's judgment, the Japanese case was so flagrantly contrary to international law, justice, the principle of self-determination, and common sense, that he thought the Japanese should be allowed to leave Paris. Lansing thought that, in fact, the Japanese would not leave, because they needed the international recognition that participation in the conference had given them. But he thought in any case that it was inconceivable that Wilson should agree to hand a piece of China to Japan.

General Bliss spoke for all of the Lesser Three in a letter to the President: "If it be right for Japan to annex the territory of an Ally, then it cannot be wrong for Italy to retain Fiume taken from the enemy.

"If we support Japan's claim, we abandon the democracy of China to the domination of the Prussianized militarism of Japan."

Ray Stannard Baker, summoned to Wilson's study to give the president some materials on the Shantung question, "pinned up a good map on the wall of the President's study and made as strong a case as I could for the Chinese position, urging some postponement at least. The President listened with that intensity of attention which is sometimes disconcerting, and when I had concluded making my points—which I had written down beforehand, to make them as brief and clear as possible—the President said:

" 'Baker, the difficulty is not with the facts of the controversy, but with the politics of it.' "

Balfour came up with the solution. In a memorandum that he prepared for the Big Three, Balfour noted that he understood that "if Japan received what she claimed in regard to Shantung, her representatives at the plenary meeting would content themselves with a survey of the inequality of races and move some abstract resolution which would probably be rejected. Japan would then merely make a protest. If, however, she regarded herself as ill-treated over Shantung, he was unable to say what line the Japanese might take."

The deal was made. Shantung was given to Japan. The Japanese stayed. The league was saved once again. The diplomats—even those who had urged Wilson to give Shantung to Japan—were disgusted. No one resigned, but the Chinese representative, Wellington Koo, did let it be known that he would not sign the treaty—and he did not. The Chinese, he said, would kill him. "If I sign the Treaty," he explained to Colonel House, "—even under orders from Peking—I shall not have what you in New York call a Chinaman's chance."

Still, although they won the Japanese signature, the president and his European allies had not won the affection or trust of the Japanese. On the contrary, they reinforced an impression that the Japanese could not get what they wished from the West through peaceful negotiations—and laid the ground for the Japanese invasion of Manchuria in the 1930s.

THE ZIONISTS

Mr. Chaim Weizmann appeared on behalf of the Anglo-Saxon Jewish community, Nahum Sokolow for Eastern Europe, and Sylvain Lévi for Western Europe. Lévi said that the French Zionists were not asking for an independent Zionist state, but only for the right to settle Jewish communities in Palestine on an equal basis with the neighboring Moslems and Christians. Weizmann and Sokolow listened impatiently to Lévi; they both favored an independent state.

Auguste Gauvin, a writer for the journal *Débats* and self-appointed spokesman for the moderates, sided with Lévi. Jews and Arabs were so scrambled together in Palestine, Gauvin said, that it was beyond the powers of the conference to unscramble them. "Very few Jews," Gauvin concluded lightly, "want to go to their Holy Land and ours, and also unfortunately the sanctuary of the Arabs, except as tourists or to make a religious pilgrimage. Perhaps the whole question could be solved if it was placed in the hands of a competent tourist agency."

Feisal (through Lawrence of Arabia) presented the counterargument: "If the views of the radical Zionists . . . should prevail, the result will be ferment, chronic unrest, and sooner or later civil war in Palestine. But I hope I will not be misunderstood. . . . I assert that with the Jews who have been settled for some generations in Palestine our relations are excellent. But the new arrivals exhibit very different qualities from those 'old settlers,' as we call them. . . . For want of a better word I must say that the new colonists almost without exception have come in an imperialistic spirit."

Balfour was agitated. His declaration to the House of Commons on November 2, 1917, had become a centerpiece of controversy. The Balfour Declaration, which many delegates to Paris took to be the promise of a Jewish state, "was not inspired by sentiment," Balfour said plaintively, "although I am free to admit I think we owe the Jews something substantial for the way, in all quarters of the world and on many battlefronts, they have rallied to the support of the Allies." Balfour understood—whether in terms of Jews, Arabs, or Palestinians—that a people without a turf are, according to the first law of politics, powerless—and destined either to be preyed upon or to become outlaws or guerrillas. All politics is based upon having and holding a turf as base. No one without a turf can be safe.

But Balfour was far more interested in a sort of justice or sentiment that preserved a balance of power in the Middle East favorable to the British Empire. "Not the least of my grievances is the fact that neither my critics nor my friends have really read my declaration. . . . I came out for a Jewish homeland in Palestine in so far as it could be established without infringing on the rights of the Arab communities, nomad as well as sedentary. Indeed I thought that in the terms of my declaration the rights of the Arabs were safeguarded as never before.

"... I thought that our war aim was to give equal rights and even-handed justice to all the oppressed. May I not say that was our rallying cry and that it reverberated throughout the world? ... It was, I thought," Balfour concluded disingenuously, "merely a happy coincidence that this belated act of justice to the Jews would establish their national home at the Eurasian crossroads and would prove a protection to the wasp waist of our empire, Suez."

THE BOLSHEVIKS AGAIN

"My life is rather unsettled," Seymour wrote home, "as I am on call at any moment, on account of the revolution in Budapest.... We got news of the revolution on Saturday night at Le Rond's dinner. This was a very sporty affair at the Cercle Interallié, which is one of the old houses on the Faubourg St.-Honoré next to the British Embassy with beautiful gardens opening out on the Champs Elysées. There must have been about 20 there, and I was amused as I came into the room (I was rather late) to find that I knew every one of the group....

"I have not had dinner in the Crillon for nearly a week. In the afternoon we went to the Madeleine, where there was lovely music—Gregorian chants beautifully sung—and a very long but interesting sermon. We got out at 4:30 and walked for an hour, ending up at Latinville's on the rue la Boétie, where one gets about as good cakes as are now to be had in Paris."

Nicolson was dispatched eventually to Budapest to see with his own eyes the hunger, fuel shortage, collapse of order, broken windows, unmowed lawns and litter, disillusion, boarded doorways, staring crowds, rage, theft, unclothed children, and civil war that the peace conference was trying to sort out—and to report to Paris what might be done. The Communists had taken over—some blamed the slowness of the diplomats in Paris to settle on some final peacetime order. It was the first Communist revolution in Europe, and Hungary was led by an unknown, Béla Kun.

One day Béla Kun was in jail, undergoing the customary police beating. Two days later he was the effective head of state of the Hungarian Soviet Republic—cabling Lenin for instructions about what to do next—and, soon, dispatching revolutionaries to Bulgaria, Austria, Rumania, and Germany. Seymour wrote home: "If no prompt action is taken it looks as if Vienna would be the next to go Bolshevik and after that probably Prague."

The mission to Béla Kun was headed by General Jan Smuts, Slim Jannie, who had fought against Britain in the Boer War, and then, as minister of defense in the new South African government, had shown himself to be such an agreeable character that Lloyd George had asked him to join the British war cabinet. He was a League of Nations man, conciliatory, patient, cool under fire.

When the train passed through Basel, it was snowing. In Austria, the train stopped frequently. Nicolson noticed out of the window that the suburban trains were crowded, with nearly all their windows broken. "Everybody looks very pinched and yellow: no fats for four years." In Vienna, paper was strewn about, windows broken, and the people looked "dejected and ill-dressed." Nicolson was stricken with embarrassment by his neat English clothes and his "plump pink face." Crowds followed the members of the mission through the streets; policemen accompanied them everywhere.

"Go off to Sachers to luncheon." Smuts was enraged, calling the extravagant lunch a "gross error in taste." He declared that henceforth the members of the mission would eat only their own army rations "and not take anything from these starving countries. His eyes when angry are like steel rods. But it was a good luncheon all the same."

In Budapest, they met Béla Kun: "a little man of about 30: puffy white face and loose wet lips: shaven head: impression of red hair: shifty suspicious eyes: he has the face of a sulky and uncertain criminal. He has with him a little oily Jew—fur-coat rather moth-eaten—stringy green tie—dirty collar. He is their Foreign Secretary."

Béla Kun and his contingent had come to the railroad station to confer with Smuts aboard the mission's train. The cars sat on a siding just outside the station. While Smuts and Béla Kun talked, the foreign secretary was ushered in to talk to Nicolson. "He takes the high culture line. . . . He quotes, with great irrelevance, 'I stood in Venice on the Bridge of Sighs.' The rain patters on the roof of our carriage."

Smuts told Nicolson that Kun was nervous. His Red Army was really run by people from the old regime; he had come into power not so much as a Communist but rather as a nationalist. He was caught in the middle: if he let the Communists down he would lose the people; if he let the old guard down he would lose the army. He hoped the Smuts mission would come on into town and show, by its presence, that the Béla Kun regime was taken seriously by the world. "He has, it seems, hoisted a huge Union Jack and a huge Tricolour" atop the Hungaria Hotel, Budapest's finest. But Smuts would not budge from the train.

Along with official recognition for his regime, Kun wanted a modification of Allied plans regarding the Rumanian frontier. He suggested a conference in Vienna or Prague; Smuts suggested that Kun come to Paris. Kun went off to consult his cabinet.

When Kun returned, he "sat there hunched, sulky, suspicious, and frightened. . . . The Spanish and Swiss Consuls . . . confirm what everybody says, namely, that Béla Kun is just an incident and not worth treating seriously." Smuts handed Kun a document that called for Allied occupation of a neutral zone between Hungary and Rumania. The signature of such a document would itself constitute a kind of recognition of Kun's regime. But Kun was suspicious still. He needed to consult his cabinet.

Nicolson went out for a drive. The car stopped at the Hungaria. The Red Guards said that the British were invited in for tea. The British thought they would decline, but when they noticed that the guards were frightened, they agreed to the invitation. In the foyer of the hotel many people were having coffee and lemonade at little tables. They were well dressed. An orchestra played. It was old Budapest, music, pastry, conversation. But there was no conversation. "It is some time before I realize what is wrong . . . there is something uncanny about it and unreal . . . each single table is absolutely silent. Not a word do they address to each other as they sip their lemonade. If one looks up suddenly one catches countless frightened eyes." It was, Nicolson concluded, a put-up job; and whoever had staged this little vision of old Budapest had forgotten to tell the performers that they must make conversation at the tables.

Béla Kun returned to the train, and handed a note to Smuts. Kun accepted Smuts's terms, but added a new clause concerning withdrawal of the Rumanian Army. Evidently Kun thought Smuts's original document was merely the first stage in negotiations.

Smuts handed the paper back to Béla Kun. "No, gentlemen," he told the little group of Hungarians, "this is not a note which I can accept. There must be no reservations." Kun seemed to think that Smuts would make a counterproposal. But Smuts had decided he did not need to take Kun seriously, that Kun was not sufficiently ruthless to be dangerous, that the best thing for the Allies to do was nothing at all.

"Well, gentlemen," said Smuts, "I must bid you good-bye."

"They do not understand. He conducts them with exquisite courtesy onto the platform. He shakes hands with them. He then stands on the step of the train and nods to his A.D.C. They stand in a row upon the platform, expecting him to fix the time for the next meeting. And as they stand the train gradually begins to move. Smuts brings his hand to the salute. We glide out into the night, retaining on the retinas of our eyes the picture of four bewildered faces looking up in blank amazement."

BULLITT'S RETURN

When Bullitt returned to Paris from Moscow, believing that he had handled the Russian negotiations with brilliance, produced a tour de force of diplomacy, and found a way to avert what would otherwise have become the greatest conflict of his time, he rushed to see President Wilson at once. He was stunned to be told that Wilson could not see him at the moment because the president had a headache.

Bullitt sought out Lloyd George. The mission to Moscow had, after all, been undertaken equally on behalf of the British, and he thought that he would break the good news to the prime minister, whose liberal background might, in any case, incline him to take a leading role in pressing the Russian negotiations to a successful conclusion. But Lloyd George declined to receive Bullitt and, as

Richard Watt has written, "went so far as to imply that the British government had never even heard of him and his mission."

The French were positively delighted not to discuss the Moscow mission with Bullitt. When Bullitt called on Colonel House, House referred him to the staff at the Crillon, who were not interested in his report.

The Big Three, who had been staunchly counterrevolutionary only a few weeks before, had somehow drifted into a new position altogether: they had come, simply, by design or distraction, to ignore the revolutionary movements that sputtered and raged throughout the world—and the people who were driven to embrace them. If Bullitt had been able to talk to Lloyd George or to Wilson, if the diplomats in Paris had been able to focus on the meaning of the revolution in Russia, or if the socialists had had any influence on the formulation of plans for the postwar world—it might not have made any difference anyway.

THE BELGIANS

The Belgians kept insisting that they were being unfairly treated. Belgium had borne the brunt of the destruction of the war, but it seemed that France was to get first claim on all the funds for rebuilding and restoration, the reparations and indemnities. It began to appear that it had been foolhardy for the Belgians to resist the Germans: now that the war was over, Belgium did not have the leverage of a great power to insist on its due for the sacrifices it had made.

M. Hyams, the Belgian foreign secretary, irritated Clemenceau one day by taking a particularly long time to argue his case.

"Come on, get down to the point," said Clemenceau.

Hyams talked on, working himself into a passion, banging on the table to emphasize his points.

"You will hurt your hand in another minute," Clemenceau said; "if you keep on banging like that, we shall not hear what you say when you do arrive at your point."

Finally Hyams sat down, having argued in vain for his country, prepared to go on arguing in vain, evidently feeling deeply discouraged. "Is there any further service," he asked, "you think I could render my country?"

"Yes," said Clemenceau.

"What?"

"Go and drown yourself."

In the future, if the Germans were to invade Belgium again, who could blame the Belgians if they simply waved the Germans on toward Paris?

THE EMPTY ROOM

The conference seemed to have ended, and yet meetings continued to be called and problems continued to be referred to committees. Nicolson attended a meeting of the Council of Five, "a scrubby affair compared to the old Clemenceau–Ll. G.–Wilson days. There is a feeling of 'another place.' The emptiness of the room is emphasized by the absence of the Italians." Only Lansing, Pichon, Hardinge, and the Japanese were there, discussing issues that seemed stale and inconsequential. "The secretaries and experts have become more familiar and take liberties which they would never have dared in the hot silence of the old Ten. Even the interpreter is not Mantoux, but a dim diffident person in pince-nez."

Keynes could no longer resist the temptation to write a parody of the minutes of a meeting of the Council of Three:

"The question before the Council was whether Belgium should have priority in Indemnity payments and should receive from Germany the 'costs of the war.'

"Three Belgian Delegates addressed the Council, each in a set speech.

"M. Hyams read a number of letters to which nobody paid attention. M. Clemenceau slept. President Wilson read the paper. Mr. Lloyd George kept up a running fire of comments, to the effect that M. Hyams was in his best form, was a poseur of the old type, and was attempting blackmail.

"M. Van den Heuvel delivered his oration in a falsetto voice which attracted the attention of the British Prime Minister, who compared it to a number of other voices, human and animal, that he remembered to have heard. . . .

"M. Vandervelde very nearly lost the chance of speaking at all as M. Clemenceau at this stage of the proceedings woke up and was inclined to interrupt. M. Vandervelde insisted however on delivering the speech. . . .

"Mr. Lloyd George remarked that this fellow was really very good: but that he talked a good deal more about Belgium's right than about Belgium's fight. The Belgians, in point of fact, never fought at all. They refused to fight. And now they were trying to bully. Mr. Lloyd George would not endure being bullied. How many dead had Belgium in comparison with Australia?

"The Belgian delegates having delivered their speeches, M. Clemenceau was woken up. President Wilson put down the paper, and remembering the Fourteen Points reminded the assembly that his conscience could not allow Belgium to claim the costs of the war.

". . . It was then discovered that the French Delegates were attempting to fix up with the Belgians an arrangement that would be considerably to the advantage of the French. Mr. Lloyd George was warned and immediately protested. This woke up everybody. There was a general melee in the middle of the room, where explanations and protests, avowals and disavowals, were tossed about in noisy confusion. Nothing of what was said could be clearly distinguished above the storm except the cries of M. Clemenceau who wailed continuously, 'Kill them, kill them.' Suddenly Mr. Lloyd George emerged from the tumult and flounced out of the room in a passion, winking to himself."

❦

OPEN DIPLOMACY

A plenary session was called for three o'clock on the afternoon of April 28. The full delegations arrayed themselves around the horseshoe table and commenced at once to whisper, confer, rustle papers, and exhibit as much boredom and inattention as they could muster, while the journalists stood on their chairs at the back of the hall to try to be the first to get the inside story.

Baron Makino rose and made "a very eloquent and dignified appeal," as Shotwell said, for racial equality, but, "recognizing that this was not the time to push his case withdrew all opposition to the covenant in its present form."

Léon Bourgeois read a long and tedious speech about the need to assure security for France by means of a general agreement on disarmament, and, although his delivery had about it "a certain solemnity," none of the delegates bothered to comment on the proposal, and the French themselves declined to put forward any proposal requiring a vote.

One moment stood out from the others for its apparent spontaneity. Pichon rose unexpectedly and proposed Monte Carlo for membership in the League of Nations. Evidently no prior deal had been made about Monte Carlo, and the conference was taken by surprise. Clemenceau "straightened up," said Shotwell, "angry and alert and in a rasping voice asked Pichon what was the meaning of it. Pichon replied nervously and haltingly that he didn't know any reason why Monte Carlo should not be made a member of the league."

Clemenceau replied without hesitation, but somewhat vaguely, "Well, I know one anyway." And then the Tiger focused his attention elsewhere in the room, while Pichon sat down again confused, and for the remainder of the session, Clemenceau kept his back turned to the French delegation.

A delegate from Panama delivered a long speech in broken French about certain principles of international law—a speech that no one quite caught—and then a delegate from Honduras delivered another long speech, this one in Spanish, protesting the way in which the conference had sanctified the Monroe Doctrine.

"Neither of these," Shotwell said, "was translated."

THE UKRAINIANS

"There is undeniably a crisis in our archives," Stephen Bonsal wrote in his diary. "There simply isn't any more room in our safe for the countless memoranda that I have drawn up . . . from the authorized Ukrainian delegates and from the free-lance volunteers who also abound." As Bonsal looked at the mess of memoranda, he was forced to admit, too, that few of them—possibly none of them—had been attentively read by the commissioners.

"In my judgment, if we are to bring the blessings of peace to Eastern Europe, forty million of its inhabitants should not be ignored. But what was I to do with this mass of neglected and also I must admit often quite contradictory information? The dossier weighs about ten pounds."

Presently, a memo came from Captain Patterson, who looked after some of the housekeeping details at the Hotel Crillon. Memoranda should not be thrown into wastebaskets, Patterson's memo said, lest they fall into the hands of spies. Rather, all papers should be taken down to the cellar and burned.

Bonsal took the Ukrainian papers down to the furnace in the cellar, but the Ukrainian dossier "did not go up in flames—it simply curled up and smoked and smouldered."

Nor could Bonsal get rid of the Ukrainians themselves. The next day a group of them called on Bonsal and made another appeal for an independent Ukraine, saved from the clutches of the Russians, and established on both banks of the Dnieper. The Russians, they said, wanted to destroy their belief in God; the Germans tried to rob them of their language; they could side with neither the one nor the other; they must be independent—and yet, they needed backing for this independence. "The Allies, thanks to America, have won the war; but will they win the peace?"

Bonsal had his instructions, and he told the Ukrainians what he was constrained to tell them: "You must place your trust in the League of Nations, which is being fashioned now by the forward-looking peoples. Its purpose is collective security and freedom for all. . . . It will be watchful and ready to curb any movement that threatens the peace of the world."

🌿
DINNER AT THE RITZ

Nicolson sat next to Proust. "Very Hebrew. . . . He asks more questions. I am amused by this. I suggest to him that the passion for detail is a sign of the literary temperament. This hurts his feelings. He says, 'Non pas!' quite abruptly and then blows a sort of adulatory kiss across the table at Gladys Deacon. But he soothes down again later. We discuss inversion. Whether it is a matter of glands or nerves. He says it is a matter of habit. I say, 'Surely not.' He says, 'No—that was silly of me—what I meant was that it was a matter of delicacy.' "

Carlo Placci was there. Placci told Nicolson that the English do not understand the Italians. Placci said that the Italians feel about the Croats the way the English feel about the Germans. Nicolson replied that he regarded the Germans "as a perfectly delightful people of great culture but having suffered from bad government."

"You are not serious," Placci said. "That is the worst of your public school education. You are never serious."

Placci said that Britain and France had gotten all they wanted out of the war and now were pushing Italy to one side. As for Wilson, said Placci, he had violated his Fourteen Points repeatedly for Britain and France and now, with Italy, he was trying "to regain his virginity."

PART SIX
THE GERMAN COUNTEROFFENSIVE

THE GERMAN DELEGATION

On April 28, a special train left Berlin to take the 160 members of the German delegation to the Paris Peace Conference. The train steamed through Germany and Belgium at a good clip, but then, as it entered the regions of the battlefields of northern France, the French authorities had the train slowed to fifteen kilometers an hour. In some villages, the German train was stopped altogether, and held, waiting, until the Germans had had time to go to the windows and look out on the devastated streets and homes. Then the journey was resumed, slowly, through ravaged farmlands—to another village, where the train would stop again, and wait. Like many of the English and American delegates, many of the Germans had had no idea of the devastation of the war until they were compelled to tour slowly through these battlefields.

The delegation was led by the German foreign minister, Count Ulrich von Brockdorff-Rantzau, a slender, monocled offspring of generations of generals and diplomats, a monarchist who had recently discovered a profound love of democracy in his heart, a high-strung and condescending man, sometimes haughty, sometimes charming, sometimes bantering, often abrupt. It was said that he slept during the day and wrote at night, that he liked definite decisions, clear-cut policies, detested compromise, would drink cognac at any hour, and enjoyed exercising his cutting wit on anyone at hand. He had no close friends, and he was the epitome of all that Clemenceau, Lloyd George, and Wilson hated about Germans.

While Brockdorff-Rantzau traveled aboard the train to Paris, he was confidentially briefed about what to expect at the conference by an American, Colonel Conger, sent by President Wilson.

"Clemenceau will make a speech," Conger told Brockdorff-Rantzau, "and then you will probably have an opportunity of saying a few words. Much will depend on your general attitude."

The foreign minister wasted no charm on Conger. He mentioned Wilson's Fourteen Points and said, "Those are my fundamental principles."

The colonel had not been delegated to talk abut the terms of the treaty. However, he told Brockdorff-Rantzau, if he did not accept the terms, "You will be compelled to sign."

"I am relying," the count replied, "on the President's word of honor."

The Weimar government, and the German people generally, proceeded on the basis that they had not surrendered unconditionally, but that they had ceased fighting on the understanding that a peace agreement would be based on Wilson's Fourteen Points. The Germans understood that their acceptance of Wilson's terms was legally binding—on the Allies as well as on themselves.

The Germans expected, therefore, to have to make some unpleasant sacrifices: the Fourteen Points specifically mentioned that Alsace-Lorraine would be returned to France—but they did not regard their situation as impossible. They relied on Wilson's promises of a peace of justice, not of vengefulness, and on the repeated words of Allied leaders that their war was not with the German people but with the militarist, monarchist German government that had recently been replaced by the Weimar Republic.

In addition to these ingenuous expectations of justice and mercy, some members of the German government entertained more opportunistic notions. Brockdorff-Rantzau, for one, stressed to his colleagues the divisions among the Allies and thought that the disagreements among Clemenceau, Lloyd George, and Wilson could be exacerbated, that the Big Three could be pitted against one another so that the Germans could finesse even more favorable terms from the victors.

Moreover, Brockdorff-Rantzau was determined not simply to rely on Wilson's ethical pronouncements but to insist on them, to embarrass the Allies with them, to exploit them, to drive them back down the gullets of the victors. The Fourteen Points, in Brockdorff-Rantzau's view, were Germany's last weapons of war.

In preparation for the conference, the government had named a special committee to study the probable topics to be covered there. Because the Germans had no idea what stance the Allies would take on which issues, the special committee churned out an interminable succession of position papers, all thoroughly researched, painstakingly documented, and dreadfully inclusive. And when they had finished their assigned topics and discovered they had still more time, the researchers set about thinking of other possible topics and filling yet more volumes with possible replies to imagined charges, injustices, judgments, and demands.

Brockdorff-Rantzau did not need a committee, however, to instruct him on what he took to be the essential issue: he understood that the Allies would allege that Germany alone bore responsibility for starting the war. He understood, too, that on the basis of that charge the Allies would feel they could justify any penance they wished to inflict on Germany. The issue of war guilt was crucial, and Brockdorff-Rantzau had a very clear view on the matter: the war was the result of great historical and economic trends that had propelled all the European nations toward conflict; and, if there were any individuals responsible for starting the war, they could certainly be found in almost every country, but especially in Russia, Serbia, and France.

When the German train arrived at the Versailles terminal, a Colonel Henri of the French Army stepped forward to greet the delegates. "I have been ordered," Henri said perfunctorily, "to see to your reception."

The Germans were escorted through a crowd of photographers to waiting cars that took them to a splendid old hotel, set in a park, the Hotel des Reservoirs. Their luggage was dumped unceremoniously in the courtyard and they were left to find their own way to their rooms. The Hotel des Reservoirs, the Germans learned, was where the French peace commission had been installed in 1871 when they had come to Versailles to seek favorable terms from Bismarck.

Sentries with loaded rifles patrolled the gates in front of the hotel, and the Germans were restricted to walks in the park. They were surrounded by barbed wire. Thus, they waited. They got up in the morning at seven-thirty, had breakfast in the dining room, strolled in the park, and talked in the lobby. In the afternoons, committees assigned to specific topics met and talked and went on with their tedious researches. The Germans had been informed by their experts that their rooms might be bugged, and that the only way to prevent spies from picking up their conversations was to play music. And so, for several days, until the hotel had been checked thoroughly for microphones, the corridors shook with the music that emanated from phonographs in each of the committee meeting rooms.

In the evenings, the six principal German delegates would meet in Brockdorff-Rantzau's room, drink brandy, keep warm in front of the smoky fireplace, and chat. In time, as he waited in vain for the Allies to present him with the finished treaty, Brockdorff-Rantzau came to wonder whether the Germans had been brought to Versailles simply to sit and wait in the old hotel as some elaborate form of humiliation.

FINISHING THE TREATY

"The President has had a hard day," Baker wrote in his diary. "The Three put nearly the finishing touches on the treaty so that it can now go to the printer; but the troublesome Belgian and Italian problems remain unsettled. . . . I have never seen the President look so worn and tired. A terrible strain, with everyone against him. He was so beaten out that he could remember only with an effort what the council had done in the forenoon."

Brockdorff-Rantzau had said that the German delegation would return to Berlin if they were not soon presented with the treaty. The Big Three hurried to get all the provisions down on paper and off to the printer so that they could present the treaty to the Germans on May 7—and yet, occasionally, still, they could not quite remember what they had decided on one issue or another, or whether they had discussed a topic that had been reported out of committee. Because they did not have time to go over the committee reports, they sometimes simply passed on a committee recommendation to the printer to be incorporated into the treaty, although the committee had meant its language to be taken only as a suggested starting point, perhaps the most extreme position on an issue that might then be trimmed back to a more moderate treaty provision.

Lloyd George, meantime, sent for the Italian ambassador and told him that if Orlando and Sonnino did not return to Paris by the morning of the seventh, the Big Three would consider the secret Treaty of London null and void.

"Would you mind repeating that?" said the Italian ambassador, ashen-faced.

Lloyd George repeated his threat.

The ambassador hurried away: the next day the diplomats in Paris heard that the Italians were coming back to Paris as quickly as they could—"fuming," some said. The printer was undone by the news; portions of the treaty had already been printed. Italy's name, as one of the Allied powers, would have to be added by hand.

Riddell drove out with Bonar Law for lunch at the Hotel du Forêt near Fontainebleau. Bonar Law said that he thought Lloyd George "had got the better of Wilson, who had had to give up most of his Fourteen Points."

General Bliss was completely disgusted with the treaty—as much as he knew of it. He did not know much—nor, for that matter, did anyone else, given the haste with which the treaty was being pasted together at the last minute. No one had read the whole treaty. "It is strange," Bliss wrote to a friend, "but true that the plenipotentiaries of the many nations supposed to be making the treaty of peace, will not know what is in the treaty any sooner than the Germans will know."

❦

THE PRINTED TREATY

"I am much troubled over our peace terms," Slim Jannie Smuts wrote to a friend. "I consider them bad. And wrong. And they may not be accepted. The world may lapse into complete chaos. And what will emerge? I don't know what to do."

Bonar Law said he was doubtful whether the Germans would accept the terms they were being offered. Churchill said that the Germans would be traitors to their country if they did accept the peace terms. In the event that the Germans refused, Foch was being asked to get the army ready. Bonar Law was not quite sure what the military could do. "They could occupy Westphalia," said Churchill, "but what is the good of that?"

"I am not enamored of our so-called peace terms," Smuts wrote in another letter. "Sometimes they appear to have been conceived more in a spirit of making war than of making peace."

In any event, the treaty was to be presented—this was definite—to the Germans at three o'clock in the afternoon on May 7, at the Trianon Palace at Versailles. Marshal Foch telephoned Field Marshal Sir Henry Wilson. Foch had gotten an advance look at the treaty, he said, and it was an immense volume that spoke of "the 'German Empire,' commenced with the League of Nations, did not allot the German colonies to anyone . . . was a mass of cross references, paragraphs changed, Articles substituted, etc., etc., with the net result that no one could possibly know what he was signing unless he could study the book as a whole. That nobody had studied it, that Tiger and Lloyd George had no notion what was in the book. . . ."

Not only did Sir Henry have no idea what was in the treaty, but he was even more dismayed by the thought that every day "instance after instance crops up of the shifting base on which we are building. Now the Esthonians—a small State—threaten to make a separate peace with the Bolsheviks, now the Finns are marching on Petrograd, now the Yugos are attacking the Austrians and have taken Klagenfurt, now the Rumanians are throwing the Hungarians over the Theiss, now the Bulgars are becoming truculent and have imprisoned some Greeks—and so on *ad infinitum*. And Paris remains paralytic and impotent."

Soon enough, Sir Henry was even more amazed and horrified. At a meeting of Bonar Law, Billy Hughes, Smuts, and a few others, Lloyd George read out some extracts from a "summary of the treaty." The prime minister could not read passages from the treaty itself, Sir Henry said, because "no one has ever seen it in its completed form, for it does not exist." Both Bonar Law and Smuts had been trying to get hold of complete copies, but could not. It was, they told Sir Henry, a "hopeless mess." So, Sir Henry realized, the

Allies were going to hand over the terms of the treaty to the Germans "without reading them ourselves first. I don't think in all history this can be matched."

Meanwhile, Lloyd George was saying to the British delegates that he thought the covenant for the League of Nations was a "ridiculous and preposterous document." And, Sir Henry noted, "the treaty opens with the league! And there were serious differences of opinion at the meeting on several questions of *principle!* And this at this hour." Sir Henry spoke to Balfour about all this—"and he, of course, like the others, has not seen [the treaty].... He was openly joking, in front of ladies, etc., about the farce of the whole thing—and yet he has to sign!"

In the afternoon of May 6, the major powers invited the minor powers to a meeting to "consult" on the final terms of the treaty. Because the full treaty was still not available, the minor powers had to content themselves with listening to André Tardieu read a forty-four-page summary of the treaty aloud. Since most of the delegates present did not understand French—and the length of Tardieu's presentation precluded the possibility of translation—few of the delegates understood at all what was being said.

The Italians, who had by this time returned to Paris, got around Clemenceau's gavel to announce that they reserved their own freedom of action on the matter of Fiume. The Chinese protested about Shantung. The Portuguese protested that they had never before signed a treaty that did not in some fashion call for the blessing of God on its provisions.

Marshal Foch demanded the floor. He must object, he said, to the imposition of a fifteen-year limit on French occupation of the Rhineland. "The Rhine alone is important," he said. "Nothing else matters." Otherwise a resurgent Germany would once again threaten the very existence of France.

Clemenceau, enraged that his own military chief had dared to criticize the treaty in public, gaveled the session to adjournment.

Late that evening, the printer commenced to put together the finished, printed treaty: it consisted of 440 articles, detailed in some 200 pages, 75,000 words, bound in a white cover. In the middle of the night, messengers carried copies of the bound treaty to the principal delegates around Paris. Herbert Hoover received his copy at four o'clock in the morning. "Hoover immediately read it through," according to Richard Watt, "and was horrified at its harshness. Unable to sleep, he dressed at first daylight and walked the deserted Paris streets. Within a few blocks he met others—Smuts and then John Maynard Keynes of the British delegation. 'It all flashed into our minds,' Hoover said, 'why each was walking about at that time of the morning.' "

When Lansing looked at his copy, he dictated an aide-mémoire: "For the first time in these days of feverish rush of preparation there is time to consider the treaty as a complete document. . . . The impression made by it is one of disappointment, of regret, and of depression."

All of the most extreme provisions the Allies had contemplated seemed to have made their way into the finished treaty: provisions that committees had thought would be compromised and modified into less harsh terms, provisions that had been meant as "maximum statements" to be worked back from; provisions that might be traded off against one another, one dropped as a bargaining concession in order to retain another—it seemed that every one of them had simply been thrust into the treaty and printed. Although any single provision might not seem unduly severe, when they were all added together—when the various committee members saw what other committees had had to add to the treaty—the cumulative effect was horrible. In every instance, it seemed, the scales had been tipped against Germany: the treaty was a work of malice.

Nothing was to be done that morning. The treaty was now in print. Nothing was left for the delegates to do but spend the morning in shocked recognition of what they had done—and proceed to present their consensus to the Germans.

At two o'clock Riddell set out at the leisurely, legal speed for the Trianon Palace, "driving through the Bois de Boulogne, St.-Cloud, and the lovely woods of Versailles. There was nothing to show that this was a momentous day in the world's history. Then suddenly I heard behind me the insistent and prolonged note of a motor horn. It was Clemenceau in his [chauffeur-driven] Rolls-Royce, driving to Versailles at fifty miles an hour, one gloved hand on each knee and 'a smile on the face of the Tiger' that made one feel that the drama was really beginning. He was gone in a flash."

THE PRESENTATION OF
THE TREATY

Count Brockdorff-Rantzau, pale, perspiring, wearing a black frock coat and using a slender walking stick, led his delegation slowly, deliberately down the narrow corridor from the rear entrance of the Trianon Palace Hotel at Versailles, past half-opened doors through which maids and menservants peered to catch a glimpse of the Germans, past the cloakroom, bar, smoking rooms, and then through the entrance, at last, to the conference room. There he stopped, dazzled and disoriented by the sudden explosion of sunlight reflected in the vast mirrors, the chandeliers, the white walls, sunlight entering through the great glass door and eight large windows. Brockdorff-Rantzau was momentarily bewildered by the reflection from outdoors, through this sea of light, of trees and flowering shrubs, green lawns and sky.

Colonel Henri announced in sharp, ringing tones: "Messieurs les délégués allemands!"

Brockdorff-Rantzau was aware of the sounds of scraping chair legs, the sounds of leather soles on the polished floor: the representatives of the Allied powers were rising to receive the German delegation. Brockdorff-Rantzau bowed. The room he had entered was about seventy-five feet square. Two windowed walls were thrown open; the third wall was white; the fourth wall was mirrored. About two hundred people filled the room. The tables at which the Allied plenipotentiaries sat were arranged around three sides of the room. On the fourth side, set apart, was a small table for the Germans.

Brockdorff-Rantzau moved stiffly to the table, followed by his associates and their secretaries and two interpreters. The foreign minister looked ill, Lord Riddell thought. "He walks with a slight limp. His complexion is yellowish, and there are black rings under his eyes which are sunk deep in his head."

As soon as the Germans were seated, Clemenceau stood.

"Gentlemen," said Clemenceau, "plenipotentiaries of the German Empire, it is neither the time nor the place for superfluous words. . . . The time has come when we must settle our accounts. You have asked for peace. We are ready to give you peace."

Brockdorff-Rantzau was not certain, even at this moment, whether the Allies intended now to have a peace conference in which victors and vanquished sat down and bargained over the final terms—as had occurred at the Congress of Vienna, when Talleyrand had played the victors off against one another so brilliantly that he demolished the whole treaty—or whether this was to be an imposed, or dictated peace. Brockdorff-Rantzau's uncertainty was soon resolved.

"We shall present to you now a book which contains our conditions. You will be given every facility to examine those conditions . . . you will find us ready to give you any explanation you want, but we must say at the same time that this peace which we are about to discuss has cost all the nations here assembled too much, and we are unanimously resolved to make use of every means in our power to ensure that we obtain every justifiable satisfaction that is our due." The Allies would be pleased to receive, within a period of fifteen days, any "observations"—in writing—that the Germans cared to make.

Then, with his customary brusqueness, Clemenceau demanded whether anyone wished to speak.

Brockdorff-Rantzau raised his hand like a schoolboy and took from his papers, which contained two possible speeches, the more hostile reply.

"Gentlemen," he began, "we are deeply impressed with the sublime task which has brought us hither . . ."

None of the German diplomats had noticed, apparently, until this moment, what a dreadful public speaker Brockdorff-Rantzau was. He seemed dexterous and graceful in intimate meetings, but he was unaccustomed to making speeches. His voice was high-pitched and harsh, and, when it came to some words, he positively hissed. He had a nervous tremor in his voice, and his knees were shaking.

Most of the diplomats in the room were shocked and offended that Brockdorff-Rantzau did not stand to address the gathering. Especially since Clemenceau had stood to address the Germans, Brockdorff-Rantzau's reply while seated appeared to be a deliberate affront to the Allies. A number of the diplomats found excuses for Brockdorff-Rantzau's behavior, saying that he must have been too nervous to stand, or had, under the pressure of the moment, forgotten.

In truth, Brockdorff-Rantzau had not stood up because he had seen in the French papers that morning the diagram of the arrangement of tables for the meeting and noticed that the German table was designated as the "banc des accusés." The count had sensed "in spirit," one of his colleagues said, "the words 'the prisoner will stand up,' and it was for that reason he kept his seat."

Only Balfour seemed unperturbed by the German's behavior. Later, when Nicolson asked Balfour whether the latter shared the general horror and indignation, Balfour replied, "What indignation?" "Oh, about Brockdorff-Rantzau's conduct." "What conduct?" "His not standing up when replying to Clemenceau." "Didn't he stand up? I failed to notice. I make it a rule never to stare at people when they are in obvious distress." Balfour, said Nicolson, "makes the whole of Paris seem vulgar."

"   to give a durable peace to the world. We are under no illusion as to the extent of our defeat and the degree of our want of power . . ."

Clemenceau broke in. He could not understand the translators, "Speak up! I can't hear a word!"

The translators spoke up, repeating what they had said. "Come nearer," Clemenceau demanded—and the translators stepped forward into the space in the middle of the horseshoe table. But Brockdorff-Rantzau had only one copy of his speech, and so, after each sentence, he had to give his manuscript page to the translators—to the French-speaking translator first, and then to the English-speaking translator—so that the speech proceeded in fits and starts, tediously, a sentence at a time, amid a rustle of papers, and the English-speaking translator, ill at ease, was seen to wipe the perspiration from his hands.

"We know," said Brockdorff-Rantzau, "the power of the hatred which we encounter here. . . .

"It is demanded of us that we shall confess ourselves to be the only ones guilty of the war."

Clemenceau tapped slowly on the table with an ivory paper knife.

"Such a confession in my mouth will be a lie." (Here the foreign minister seemed to hiss.)

Wilson toyed absently, as usual, with a pencil.

"We are far from declining any responsibility for this great world war having come to pass, and for its having been made in the way in which it was made . . . but we energetically deny that Germany and its people, who were convinced that they were making a war of defense, were alone guilty...."

Lloyd George squirmed in his chair, as he often did when he was annoyed, as though he might suddenly get up and hit someone.

"I ask you when reparation is demanded not to forget the armistice. It took you six weeks till we got it at last, and six months till we came to know your conditions of peace.... The hundreds of thousands of noncombatants who have perished since November 11 by reason of the blockade were killed with cold deliberation after our adversaries had conquered and victory had been assured to them. Think of that when you speak of guilt and of punishment."

Lloyd George found an ivory paper knife and turned it over and over in his hand until, at last, he snapped it in two. Wilson leaned over to him and whispered something. Some of the other Allied diplomats whispered among themselves. "The Germans are really a stupid people," Wilson said later. "They always do the wrong thing.... This is the most tactless speech I have ever heard." "Beasts they were," said Balfour, "and beasts they are."

By the time Brockdorff-Rantzau finished speaking, the whole room was murmuring with outrage. When the foreign minister at last subsided, Clemenceau broke in: "Has anybody any more observations to make? Does no one wish to speak? If not, the meeting is closed."

Brockdorff-Rantzau rose. Everyone in the conference room rose. Brockdorff-Rantzau turned and led his delegation back out the door, back through the narrow corridor, and out to where their cars waited for them. While the secretaries gathered up the diplomats' coats and hats, Brockdorff-Rantzau stood on the steps, looking out into the gardens, leaning on his walking stick. He ignored the photographers. Reserved, remote, somewhat contemptuous, he put a cigarette between his lips, which trembled slightly, lit it nonchalantly, and strolled on down to his limousine.

The "predominant feeling," Walter Simons wrote home to his wife in Germany, "was that of a great unreality. Outside of the big window on my right there was a wonderful cherry tree in bloom, and it seemed to me the only reality when compared with the performance in the hall."

Lloyd George was enraged, Frances Stevenson wrote in her diary, "& it was some time before he became himself again. The Germans were very arrogant and insolent, & Brockdorff-Rantzau did not even stand up to make his speech.... D. said that he felt he could get up & hit him, & he had the greatest difficulty in sitting still."

Yet, soon enough, the prime minister recovered his good cheer. "Went down to St.-Cloud with D. for golf & stayed there to tea," Miss Stevenson wrote in her diary the next day. "A perfect afternoon, D. in very good spirits, though he did not play golf well. . . . Everyone seems delighted with the peace terms, & there is no fault to find with them on the ground that they are not severe enough. Someone described it as 'a peace with a vengeance.' "

A READING OF THE TREATY

Back at the Hotel des Reservoirs, Brockdorff-Rantzau assembled the German delegation in the hotel's dining room. No one spoke. The feeling among those who had accompanied Brockdorff-Rantzau to the Trianon was that he had made a dreadful mistake in choosing to deliver the harsh speech. The foreign minister had been given only one copy of the treaty: the binding was torn apart, and sections were handed out to twenty translators to render into German. The delegates waited to read the terms.

By midnight, the translators had finished a rough translation. A courier was dispatched to take a mimeographed copy to Berlin. The delegates at the Hotel des Reservoirs took copies off to various corners to read. Dismay spread among the delegates: the treaty was much worse than they had imagined it might be. As they drifted back together in the early morning to talk about what they had read, they had already begun to refer to the treaty as a *Diktat*.

Within two days, in Berlin, thousands of copies of the treaty had been printed and were being hawked on the streets to a populace whose reaction was enraged and violent. On the streets outside the American military mission, crowds milled about, shouting a bitter, derisive chant about the loss of the Fourteen Points.

In the Great Hall of the University of Berlin, the National Assembly—transported from Weimar for the occasion of receiving the treaty in the German capital—heard first from Philipp Scheidemann, chancellor, who waved a copy of the treaty in the air and, to the unanimous applause of the assembly, cried: "This treaty is, according to the conception of the government, unacceptable. . . . What hand would not wither that binds itself and us in these fetters?"

"This peace," said the speaker from the Majority Socialist party, "is nothing more than a continuation of the war by other means. It is truly a product of a half-year's secret diplomacy."

"If our army," said Conrad Haussmann of the Democrats, "and our workmen had known on the fifth and ninth of November that the peace would look like this, the army would not have laid down its arms and all would have held out to the end."

Hugo Haase, of the Independent Socialist party, broke the spirit of unanimity only briefly when he recalled to the Assembly that the Germans had imposed a harsh treaty on the Russians at Brest-Litovsk in 1917—as harsh a treaty as this one the Allies had presented to Germany. But Haase, too, condemned the Versailles treaty, and the attacks continued without further abatement. "French revenge and English brutality" were remarked—and the utter hypocrisy of Woodrow Wilson.

Felix Fechenbach, president of the Assembly, said, "The unbelievable has happened; the enemy presents us a treaty surpassing the most pessimistic forecasts. It means the annihilation of the German people. It is incomprehensible that a man who had promised the world a peace of justice upon which a society of nations would be founded, has been able to assist in framing this project dictated by hate."

The speeches against the treaty continued for five hours without cease, and finally, when there was no more to be said, the exausted members of the Assembly rose before adjournment to sing: "Deutschland über Alles."

❧

BROCKDORFF-RANTZAU REPLIES

Although many of the Germans at Versailles wished simply to pack up and go, in order to show their disgust with the treaty, Brockdorff-Rantzau held them at the Hotel des Reservoirs and instructed them to draft their "observations" on the treaty for presentation to the Allies. Brockdorff-Rantzau's idea was clear and precise: the Germans had ceased fighting the war because of the "pre-armistice agreement" that a peace would be made in accord with Wilson's Fourteen Points. Now the Germans would insist the Allies must stick to their original, and binding, agreement. The German delegation would show, point by point, each particular of the treaty that did not agree with Wilson's Fourteen Points, and insist that the treaty provisions be changed.

Unfortunately, once the German experts set to work on the treaty, they fell afoul of the same confusion that had beset the Allied experts: the treaty was divided up among different experts; each group prepared its notes and handed them along for transmittal to the French; none of the experts from other areas conferred on overlapping concerns; often Brockdorff-Rantzau did not have time to read the notes before they were dispatched to Clemenceau; some notes protested on issues that had nothing to do with the Fourteen Points, some notes contradicted the Fourteen Points on which the Germans were now relying; haste sowed more confusion; and, finally, it seemed the Germans were determined to pick at every nit in the treaty, tediously, annoyingly, to stray from major issues into every minor vexation and slight that they could recall.

The notes were sent over to Clemenceau daily, sometimes several a day. Each note was given to a committee, which formed a response, usually a rebuttal. Sometimes Clemenceau, Lloyd George, and Wilson would gather to agree on a response. Sometimes Wilson would sit down at his own typewriter to peck out a reply. Sometimes a secretary or aide would write up something quickly; it would be typed, signed by Clemenceau, and sent back over to the Hotel des Reservoirs.

The exchange of notes descended almost at once into a wrangle over precedents and counterprecedents, old grudges from 1871, bitterness about the treatment of prisoners, accusations about torture, rape, starvation, sexual assaults on children, the murder of an old German peasant woman with a hatchet, the murder of a French farmer with a pruning knife—and many other issues that were beyond the powers of anyone to make good.

As for the question of war guilt, the Germans repudiated absolutely the imputation that they were solely responsible for starting the war. As they understood it—from what their government had said during the war, and from what they were able to discern independently, the German people had been attacked by czarist Russia, and the Germans had invaded France only to forestall an invasion that the French (still bitter from 1871) planned to launch against Germany. The war had been a dreadful tragedy. Of course the German government had been bad (had not some others been bad, too?)—but it was hardly wholly responsible for the war; and, in any case, it had been replaced.

As for the demand that the Germans hand over Kaiser Wilhelm II (who was, anyhow, in Holland) to be tried for "a supreme offense against international morality," that was odious. As for the notion that the Germans should also hand over for trial any other Germans that the Allies might choose, at their discretion, to accuse of having "committed acts in violation of the laws and customs of war" (whatever they were), that was out of the question. The Germans proposed instead that an independent "commission of inquiry" be set up; Germany would make its case openly before the commission; and then the world might judge just where responsibility for the war lay.

As for the provisions that Germany disarm: the best part of the imperial navy—nine battleships, five battle cruisers, seven light cruisers, fifty destroyers—were already being held captive at the British base at Scapa Flow. All German submarines had been surrendered. All submarines under construction had been broken up in the shipyards. And the treaty provided that the navy was to be reduced even further—to be restricted to a few old, and obsolescent, ships.

The German Army was to be reduced to seven infantry divisions and three cavalry divisions—96,000 soldiers and 4,000 officers—an army perhaps large enough to ensure internal order, to put down Communist riots and attempted coups, but certainly not large enough to invade any other country, and probably not large enough to protect Germany against invasion by any one of its neighbors, possibly even the smallest of its neighbors. Germany was to have no air force, no schools to educate military officers, no military societies, no shooting clubs, no associations of former soldiers. The number of guns to be permitted to the army was itemized exactly: 204 field guns and 84 howitzers, a small, specified number of mortars, rifles, and carbines, and 56 million rounds of small-arms ammunition. Germany might not have any tanks, poison gas, or aircraft of any kind. The officer corps was to be disbanded; the cadet schools were to be closed; and an Allied commission would have the right to go anywhere in Germany at any time to inspect any place to make certain that the military terms of the treaty were being obeyed.

To these disarmament provisions, Brockdorff-Rantzau protested with disdainful mildness. He observed that the Germans understood that such provisions were only the beginning of a general agreement for global reduction in armaments.

Next, according to the treaty, Germany must cede all vessels of her merchant marine that exceeded 1,600 tons gross, half of the vessels exceeding 1,000 tons, and a fourth of all trawlers and fishing boats. This provision included not only those ships sailing under German flag, but any ship flying another flag but owned by a German; the provision included ships afloat and ships under construction. In addition, Germany was required to build ships for the Allies—200,000 tons a year for five years—as requested.

"Thus," said Keynes, stating the argument of the Germans, "the German mercantile marine is swept from the seas and cannot be restored for many years to come on a scale adequate to meet the requirements of her own commerce."

As for colonies, Germany was required to cede "all her rights and titles over her overseas possessions"—including not only government possessions but also private property, whether of individuals or corporations. "So far as I know," said Keynes, "there is no precedent in any peace treaty of recent history for [such] treatment of private property."

But, more than all this, more sacred to a nation than its army or merchant marine or overseas interests is its own soil. Alsace and Lorraine were taken from Germany—as nearly everyone recognized they should have been. The Germans protested—illogically by their own terms, since the Fourteen Points specifically mentioned the need to restore Alsace-Lorraine to France—to no avail. The Saar Basin, which contained more coal than the whole of France, was taken from Germany and given to France. In the west, small bits of territory around Eupen and Malmédy were ceded by the Germans. In the north, a portion of Schleswig was to be ceded, depending upon a plebiscite, to Denmark. Danzig was taken from Germany and made into a free city in order to provide Poland access to the sea. A slice of East Prussia was to be submitted to plebiscite. In another slice of territory, that between the Nogat and Vistula rivers, the inhabitants would vote for German or Polish citizenship. A slice of territory around Memel, in the northeastern part of Prussia, was ceded. Upper Silesia was to be subject to plebiscite. What was formerly Prussian Poland—or, as the Germans said, Polish Prussia—was taken from Prussia and joined with the Polish kingdom of Russia to form the new Poland. In addition, Germany was to place under lease or international control the ports of Hamburg and Stettin, the Rhine, parts of the Moselle, the Elbe, the Oder, the Niemen, and the Danube.

Stripped of its armed forces, many of its mines, reduced in population by six and a half million, deprived of one-tenth of its factories, and of one-sixth of its farmland, deprived of its merchant marine, its colonies, and slices of its heartland, obliged to devote part of its industrial might to building ships for the Allies and to providing coal for France, Germany was then required to agree to pay reparations that might be any sum the Allies would care to name in the future.

Under the circumstances, said Brockdorff-Rantzau, there could be no way for Germany to revive her industry. And so there would be no way to give work and bread to her people. And so the catastrophe of starvation could not be far off for his people, the foreign minister said.

"Those who will sign this treaty," said Brockdorff-Rantzau, "will sign the death sentence of many millions of German men, women, and children."

❧

THE ALLIED RESPONSE

"And so," Jan Smuts wrote in anguish to a friend, "instead of making peace, we make war, and are going to reduce Europe to ruin. The smaller nations are all mad; they want credit, not for food for their starving population, but for military expenditure. It is enough to reduce one to complete despair. Poor old Europe, the mother of civilization."

In general, the British tended to blame Clemenceau; but Nicolson acknowledged, in a letter to his wife, that Lloyd George and the

British were at least equally responsible. "If I were the Germans I shouldn't sign for a moment."

Balfour was incensed: " 'Those three all-powerful, all-ignorant men' "—Nicolson quoted him as saying—" 'sitting there and carving continents with only a child to lead them!' I have the most uneasy suspicion that the 'child' in this case signified myself. Perhaps he meant Hankey. I hope he meant Hankey.... Yes ... let us assume that it was Hankey."

Balfour threatened to resign. So did Keynes, Lord Curzon, E. S. Montagu, and the maharajah of Bikaner.

"Lunch with Smuts," Nicolson noted in his diary for May 13. "He is very pessimistic. His view is that the world-crisis is one between government (he pronounces it 'gurment') and anarchy. The former, in his opinion, has shown itself incapable of constructive or directive thought.... He feels that all we have done here is worse, far worse, than the Congress of Vienna. The statesmen of 1815 at least knew what they were about. These don't."

"Under this treaty," Smuts wrote home, "the situation in Europe will become intolerable and a revolution must come, or again, in due course, an explosion into war.

"Germany is being treated as we would not treat a Kaffir nation.... I am bitterly disappointed in both Wilson and Lloyd George, who are smaller men than I should ever have thought. But one only judges a man properly in a great crisis, and I must say that these two are, in my opinion, being found but weak and light in the great balance. If the Germans do not accept, the hunger blockade will again be enforced, even though countless women and children have to die....

"The Germans behaved disgracefully in the war and deserve a hard peace. But that is no reason why the world must be thrust into ruin."

To a friend, Smuts wrote: "Many Americans are on my side, but of course they are smaller fry and are afraid of Wilson. They tell me very bitter things of him. 'Making the world safe for Democracy!' I wonder whether in this reactionary peace—the most reactionary since Scipio Africanus dealt with Carthage—he still hears the mute appeal of the people to be saved from the coming war.... What a ghastly tragedy this is!"

Among the Americans, Ray Stannard Baker noted in his diary, Bernard Baruch said that the treaty was unworkable "because of the economic terms. Herbert Hoover agreed with him." Secretary of State Lansing was anxious to let his colleagues know that the American commissioners—himself, General Bliss, and Henry White—had been too little consulted by President Wilson and had really not even known what was being put into the treaty.

Norman Hapgood, Henry Morgenthau, Felix Frankfurter, and Lincoln Steffens came to call on Baker, and told him that the president could still get the liberals of the world to rally behind him if some changes were made in the treaty. Baker dutifully relayed this message to Wilson, who replied, "Baker, it is like this. We cannot know what our problem is until the Germans present their counterproposals [in a complete, coherent form]." When Baker reported this exchange to Steffens and the others, one of them said, "Apparently he wants no help."

"He never does," one of the others said.

It seemed to Baker, however, that the president was "in the best spirits in weeks." The tension was gone. "For better or worse something had been done." Wilson, with the help of Dr. Grayson, rearranged the purple and green furniture in the sitting room.

Smuts composed a letter to Lloyd George, a letter that Smuts hoped would cause the prime minister to reconsider the treaty in its entirety. "My dear Prime Minister," he wrote, "The more I have studied the peace treaty as a whole, the more I dislike it."

The occupation of the Rhineland, said Smuts, was a mistake. Not only would the Germans resent such occupation, but, because Germany was obliged to pay the cost of maintaining the French troops who occupied the Rhineland, the French would probably garrison their entire army there and force the Germans to pay most of the French military budget. The provision that allowed the French to continue to occupy the Rhineland until Germany had satisfied all other treaty obligations was based on a delusion. Germany would never be able to satisfy all the treaty obligations: the French would be entitled to occupy the Rhineland forever.

As for reparations payments, they were calculated to "kill the goose which is to lay the golden eggs." Furthermore, if Germany were to be stripped of the Saar Valley and of Upper Silesia—its two principal sources of coal—the Germans would be utterly unable to revive their factories. Germany could do nothing but die, or become desperate.

As for the cessions of territory from Germany to Poland: Poland was a "house of sand." No foreign policy—certainly not Britain's—should be based on the absurd notion that Poland would be a sound nation. The frontiers that the treaty provided for Poland were "a cardinal error in policy which history will yet avenge."

As for the penalties section of the treaty: to expect the Germans to hand over anyone that the Allies might choose to name was a travesty. It was absurd, too, to reduce the German military to such proportions that the Germans would not even be able to maintain internal order—and this at a time that Germany was in dreadful turmoil.

Finally, the treaty was marred by what Smuts called innumerable "pinpricks"—annoying, unnecessary little clauses, such as those that called for international regulatory bodies to oversee German transportation, that were only calculated to provoke resentment.

"The final sanction of this great instrument," Smuts concluded on the treaty, "must be the approval of mankind"—an approval, as it was, that could not be obtained.

❦

THE BROKEN PROMISE

"Humanity can evolve an antidote for the tyrant and the despot," one socialist journal declared. "It recovers hardly from the statesman who proclaims a high ideal, only to stand impotently by while it is shattered to pieces before his eyes."

According to the *Nation*, the American people would have to display "blindness and moral callousness beyond belief " to approve of the treaty, and, according to the *New Republic*, the treaty could only form the "prelude to quarrels in a deeply divided and hideously embittered Europe."

On May 15, five young aides in the American delegation got together and submitted letters offering to resign their posts. Adolf Berle said that he felt President Wilson's principles had been abandoned in letter and in spirit; Joseph Fuller said that America had "bartered away her principles in a series of compromises with inter ests of imperialism and revenge"; Samuel Eliot Morison said that American interests, as well as American ideals, had been violated; John Storck declared that the treaty would make Germany "eager for revenge"; and George Bernard Noble said that the peace, in which American ideals were "sacrificed on the altar of imperialism . . . would be provocative of future wars." Because such a set of resignations would have been embarrassing, they were not accepted.

"It must be admitted in honesty," Secretary of State Lansing wrote at the time, "that the League is an instrument of the mighty to check the normal growth of national power and national aspirations among those who have been rendered impotent by defeat. Examine the Treaty and you will find peoples delivered against their wills into the hands of those whom they hate, while their economic resources are torn from them and given to others. Resentment and bitterness, if not desperation, are bound to be the consequences of such provisions. . . . This war was fought by the United States to destroy forever the conditions which produced it. Those conditions have not been destroyed. They have been supplanted by other conditions equally productive of hatred, jealousy, and suspicion."

On May 17, Bullitt sent a letter of resignation to Lansing. The treaty violated American principles and interests in so many instances—in the settlement over Shantung, Fiume, the Saar, the giving of territory to Poland, and many other particulars—that the treaty betokened "a new century of war" that the league would be "powerless" to prevent. The United States, said Bullitt, should refuse to guarantee France's borders, refuse to join the league, and refuse to sign the treaty.

"It is my conviction," he said, in remarks directed to Wilson, "that if you had made your fight in the open, instead of behind closed doors, you would have carried with you the public opinion of the world, which was yours; you would have been able to resist the pressure and might have established the 'new international order . . . ' of which you used to speak. I am sorry you did not fight our fight to the finish."

Bullitt's resignation was accepted at once by Lansing. It did not serve to change Wilson's mind or help to save the world from disaster, but it was used later—by the Republican senators back home— "to fight President Wilson and the Democrats," as Bullitt's fellow traveler Lincoln Steffens said, "and to help elect the Republicans."

THE AUSTRIANS ARRIVE

When the Austrian plenipotentiaries arrived in Paris to receive their treaty from the Allies, the reception was uncommonly cordial: the Austrians were installed in luxurious quarters at the Villa Henri IV, from which they had a superb view of the whole city of Paris; the mayor of Saint-Germain issued a proclamation calling for Parisians to display that courtesy that had always been—or so the mayor said—the pride of Paris.

The Austrians were hoping, among other things, that the Allies would not take away the Tyrol and its 250,000 German inhabitants and give them to Italy, and that the Allies would not insist on a provision in the treaty that would forever bar Austria from joining in a union with Germany. But Chancellor Renner, the head of the Austrian delegation, was careful to appear agreeable and inoffensive. He smiled whenever he found a suitable opportunity, apologized for not speaking French, referred to the Allies as "this illustrious tribunal," and—a word the Germans had refused to employ—as "victors."

The Allies, for their part, were delighted with the Austrians, impressed by the deference and graciousness of Chancellor Renner; even Clemenceau was polite to the Austrians: no one wished to have a repetition of the German debacle.

THE ITALIANS AGAIN

The Italians, having returned to Paris, concentrated their efforts on obstructing the completion of a treaty to present to Austria. Among other things, the Italians disputed the correctness of giving the Klagenfurt district to Yugoslavia. If Klagenfurt was given instead to

Austria, then Italy might expect Austria to be content to have the Italians control the Brenner Pass—through which Italy had often been invaded. On the other hand, the Italians might be satisfied with the Adalia zone, leaving open the possibility of an independent Turkey embracing all Anatolia, adjacent to a Greek zone.

If, on the other hand, Turkey was moved entirely out of Europe and Armenia, and Greece was given the Smyrna-Aivali zone with a mandate over most of the vilayet of Aidin, then Italy could have a mandate over South Asia Minor from Marmaris to Mersin, in addition to Korea.

Whether or not such a settlement would be affected by a decision to give the Serbs improved defensive positions for the Vordor railway and in the Strumnitza enclave was a moot question, and one that could perhaps not be definitively resolved until agreement was reached on whether to form a Union of Northern Albania into an autonomous state under Yugoslavia, to reserve central Albania for Italy, Southern Albania for Greece, and to neutralize Koritsa— which appeared to be the only way to save Ipek and Djakovo for Northern Albania.

When the Italians arrived to talk about all this with Lloyd George, they were shown into the drawing room, and sat down around a map with members of the British delegation. "The appearance of a pie about to be distributed," said Nicolson, "is thus enforced."

The Italians asked for Scala Nuova.

"Oh, no!" said Lloyd George. "You can't have that—it's full of Greeks!"

The prime minister went on to point out that there were more Greeks at Makri and a wedge of them on the coast toward Alexandretta.

"Oh, no," Nicolson whispered to him, "there are not many Greeks there."

"But, yes," said Lloyd George, "don't you see it's colored green?"

"I then realise," wrote Nicolson, "that he mistakes my map for an ethnological map, and thinks the green means Greeks instead of valleys, and the brown means Turks instead of mountains. Ll. G. takes this correction with great good humour. He is as quick as a kingfisher. Meanwhile Orlando and Sonnino chatter to themselves in Italian."

When the Italians confronted Wilson and Clemenceau in conference, the atmosphere was not so jolly. Clemenceau, Seymour
noted, "was irritable and brusque." When Sonnino tried to avoid
being pinned down among all the delicious variables, Clemenceau
was abusive: "You must want one thing or the other, Monsieur le
Baron Sonnino."

And when Sonnino tried to slip away from the point by di-
gressing on whether the Slovenes should or should not be referred
to as "enemies," Lansing took him on rudely.

"I am appalled," Sonnino burst out at last, his hands trembling
so that the little table in front of him shook, "by the atmosphere of
hostility which Italy encounters in this room."

"Oh, no," Balfour said, the inflections of habitual boredom rising up through the expression of concern, "surely not."

The issue of Klagenfurt, like so many other issues, was not
quite solved. A plebiscite was called for—and then the rumor
reached the British delegation that, under the circumstances, the
Serbs could not be present for the ceremony at which the Austrian
treaty was given to Renner. Nicolson rushed over to see Ivan Ritter
von Zolger of the Yugoslav delegation.

It was unfair, Zolger explained to Nicolson, to call for plebiscites in areas that would go against the Yugoslavs, such as Klagenfurt, and refuse to call for plebiscites in areas such as Gorizia and
Gradisca, which would vote in the Yugoslavs' favor. A compromise,
however, was possible: plebiscites could be conducted in one of two
ways—the entire district could vote, and a simple majority would
determine the outcome; or the district could vote commune by
commune. If the first method were followed, the Yugoslavs would
lose; if the second method were followed, the Yugoslavs would get
at least the southern portion. Nicolson promised Zolger that the
treaty would specify the second method.

Unfortunately, the treaty was to be presented to the Austrians
at once. President Wilson's agreement must be obtained immediately. But President Wilson was out. Then, when one of the young
English aides caught up with the president on a stairway, Wilson
was in a bad temper. He had just had a flat tire. Having had to
change a tire, he would change nothing else.

Clemenceau was told of the emergency. He thought the issue
could be resolved at some future date. Before he handed the treaty
to Chancellor Renner, Clemenceau opened the document to the

page on which Klagenfurt was mentioned—and tore out the page.

In all the last-minute haggling over the Italian claims, Nicolson was riven by one moment in the negotiations. Lloyd George and Balfour and others were talking of possible mandates with Orlando and Sonnino. To make certain they were all correctly following the league provisions, they got out the league covenant regarding mandates. They observed, Nicolson recalled, "that this article provides for 'the consent and wishes of the people concerned.' They find that phrase very amusing. How they all laugh! Orlando's white cheeks wobble with laughter and his puffy eyes fill with tears of mirth."

THE GERMAN COUNTERPROPOSAL

On May 29, Brockdorff-Rantzau presented Clemenceau with a comprehensive reply to the proposed treaty. The German reply, Riddell said to Lloyd George, was "almost as long as a novel," consisting of about 65,000 words that had been printed up by a trainful of German typesetters and compositors brought especially to Versailles for the purpose.

In the German counterproposal, which amounted, in effect, to a complete, and completely revised, treaty in itself, the Germans sought to enter the League of Nations at once, and on an equal basis with the other members. The Germans agreed to disarm themselves, provided that their disarmament was the prelude to general disarmament. The Germans could not, under any circumstances, agree to cede Upper Silesia and the Saar Valley; instead, the Germans agreed to supply France with coal. Before Germany would consent to surrender any territory at all, a plebiscite must be conducted in the disputed territory: this provision was meant specifically to include even Alsace and Lorraine. Germany could not undertake to oppose Austria's wish for possible union with Germany. Germany objected to the cession of large portions of territory to Poland. Germany was prepared to make Danzig, Memel, and Konigsberg "free ports," so that Poland might have access to the sea, but Germany could not agree to cede Danzig to Poland. Rather Germany would agree to plebiscites in these three instances—but under a revised system of voting more favorable to Germany. Germany agreed to cede Shantung, but objected otherwise to the loss of her colonies and suggested the establishment of a special committee to hear the German case for mandates over former colonies.

Germany agreed to pay reparations in the specific amount of $25 billion, a figure calculated to be acceptable to the public in Britain and France. In the way in which the reparations were to be paid, however, Germany was, as Keynes said, "rather disingenuous." The Germans apparently assumed that "public opinion in Allied countries would not be satisfied with less than the *appearance* of $25,000,000,000; and . . . they exercised their ingenuity to produce a formula which might be represented to Allied opinion as yielding this amount, whilst really representing a much more modest sum. . . . The German tactic assumed, therefore, that [the Allies] were secretly as anxious as the Germans themselves to arrive at a settlement which bore some relation to the facts, and that they would therefore be willing, in view of the entanglements which they had got themselves into with their own publics, to practice a little collusion in drafting the treaty."

The Germans offered to pay the $25 billion over a period of time, but not to pay any interest on the outstanding debt. (This would have cut their burden in half if, for instance, they would otherwise have paid their debt over a period of thirty-three years at five percent interest.) Secondly, the Germans were to receive credit against that $25 billion for the imperial navy that they had handed over to the Allies, for the value of railways and state property in any ceded territories, and for the value of any loans that Germany would forgive former wartime allies. If, for instance, Germany were to lose Alsace and Lorraine to France, then the value of state property in Alsace and Lorraine would be deducted from the $25 billion. Keynes figured that all these conditions would reduce the value of reparations to $7 billion, as opposed to the $40 billion in gold and property and other valuables that he calculated Germany would be liable to surrender under the provisions of the treaty as written by the Allies.

But Germany had another condition for agreeing even to this reduced figure. She would pay these reparations if she were allowed to keep her merchant marine and her colonies, and if "all interferences during the war with her economic rights and with German private property, etc., shall be treated in accordance with the principle of reciprocity"—in other words, said Keynes, providing that "the greater part of the rest of the treaty" be abandoned.

Riddell read through this German document while Lloyd George listened to Chopin. "The Germans," Lloyd George said to Riddell, "allege that where the principles laid down in the Fourteen Points work in favour of the Allies, they have been applied in preparing the peace terms, but where they work in favour of Germany, some other principles have been introduced and acted upon—military strategy or economics, etc. Of course there may be some ground for that argument."

"I can't say," said Riddell. "I have not examined the terms with sufficient care, but it is obvious that the Allies could not permit such a question to be debated. They could not debate objections based on an implied charge of humbug and hypocrisy."

"Yes," Lloyd George replied quickly, "I quite agree."

Field Marshal Sir Henry Wilson was impressed with the German counterproposal. "It was very clear," he noted in his diary, "that the feeling was that the Boches had made out a good case, and in several particulars an unanswerable case. The Frocks," as Sir Henry liked to refer to the frock-coated diplomats, "are in a beastly mess. The Boches have done exactly what I forecast—they have driven a coach and four through our Terms, and then have submitted a complete set of their own, based on the 14 points, which are much more coherent than ours."

Jackie Fisher, first lord of the admiralty, looked over the German counterproposal and declared that the German document was in itself "the most brilliant treaty that victors had ever imposed upon conquered." And the Germans had written it in three weeks.

MEMORIAL DAY

On the afternoon of May 30, Memorial Day, President Wilson drove out to dedicate a new cemetery at Suresnes, west of Paris, for American soldiers. The cemetery was placed atop a hill, Mont Valerian, from which the whole of the Seine Valley could be seen. It was a beautiful day, and those who heard the president said it was his finest speech—"so perfectly turned," Ray Stannard Baker said, "so sure, so musical."

"It would be no profit to us," the president declared, "to eulogize these illustrious dead if we did not take to heart the lesson which they have taught us . . . they have done their utmost to show their devotion to a great cause, and they have left us to see to it that this cause shall not be betrayed, whether in war or in peace . . . they came . . . to see to it that there should never be a war like this again."

It was a hot, dusty day in the cemetery. Several thousand, mostly soldiers, had come to hear the president speak. A few of the graves had been decorated with wreaths. Some of the soldiers stood back among the acacia groves at the edge of the cemetery.

"The peoples of the world are awake and the peoples of the world are in the saddle. Private counsels of statesmen cannot now and cannot hereafter determine the destinies of nations. If we are not the servants of the opinion of mankind, we are of all men the littlest, the most contemptible, the least gifted with vision. If we do not know our age, we cannot accomplish our purpose, and this age is an age which looks forward, not backward; which rejects the standards of national selfishness that once governed the counsel of nations and demands that they shall give way to a new order of things in which the only questions will be, 'Is it right?' 'Is it in the interest of mankind?' "

The crosses on the soldiers' graves were all of wood, all new, each bearing a name and number, and a great profusion of flowers had been provided for the occasion, and they had been strewn generously, dazzlingly over the graves, and, by this time, had become half-withered in the sunlight.

"I sent these lads over here to die," the president was saying— and the audience was forcibly struck by the thought he expressed. ("I can never forget the impact," said Ray Stannard Baker, "of his final words.")

"Shall I—" the president said, "can I—ever speak a word of counsel which is inconsistent with the assurances I gave them when they came over?"

THE BRITISH RETREAT

On June 1, Lloyd George startled his colleagues by summoning the whole of the British cabinet to Paris to discuss whether the treaty ought to be revised. E. S. Montagu, who had been in London, returned to Paris with Jackie Fisher and Sir Austen Chamberlain, and the three men passed around a copy of the German counterproposal among them. They were all agreed, Montagu recalled, that "the Germans had made out a case requiring considerable modification of the treaty." Among other things, it was clear that the treaty, in devastating Germany, gave France a potent boost toward continental hegemony.

At dinner with the prime minister, Churchill led the attack on the treaty, but the drift of dinner-table conversation was all against the treaty in any case. Fisher said that if the Allies attempted to force their version on the Germans, and the Germans refused to sign, there would be no treaty at all, "that if we went home with no peace although we could have achieved this peace [based on the German counterproposal], we should have risked all to gain nothing."

At breakfast the following morning, Smuts attacked the treaty violently, and Churchill followed with more negative remarks, as did Sir George Foster, the Canadian minister of trade. "The strangeness about the proceedings," Montagu thought, ". . . was the unanimity."

"We lunched with Arthur Balfour," Montagu noted, "where the conversation was amazing and Arthur Balfour, as usual, charming, tired and wholly useless. Fisher gave a brilliant exposition of the impossibility of restoring an original Poland. Arthur Balfour roused himself and suggested the same arguments might have applied against the unification of Italy. We demanded that this should be reasoned: he did it elaborately. Bob Cecil wound up saying: 'Is that all, Arthur? Then it's all nonsense.'"

In the evening, Lloyd George charged Balfour with answering all the arguments that the members of the cabinet and others had made against the treaty. Balfour replied to Smuts and Fisher and Churchill, to all the arguments in turn, and he even attempted a detailed rebuttal of the criticisms on reparations—claiming, with stunning implausibility, that the burden would fall heavily on those German workers who made goods for export, such as bootmakers, but not at all, for instance, on railway workers.

In the end, the patience of Balfour's colleagues was exhausted, and he was finally silenced, Montagu said, with a "howl of derision."

Lloyd George concluded: he would go to Clemenceau and Wilson and insist upon revising the terms dealing with German admission to the League of Nations, with reparations, with the costs Germany was to pay covering the French army of occupation in the Rhineland, and with the cessions to Poland of territory in the east. He wished, Lloyd George declared staunchly to the cabinet, to have the authority to tell Clemenceau and Wilson that, if these terms were not revised, the British Army and Navy would not be available to enforce the treaty.

CLEMENCEAU REPLIES

When Lloyd George took his proposals into a meeting with Clemenceau and Wilson, the Tiger savaged Lloyd George. The British were not suggesting any concessions, Clemenceau observed, at the expense of Britain. Lloyd George did not suggest that Britain return some of its captured German ships to Germany; Britain did not volunteer to return any German colonies to Germany; Britain did not propose to restore Germany's merchant marine or otherwise assist Germany in reviving her overseas trade.

As for the suggestion, among others, that the period of the occupation of the Saar Valley be reduced from fifteen years, Clemenceau said that he would not consider reducing the period even to fourteen years, three hundred and sixty-four days.

"Historically," Clemenceau wrote in his memoirs, "England was our oldest enemy." France and England had been allies, and they might well live together in peace. But, "for centuries France and Great Britain have disputed the possession of both the civilized continents and of those yet to be civilized." Clemenceau hardly intended to submit to "the 'traditional British policy,' which consists in keeping the continent of Europe divided for the benefit of the islander."

Clemenceau assigned André Tardieu the task of bucking up American resistance to the British, and Tardieu wrote Colonel House: "Could the Allies suppose that this text would be satisfactory to Germany? Of course not ... Germany protests, as it was certain she would. ... Is it an unjust treaty? Count Brockdorff believes it is. If we change it, we admit that we think as he does. What a condemnation of the work we have done during the past sixteen weeks!" The Allies were dealing, said Tardieu, with "an adversary who respects only firmness." This was no time to show weakness. "Thus on the general principle my opinion is this: a week ago, we ought to have answered the Germans, 'We will change nothing.'"

"We know the Germans better than you," Clemenceau told Wilson and Lloyd George. "Our concessions will only encourage their resistance while depriving our own peoples of their rights. We do not have to beg pardon for our victory."

❧

WILSON'S REACTION

On June 3, said Seymour, "we had a grand meeting this morning of all the American delegates. It was the first time they had all been together and in many ways it was the most interesting morning I have had over here." The meeting took place in Lansing's study at the Hotel Crillon. Thirty-eight men were present; Wilson, Lansing, Bliss, White, and Colonel House sat in large armchairs; the experts sat facing them in a semicircle. "Wilson as usual was very genial," Seymour said, "and came around the small circle shaking hands with each of us and saying some words to everyone on his particular work."

The president opened the meeting by saying that he had not come to express opinions, but rather to hear them. He wanted to know what reactions they all had to the German counterproposal, specifically their reaction to the four points that had made the "greatest impression on our British colleagues." Genial, smiling, gracious, Wilson evidently expected to hear his aides and associates dismiss the British reaction and reassure him that the treaty was fine.

Norman Davis and Thomas Lamont, two young economics experts, thought that the reparations provisions definitely needed to be changed. The Allies needed to return to the idea of a fixed sum, the young men said; otherwise the prospects of the German economy would be too uncertain; Germany would not be able to get necessary foreign credits; German industry could not be started up again.

Lansing spoke up then, to suggest that Wilson ask each group of experts to prepare "a memorandum of what might be conceded"—but Wilson was all but alarmed by the suggestion. He did not wish to open the floodgates of criticism, for fear that, once begun, the criticism could not be stopped. He did not want the members of the American delegation to misunderstand him; he might favor some minor revisions in the text of the treaty, but he would not favor revision merely because the terms seemed hard. "The terms *are* hard," the president said. "Nations should learn once for all what an unjust war means. We don't want to soften the terms, but we do want to make them just. Wherever it can be shown that we have departed from our principles we ought to have rectifications."

Herbert Hoover agreed, and he wanted the president to know that "whatever the course you may choose I am, for what I am worth, prepared to stand by." Yet, Hoover asked, just the same, in order to make certain that the Germans would sign the treaty, "Apart from all questions of justice, how far does the question of expediency come in?" It was "pretty difficult" sometimes to determine just what justice might be. But to "get something rather than lose all" it might be prudent to change the terms for reparations, the Saar Valley, and Upper Silesia.

White chimed in to suggest that one or two quite small modifications would take care of the difficulties over the Saar.

Wilson was not confronted, as Lloyd George had been, by a

Smuts or a Jackie Fisher, but, as the discussion in the American delegation wore on, and it seemed that nearly everyone had some small, annoying criticism to make, Wilson lost his patience. He had had enough of the British, of Lloyd George's incessant changes of mind.

"The time to consider all these questions," Wilson told his delegation, "was when we were writing the treaty, and it makes me a little tired for people to come and say now that they are afraid the Germans won't sign, and their fear is based upon things that they insisted upon at the time of the writing of the treaty; that makes me very sick.

"And that is the thing that happened. These people that overrode our judgment and wrote things into the treaty that are now the stumbling blocks, are falling over themselves to remove these stumbling blocks. Now, if they ought not to have been there, I say, remove them, but I say do not remove them merely for the fact of having the treaty signed. . . .

"Here is a British group made up of every kind of British opinion, from Winston Churchill to Fisher. From the unreasonable to the reasonable, they are all unanimous, if you please, in their funk. Now that makes me very tired. . . ."

The meeting was adjourned.

IMPRESSIONS OF THE BIG THREE

All of the diplomats had, by this time, lost some of their luster. Ramsay MacDonald told Riddell about meeting an American one Sunday who had said that the trustees at Princeton could not stand Wilson "because he was always forming policies in secret without consultation with anyone and then endeavoring to force them upon the institution." More than that, the anonymous gossip said, "Wilson is the sort of man who when he is shaving in the morning thinks of a phrase, and then takes his typewriter and enshrines it in a speech. The sort of man with whom words precede thoughtful decisions instead of a plan of action being succeeded by words of exposition and advocacy."

Lloyd George, said Wilson, was a "chameleon." "He comes in to our conferences bright with the color of the last man he has talked with, and without regard to the subject we may have before us, breaks in with the observation, 'It has just occurred to me'—everything apparently has just occurred to him—or 'I have just been informed'—and delivers himself on some subject quite foreign to the business at hand."

Bonar Law, Seymour said that the gossips were saying, "cares but doesn't know; Balfour knows but doesn't care; Lloyd George neither knows nor cares."

Lloyd George said that he could not understand Wilson. "I am not quite sure whether he is always what he appears to be in private. He always seems to keep on the mask. Now with Clemenceau it is different. Like all public men he has got his public attitude and point of view. He presents in public a certain appearance, but in private you feel that he is not posing, consciously or unconsciously. He is what he appears to be."

Lloyd George was tickled by a story from someone who was riding with Clemenceau in the Bois de Boulogne. "They passed some beautiful women, who kissed their hands to him. The old man returned the compliment and then remarked, 'It is hard, is it not, that one has never made a success until now, when it is too late?' "

Riddell asked Lloyd George whether he would rather have Clemenceau's tongue or a million pounds.

"I am not so sure. That terrible tongue has not been an unalloyed blessing. A tongue like that makes many enemies and spoils many friendships, whereas a million pounds is not so dangerous."

"D. & I had a long talk," Frances Stevenson wrote in her diary. "I know Stern would marry me if I gave him the slightest encouragement & if he thought I would leave D. It is a great temptation in a way for although I don't love him we are good friends & I know he would be very kind to me. . . . People will not be so anxious to marry me in 10 years' time. On the other hand I know I should not be happy now away from D. & no-one else in the world could give me the intense & wonderful love that he showers on me. He was very sweet about it, & says he wants to do what is best for me. But I can see that he would be unhappy if I left him, so I promised him I would not."

As for the fraudulent operatic performer Orlando, what could be said? For not getting hold of the territories he wanted, he was, as he knew he would be—and to the astonishment of Clemenceau, Lloyd George, and Wilson—fiercely criticized by the politicians and journalists back in Rome, including Mussolini, and, on June 20, voted out of office.

❧

THE FORMAL ALLIED RESPONSE

The Allies replied to the Germans in a document of some twenty thousand words. They stated that Germany would be welcomed into the League of Nations just as soon as she proved herself stable and possessed of the will and ability to honor international agreements. No plebiscite would be conducted in Alsace and Lorraine, because the inhabitants there had not asked for a plebiscite. France would not pay for any German property taken in Alsace and Lorraine, because the Germans had not paid for any French property in 1871. As for Danzig, it had been annexed by Prussia against the will of its inhabitants; it would not now be given to Poland, because it did have a predominantly German population, but neither would it be returned to Germany. The Allies would make a concession on Upper Silesia: a plebiscite would be arranged. No German colonies would be returned, but the Allies would make another concession concerning the German military: the army would be reduced to 100,000 men not at once but over a period of time, the reduction to be completed by March 1920. As for the responsibility for the war, the Allies repeated their conviction that Germany forced the war on Europe. The kaiser would be tried. "The arraignment framed against the kaiser has not a juridical character as regards its substance, but only in its form. The ex-emperor is arraigned as a matter of high international policy as the minimum of what is demanded for a supreme offence against international morality, the sanctity of treaties and the essential rules of justice."

The Allies charged Germany, in fact, with having built up enormous armaments that had been intended, from the first, to wage offensive war, with a system of espionage in foreign countries that not only gathered information but attempted to foment trouble and to subvert foreign governments, with encouraging Austria-Hungary, a subservient ally, to make war on Serbia, with spurning every effort that others had made to bring the disputants together to resolve their differences in a spirit of conciliation, with violating Belgium's neutrality, with pursuing the horrors of war with a particular savagery, with introducing poison gas, with bombarding cities that had no military significance, with the destruction of the life and property of noncombatants and civilians by way of submarine war, with pillage and destruction of foreign countries for the wanton purpose of harming competitors, with pursuing a war that had brought adversary nations into a staggering indebtedness of millions of dollars, with responsibility for the death of millions of soldiers, the wounding of other millions, and the death or maiming of countless others—of the death by famine, disease, and starvation, sea and air raids of perhaps one million civilians in Serbia and Austria, perhaps two million in Russia, perhaps six million throughout Europe who succumbed to the Spanish flu, of civilian casualties that perhaps numbered, in all, as high as twenty-two million. The Germans must not think, said the reply of the Allies, that they had shed all responsibility for this terrible calamity merely by voting in a shaky republican government at the last moment. "They cannot pretend, having changed their rulers after the war was lost, that it is justice that they should escape the consequences of their deeds."

WEIMAR

Count Brockdorff-Rantzau glanced over the Allied reply to the German counterproposal and announced that his delegation would leave for Weimar that evening. The Germans packed hastily, taking only official documents with them. Crowds gathered outside the Hotel des Reservoirs. By the time the first of the limousines arrived to begin taking the Germans to the train, a large mob had collected. Brockdorff-Rantzau was the last to leave: his car drove slowly through the crowd, whose members began to whistle and shout—and then to throw stones. One of the stones broke a window in a car accompanying Brockdorff-Rantzau and inflicted a head wound on one of the secretaries. French police moved in and made a path for the cars.

The train trip to Weimar was painfully slow: it took a night, a day, and another night. Brockdorff-Rantzau met with his committee aboard the train and saw to the drafting of a memorandum for the National Assembly. When the delegation arrived at Weimar, early on the morning of June 19, Brockdorff-Rantzau drove at once to the former Grand Ducal Palace, where the cabinet was assembled, waiting for his report, in one of the drawing rooms.

"There are two slogans," Brockdorff-Rantzau said, "which I was up against during the whole of the war: 'Hold out!' and 'Time is on our side!' It is these same two slogans, strangely enough, that I find now I must adopt myself."

In two or three months, said Brockdorff-Rantzau, "our enemies will be at loggerheads over the division of the spoils." For the moment, he said: "If we refuse to sign, we shall be in purgatory for a time, for two or at the most three months. If we sign, it means a lingering disease, of which the nation will perish."

To buttress these conclusions, Brockdorff-Rantzau presented the cabinet with the memorandum that the delegation had prepared aboard the train from Versailles. The delegation was unanimous: the terms were "unbearable," and the German government must "refuse the treaty." To sign, especially to sign a treaty that accepted the guilt for starting the war, would be "both hateful and dishonourable."

❦

ERZBERGER

Brockdorff-Rantzau might have carried the cabinet with him, had it not been for Matthias Erzberger. Erzberger was so often precisely right about what could be accomplished—and, while the German delegation wrangled in Paris with the Allies, about what could be achieved in the final peace treaty—that his opponents believed he was connected in some sinister fashion with enemy spies. In fact, he was in touch, daily, with a young French academic, Hesnard, who was in Weimar; and Hesnard was in constant contact with his mentor back in Paris, Haguenin, a former professor at the University of Berlin; and Haguenin was in direct and confidential contact with Clemenceau.

Professor Hesnard bore a single message to Erzberger: when it came time to enforce the treaty, the Allies would be lenient. To be sure, Hesnard emphasized, he was in no official position to give any formal interpretation to the treaty; but, inevitably, theory and practice were two different things.

In the meantime, the American Colonel Conger also managed to hold conversations with Erzberger. Conger was not, he assured Erzberger, able to speak officially. As a general staff officer he was merely able to travel anywhere he wished, and he had some observations that he thought Erzberger might find useful. Conger told Erzberger that the Germans should not for a moment believe that President Wilson was in any way at odds with the French and British. Wilson was in complete agreement with the others; there was no hope whatever of any modification of the treaty terms; indeed, Erzberger should know that American troops were fully prepared and waiting to take part in an Allied invasion of Germany if the treaty were not signed.

Erzberger thought, however, that the French could not support such an invasion. Was it not true that the French would not agree to start up the war again? On the contrary, said Conger, the French would like nothing better.

In subsequent conversations, Erzberger tried to pry Conger open by suggesting that French and British emissaries had been sent to convey different messages—but Conger was not thrown off. Then Erzberger said that he himself favored signing the treaty, but he thought the cabinet would not go along with him. President Ebert had said, said Erzberger, "I am not so sure that we won't fight when the time comes." Still, Conger was not unsettled; rather, he insisted, calmly, that Germany must sign. Again, he said, he could not speak officially, but in his opinion "the treaty was interpreted too literally by the Germans, that, after signature, and as it became apparent that Germany was doing her utmost to live up to the terms of the treaty, it would receive more and more a liberal interpretation favorable to Germany."

In time, Erzberger was persuaded that Germany must accept

the treaty, no matter what its terms were. If the Germans accepted the treaty, the worst that could happen was that the tax burden would be extremely oppressive; the Germans in the east might rise up in arms; perhaps a military coup would be attempted against the government. Still, Erzberger thought the coup would fail, because of the overwhelming desire most Germans had for peace; uprisings and attempted Communist revolution would fail because food and raw materials would be moving into the country again.

If the Germans did not sign the treaty, Erzberger said, the Allies would resume their blockade, and the Allies' armies would invade from the west, the Poles and Czechs from the east. Germany would be split apart; the German Army could no longer resist; a state of famine would spread throughout Germany; the Communists would rise up in riot and revolution. "Plundering, death and murder would be the rule of the day. In the general confusion, there will no longer be a communication system. The breakup of Germany will follow. . . . The individual free cities will not be able to resist the pressure of the Allied offers to agree to peace terms with them. . . . Smaller German states too would declare themselves independent and seek to establish relations with our opponents. The main map of the German Reich would then disappear, and in its place a checkered collection of little states would appear, as has always been the dream of France."

If the terms of the treaty could not be fulfilled, that was all to the good. In time, the terms would be abandoned by the Allies, and nothing would have been lost. "If someone had me handcuffed and was pointing a revolver at me," Erzberger said, "demanding that I sign a piece of paper on which I promise to fly to the moon in forty-eight hours, then any sane person, in order to save his life, would sign the paper."

ፘ

"A MILITARY POINT OF VIEW"

The German Army did not care to surrender. As time went on, the officer corps came more and more to believe that the army would have won the war, or at least held the Allies to a stalemate, had they not been "stabbed in the back" by the cowardly civilians who dominated the new Weimar Republic.

Because the politicians were aware of the sentiment sweeping through the army, the government leaders felt they could not sign the treaty unless and until they had received, in writing, a statement from the army saying whether or not it was prepared to defend Germany against a renewed Allied invasion.

General Wilhelm Groener, the chief of staff of the army, was prepared to arrange the army's acquiescence to the treaty. The son of a noncommissioned officer, a career officer himself, Groener was dedicated to the preservation of the army, and understood that it could only destroy itself by attempting at this date to resist an Allied invasion. Yet, Groener, for all his clarity of thought and competence, could not command the devotion and loyalty of the officer corps. Reverential feelings were reserved for old Field Marshal Paul von Hindenburg, still the titular head of the German Army.

Groener had been responsible for much of the untainted respect Germans had for Hindenburg. Groener had insisted that Hindenburg never be brought into political arguments, that the field marshal's honor always be protected, that the army must understand that one chief of staff or another might err from time to time in his strategy but the field marshal was never wrong, that Hindenburg must be preserved to represent the undying spirit of the army, and its dedication to the future of Germany.

Now, if Hindenburg could be persuaded to declare that the army could not defend Germany, the officer corps would have to submit. The field marshal was accustomed to sign anything that Groener placed before him. The field marshal had, in fact, sunk into a "dreamlike passivity," as Richard Watt has called it, because he was in his seventies, because he always delegated great powers to his chief of staff, and because he was still undone by the fact that he had assisted in helping get rid of the kaiser, to whom he still referred as "his majesty, my King and my master."

Before Groener called on Hindenburg, the chief of staff conducted a confidential poll of the local commanders of the military zones into which Germany was divided. Groener's aides asked the commanders whether they thought the Germans would be willing to resume war, whether volunteers would present themselves, what resistance the people would offer to enemy occupation, and whether the people in their area would remain steadfast under the pressure of occupation. To all of these questions, the local commanders gave

discouraging replies. They felt the German people would not tolerate a resumption of war, that they would not volunteer to fight, that
only in the east would the people resist, and that Communist insur-
rections would probably occur in every major city.

On the evening of June 16, Groener took his information to
Hindenburg, who was living in Hanover, at a dignified distance
from the fray. When Groener told the field marshal what he knew of
the politics of the moment, and of the attitude of the people, Hindenburg was silent for a time. He then asked whether an appeal
might be made to the officers to "ask a minority of our citizens to
sacrifice themselves to save our national honor?"

Groener replied that such a gesture would be useless. Even
worse: the people would repudiate the military, the Allies would be
pitiless, the officer corps "would be destroyed, and the name of Germany would disappear from the map."

In the hope that his reply had moved the field marshal, Groener
then asked for instructions. Indeed, understanding the possibilities
inherent in the situation, Groener asked Hindenburg for written instructions.

Hindenburg spent the night pacing up and down in his bedroom, and he gave Groener a note in the morning to take to the cabinet. "In point of fact," said the field marshal, "I agree with you, and
I don't mind saying so openly. But I cannot and will not give up
those views which have guided me all my life."

The note that he gave Groener had been written carefully—to
avoid giving real assistance to the government, but to let it do what
it must; and, above all, to permit the field marshal to preserve his
honor.

"In case of a resumption of hostilities we are militarily in a position to reconquer, in the east, the province of Posen and to defend
our frontier. In the west we cannot, in view of the numerical superiority of the Entente and its ability to surround us on both flanks,
count on repelling successfully a determined attack of our enemies.
A favorable outcome of our operations is therefore very doubtful,
but as a soldier I would rather perish in honor than sign a humiliating peace."

DEADLOCK

In a drawing room of the Grand Ducal Palace, a cabinet meeting went on interminably. It was suggested that the German government might accept the treaty on the condition that the "war guilt" clauses were removed; yet, still, there were the matters of territory, reparations, and so forth. The debate went on. Brockdorff-Rantzau was called in once more to address himself in some detail to the notion that, if Germany held out, the Allies would collapse in disunity. He seemed less convincing than he had been before.

Then Minister of Defense Noske spoke up. He had come into possession of a note from Field Marshal von Hindenburg, which he would like to read to the cabinet. He read Hindenburg's note—putting as much emphasis as he could on the sentence declaring that Germany could not successfully defend against an Allied invasion from the west. Nonetheless, opposition to signing the treaty continued; some cabinet members still advocated refusing to sign, resuming the war. "It's all very fine," Noske said, "for us fifteen heroes to sit here and refuse to sign, but behind us there is a nation which is down and out. What is the use of heroics on the part of fifteen leaders in that situation?"

The cabinet was, and remained, about equally divided. At three o'clock in the morning of June 19, Ebert despaired: since the cabinet could not reach a conclusion, the matter would have to be referred to the full National Assembly.

Almost at once, the parties began caucusing in Weimar to determine what position to take on the treaty. Party members were informed that they must reach a decision within five days: the Allies had given a deadline to the Germans of June 24.

A group of economists and financiers submitted a report to the Assembly. If the treaty were to be accepted, "Germany will collapse economically, ... will be incapable of providing her present population with the opportunity to earn a living, and millions of Germans will die in civil conflicts or will be forced to emigrate."

The treaty was purposely designed, they said, "to ruin Germany economically."

At the same time, a group of senior military officers gathered for a council of war. Several of the generals had come to embrace a plan that called for sacrificing western Germany, withdrawing behind the Elbe, and making a last stand in the old bastion of Prussia. "This old Prussia," said General Walther Reinhardt, "must be the core of the Reich."

"From the point of view of both civil and international law," said General Groener disdainfully, "you classify yourselves as rebels. The Allies will consider you as such and treat you as such." The officer corps, somewhat chastened, then heard Minister of Defense Noske offer himself as leader of Germany if Ebert and Scheidemann and the others could not maintain themselves in office. What if the government fell, and Noske were asked, as a man who enjoyed the confidence of the military, to form a new government? In the deranged atmosphere of Weimar, even the prospect of Noske as dictator of Germany had an aura of the plausible and desirable.

Meantime, in another cabinet meeting, representatives of the various states that made up the German reich were asked to express themselves on the treaty. The representatives of Bavaria, Saxony, and Württemberg said they were prepared to sign. The prime minister of Baden said his people favored signing. The prime minister of Hesse said his people would not tolerate more war.

And yet, even so, the right-wing National People's party and the German People's party emerged from caucus to declare that they would not vote for signing the treaty, and even worse the Democratic party voted to reject the treaty. But, what was perhaps most surprising and devastating was the fact that Erzberger's own party declared it would favor signing only if the "guilt" clauses were deleted. Then, in a cabinet vote, Chancellor Scheidemann voted against the treaty, while Noske voted in favor of the treaty. Scheidemann was joined by two other members of the Majority Socialists and four members of the Democratic party. On the other side, Noske and Erzberger were joined by two members of the Center party and three members of the Majority Socialist party. At 7–7, the deadlock was complete. At one o'clock in the morning of June 20, Chancellor Scheidemann resigned. Germany had no government.

Along the frontiers of the Rhine, Marshal Foch visited the Allied troops at Cologne, Coblenz, and Mayence to make certain, should the Germans refuse to sign the treaty, that the Allied Army was ready to march on Monday, June 24, at 6:45 P.M.

୧

SCAPA FLOW

In Britain, in the harbor at Scapa Flow, late morning on June 20, an artist who was sketching the German battleship *Friedrich der Grosse*, noticed that the vessel was tilting—and, soon enough, that the sailors were lowering lifeboats. An alarm was raised, too late. The *Friedrich der Grosse* lurched, and slipped down beneath the water at 12:16 P.M. The whole German fleet, held captive in the harbor by the British, was sinking.

The fleet—five heavy cruisers, nine battleships, seven light cruisers, and fifty-odd destroyers, all disarmed—had sailed to Britain a week after the armistice and had been held, fully manned and rusting, in Scapa Flow harbor all during the peace conference. The sailors, like everyone else, were riotous at the end of the war. At one time they elected a supreme sailors' soviet, which they insisted had taken over the fleet, retaining the admiral simply as a technical adviser. At other times, they merely mutinied. "White guards" sprang up on some ships to fight the "red guards"—and the admiral of the fleet was obliged to leave his flagship and transfer his command to a less politically volatile ship.

During the spring, the ships were gradually unmanned, and, by June, they were left with only skeleton crews. The crews that were left, however, were a core of diehards. When the admiral learned from British newspapers that his ships were to be divided among the Allies, he sent a message to his ghost fleet. When he flew a certain flag from his ship, the crews were to open the sea cocks on their ships.

As the fleet sank, British seamen came out to stop the German sailors, to order them back to their ships to stop the flooding. The German sailors threw away their oars and drifted. Here and there, the British—enraged by the unending perfidy of the Germans—fired into the German lifeboats, killing some of the German sailors.

But, quickly enough, the British saw the pointlessness of shooting the sailors, and oars and guns were silenced. The British and German sailors turned their attention to the sinking vessels and watched the last stages of the suicide.

❦

THE GERMAN COLLAPSE

On the afternoon of June 21, President Ebert came up with a new government. He named Gustav Bauer, a former trade union leader and one of Germany's lesser-known politicians, as chancellor. He gave the other cabinet positions to Majority Socialists and Democrats, none of whom, at least, had definitely committed himself to opposing the treaty. Both Erzberger and Noske were disappointed with this new government: each had hoped to be named chancellor himself. Erzberger sulked; Noske struck up conversations with the still disgruntled officer corps.

The Bauer cabinet appeared before the National Assembly with this proposal: that the treaty be accepted on the condition that the "guilt" or "shame" paragraphs be deleted. The Independent Socialists objected at once: they had no intention of going back to war just to save the honor of the kaiser and the officer corps.

Bauer agreed to amend his proposal, to say that Germany would accept the treaty without any conditions—and then the parties on the right objected. They would not consent to unconditional acceptance of the treaty. And so Bauer proposed a compromise. The cabinet would inform the Allies that they would sign the treaty, "without, however, recognizing thereby that the German people was the author of the war."

A telegram was sent to Versailles, where it was translated and delivered to Clemenceau, Lloyd George, and Wilson by seven o'clock on the evening of the twenty-second. The Big Three gathered at Lloyd George's residence and declared themselves so irritated by the sinking of the fleet at Scapa Flow that they would not even consider letting the Germans slip away from the shame paragraphs of the treaty. Wilson sat down at his typewriter and tapped out a reply: "The time for discussion is past. . . ." The Germans had less than twenty-four hours to inform the Allies whether or not they intended to sign the treaty exactly as it was.

Erzberger was surprised. The cabinet was unsettled. The cabinet met in the middle of the night and decided the issue would have to be submitted again to the National Assembly. Meanwhile, Bauer was informed, Minister of Defense Noske had missed this cabinet meeting because he was meeting with General von Maercher to plot a military coup against the government.

The general had seduced Noske by saying, "For you, Herr Minister, I would let myself be cut to pieces, and so would my infantrymen." Noske, inspired by the vision of himself as dictator of Germany, jumped to his feet with tears in his eyes: "General," he cried, "now I too have had enough of this rotten mess!"

Unfortunately, Noske could not get Bauer to accept his resignation from the cabinet. Instead, Bauer asked Groener to ask Hindenburg again whether Germany could resist an invasion. When Bauer called back later to get Hindenburg's reply, the field marshal stepped out of the room, saying to Groener: "You can give the answers to the president as well as I."

Bauer relayed Groener's pessimistic reply to Noske, who reluctantly abandoned the military coup and remained in the cabinet. At last, Bauer took the issue again to the National Assembly—informed them again of the situation, of the Allied reply, of Groener's message. And the National Assembly, like Hindenburg and Scheidemann and Brockdorff-Rantzau and so many of the others, neatly ducked responsibility for entirely accepting defeat. They passed a resolution that said the cabinet, by virtue of the previous day's vote, already had the power to accept the treaty.

Bauer's government cabled Versailles. The Germans accepted the treaty and a delegation would arrive in five days to sign the document. The Big Three were meeting in Wilson's study when the telegram arrived. Clemenceau, Lloyd George, and Wilson were relieved by the news but not overjoyed. "Orders were given," the minutes of the meeting state, "for guns to be fired. No further discussion took place."

SHOTWELL AND SEYMOUR

"Peace!" Shotwell wrote excitedly in his diary. "The guns are firing from the batteries around Paris. They announce the end of our work." Most of the diplomats in Paris were delighted—if not with their work, then with the end of their work. Some of them were at once overcome with nostalgia for their time in Paris, and spent their next few days, as they had spent the past week while waiting to hear from the Germans, in last tours of Paris and the countryside.

Spring had passed and, almost eerily, the scars of war were already disappearing beneath the summer flowers. Near Verdun, Shotwell noticed, "weeds were beginning to grow and large expanses of buttercups were shining gaily in the sunlight." Elsewhere, he saw "patches of clover in bloom and great fields of yellow blossoms that may be some kind of clover but in any case shine very gaily in the sunshine." To the south of Paris, near Châteauroux, the road rose among the farming hills, said Shotwell, "through a lovely rolling country—poppies and bluebells in bloom."

Seymour went north, through Belgium, "following the line to Dixmuide where there are eight cafés running and not a single house standing." At Ostend, "we got good rooms on the sea front and had the best dinner I have had for five years, with perfect coffee, lots of butter and sugar." But Brussels was "the liveliest place I have seen in ten years. It is like the gayest of continental cities before the war. I never saw so many restaurants all brilliantly lighted, cafés of all kinds, dance halls . . . drinking and singing. Any kind of food or drink desired is brought at once. Prices for the most part are high, except for the dairy products such as eggs and butter. For breakfast Monday morning we had strawberries with an enormous bowl of thick whipped cream, an enormous omelet, crescent rolls, and all the butter and sugar we wanted for five francs."

The graves, said Shotwell, "still dot the little meadow down by the brook that runs through Oissery. It was nine o'clock on the sixth of September [1914] when they pushed through here . . . through

Brégy to the hamlet of Fosse-Martin. This is hardly more than a farmyard with great barns and an enormous courtyard surrounded by farm buildings. We drove right into the farmyard itself and out the gate into the lane behind, and there suddenly came upon a little cemetery of French graves which the peasant women had cared for with carnations and sweet williams."

Near Laon, just at the west end of Chemin des Dames, Shotwell was stunned to see "the whole hilltop was ablaze with masses of poppies. I never saw anything like this great wilderness of a battlefield covered with this cloak of blood-red flowers. It was inconceivably beautiful. How it has happened I can hardly understand."

"I hope," Seymour wrote home, "that Gladys has told you of our various gaieties, going to the theater last week, and up to the [restaurant] Lapin Agile. Almost every day we get off for a walk, when it is not too hot, and stop for an ice or a drink at a café or terrasse. We have been having dinner parties up in our room for various people, and enjoying the long sunset from our balcony."

ै

VERSAILLES, THE HALL OF MIRRORS

The end came on Saturday, June 28. By noon the road to Versailles was jammed with automobiles, most of them with large colored labels on their hoods and windshields. At the intersection of the Avenue de Picardie and Boulevard de la Reine, the cars with tricolor or yellow and green cockades were directed straight down the avenue, while all other cars were sent down the boulevard. Then at the intersection of the Avenue de St.-Cloud and Rue St.-Pierre, the cars with the tricolor were directed along the Rue St.-Pierre to the Avenue de Paris and on to the front of the palace, where troops in horizon-blue uniforms lined the avenues into the courtyard. Inside the courtyard were the cavalry with their pennants of red and white and the Garde Républicaine in white breeches, white crossbelts, burnished crested helmets with long black and red horsehair crinière, black riding boots, swords at rest in front of them. The limousines pulled up in the forecourt before the entrance to the marble staircase. General Pershing was among the first to arrive, followed by Secretary Lansing, General Manoury, who had been blinded in the war and who was helped from his limousine by General Alby, then the maharajah of Bikaner, Baron Makino, M. Antoine Dubost, wearing the medal of 1870 on his chest, and then, at last, arriving with General Mordacq, Clemenceau, greeted with sudden shouts and cheers, Lloyd George applauded by the attendants in the marble court, and President and Mrs. Wilson, also applauded as they stepped from their limousine to mount the stairway up into the palace and through the apartments of Marie Antoinette. The palace looked, on this day, especially ostentatious.

"I hate Versailles," Nicolson whispered to Headlam-Morley as they walked through the grand anterooms.

"You hate what?" asked Headlam-Morley, who was slightly deaf.

"Versailles."

"Oh, you mean the treaty."

"What treaty?" asked Nicolson, his mind groping for some reference to 1871.

"This treaty."

"Oh, I see what you mean—the German treaty," said Nicolson vaguely, pondering, for the first time, the notion that the document they had all just completed would be called not the Treaty of Paris but the Treaty of Versailles.

When, at last, the diplomats entered the Hall of Mirrors, 240 feet long, 35 feet wide, 42 feet high, designed by Mansart in 1678, they were thrust into a pandemonium amid the gold gilt, the frieze of little allegorical figures of children and trophies of war, the paintings of Louis le Grand on the ceiling, the great wall of seventeen windows opening into the gardens, and the facing wall of seventeen vast mirrors reflecting all these diplomats, Louis le Grand, allegorical children, journalists, eight-branched silver candelabra decorated with the labors of Hercules, Lloyd George's special contingent of fifty disabled soldiers, two grubby old men—country friends of Clemenceau's—in special chairs in the center of the spectacle, secretaries, photographers, colonels, "a mass of little humans," said the painter William Orpen, "all trying to get to different places." Sir Henry Wilson estimated the crowd at "about 1,000 people, of whom I daresay 150 were ladies, which I thought all wrong."

Along the mirrored side of the vast hall was a long horseshoe

table. At the center of the horseshoe table was the place reserved for
Clemenceau. To his left were chairs for the delegates from Britain,
the Dominions, and Japan. To his right were chairs for the representatives from the United States, France, Italy, Belgium. Chairs for
the delegations of the other nations were arrayed around the horseshoe; the reporters had already learned that the chairs reserved for
the Chinese would not be occupied.

In front of this long table "like a guillotine," said Nicolson, was
the table on which the treaty of peace lay to be signed. The treaty
existed in only one official copy, printed with a wide margin on Japanese vellum and held together with red tape. The personal seals of
the signatories had already been affixed to the document, in order to
save time, so that the delegates would only need to sign their names
next to their seals.

Tapestry-covered backless benches had been put out for seat-
ing and the delegates clustered in the aisles, pushed by one another,
and stepped over the benches as they moved about the room trying
to collect autographs on their programs. Almost everyone agreed
that the French had arranged the room badly, and Mrs. Wilson had
to content herself on a backless bench until someone filched an armchair for her. The accommodations for the press, Lord Riddell said,
were "very much like a bear garden."

At about two forty-five o'clock, Clemenceau moved purpose-
fully through the crowd and took his seat at the center of the horseshoe table. He was followed almost at once by President Wilson,
who attracted a small flurry of polite applause, and then by Lloyd
George, who took his place at the long table. Clemenceau made a
gesture to the ushers, who commenced to say "Ssh! Ssh!" as they
moved up and down the aisles. The diplomats took their seats
quickly; the chattering subsided; an occasional cough or throat-
clearing could be heard in the hall, the rustle of programs, a short
military order followed by the sound of the swords of the Garde
Républicaine being returned smartly to their scabbards, and then
the crisp order of Clemenceau breaking the silence: "Faîtes entrer
les Allemands."

"I suppose, now," Balfour had said several days before, "[the
Germans will] send us a few bow-legged, cross-eyed men to sign
the treaty." In fact, Dr. Hermann Müller and Dr. Johannes Bell—
the secretary for foreign affairs and the colonial secretary, respec-
tively, of the new German government were deathly pale and kept

their eyes fixed on the ceiling as they entered the Hall of Mirrors, in order to avoid the stares of the assembled company. None of the delegates of the Allied powers stood to receive the Germans—evidently a pointed reminder that Brockdorff-Rantzau had not stood to receive the treaty at the ceremony of May 7.

Dr. Müller, a tall man with a little black moustache, and Dr. Bell, round-faced and uncomfortable, bowed, and took their seats— their legs shaking uncontrollably once they sat down—next to the small table holding the treaty. Clemenceau spoke briefly and without pleasantries:

"An agreement has been reached upon the conditions of the treaty of peace. . . . The signatures about to be given constitute an irrevocable engagement to carry out loyally and faithfully in their entirety all the conditions that have been decided upon. I therefore have the honor of asking messieurs the German plenipotentiaries to approach to affix their signatures to the treaty before me."

The Germans leapt up to sign the treaty and were motioned to sit down again while Mantoux translated Clemenceau's speech into German. Then the Germans rose again and stepped forward to sign the document. The pen did not work. Colonel House stepped forward with a pen. Dr. Bell, either out of nervousness or haste, omitted his Christian name and signed in a heavy, perpendicular script, "Dr. Bell."

The five American commissioners signed next, led by the president. In moving Wilson's personal library from Princeton to the White House, one of his aides noticed that Wilson had tried out various inscriptions—Thomas W. Wilson, Thomas Woodrow Wilson, T. W. Wilson, T. Woodrow Wilson—before settling on Woodrow Wilson as his customary signature. The president realized he was excited when, after writing "Woodrow" with perfect ease, he had some difficulty signing "Wilson."

Wilson was followed by Lansing, House, Bliss, and White; Lloyd George was followed by Balfour, Lord Milner, Bonar Law. Clemenceau was followed by Pichon, Klotz, Tardieu, and Cambon. Then came the delegations of Italy, Japan, Belgium, and the others. The ceremony moved along with surprising swiftness—and, as the delegates formed a line in front of the signature table, conversations started up, the buzz of voices filled the hall, and a casual feeling pervaded the room as the delegates chatted with one another.

Riddell was appalled by the bad management, the sense of informality, the feeling of disorder that overtook the ceremony of the signing. Lloyd George noticed, to his disgust, that delegates were actually going up to the Germans and asking for their autographs. The more squeamish among the American and British delegates were overcome with a sense of shame that the ceremony seemed to subject the Germans to unnecessary humiliation. Nicolson pronounced the whole messy affair "horrible."

As soon as the Germans had signed the treaty, a signal was sent out to the gun battery of St.-Cyr on the southern slopes of Versailles, and the firing of the cannon was taken up by one fort after another on the hills around Paris; the waiting crowds had begun to cheer—and so, as the chatting delegates continued the signing, their signatures were accompanied by the muffled cheers and the booming of the cannon.

When the last of the signatures had been placed on the treaty, the last pen put down on the table, Clemenceau closed the session abruptly. ("Messieurs, all the signatures have been given. The signature of the conditions of peace between the Allied and associated powers and the German republic is an accomplished fact. The session is adjourned.")

The Germans rose and vanished from the hall at once through a side door; the delegates milled about to congratulate one another. Through the windows, past the terrace, the fountains could be seen: bright sunlight, open country, clear blue sky, white clouds, a squadron of airplanes in the sky, a cordon of troops holding back the crowds in the gardens. Wilson made his way through the throng of delegates; Lloyd George shook hands, smiling; Clemenceau walked among the milling diplomats, shaking hands, his eyes bleary, saying, "Oui, c'est une belle journée."

Wilson, Lloyd George, and Clemenceau appeared together out on the terrace, and the crowd burst into cheers, arms waving, car horns joining in with the booming of the cannon, well-wishers grasping the hands of the Big Three, thumping them on their backs as they wandered out onto the grass, and Wilson, finally, reached out to take Clemenceau's hand, because the old man, on this, his day of triumph, relief, and dismay, did not seem to know where he was going, and his eyes were filled with tears.

EPILOGUE

When all the diplomats had dispersed at last, and the Palace of Versailles was left to the gardeners, and the delegations returned once more to their homelands, the Europe that they left behind still trembled with the wounds and shocks of war and the insults of peace.

A generation had been decimated on the battlefields of Europe. No one had seen the likes of such slaughter before: the deaths of soldiers per day of battle were 10 times greater than in the American Civil War, 24 times the deaths in the Napoleonic Wars, 550 times the deaths in the Boer War. And still the epidemic of flu spread through Europe and America and elsewhere until it had claimed another 14 million lives among the survivors of the war.

The economy of Europe was in ruins. Food prices had risen during the war by 103 percent in Rome, by 106 percent in Paris, by 110 percent in London, and, in Germany, prices had become all but meaningless. The Germans had 40 percent less butter than in 1914, 42 percent less meat, 50 percent less milk. The destruction of factories, railroads, and shipping produced economic dislocation on such an order as to be excruciating.

Even before the treaty had been signed, the so-called Vilna dispute had erupted into a pocket war. The Polish general Joseph Pilsudski took the town of Vilna from the Bolsheviks; diplomatic negotiations returned the town to the Bolsheviks—who only had it taken from them by the Lithuanians who were driven out by a band of Polish freebooters.

The Teschen conflict, too, commenced before the Paris conference had adjourned, and then the Polish-Russian War broke out, and then the Burgenland dispute between Austria and Hungary over a strip of territory predominantly inhabited by Germans but occupied by Hungarian irregulars and assigned by the peace conference to Austria.

On June 22, 1920, Greece, encouraged by Lloyd George, invaded Anatolia, and Turkey invaded Armenia. In Italy, Gabriele d'Annunzio led an expedition into Fiume. The Italians negotiated with the Yugoslavs and gave up Fiume—but a Fascist coup overthrew the government and forced Yugoslavia to abandon its claims.

Anxiety led to the formation of the kind of interlocking set of alliances in which the world had been caught in 1914. In February of 1920, France and Poland signed a pact to come to one another's assistance in case of attack; in March of 1920, Poland and Rumania signed a defense treaty. Several weeks later, Germany was said to be in default on some of its war debts; the French occupied Düsseldorf, Duisburg, and Ruhrort. In April, Rumania joined Czechoslovakia in the Little Entente.

The war had cost $603.57 billion. Rubber was in such short supply in Europe that trucks were traveling on their rims, and fats were so scarce that housewives strained their dishwater to salvage whatever grease it might contain. International trade was in shambles: British exports were only half what they had been before the war. By 1921, the world economy had stumbled into a brief, but portentous, depression, distinguished not by uniformity but by apparent caprice. While the manufacture of gas masks and airplane wings ceased, the production of copper and wheat continued at such vigorous wartime levels that prices slumped precipitately.

And then inflation struck. In Germany, to pay for the war, the money in circulation had been quintupled; public debt was 20 times its prewar level. The exchange was 4 marks to the dollar in 1914, then 14.8 marks to the dollar in May of 1921, then 62.6 marks to the dollar in November of 1921, and then 62 *billion* marks to the dollar in October of 1923.

Prices soared. Money was worthless, as were insurance policies and savings accounts. The mortgage on a house was worth less, in paper marks, than a glass of beer.

As for war debts, in 1921, the reparations commission finally fixed Germany's debt at 132 billion gold marks to be paid over 30 years, plus 26 percent of the proceeds of German exports and some other goods—an assessment that, by 1922, was manifestly absurd. The Germans defaulted. On January 11, 1923, French and Belgian troops moved in to occupy the Ruhr district.

The Germans, in retaliation for the French military move, purposely set about inflating their currency; and the effects of German inflation spread. The French franc fell by 25 percent. An American banker, Charles Dawes, was called in to stave off disaster, and the Dawes Plan, postponing and reducing German payments, prolonged the agony.

Within the changing context of all these rising and falling currencies, Germany eventually paid 36 billion gold marks. In the same period, Germany borrowed from foreign sources about 33 billion marks that were, for the most part, never repaid. The actual effect of reparations, then, was economically negligible. Nonetheless, because the Germans believed that reparations debts, whether paid or not, were the cause of their economic troubles, the effect of the reparations clauses of the Versailles treaty was fiercely embittering to the Germans.

By 1925, France had signed treaties with both Poland and Czechoslovakia for mutual assistance in case of attack by Germany. The Weimar government in Germany had settled down to a tenuous existence, while the Protestant middle classes drifted toward the reactionary right. And gradually the world slid into the great depression of the thirties, the Japanese invasion of Manchuria, the Italian attack on Ethiopia, the German reoccupation of the Rhineland.

At the conclusion of the Paris conference, Wilson returned from Europe to do battle with the United States Senate over ratification of the treaty. Colonel House had advised the president, just before Wilson sailed for America, to be conciliatory to his Senate opponents. Of ninety-six senators, only fourteen Republicans and four Democrats were unalterably opposed to the treaty—and the majority of American citizens favored its adoption. But, before Wilson boarded the *George Washington* he said to the colonel: "House, I have found one can never get anything in this life that is worthwhile without fighting for it."

In Washington, Wilson scorned the meddlesome efforts of the Senate to "advise and consent." Some senators suggested some minor revisions—a clause, for example, that would explicitly note that the United States, as a member of the League of Nations, would not come to the aid of another country in war without an express declaration of war from Congress. Wilson would have none of it. Rather than woo the "mild reservationists" to his side by accepting their suggestions, he drove them over to the side of the "irreconcilables" by insisting that the treaty be taken just as it was, without changing a comma.

Senator Lodge, chairman of the Senate Foreign Relations Committee, decided that the first thing to be done was to read aloud the whole treaty, 268 pages long in the copy he had. And so he read it aloud, sometimes to fellow committee members; sometimes, when they had all left the room, just to the clerk of the committee; and sometimes, when the clerk could not stand it, Lodge read the treaty aloud to himself, alone in the committee room. Then the senator began to demand some documents from the president, copies of the records of the Paris negotiations, and other information. Wilson, enraged, became even more stubborn.

In September, the president set out on a twenty-seven-day crusade across America to persuade the American people to force the Senate to "take its medicine." He traveled eight thousand miles, he delivered forty speeches, and attended lunches, receptions, dinners. When he had left Washington, he was suffering from ferocious headaches, and his hands were shaking. As he went from town to town, the headaches became increasingly persistent, until he was in constant pain. Urged by Mrs. Wilson and Dr. Grayson and others to stop and rest, Wilson drove himself on, until, in Pueblo, Colorado, he was stopped by a stroke that paralyzed an arm and a leg. And then, soon after, he was assaulted by another stroke that paralyzed his entire body and deprived him of his speech.

He was returned to the White House where he recovered and languished, rose to lucidity and disintegrated in fits of bitterness, while Mrs. Wilson attended to the duties of the presidency in his name. The treaty was defeated in the Senate—but its defeat provoked such a public clamor that the senators were persuaded to bring it up again, this time in a form sufficiently amended to assure its passage. For this second vote, Wilson roused himself to send a message to his Democratic supporters in the Senate—to vote *against* the revised treaty. As the roll call was taken, Senator Brandegee, one of the "irreconcilables," turned to Senator Lodge. "We can always depend on Mr. Wilson," said Brandegee. "He has never failed us." The treaty was defeated, by a narrow margin of only seven votes.

As the Republicans and Democrats geared up for the elections of 1920, Wilson evidently thought—in spite of his devastated mind, or because of it—that he would be called to run for an unprecedented third term as president. He waited for the call to come from the Democratic convention in San Francisco, but his name was not even put before the delegates. The Democrats nominated Governor James Cox of Ohio, who lost to Warren Harding, and Wilson moved out of the White House to another home in Washington. There he lingered, with Mrs. Wilson to care for him. In his last years, he grew increasingly dour and nasty. Sometimes he would receive friends in his study, and speak well for a time; occasionally he would deliver himself of a well-turned jest or pun or comment on politics; but often he would lapse into paroxysms of tears, spitefulness, or hatred.

He was certain, when he stirred himself to focus on such matters, that his opponents would finally bring themselves to "utter destruction" and to "contempt." He had, he said, "seen fools resist Providence before."

In the end, he sank into deep self-pitying depression. In January of 1924, when Dr. Grayson wanted to go off for a week's holiday, Wilson was profoundly depressed. Mrs. Wilson found him sitting in his room with his head bowed, and asked him if he felt badly. "I always feel badly now, little girl," he said wearily. She asked if he wanted Grayson to stay. No, he said, Grayson needed the holiday. But then, he said slowly, "it won't be very much longer, and I had hoped he would not desert me."

By early February, he could no longer move from his bed. Grayson, back from his vacation, came to see his old patient. "I am," Wilson said to the doctor, "a broken piece of machinery. When the machinery is broken—"

He died on February 3, 1924, at the age of sixty-seven.

Georges Clemenceau hoped to be rewarded for his efforts on behalf of France at the peace conference by being elected to the largely honorary office of president of the French republic. Instead, he was promptly attacked by President Poincaré, Marshal Foch, the army, and the right wing, for having sold out France at the conference by agreeing to a "soft" peace. At the same time, the socialists attacked him from the left for the way he had so rudely suppressed strikes and censored newspapers and curbed free speech during the war. Caught at last between the two warring factions of the French republic, finding that there were few old friends to comfort the erstwhile "wrecker of ministries," not only was Clemenceau kept from the office of president, but his own ministry was resoundingly renounced in the elections held in the autumn of 1919.

He left France at once, to soothe his feelings by touring the Middle East. He visited Cairo, went tiger-shooting in Gwalior, made a pilgrimage to the Ganges, traveled on to the Far East, through Singapore. When he returned to France, he went at first to the Vendée. In time, he returned to Paris, to his apartment in the Rue Franklin, and settled finally into dividing his time among the Vendée, the Rue Franklin, and visits with Monet at Giverny.

In the country, he rose at dawn, tended his roses, strolled out to look at the sea, and then, until lunch was brought to him by his faithful old valet, Albert, he wrote. In the afternoons, he would go out for a ride; his chauffeur would drive about the countryside on no particular errand, and then he would return home for a walk in his garden, dinner, bedtime at eight or nine o'clock.

He wrote a biographical study of Demosthenes, seeing him as a defender of liberty, a foe of militarists, and yet a man who was never hesitant to fight to defend himself. He wrote, also, *Au Soir de la Pensée*, his great, turgid philosophical work. And it was at this time that he wrote his study of Monet's water lilies.

Monet was, himself, losing his eyesight in these years, and sinking from time to time into black depressions. Clemenceau badgered Monet to keep working, teased him out of his dark moods, visited him often, and, finally, attended his body to the grave in December 1926.

Clemenceau had resolved that he would never answer any criticism brought against his policies during the war or the peace conference, but in the end, he could not restrain himself. The problem, he wrote in *Grandeurs et Misères d'une Victoire*, was not with the treaty, but with the will of the government that succeeded his to see that the treaty was enforced. The treaty itself, for all its flaws, was good.

And yet, Clemenceau was not entirely satisfied with his defense of his actions. He revised his manuscript over and over, and could still not bring himself to rest content with his defense. Then, in mid-November of 1929, still fretting over his manuscript, he fell ill and took to his bed. His strength left him at once; he lapsed into a coma, and within a week he was dead, at the age of eighty-eight, his vindication still not finished to his satisfaction.

Lloyd George, soon after he returned from the conference to London, had to deal with nasty coal-mining and railroad strikes, and it became increasingly difficult to hide the fact that the war had had a devastating economic impact on Britain, and that reparations would not save the empire. Lloyd George tried budget cuts, an antiwaste campaign, and other improvisatory policies, but the electorate became increasingly impatient with him. In 1922, he tried to rescue his political fortunes by grandstanding, calling for an international conference in Genoa. This conference only resulted in a pact in which Russia ingratiated herself with the Germans by repudiating any claim for reparations.

Soon thereafter, it was discovered that one of Lloyd George's campaign fund-raising operations had engaged in some irregular practices. By October of 1922, he had lost his support in the House of Commons. A general election was called, and the prime minister's Liberal party was defeated, and never recovered.

He would not retire—and his faithful Carnarvonshire constituents returned him to office every time an election was called. Yet, Lloyd George's faction lost power with each election. In 1923, the Liberals held 159 of the 608 seats in the House of Commons. By 1929, Lloyd George's supporters numbered 59. His daughter Megan, his son Gwilym, and his son's brother-in-law Goronwy Owen all stood for election and won seats in Commons—but by 1931 they were Lloyd George's only followers. No one else trusted him any longer. He lived another fourteen years as a political castoff, still vexing both the right and the left by his mercurial ways.

On the one hand, Lloyd George had misgivings about the treaty, and could not quite bring himself to criticize German rearmament in the thirties; on the other hand, he opposed "appeasement" of Germany. On the one hand, he was impressed by Hitler, visited the führer at Berchtesgaden and called him "the greatest living German"; but, on the other hand, he advocated closer cooperation with Russia in anticipation of danger from Germany. When war broke out in 1939, Lloyd George turned down Churchill's nostalgic offer of a cabinet position, criticized the group who had taken over the direction of Britain's destiny, thought Britain would lose the war, thought Churchill's government would fall, and turned down the offer of an ambassadorship. Still, he always accepted an invitation for luncheon or a conversation about his political future, evidently harboring the extraordinary hope that he would himself once again be called to lead the nation in war.

In 1941, Dame Margaret Lloyd George died in Wales. When Lloyd George received the news that she was dying, he set out to be with her, but encountered a terrible blizzard along the way, and snowdrifts blocked the roads. He needed twice to be dug out of drifts as he persisted in his journey, and forty or fifty Welshmen turned out—including quarrymen and the local vicar—to clear the mountain passes to Criccieth, but still more snows filled the roads, and Dame Margaret died before Lloyd George could get to her.

After Dame Margaret's death, Lloyd George's political life and ambitions came to an abrupt end. His appearances in the House of Commons became rare. He took to sitting by the window in his study at his home in Surrey, and staring quietly and idly out at the countryside.

In October of 1943, he married Frances Stevenson, and they retired together to a small farm in Wales. His powers faded quickly; his doctor examined him and found cancer. He was not told, but he sensed that he was losing his strength. He spent much time sitting silently, absorbed in thought. He tired easily; but he still got up each morning with the question "Who's coming today?"

He died on March 26, 1945, at the age of eighty-two.

Of the Germans, Friedrich Ebert was subjected to constant abuse from the right wing, and, in 1922, when he was called a traitor to his face, he sued for slander. The court found in his favor, although it declared that when he had called a strike against the Hohenzollern monarchy in 1918, he had been, in a certain narrow sense, a traitor. In time, Ebert was drawn into more lawsuits—he had slander suits out against 150 defendants at one point—and the ceaseless plague of accusations of treason and his retaliatory litigation undid his health, and his mind, and he died in 1925, after neglecting his doctor's diagnosis of appendicitis, of peritonitis.

Philipp Scheidemann remained a member of the Reichstag, where he made speeches warning against the rise of militarism in Germany. For his pains he was put on the list of the men who had consented to the armistice in 1918, the so-called November criminals, and two men attempted to murder him in June of 1922. Scheidemann, who always carried a pistol, fell to the ground firing and scared off the would-be assassins. Thereafter, he always traveled armed and in the company of armed friends. He died of natural causes in 1939.

Matthias Erzberger was charged with fiscal irresponsibility as minister of finance. He sued for libel, and, in the trial, he was subjected to much abuse for signing the armistice and encouraging acceptance of the treaty. After he resigned, he was not left alone until, in August of 1921, he was assassinated as a "November criminal."

Count von Brockdorff-Rantzau retired from the government for several years, until 1922, when he was persuaded to become ambassador to the Soviet Union, where he remained for six years. When he died, in 1928, his last words, spoken to his brother, were: "Do not mourn. After all, I have really been dead ever since Versailles."

As for the treaty itself, it was rejected by the Congress of the United States. It was formally accepted by the French, but only grudgingly, and was pilloried, beginning at once and continuously, by both the left and the right. Formally accepted by the English, the treaty was savaged at once by Keynes in his book *The Economic Consequences of the Peace*, which set off a sustained attack on the treaty by English liberals. English shame over the treaty provisions encouraged the Germans, increasingly, to believe that they could ignore or violate it with impunity. The treaty was despised in Germany, hated by the Japanese, not signed by the Chinese, and it was the subject of denunciatory expositions in school classrooms in Hungary, Austria, Yugoslavia, and the rest of Eastern Europe.

Through all this, Hitler rose to power. He made his first public impression, and he continued to draw audiences, and hold and augment them, by delivering the same speech over and over again: a vitriolic speech entitled "The Treaty of Versailles."

No single conclusion can be drawn from all this disaster without diminishing the experience of history itself. The lesson of Versailles is protean, not simple, and as the event is turned over in the mind, a hundred different nuances and shadings appear. The experience cannot be impaled on one moral or another. Yet, certain lessons suggest themselves with an undeniable insistence.

The first, surely, is a reminder of the double maxim: it is always easier to start a war than to end one, let alone win it. And the second is that harshness and vengeance nearly always return to haunt those who impose them.

But of all the lessons that Versailles leaves us, certainly the most insistent is that of the inability of the few any longer to govern the many. The few world rulers who dominated Versailles simply could not any longer settle the fate of the many new nations. The few old imperial powers could no longer impose their will on the many new peoples who took their destinies into their own hands. The few heads of state gathered in a small room could no longer determine the world in which we live.

The failure of the diplomats of 1919—a failure that no one has since been able to repair, whose results we have lived with ever since—has been a terribly mixed legacy. The rise of Hitler, the Second World War, the riots and revolutions that plague a world without political order have been the cause of enormous bloodshed and suffering. Yet, at the same time, the collapse of the old order was a necessary prelude to the spread of self-rule, the liberation of new nations and classes, the release of new freedom and independence. The old order was, finally, an ally of old privilege, a fossil of the nineteenth century, a relic of a clockwork universe that had gone out of existence forever.

SELECTED BIBLIOGRAPHY

The essential works for any book of this sort are the conference transcripts and ancillary documents, which are, in this case, to be found in *Papers Relating to the Foreign Relations of the United States, Paris Peace Conference, 1919*, issued by the Department of State, published in eleven volumes by the U.S. Government Printing Office between 1942 and 1947. The British version of these records was edited by Harold W. Temperley, *A History of the Peace Conference of Paris*, six volumes, published by Hodder and Stoughton between 1920 and 1924. The French record of the essential negotiations is to be found in Paul Mantoux's *Paris Peace Conference, 1919, Proceedings of the Council of Four*, published in Geneva in 1964. In addition to these three works, I have relied heavily on the twenty-one-volume *My Diary at the Conference of Paris*, by David Hunter Miller, privately printed in New York in 1924.

In general, however, I have tried to draw the book primarily from diaries, letters, and memoirs, and particularly from those of Shotwell, Seymour, Nicolson, and Keynes. For permission to quote from their writings, I am indebted to Macmillan for James T. Shotwell's *At the Paris Peace Conference*, published in 1937; to Yale University Press for Charles Seymour's *Letters from the Paris Peace Conference*, published in 1965; to Houghton Mifflin for Harold Nicolson's *Peacemaking 1919*, published in 1933; and to Harcourt, Brace for John Maynard Keynes's *The Economic Consequences of the Peace*, published in 1920.

Although most of the essential diaries and letters from the Paris Peace Conference have by now been published, some interesting collections of papers are at Yale (those of Gordon Auchincloss, William H. Buckler, Vance McCormick's diary, Frank L. Polk, William Wiseman), at the Library of Congress (Newton D. Baker, Ray Stannard Baker, Tasker H. Bliss, George Creel, Norman H. Davis, Breckinridge Long, William G. McAdoo, Roland S. Morris, Elihu Root, Henry White, and Woodrow Wilson) and at Princeton (Ray Stannard Baker, Arthur Bullard). And, although the papers of Ray Stannard Baker, Tasker Bliss, and Henry White have been partially published, I found it useful to compare—particularly in Baker's case—the published and unpublished versions.

I have not listed below all of the secondary works that I consulted in the course of doing this book, but I have tried, rather, to acknowledge my debts to those on which I most often leaned. I would like to acknowledge a particular indebtedness to two very fine secondary works on which I relied heavily, Richard Watt's *The Kings Depart,* published in New York by Simon and Schuster in 1968, and Arno J. Mayer's *Politics and Diplomacy of Peacemaking,* published in New York by Vintage Books in 1969.

ALBRECHT-CARRIE, RENÉ. *Italy at the Paris Peace Conference.* New York, 1938.
AMERY, L. S. *My Political Life.* London, 1955.
ANSCOMBE, G.E.M. *An Introduction to Wittgenstein's Tractatus.* London, 1959.
BAILEY, THOMAS A. *Woodrow Wilson and the Great Betrayal.* New York, 1945.
———. *Woodrow Wilson and the Lost Peace.* New York, 1944.
BAKER, RAY STANNARD. *American Chronicle.* New York, 1945.
———. *What Wilson Did at Paris.* New York, 1919.
———. *Woodrow Wilson, Life and Letters.* New York, 1937–39. 8 vols.
———. *Woodrow Wilson and World Settlement.* New York, 1923.
BALAKIAN, ANNA. *André Breton.* New York, 1971.
———. *Surrealism, The Road to the Absolute.* New York, 1970.
BARNES, GEORGE N. *From Workshop to War Cabinet.* London, 1924.
BARNES, JAMES STRACHEY. *Half a Life.* London, 1933.
BARR, ALFRED H., ed. *Fantastic Art, Dada, Surrealism.* New York, 1947.
BARUCH, BERNARD M. *The Making of the Reparation and Economic Sections of the Treaty.* New York, 1920.
BEAVERBROOK, W.M.A. (Lord Beaverbrook). *Men and Power, 1917–1918.* London, 1956.
BENEDIKT, MICHAEL. *The Poetry of Surrealism, An Anthology.* New York, 1974.
BIRDSALL, PAUL. *Versailles Twenty Years After.* New York, 1941.
BLACK, MAX. *A Companion to Wittgenstein's Tractatus.* Cambridge, England, 1964.
BLAKE, ROBERT. *The Unknown Prime Minister: Life and Times of Andrew Bonar Law.* London, 1955.
BLUM, JOHN MORTON. *Woodrow Wilson and the Politics of Morality.* Boston, 1956.
BONSAL, STEPHEN. *Suitors and Suppliants.* New York, 1946.
———. *Unfinished Business.* Garden City, New York, 1944.
BORDEN, HENRY, ed. *Robert Laird Borden: His Memoirs.* London, 1938.
BRUUN, GEOFFREY. *Clemenceau.* Cambridge, Massachusetts, 1943.
BULLITT, WILLIAM C. *Testimony Before the Committee on Foreign Relations, United States Senate, of William C. Bullitt.* New York, 1919.

BURNETT, PHILIP MASON. *Reparation at the Paris Peace Conference from the Standpoint of the American Delegation.* New York, 1940. 2 vols.

CALLWELL, C. E. *Field-Marshal Sir Henry Wilson: His Life and Diaries.* London, 1927.

CAMBON, PAUL. *Ambassadeur de France, 1843–1924, par un Diplomate.* Paris, 1937.

CECIL, E.A.R.G. (Viscount Cecil of Chelwood). *A Great Experiment.* London, 1941.

———. *All the Way.* London, 1949.

CHURCHILL, RANDOLPH S. *Lord Derby.* London, 1959.

CHURCHILL, WINSTON S. *Victory.* London, 1946.

———. *The World Crisis: The Aftermath, 1918–1929.* New York, 1929.

CLEMENCEAU, GEORGES. *American Reconstruction, 1865–1870.* Edited by Fernand Baldensperger. New York, 1928.

———. *Claude Monet, The Water Lilies.* Translated by George Boas. New York, 1930.

———. *Clemenceau, The Events of His Life as Told by Himself to His Former Secretary, Jean Martet.* Translated by Milton Waldron. New York, 1930.

———. *Demosthenes.* Translated by Charles Thompson. Boston, 1926.

———. *Grandeur and Misery of Victory.* Translated by F. M. Atkinson. New York, 1930.

———. *In the Evening of My Thought.* Translated by Charles Thompson and John Heard, Jr. Boston, 1929. 2 vols.

CLOUGH, SHEPARD B. *European Economic History.* New York, 1968.

COOPER, JOHN M., ed. *Causes and Consequences of World War I.* New York, 1972.

COOTE, SIR COLIN. *Editorial.* London, 1965.

COX, FREDERICK J. "The French Peace Plans, 1918–1919; The Germ of the Conflict Between Ferdinand Foch and Georges Clemenceau." *Studies in Modern European History.* New York, 1971.

CREEL, GEORGE. *Rebel at Large, Recollections of Fifty Crowded Years.* New York, 1947.

CRONON, E. DAVID, ed. *The Cabinet Diaries of Josephus Daniels, 1913–1921.* Lincoln, Nebraska, 1963.

CZERNIN, FERDINAND. *Versailles: 1919.* New York, 1964.

DÉAK, FERENCZ. *Hungary at the Paris Peace Conference.* New York, 1942.

DUGDALE, BLANCHE. *Arthur James Balfour.* London, 1936.

ELCOCK, HOWARD. *Portrait of a Decision: The Council of Four and the Treaty of Versailles.* London, 1972.

ERLANGER, PHILIPPE. *Clemenceau.* Paris, 1968.

FERRIS, PAUL. *The House of Northcliffe.* London, 1971.

FOCH, FERDINAND. *Memoirs of Marshal Foch.* Translated by Colonel T. Bentley Mott. Garden City, New York, 1931.

GEFFROY, GUSTAVE. *Georges Clemenceau.* Paris, 1919.

GEORGE, ALEXANDER, and GEORGE, JULIETTE. *Woodrow Wilson and Colonel House.* New York, 1956.

GOLLIN, ALFRED. *Proconsul in Politics.* London, 1964.

GRAVES, ROBERT. *Goodbye to All That.* New York, 1957.

GRAVES, ROBERT, and HODGE, ALAN. *Long Weekend: A Social History of Great Britain, 1918–1939.* New York, 1963.

GRAYSON, CARY T. *Woodrow Wilson: An Intimate Memoir.* New York, 1960.

HANCOCK, W. K., and VAN DER POEL, JEAN, eds. *Selections from the Smuts Papers.* Cambridge, England, 1966. 4 vols.

HANKEY, MAURICE P. *The Supreme Control at the Paris Peace Conference, 1919.* London, 1963.

HANOTAUX, GABRIEL. *Le Traite de Versailles, du 28 juin 1919.* Paris, 1919.

HANSEN, HARRY. *The Adventures of the Fourteen Points.* New York, 1919.

HARDEN, MAXIMILLIAN. *I Meet My Contemporaries.* New York, 1925.

HARDINGE (Lord Hardinge of Penshurst). *Old Diplomacy.* London, 1947.

HELMS, *Captains and the Kings.*

HENDRICK, BURTON J. *The Life and Letters of Walter Hines Page.* Garden City, New York, 1924–26. 3 vols.

HOARE, ROBERT. *World War One.* London, 1973.

HOOVER, IRWIN. *Forty-two Years in the White House.* New York, 1934.

HUGHES, WILLIAM. *Policies and Potentates.* London, 1949.

HYNDMAN, H. M. *Clemenceau, the Man and His Time.* New York, 1919.

JANIK, ALLAN, and TOULMIN, STEPHEN. *Wittgenstein's Vienna.* New York, 1973.

JONES, THOMAS. *Lloyd George.* London, 1951.

KENNY, ANTHONY. *Wittgenstein.* Cambridge, Massachusetts, 1973.

KEYNES, JOHN MAYNARD. *Two Memoirs, Dr. Melchior: A Defeated Enemy and My Early Beliefs.* London, 1949.

LANSING, ROBERT. *The Big Four.* Boston, 1921.

———. *The Peace Negotiations.* Boston, 1921.

LEDERER, IVO J., ed. *The Versailles Settlement, Was It Foredoomed to Failure?* Boston, 1960.

———. *Yugoslavia at the Paris Peace Conference, A Study in Frontiermaking.* New Haven, Connecticut, 1963.

LINK, ARTHUR S. *Wilson the Diplomatist.* Baltimore, 1957.

———. *Wilson, the Road to the White House.* Princeton, New Jersey, 1947.

———. *Woodrow Wilson and the Progressive Era.* New York, 1954.

LIPPARD, LUCY R., ed. *Surrealists on Art.* New York, 1970.

LLOYD GEORGE, DAVID. *Memoirs of the Peace Conference.* New Haven, Connecticut, 1939. 2 vols.

———. *The Truth About the Peace Treaties.* London, 1938.

———. *War Memoirs.* London, 1933–36. 6 vols.

LLOYD GEORGE, FRANCES. *The Years That Are Past.* London, 1967.

LUCKAU, ALMA. *The German Delegation at the Paris Peace Conference.* New York, 1941.

MAIER, CHARLES S. *Recasting Bourgeois Europe.* Princeton, New Jersey, 1975.

MALCOLM, SIR IAN. *Vacant Thrones.* London, 1931.

MANGIN, CHARLES. *Comment Finit La Guerre.* Paris, 1920.

MARSTON, F. S. *The Peace Conference of 1919, Organization and Procedure.* New York, 1944.

MCDOUGALL, WALTER A. *France's Rhineland Diplomacy, 1914–1924.* Princeton, New Jersey, 1978.

MIDDLEMAS, KEITH. *Whitehall Diary*. London, 1969.

MIQUEL, PIERRE. *La Paix de Versailles et l'opinion publique française*. Paris, 1972.

MORDACQ, JEAN JULES HENRI. *Le Ministère Clemenceau. Journal d'un témoin, novembre 1917–janvier 1920*. Paris, 1930–31. 4 vols.

MORISON, ELTING E., ed. *The Letters of Theodore Roosevelt*. Cambridge, Massachusetts, 1954.

MOTHERWELL, ROBERT, ed. *The Dada Painters and Poets, An Anthology*. New York, 1951.

MULDER, JOHN M. *Woodrow Wilson: The Years of Preparation*. Princeton, New Jersey, 1978.

NOBLE, GEORGE BERNARD. *Policies and Opinions at Paris, 1919*. New York, 1935.

NOWAK, KARL FRIEDRICH. *Versailles*. New York, 1929.

ORPEN, SIR WILLIAM. *An Onlooker in France, 1917–1919*. London, 1924.

OWEN, FRANK. *Tempestuous Journey*. London, 1954.

PALMER, FREDERICK. *Bliss, Peacemaker, The Life and Letters of General Tasker Howard Bliss*. New York, 1934.

RECOULY, RAYMOND. *La Barrière du Rhin*. Paris, 1940.

———. *Le Mémorial de Foch*. New York, 1929.

RICHTER, HANS. *Dada, Art and Anti Art*. New York, 1965.

RIDDELL (Lord Riddell). *Lord Riddell's Intimate Diary of the Peace Conference and After, 1918–1923*. London, 1933.

ROBERTS, MARTIN. *The New Barbarism?* Oxford, 1975.

ROSKILL, STEPHEN. *Hankey: Man of Secrets*. Vol. II, 1919–31. London, 1972.

SEYMOUR, CHARLES, ed. *The Intimate Papers of Colonel House*. London, 1928. 4 vols.

SPERANZA, FLORENCE C., ed. *The Diary of Gino Speranza, Italy, 1915–1919*. New York, 1941.

STEFFENS, LINCOLN. *The Autobiography of Lincoln Steffens*. New York, 1931.

SYLVESTER, A. J. *The Real Lloyd George*. London, 1947.

TARDIEU, ANDRÉ PIERRE. *The Truth About the Treaty*. Indianapolis, 1921.

TAYLOR, A.J.P., ed. *Lloyd George: A Diary by Frances Stevenson*. London, 1971.

———. *Lloyd George: Rise and Fall*. London, 1961.

TERRAIL, GABRIEL. *Le Combat des Trois*. Paris, 1922.

THOMPSON, CHARLES T. *The Peace Conference Day by Day*. New York, 1920.

TILLMAN, SETH P. *Anglo-American Relations at the Paris Peace Conference of 1919*. Princeton, New Jersey, 1961.

TRACHTENBERG, MARC. "Reparation at the Paris Peace Conference." *The Journal of Modern History*, Vol. 51, No. 1 (March 1979), 24–55.

TRASK, DAVID F. "General Tasker Howard Bliss and the 'Sessions of the World,' 1919." *Transactions of the American Philosophical Society* (new series), Vol. 56, Pt. 8, Philadelphia, 1966.

TZARA, TRISTAN. *Seven Dada Manifestoes and Lampisteries*. Translated by Barbara Wright. London, 1977.

VANSITTART, R.G.V. (Lord Vansittart). *The Mist Procession*. London, 1953.

WALEY, S.D. *Edwin Montagu*. New York, 1964.

WATSON, D. R. *Georges Clemenceau*. London, 1974.

WILLIAMS, WYTHE. *The Tiger of France*. New York, 1949.

WILSON, EDITH BOLLING. *My Memoir*. New York, 1938.

WILSON, WOODROW. *George Washington*. New York, 1969.

NOTES

PROLOGUE
Pages xv through xviii

Shotwell's meeting with Scott is in Shotwell's diary for January 12. The atmosphere of Paris is described by Smuts in a letter to M. C. Gillett on January 18. The note about Sylvain Lévi comes from Shotwell, January 25. Statistics on the war are taken from Roberts, 48–49, 68, and on economic conditions from Clough, *passim*. The quotations on the Somme are from Roberts, 38, and on the situation of wagons from Roberts, 70.

THE SAVIOR
Pages 3 through 16

That Wilson was superstitious about the number 13 appears in Wythe Williams, 176, among other places. The arrival is described in Seymour's *Letters*, December 14, and in Thompson, 1–9. Grayson's observations come from "A Personal Glimpse," 80. Wilson's childhood is related in George and George, 3–14, *passim*. The Freud-Bullitt study, although unreliable, remains interesting on Wilson's relationship with his father. The neurological data come from an essay by Edwin A. Weinstein, 315–46 in Cooper's *Causes and Consequences of World War I*. Wilson's student career and years at Princeton are recounted in George and George. The situation in Germany at the end of the war is taken from Watt. The domestic opposition to Wilson is suggested with particular vividness in Theodore Roosevelt's *Letters*, especially 1380–1419. Wilson's own observations on George Wash

275

ington come from his biography of the first president, 3–4, 46, 101 ff. The impressions of Wilson's first appearance in Paris come from Thompson, 13–14, Seymour, 36–37, Shotwell, 86, Arno Mayer, 171, and from coverage in the London *Times* on December 14.

THE TIGER
Pages 17 through 27

The description of Clemenceau as a Chinese mandarin is Lansing's, 32–33 of *The Big Four*. Clemenceau's background comes from Bruun and from an unpublished manuscript by Bernard Weisberger. The quotations about his father are from Martet, 294 ff. Clemenceau's love of slang is noted in Williams, 49. Clemenceau's remarks about Andrew Johnson are from his own *American Reconstruction*, 39 ff. His comments on Monet are in his book on the water lilies, 9–10, 22–23, 31–32. His praise of the French countryside is quoted in Bruun, 119. His tendency to expose himself to fire was noted by Bruun, 147. His declaration, "Je fais la guerre," is quoted by Williams, 150, among others. His encounter with the chamber of deputies is recounted by Arno Mayer, 177–86.

HOTEL CRILLON
Pages 27 through 29

Impressions of the Crillon come from a dispatch of December 10 to the *Washington Post* from Raymond G. Carroll; from Seymour, 105 and 42; from Shotwell, 87–88 and 120. Clemenceau's meetings with Wilson are recalled in House, vol. IV, 253. Clemenceau's remark in the chamber is quoted in Seymour, 85.

THE GOAT-FOOTED BARD
Pages 29 through 35

Wilson's arrival is detailed in Thompson, 55–61, and Mayer, 190 ff. Hughes's recollections are in his *Policies and Potentates*, 233 ff. The Gollin quote is from *Proconsul in Politics*, 384–87; Sir Colin Coote's assessment comes from *Editorial*, 96–97. L. S. Amery's comes from *My Political Life*, 395–96. Churchill's is from *Victory*, 87–90. Keynes's is from *Essays in Biography*, ed. by Sir Geoffrey Keynes, 32–39. Rowland (59, 120, 129, 229–30, and 642) wrote of Lloyd George's relationships with women. Keynes (*Economic Consequences*), Nicolson (19–24), and Watt (46–47) wrote about the election in Britain.

CROSSING THE CHANNEL
Page 35

Vansittart, 208.

HOTEL MAJESTIC
Pages 35 through 37

Keynes's remarks on the Majestic are on 12–13 of his essay on Dr. Melchior. Nicolson's observations are from 44–47 of his diary; he mentions the handbook on the Congress of Vienna on 80. Other comparisons to 1815 are from Baker, vol. I, 104 ff.

LA SCALA
Pages 37 through 38

Wilson's tour of Italy is in Mayer, 211 ff. The description of Orlando is from Barnes, 238. The description of Sonnino is from Lansing, *The Big Four*, 106–7.

THE BRITISH DELEGATION
Pages 39 through 41

Riddell's socialist observations occur on page 10 of his diary. The British concern that their phones were being tapped is mentioned by Sylvester, 31. Lloyd George's amusement at the chart was recorded by Nicolson, 26. The notes on the Folies come from Seymour, 89. Shotwell wrote about the Majestic on 111 and 121. Eyre Crowe is recalled by Nicolson, 246. Shotwell tells the Balfour story on 122.

PRECONFERENCE ANALYSIS
Page 41

Nicolson, 48–52.

JANUARY 18
Pages 45 through 50

Shotwell's description is on 126 of his diary. The appearance of the Quai d'Orsay is taken from Thompson, 106, and Hansen, 32–37. Lord Escher's rundown on the French appears in Randolph Churchill's biography of Lord Derby, 356. The observations on Dutasta appear on 119–20 of Nicolson. Clemenceau's treatment of Pichon is in Miller, February 27. Lloyd George's comment on Pichon is from Riddell, 20. The description of Bonar Law is from Beaverbrook, xix; of Milner from Beaverbrook, xx–xxi; of Hankey from Vansittart, 164; of Bliss from Baker's *American Chronicle*, 379–80; of Henry White from *American Chronicle*, 381–83, with the manuscript note from page 357 of "Unpub. Mss. Mission to Europe," Library of Congress, R.S.B. Papers, Container 171; of Lansing from *American Chronicle*, 378, and Hansen, 192; of Mantoux from Sylvester, 29–30, and Frances Lloyd George's *The Years That Are Past*, 80–81, and Seymour, 155; of Clemenceau's manner of presiding from Lansing, *The Big Four*, 17–19, Thompson, 123, and Nicolson, 242.

PROTOCOL
Page 50

Nicolson, 245.

THE FEW AND THE MANY
Pages 50 through 52

Nicolson's remarks on open diplomacy are from Nicolson, 123. Lloyd George's tardiness was described by Amery, 178–79. The meeting room and Clemenceau were described by Shotwell, 175–78. Clemenceau's manner of presiding was described by Nicolson, 242, J. Barnes, 227, Cecil, 66.

BASIS OF NEGOTIATIONS
Pages 52 through 54

The armistice terms were mentioned in Riddell, 5. Wilson's Fourteen Points are discussed by Nicolson, 39–42, and Keynes, 56–67.

THE AIMS OF CLEMENCEAU
Pages 54 through 56
Clemenceau's aims are discussed by Mayer, 78–87. The most interesting work done on the Paris Peace Conference during the past decade has been a thorough-going reconsideration of French aims. Only a little of it has been published. Some of the best has been by Walter A. McDougall, Charles A. Maier, and Marc Trachtenberg.

THE AIMS OF LLOYD GEORGE
Page 56
Lloyd George's aims were considered by Nicolson, 83, and Seymour, 137. See also Mayer, *passim.*

THE AIMS OF WILSON
Page 57
Wilson's aims were considered by J. Barnes, 326, Thompson, 146. But see especially Mayer, *passim.* The Lloyd George remark comes from Riddell, 58.

THE AIMS OF ORLANDO
Pages 58 through 59
Orlando's aims were considered by Watt, 51–59 and 100, Nicolson, 160–62, Gino Speranza, volume II of his diary, 239, and, again, Mayer, *passim.*

THE AIMS OF OTHERS
Pages 59 through 60
The stories about Chekri Ghanem and suffrage come from Shotwell, 178–79.

THE TRANSCRIPT
Pages 60 through 61
Sylvester, 29.

THE LEAGUE OF NATIONS, I
Pages 61 through 64
On the league meetings, see Lloyd George, 281, and Thompson, 174–86. On Nicolson's belief in Wilsonism, Nicolson, 36. On Wilson as a "quaint bird," Riddell, 13. Clemenceau's cracks about Wilson come from Seymour, 115. The observations on Smuts are from Nicolson, 317; on Cecil from Shotwell, 111; on Cecil's plan for the league from Lansing, *The Peace Negotiations,* 88; on Léon Bourgeois from Cecil, 64–65.

THE LEAGUE OF NATIONS, II
Pages 65 through 66
"Who is Mandatory?" comes from Thompson, 160 ff. The Hughes stories come from Riddell, 17, Baker's *Woodrow Wilson and World Settlement,* vol. I, 254–55, Hughes, 237–48, and Sylvester, 36.

PRIMITIVE PEOPLE
Pages 66 through 67
Shotwell's encounter with Milner is related in Shotwell, 171–72.

GRAND TURK
Pages 67 through 68

Riddell, 19.

WILSON'S TOUR OF THE BATTLEFIELDS
Pages 68 through 70

The controversy over Wilson's visit to the battlefields is related by Thompson, 91 and 153, and Nicolson, 249–52 and 260–61. The Hughes quote comes from Hughes, 234–35. Shotwell's account of his visits to the front come from pages 247–48 and 342 of his diary.

SACRIFICES
Pages 70 through 71

Klotz's reading of the pamphlet is mentioned by Baker, *Woodrow Wilson and World Settlement,* vol. I, 170. Lloyd George's ideas were noted by Riddell, 23 and 43. Clemenceau's statement was reported by Harden, 46.

LLOYD GEORGE TO THE FRONT
Pages 71 through 74

Lloyd George's drives to the front were mentioned by Frances Stevenson in *The Years That Are Past,* 160. Lloyd George himself wrote about it on pages 2110 ff. of his memoirs. The Graves passage is from *Goodbye to All That,* 163, 114, 154–56. The passage from the Michelin guide comes from 143 ff. of the Verdun guide for 1931.

THE AGE OF THE SMILE
Pages 74 through 75

The smiling age was characterized by Riddell on page 16. Beaverbrook's remarks on Churchill come from Beaverbrook, xiv.

THE LEAGUE OF NATIONS, III
Page 76

Hughes, 246 ff.

INITIATIVE
Pages 76 through 78

Lansing, 56–59.

THE GERMANS
Pages 78 through 79

Nicolson, 95–100, *passim.*

AUSTRIA-HUNGARY
Pages 79 through 82

Seymour, 123–28. For his attitude toward Austria, see Nicolson, 34. On Bratianu, Seymour, 142, and Nicolson, 248. For the session on January 31, see Nicolson, 253 ff.

IMPROVISATION
Page 83

Nicolson, 242.

THE MPRET OF ALBANIA
Pages 83 through 84

See *The Mask of Merlin*, 169 ff.

FEISAL, AND LAWRENCE OF ARABIA
Pages 84 through 87

Feisal and Lawrence are mentioned by Hughes, 221–23, by Lansing, 164–68, by Nicolson, 142 and 327, by Shotwell, 130.

THE NEWS
Pages 87 through 88

Observations about the news are based on the papers of the time, especially the *Washington Post*, the *London Daily Mail*, the *Illustrated London News*, and *Figaro*, and on Graves and Hodges, 19–49, *passim*.

A RIOT IN A PARROT HOUSE
Pages 88 through 89

Nicolson, 152–55, 269, 271.

THE LEAGUE OF NATIONS, IV
Pages 89 through 91

For the attack on Wilson in *Figaro* and the attendant fuss, see Thompson, 187 ff. and Nicolson, 78–79 and 201–2.

COLONEL HOUSE
Pages 91 through 93

For House, see George and George, 75–85, 92–93, 124–31, and for the concluding quote, see Baker's diary for April 28.

THE ANCIENT GREEKS
Page 94

Martet, 94–96.

THE LEAGUE OF NATIONS, V
Pages 94 through 96

For the essential diplomacy by Cecil, see David Hunter Miller's diary for February 13.

THE ASSASSINATION
Pages 99 through 101

For the incident itself, see Roskill, 63, Watt, 83–84, Nicolson, 264–65, and Baker's *Woodrow Wilson and World Settlement*, vol. I, 297. For Balfour wondering at the significance, see Vansittart, 211. For Clemenceau's duels, see Williams, 38 ff. and 262, and Bruun, 49. For the story about Sarah Bernhardt, see Martet, 38.

SABOTAGE
Pages 102 through 103

For the description of Balfour, see Beaverbrook, xi–xii, Sylvester, 22, and J. Barnes, 310. For the way Balfour took charge, see Roskill, 64–65, and Baker, *What Wilson Did at Paris,* 47 ff. For the quote on Balfour as Richelieu, see Nicolson, 32.

ENTROPY
Pages 103 through 105

For "sops to vanities," Vansittart, 202. For the committee work, see Watt, 66–73, Nicolson, 266–74 and 277, and especially Seymour, 167 ff.

THE SMART SET
Pages 105 through 108

For tea, see Seymour, 178. For Fisher and Augustus John, see *The Years That Are Past,* 154–58. For Paris putting on her act, Vansittart, 204. On Paderewski's band, *The Years That Are Past,* 149. For Sarah Bernhardt, *The Years That Are Past,* 153. For Criqui, Vansittart, 206. For the chemise, Frances Stevenson's diary, 171. For the Nicolson stories, see his diary, 314, 341. Seymour's estimates of his peers are on 61–62, 129–30, 171, and 190 of his *Letters.*

PROUST
Pages 108 through 109

Nicolson, 131, 156, 275.

SHELL SHOCK
Pages 109 through 113

The Proust quote is from Balakian's *Breton,* 46. The cloaca quote is from Balakian's *Breton,* 20. For the remainder of the chapter in general, see Balakian's *Breton,* 23–64, *passim.* In general, and for the way *Les Champs Magnétiques* was written, see Lippard, 14–19. Apollinaire's poem is from Apollinaire's *Selected Writings* and was translated by Roger Shattuck. The poem by Robert Desnos was translated by Michael Benedikt and appears in *The Poetry of Surrealism.*

MISSION TO MOSCOW
Pages 114 through 118

For the background on the trip, see Watt, 74–82, 98–99. For the trip itself, see Bullitt's Senate testimony and Steffens's *Autobiography,* 790–803.

POLISH JOKES
Page 119

Shotwell, 189–90. For Lansing's characterization of Paderewski, see Lansing's *The Big Four,* 201.

MISSION TO GERMANY
Pages 120 through 130

Keynes told this story in *Dr. Melchior.* Observations on Erzberger and the German government come from Watt, especially 275–79, 283–91, 307–9, and 455–61.

TRACTATUS LOGICO-PHILOSOPHICUS
Pages 130 through 133

For Wittgenstein's background, see Kenny, 1–8, and Janik and Toulmin, 220–22 and 243–44. For the *Tractatus*, see especially pages 54–73 of Kenny.

NOIR CACADOU
Pages 133 through 138

For Tzara's recollection, see Richter, 227–28. The observations about Eggeling come from page 63 of Richter. For Huelsenbeck's poem, translated by Ralph Manheim, see Motherwell. Tzara's *poème simultané* is on page 30 of Richter. For the general remarks about dadaism, see Richter, 25, 34, 43–44, 57–58. The Schwitters story appears in Richter, 137 ff. The material by and about Ernst comes from Lippard, 128 and 47. For Arp's poem, see Richter, 52. For the disintegration of the evening, see Richter, 78.

WILSON'S RETURN
Pages 141 through 143

Edith Wilson, 245–46.

WILSON'S COUNTERATTACK
Pages 143 through 144

Edith Wilson, 247. For Lloyd George's annoyance with Wilson, see Stevenson's diary for March 15 and Riddell, 32. Baker's observations come from page 392 of *American Chronicle* and page 311 of *Woodrow Wilson and World Settlement*.

WILSON WOUNDED
Pages 144 through 146

On the Monroe Doctrine, see Watt, 86–89, and David Hunter Miller's diary for March 18, and a letter from the editor of the *Atlantic Monthly*, dated March 27, in Container 97 of the Ray Stannard Baker papers in the Library of Congress. Wilson's peculiar apologetic manner was noted by Sylvester, 35.

THE COUNCIL CHAMBER
Pages 146 through 149

For Keynes on Wilson, see *The Economic Consequences of the Peace*, 40–45. For Keynes on Clemenceau, see *Economic Consequences*, 29–32.

WEEKEND AT FONTAINEBLEAU
Pages 149 through 152

Sylvester, 37–38. Hankey, 71–77. For Sir Henry Wilson, Callwell, 176–77. See also Riddell, 36 and 39. On Beer, see Seymour, 11. On Kerr, see Shotwell, 223. For the memorandum, see Rowland, 485. And for Frances Stevenson's concluding remarks, see her diary, 175–76.

THE BIG FOUR
Pages 152 through 154

On the arrangement of the room, see Helms, 112. For the issues and Orlando's language problems, see Watt, 89–95. For the structure of the conversations and the lack of a recording secretary, see Lansing, 61, Sylvester, 30, Hardinge, 232, and Bliss, 46. For Lloyd George's calculations, see Rowland, 486–88.

WILSON FALTERS
Pages 154 through 155

Hoover, 81. On Wilson's suspiciousness, *The Truth About the Peace Treaties*, vol. I, 244. For the muscle twitch, see Watt, 93. For the laugh, see Lansing's *The Big Four*, 68.

THE TIGER'S TIGER
Pages 155 through 157

For Foch, see Watt, 90, Riddell, 35, Shotwell, 208, and especially Frederick J. Cox's essay, "The French Peace Plans, 1918–1919."

THE SQUEEZE
Pages 157 through 160

On the French delay, see Baker's *American Chronicle*, 398. See George and George, 253–54, Watt, 93–95, and Thompson, 260–61. For Keynes, see *Economic Consequences*, 120–21. Wilson's last words are quoted in the Freud-Bullitt study, page 14, *Encounter*, January 1967.

WILSON YIELDS
Pages 160 through 164

See Thompson, 278–79, and David Hunter Miller's diary for these several days. The formal negotiations, here as elsewhere, are recounted, under the appropriate dates, in the Department of State records of the conference. Lloyd George's remark that the British had what they wanted is on page 42 of Riddell. The assessment of Headlam-Morley comes from Shotwell, 185 and 210; of Haskins from Seymour, xxviii. See also House's diary for the several days before and after April 1. The remark about a "positive break" is from Baker's *Woodrow Wilson and World Settlement*, vol. II, 41.

WILSON BREAKS
Pages 164 through 166

The onset of Wilson's stroke was described on page 42, vol. II of *Woodrow Wilson and World Settlement*. Grayson's medical opinions appeared on page 17 ff. of *Physical Culture* for March 1919, vol. XLI, no. 3. The neurological data on Wilson come from Weinstein, in Cooper's *Causes and Consequences of World War I*, 315–46.

WILSON'S DEFEAT
Pages 167 through 169

For the conduct of the negotiations, see House's diary for the first few days of April and Baker's *Woodrow Wilson and World Settlement*, vol. II, 45. For Clemenceau's joy over Wilson's illness, see Frances Stevenson's diary for April 5. For House's wish that Clemenceau would pass the germ to Lloyd George, Baker's *American Chronicle*, 400. For the remainder of the negotiations, see House; and for this, and the next several days, see also Temperley and the Department of State records of the negotiations.

WILSON RALLIES
Pages 169 through 170
See House for April 6 and Freud-Bullitt, 15–16. For the comments by White and Lansing, see Thompson, 291.

APRIL 7
Pages 170 through 171
See House for April 7. For Baker's encounter with Wilson, see Baker's *American Chronicle*, 403.

THE SAAR
Pages 171 through 172
House, April 8.

THE MONROE DOCTRINE
Pages 172 through 173
American Chronicle, 405, and Thompson, 296.

THE DEAL
Pages 173 through 174
House, April 12 through 15.

WILSON'S NIGHTMARES
Pages 174 through 175
Hoover, 98–99, and Weinstein, *passim*.

BENEFACTORS OF HUMANITY
Pages 175 through 176
House for April 15 and Bonsal, 261.

FIN DE LA SAISON
Pages 179 through 180
For Seymour, see page 201 of his *Letters*.

THE HOUSE OF COMMONS
Pages 180 through 182
See Ferris, 219–27, and Blake, 406–9. For Lloyd George's comments, see Riddell, 52 and 66. For the concluding remarks, Frances Stevenson, 180.

THE ITALIANS
Pages 182 through 188
For the "Lesser Three," Seymour, 207. On Tardieu, see Bonsal, 104. For the meeting, see Temperley and the Department of State records for April 20. For Wilson's remark about Italians in New York, see Bonsal, 104. On Orlando's tears, see Riddell, 53. For Clemenceau's remarks to House, Bonsal, 101. For House's re-

marks to Wilson, Bonsal 105. For Riddell's remarks on Wilson's appeal to the Italian people, Riddell, 57. For the text of Wilson's appeal, the Department of State records. For Orlando's position that the Italians could "choose between Wilson and me," see Watt, 104. For Clemenceau's remark that the French papers were bribed by the Italians, Seymour, 212. For D'Annunzio and Mussolini, Mayer, 706-7.

THE JAPANESE
Pages 188 through 191
On Makino, see Bonsal, 228. For Lansing's remark about blackmail, see *The Peace Negotiations*, 244. For the Japanese appearance and timing, Bonsal, 234 ff. For House's involvement, see his diary, 466-67. Hankey's letter to Lady Hankey is in Roskill, 83. For Ray Stannard Baker's part, see *American Chronicle*, 413. Balfour's memorandum is quoted in House, 468. Wellington Koo's remark is in Bonsal, 243-44.

THE ZIONISTS
Pages 191 through 193
Bonsal, 52-56, 61.

THE BOLSHEVIKS AGAIN
Pages 193 through 196
Seymour, 185. Nicolson, 291-304.

BULLITT'S RETURN
Pages 196 through 197
Watt, 98-99.

THE BELGIANS
Pages 197 through 198
Sylvester, 28.

THE EMPTY ROOM
Pages 198 through 199
Nicolson, 323-24, Roskill, 85-87.

OPEN DIPLOMACY
Pages 199 through 200
Shotwell, 296-97.

THE UKRAINIANS
Pages 201 through 202
Bonsal, 140-43.

DINNER AT THE RITZ
Page 202
Nicolson, 318-19.

THE GERMAN DELEGATION
Pages 205 through 208

Nowak, 178–95, 199, and Watt, 393–404.

FINISHING THE TREATY
Pages 208 through 209

Baker's diary for May 3. For Lloyd George, see Riddell, 66. For Bliss, see *Bliss, Peacemaker*, 396.

THE PRINTED TREATY
Pages 209 through 212

For Smuts, see his letter to A. Clark for May 2. For Bonar Law, see T. Jones for April 14. For Smuts's second letter, see his letter to A. Clark for May 7. For Foch, see Callwell, 187. For Sir Henry's reactions, see Callwell, 187–91. For the meeting and the last-minute reactions, see Watt, 406–7. For Riddell's drive to the palace, see Riddell, 70.

THE PRESENTATION OF THE TREATY
Pages 213 through 217

For Brockdorff-Rantzau, see Watt, 409, and Nowak, 214. For the room, see Watt, 408. For Riddell's impression of Brockdorff-Rantzau, see Riddell, 71. For Clemenceau's speech, Watt, 409. Brockdorff-Rantzau's reply, Watt, 411, Nowak, 217–25, Nicolson, 329–30, and Riddell, 72. For the fidgeting of the Big Three, Riddell, 73. For Walter Simons's reactions, Alma Luckau, 115 ff. Wilson's remark is quoted by Watt, 411–12. The German leavetaking is described by Nowak, 225. For the conclusion, see Stevenson's diary for May 8.

A READING OF THE TREATY
Pages 217 through 218

Watt, 412–16.

BROCKDORFF-RANTZAU REPLIES
Pages 218 through 222

Watt, 416 ff., 441 ff. See also Keynes, 56–112 *passim*, Nowak, 226 ff., and, for the last line, Thompson, 379 ff.

THE ALLIED RESPONSE
Pages 222 through 225

The Smuts quote is from his letter to M. C. Gillett of May 14. Nicolson's letter appears on page 350 of *Peacemaking*. Balfour is quoted on page 342 of Nicolson. The Smuts letter is to "Dearest Mamma," on May 20. For Baker's observations, see *American Chronicle*, 430. The Smuts letter to Lloyd George is from May 14.

THE BROKEN PROMISE
Pages 225 through 226

Mayer, 877. For the succeeding reactions, see also Mayer, 772 ff. For the reaction to the first resignations, see the Minutes of the American Commissioners for May 19 in vol. 11 of the Department of State records. Bullitt's letter of resignation is quoted on pages 800–1 of Mayer.

THE AUSTRIANS ARRIVE
Page 227
Thompson, 372–73, 387–88, Nicolson, 328–51, Watt, 436.

THE ITALIANS AGAIN
Pages 227 through 230
Nicolson, 330–34, Thompson, 372–73, Seymour, 224–27. J. Barnes, 315, confirms Nicolson's story about the laughter.

THE GERMAN COUNTERPROPOSAL
Pages 230 through 232
Riddell, 83. The details of the counterproposals are given in Watt, 421 ff. For the British reactions to the counterproposals, see Waley, 211–15, and Callwell, 95.

MEMORIAL DAY
Pages 232 through 233
Baker, *American Chronicle*, 436–37.

THE BRITISH RETREAT
Pages 234 through 235
See Amery, 177–78, and, for Montagu's remarks, Waley, 211–12.

CLEMENCEAU REPLIES
Pages 235 through 236
House, 492–93. For Clemenceau's assessment of England, see pages 201–2 of his *Grandeur and Misery of Victory*.

WILSON'S REACTION
Pages 236 through 238
Seymour, 253–56. For general remarks, see Mayer, 802–4. For Wilson's acknowledgment that the terms were hard, see Ray Stannard Baker, *American Chronicle*, 442. For Wilson's reply, see House, 490–91.

IMPRESSIONS OF THE BIG THREE
Pages 238 through 240
For Wilson at Princeton, see Riddell, 79. For Wilson on Lloyd George, see Baker's diary for June 13. For Seymour on Bonar Law, Seymour, 227. For Lloyd George on Clemenceau, Riddell, 93. For Frances Stevenson, see her diary for May 23.

THE FORMAL ALLIED RESPONSE
Pages 240 through 241
Hansen, 338 ff., Watt, 451–53. See also Nicolson, 361–63.

WEIMAR
Pages 241 through 242
Nowak, 264 ff., and Watt, 454–55.

ERZBERGER
Pages 242 through 244
Watt, 455 ff.

"A MILITARY POINT OF VIEW"
Pages 244 through 246
Watt, 462 ff., Nowak, 266 ff.

DEADLOCK
Pages 247 through 249
Watt, 479 ff.

SCAPA FLOW
Pages 249 through 250
Thompson, 397, Watt, 486–89.

THE GERMAN COLLAPSE
Pages 250 through 251
Watt, 484 ff., Roskill, 95, Callwell, 200, Ike Hoover, 85.

SHOTWELL AND SEYMOUR
Pages 252 through 253
Shotwell, 332, 349, 350, 362, 370–73, and Seymour, 262–65.

VERSAILLES, THE HALL OF MIRRORS
Pages 253 through 257
For the look of the roads, see Hansen, 348–49. For the arrivals of the delegates, see Nicolson, 366, and Shotwell, 382. For the appearance of the room, see Hansen, 308–9, Sir William Orpen, 120–21. For the tables, see Nicolson, 366, and for the appearance of the document itself, see Hansen, 353. Riddell's remarks are on pages 100–1 of his diary. Balfour's remark is in Baker's *American Chronicle*, 450. The German entrance was described by Baker in *American Chronicle*, 454–55, and by Hansen, 345 ff. The signatures were described by Hansen, page 356. Wilson's signature was described by Ike Hoover, 111.

EPILOGUE
Pages 259 though 268
The economic statistics come from Clough, *passim*. The political history comes from Roberts. The end of Wilson's life is taken from George and George, of Lloyd George's from Owen, Clemenceau from Erlanger, and the Germans from Watt.

INDEX